HAVEN

CERIL N DOMACE

To Mary Jane Heyman, I did always promise I'd dedicate this to you.

Also to my parents, my siblings, my friends, and the people who suffered through the early drafts. Without you, it never would've gotten this far.

And especially to Danielle German, I hope you're happy. This is all your fault.

First Printing: 2021

Print ISBN: 978-1-7364301-0-1

Edited by Tiffany Kaye with Writers Untapped

Book Cover Design by ebooklaunch.com

For information about purchasing and permissions, contact Ceril N Domace at cerilndomace@gmail.com

www.cerilndomace.com

CHAPTER ONE

IN WHICH THERE IS CHANGE

"The Change can happen at any time, to anyone, regardless of age, race, or sex. At this point, fae are more vulnerable than at any other time in their new lives. Within a week, the mortality rate drops by one-third as those who Change adapt to their bodies. Any nonphysical abilities do not take effect until the physical changes are complete, which may take anywhere from an hour to a week, depending on which species they become. New muscle and bone growth are rapid, and subjects report experiencing immense pain which may lead to self-mutilation. Approximately 70 percent of those undergoing the Change lose control and attack those around them."

—Studies of the Fae Folk by Gabriel Clark, Lord Gabriel

Owen picked Ashley up and spun her in a circle as fast as he could as they walked out of the theater after her violin recital. "Congratulations, Ash, you were amazing!"

"Dad, put me down," Ashley squealed, failing to hold back her laughter. "People are staring!" Her giggles failed to dissolve as he set her back on the ground and she tried to brush her blonde hair back into place.

Chuckling, Owen spun to face Arthur, Dorothy, and the twins, Jen and David. "All right," he yelled, clapping his hands together, "who's ready for ice cream?"

1

As one, the kids—except Ashley—jumped up and down and chanted for ice cream. Ashley rolled her eyes and inched away from her siblings. At twelve, she had recently decided she was far too old for such childish behavior. The argument would have had more merit if Arthur weren't sixteen and unashamed about his love for anything frozen and dairy.

"I guess someone doesn't want ice cream," Owen said, winking at his wife, Tiffany.

Tiffany grinned devilishly. "That means more for us, honey."

"Mom, Dad," Ashley yelled over her family's laughter. "That's not true!" Seeing that her words had no effect, she ran to Arthur's ancient sedan, mousy blonde hair flaring out behind her. She threw herself against the side without noticing how the mud rubbed off on her new recital dress and her coat.

"Hey Dad, I can take the girls and David to DQ if you want," Arthur offered as he unlocked his car so Ashley could get in. Running a hand through his black hair, he cast a sidelong glance at the twins, who were bickering about something that had happened in Tae Kwon Do that day. "You look like you could use a little peace and quiet."

Owen rubbed the back of his neck and looked to Tiffany for her input. The recital hadn't been kind to her. Ashley's performance aside, middle-schoolers weren't known for their ability to stay on pitch, and judging from the way her expression became pinched whenever she thought the others weren't looking, the sharp notes made for prime migraine material.

She shrugged. "We'd have to take Dorothy because her carseat's in the minivan, but . . . Jen, David, do you want to ride with us or Arthur?"

The twins exchanged a look and with no hesitation said they wanted to ride with Arthur. He let them choose the music, which at eight years old, that was all they cared about. Also, the heat in his car worked better.

Owen nodded. "Be careful, the roads are icy. We'll go to the Dairy Queen on Broadway instead of the one on Twelfth. The crowds will be smaller there."

Tiffany laughed as she pulled her blonde hair back into a ponytail and readjusted her headband. "Dear, only you would drive halfway across town to avoid a crowd."

"It's just common sense. We'll still get our ice cream before everyone else, and we'll be on time for certain people to go to bed," he said with a sidelong glance at Dorothy.

"Sure, Dad. Keep telling yourself that," Arthur said as he shoved his siblings toward his car.

Owen shook his head and pouted at Dorothy. "Did you hear that? I get treated horribly."

"Mommy says you deserve it, Daddy," Dorothy said, brown eyes turned toward the sidewalk as they walked along.

Owen, squawking in mock outrage, swung Dorothy up in his arms. "Does she say that, now? Well, what do you think, little Dot?"

"Daddy is the best. You give the best hugs." Dorothy giggled, all smiles as she snuggled into his arms.

"Oh, really—" He gasped, widening his eyes to pull the largest giggle from Dorothy. "Even better than your mommy's? But she gives great hugs."

Dorothy nodded and whispered, "Don't tell her, but you smell better."

He threw back his head and roared with laughter, refusing to tell Tiffany why as they reached the minivan.

***

As Owen, Tiffany, and Dorothy walked through the door and into the nearly empty restaurant, Jen ran up to them, brown eyes darting between them, short blonde hair hopelessly mussed, and words already pouring from her mouth.

"What took you guys so long? We've been waiting forever. Can we order now? I want ice cream and—" She would have kept going had Owen not cut her off so they could order.

Out of the corner of his eye, Owen saw Tiffany rub her temples for the third time in less than three minutes as he lined the kids up in front of the cashier. He caught her eye and silently asked if she wanted him to hurry the kids along. Her headaches were legendary, and judging by the way she set her jaw, this one would be a killer.

She shook her head, glanced toward Dorothy and Arthur, who were currently engaged in an enthusiastic game of patty cake, and tapped her temple. The noise wasn't agreeing with her, but she would be fine.

Still, it was fortunate that it didn't take long for the food to arrive, as Arthur swore he was going to lead the twins in open revolt if he had to wait any longer. This was, of course, in between dramatic declarations that he was starving and likely to pass out at any given moment.

"I almost messed up on the first run," Ashley gushed between bites of her blizzard. "I was scared I would ruin the whole show, but I didn't, and Mr. Nelson said it was the best he'd ever heard me play, way better than Felicia."

Owen hadn't seen her smile like this since she'd started preparing for the recital, and it was wonderful to see it again now that its weight was off her shoulders.

"You were great, Ashley. I've never heard you play so well," Tiffany said, reaching over to ruffle her oldest daughter's hair. She wasn't eating, even though she and Owen had purportedly ordered something to share. Cold foods made her headaches worse.

Owen nodded, a broad smile lighting up his face. "I agree. All that time you spent practicing paid off. You sounded wonderful."

Ashley smiled as she soaked in her parent's praise, happy to be the center of attention for once. "Though, of course, someone"—she glared at Arthur, who'd made a point to hoot and holler at the end of her performance—"almost ruined it all. Everybody saw you, you know? I was so embarrassed. I literally died."

"Maybe so, but I was doing it for the good of everyone," Arthur answered, his lips twitching.

Ashley tilted her head and asked what he meant.

Arthur leaned back and crossed his arms. "Well first, you see, I had to let everyone know that the best musician of the whole night was my little sister."

Ashley ducked her head while Owen braced himself for what he knew was coming.

"And second, I had to stop you from getting an even bigger head." He jumped away in time to dodge Ashley's retaliatory punch.

Deciding to intervene before one of Ashley's surprisingly strong right crosses connected, or Arthur ended up with the remains of her blizzard dyeing his hair white, Owen spoke up. "Enough. Finish your food. It's getting late and some people have to go to bed."

"We know it's past your bedtime, old man. No need to point it out," Tiffany said, smiling as she poked his ribs. The sparkle in her blue eyes was almost enough to outshine the stars. Cor but he loved her when she was like this.

"Hey, I need my beauty sleep," he said, brushing imaginary bangs off his forehead and batting his eyes at Tiffany. "You think I'm this good looking naturally? Besides, if anyone here gets grumpy when she doesn't get enough sleep, it's this"—he kissed her—"lovely woman beside me."

Unsurprisingly, Arthur led the chorus of groans coming from the under-eighteen portion of the table. That boy didn't have a serious bone in his body.

"We can be far worse if we want to," Owen said, grinning. "We will if you don't hurry." Tiffany played along, scooping up the last bite of their allegedly shared dessert and feeding it to him before kissing his cheek.

"Quick, I know where this is going," Arthur said, shoving the last of his waffle cone into his mouth and hurrying his siblings along.

Owen knew they could have stayed longer, but Tiffany hadn't been looking well. Try as she might to hide it from him, he knew her. Her headaches had been worse than usual recently, both in frequency and intensity, and she'd want to go to bed. He helped her into her coat and held her hand as they walked to the car, eager to get home.

As Owen and Tiffany followed their children outside, Tiffany shuddered, dropped Owen's hand, and clutched her sides. "Owen. I … I hurt … everywhere," she whimpered. She cried out as she fell to the ground and curled into a ball. The sound reached the cars, alerting the kids and bringing them racing back. Their voices overlapped as each demanded answers.

"What's wrong with Mom?" Arthur asked, grabbing his father's arm, the first to turn his attention to Owen instead of Tiffany.

"I don't know—" he started to say, his stomach tightening into knots, but was interrupted by Tiffany's screams. Her whole body jerked as she convulsed. Cursing in Welsh under his breath, Owen frantically looked around for anyone who could help. No luck and it'd take too long for an ambulance to get here.

"I'm taking her to the emergency room," he said, gathering her into his arms. He took a deep breath and tried to slow his racing heart. It wouldn't do any of them any good if he panicked. "Arthur, take the minivan, and get your brother and sisters home."

Arthur's eyes may have looked like dinner plates, but he set his jaw as he switched keys with Owen, then shepherded his scared siblings away. Satisfied the kids were taken care of, he refocused on Tiffany.

He cradled her to his chest as he rushed to the car, barely managing to hit the unlock button without dropping her. Once he managed to get the door open, he lay her across the back seat as if she were made of glass. He dove into the driver's seat and peeled out of the parking lot, driving as fast as he dared on the icy roads.

Fear laced its frozen fingers through his chest as Tiffany's shrieks increased in volume and frequency. St. Gabriel's Hospital was on the other side of town; he couldn't think with her screams echoing in his ears.

Lights flashed in his rearview mirror and he unleashed a string of curses. He accelerated as her cries rose to a crescendo, then stopped. His heart froze. He hadn't thought there was a worse sound than the scream of a loved one, but the silence after was infinitely worse. He dared a glance into the back seat. A strange combination of relief and panic filled his heart when he realized she was moving, that she wasn't—

He tore his eyes away and focused on the road. The sirens that had been a counterpoint to Tiffany's screams wailed behind him. There was movement in the back seat, the sound of cloth ripping. Something slammed into the back of Owen's head and knocked him into the steering wheel. The car hit a patch of ice and skidded out of control across the freeway. The last thing he was aware of was a screech that turned his stomach to stone.

***

Blue lights, screaming, red flashes. Tiffany was screaming. There was something wrong with Tiffany. He drifted in a haze, each second separate and distinct from the rest. He couldn't—he couldn't see anything beyond the blur in front of his eyes. Worst of all, he couldn't move. Something was holding him down.

Voices drifted in and out, asking him his name and what he had been doing. They were taking him to a hospital. Good. They would take care of . . .

***

The acrid scent of antiseptic brought Owen back to consciousness and chased away the last vestiges of sleep. He cracked his eyes open and the lights twisted like blades into his skull. Squeezing them shut again, he waited for the nausea to pass. His dizzy thoughts continued to drift from topic to topic, trying to collect themselves.

Ice cream. Kissing Tiffany before they—His eyes flew open and he shot up, ignoring the light and forcing down the wave of nausea. Tiffany. He'd been taking her to the hospital, and there had been a crash. He looked around, desperate for answers, but he was alone. Where was she? Were they operating on her? Why was no one here? Where were his kids? Were they safe?

He slammed the call button over and over again, desperate to get someone to his room. After an eternity, an Asian man in blue scrubs charged into the room, breathing hard. He darted to Owen's side and tried to ease him back down.

Owen grabbed the nurse's arm and begged him for any information about Tiffany, but the man remained steadfast. "That would be something to discuss with Dr. Prather, sir," he said, not meeting Owen's eyes as he forced him back onto the bed.

Owen let himself be pushed back onto the bed, his mind already a world away. Tiffany—why wouldn't they tell him where Tiffany was?

His mind was stuck in a replay of those final moments, and he prayed memories were wrong. Tiff hadn't been wearing a seatbelt; perhaps she'd been thrown from the car. Her symptoms, they meant something serious had happened, didn't they? Her screams rang in his ears. Why wouldn't they tell him where his wife was?

***

He might have lain there forever, watching the world drift in and out of focus, if a child hadn't run past the open door, trying to escape a nurse with a needle. The kids. Where were they? Why weren't they here? He'd been awake for ages; someone should've called home to them.

"Please, where are my children? Who's taking care of them?" he asked hoarsely.

The doctor, a middle-aged white woman with graying brown hair, stopped her discussion with Nurse Yang and came to Owen's bedside. Owen wasn't sure where she'd come from; he'd stopped paying attention when he realized they weren't going to tell him where Tiffany was.

Carefully, like she was worried her words would damage his bruised body, she spoke. "Mr. Williams, my name is Dr. Janice Prather. I've been taking care of you since you came in. Do you know why you're here?"

"I was taking my wife to the hospital and we got into an accident," he said in a hoarse voice. His fists shook and it took a colossal amount of effort to keep them at his side. "Please, what happened to my wife? She was screaming. And where are my children?"

"Mr. Williams, I need you to answer a few questions—"

Owen lost his last shred of patience and surged up, making a grab for the doctor's arm. "I'll answer your bloody questions after you tell me where my family is." Desperation gave him strength he didn't know he had, enough to ignore his body's screaming.

Dr. Prather pulled her arm free from his grip and began again, keeping her distance from him while gesturing for the nurse to hold him down. Her high-pitched voice grated on his already frayed nerves. "Mr. Williams, I promise I'll answer your questions, but first you need to answer mine." She stopped and looked sternly at Owen. "Now, will you stop shouting so we can all move along with our day?"

Owen answered her barrage of questions about his medical history as succinctly as possible, resisting the urge to flinch every time she spoke. He even managed to get something out of it, even if it was only a list of his injuries. He'd sustained a moderate concussion and broken one of his ribs. As he'd been unconscious most of the night, they wanted to run a few tests before letting him go.

It took an eternity, but finally the last pointless question about his medical history was answered and Owen was free to get some answers of his own.

"Mr. Williams, what do you know of the fae?" Dr. Prather asked. She had set her clipboard aside and was looking him in the eye.

Frowning, Owen tried to remember what he had been taught about fae in secondary school. "Not much. They showed up fifty years ago, went to war with the U.S. after they discovered they were being experimented on, and isolated themselves in their havens after the war. No one in the States has had much contact with them in years." He paused and narrowed his eyes. "What does this have to do with Tiffany?"

"Do you know how the fae multiply?" Doctor Prather asked without meeting his eyes.

"Of course," Owen said, nodding. "The first fae were human—"

His heart stopped. It couldn't be possible. Tiffany was not fae. He looked at Dr. Prather, who would have looked sympathetic if her eyes weren't filled with disgust. "But there hasn't been a Change in five years. It's why the bloody Relocation Act passed—" Owen's wide eyes begged the woman to tell him he was mistaken, that it was all some big joke.

"Mr. Williams, I know this is hard to accept, but your wife was in the process of becoming one of the fae when she died." Her lips pulled back in a grimace like the word had left a bad taste in her mouth "A gryphon, specifically."

He pressed a hand to his forehead, trying to catch the breath that had disappeared from his lungs. "What do you mean was? Fae can't die, can they? Everyone says they're immortal."

Dr. Prather pursed her lips. "It has long been documented that the fae are extremely vulnerable while they are changing." Her smile bared too many teeth to be kind, and her eyes still didn't match it. "To put it bluntly, your wife's neck was broken in the crash. She was only part way through the Change when your car flipped."

In that moment, Owen knew what drove Orpheus to delve into Hades to retrieve Eurydice. He knew why Romeo had laid down at Juliet's side in that cold tomb. All light had gone from the world and all joy vanished with the memory of her smile.

"Why didn't she tell me?" he asked hollowly, latching onto the first thought that made its way through the noise. The words may as well have come through cotton for all he could hear them. "I mean, they know what they, the fae, they know what they are, right?"

"What little research we have on the fae, most of it having been confiscated after the war, says the fae had no idea who would Change,"

9

Dr. Prather said. Her lips turned down and a touch of scorn entered her voice. "They wouldn't even find out they could Change until the process had already begun."

Owen couldn't believe it. He couldn't reconcile the image of his kind, intelligent wife with what he knew about the fae. They were emotionless monsters, living weapons whose only purpose was destruction, everyone knew that. Tiff couldn't even kill bugs. She would . . . *had* called him in from his workshop to get rid of spiders in the bathroom. Dear God, what would he tell the kids?

The kids. His mind ground to a screeching halt. Where were the kids? He'd asked earlier but no one answered him. "Where are my children?" he asked, voice rasping uncomfortably.

Dr. Prather glanced at Nurse Yang, who until this point had been hovering at the edges of the room. He, at least, got right to the point. "Mr. Williams, there wasn't anyone home when the police went to your house. The minivan registered to you was in the garage, but your children weren't on the premises."

Seized with blind panic, Owen tried to leap from the bed. "What? Where are they? Who the hell is out looking for them?" he shouted. Muscles screaming, he fought against Nurse Yang and Dr. Prather as they tried to force him back down. "Let me go. I need to find my kids."

His wife was gone, and he would be cold in his grave before he lost his children too. He'd get out of this bed and search for them himself if they would let him out of this bloody hospital.

"Mr. Williams. Owen," Nurse Yang yelled. "You won't be any use to your children if you kill yourself trying to help them. You need to stay in bed for now. The police and agents from the Committee for Fae Relations are using every resource at their disposal to find them. There's nothing more you can do." He locked eyes with Owen, who reluctantly settled down.

"I can leave after you run your tests, right?" Owen asked. He itched to get out there, to help look, and these two were all that stood in his way.

"Provided there are no complications, and your scans turn out all right," Dr. Prather said, "I don't see why not. After all, the police still need to take your statement about the events of last night."

Owen grudgingly agreed to the tests, still glaring at the two of them. The sooner they were done the sooner he could leave.

"Now that that's out of the way . . ." Dr. Prather turned and clapped her hands.

She continued speaking, but her words faded away as Owen pulled himself to his feet. He barely noticed her leave as nausea threatened to empty his stomach. Nurse Yang guided him into a wheelchair, and as he was wheeled out of the room, he resigned himself to hours of being poked, prodded, and scanned.

***

"Mr. Williams, tell me again about the last time you saw your children." The officer's accusing voice bounced off the walls of the small, windowless room.

"For the last time," Owen said, massaging his temples. "When Tiffany collapsed, I sent Arthur home with his siblings. He knows to contact our neighbors, the Jamesons, if something happens to Tiff or me." They had to have been sitting here for an hour. It never would've taken this long if they were in Wales. At least there Owen wouldn't've been treated like a pariah by those who knew what happened to Tiffany. Why had he let her convince him to move to Kansas?

"As you've said before. What happened next?" It was like the officer, whose name he couldn't bother to remember, was convinced he was hiding some dark secret.

"The car skidded and flipped. I woke up in the hospital and heard the kids were missing. That's all I know," he said, hoping beyond hope this was the last of the questions. The officer had left no stone unturned in his quest for answers, ripping through defenses and delving down paths that had nothing to do with the matter at hand as he picked through Owen's memories.

"And the Jamesons, you wouldn't have any reason to be wary of them, would you? Fred Jameson is on public record as a member of various anti-fae groups."

"Not that I know of, no," Owen said. Of course that wouldn't be the last one. "Fred may be a daft old geezer, but he wouldn't hurt the kids. They've known us for years." His stomach tied itself in knots at the implications behind the officer's questions. The Jamesons were their friends, even if Mr. Jameson had hated anything to do with the fae since the war. Besides, he wasn't the kind of man who'd take his anger out on children.

Looking over his notes, the officer nodded. "Well, Mr. Williams, that about wraps up my questions. We'll keep you updated as the search continues." He stood and walked toward the door, pausing at the threshold. "I am sorry about your wife. I don't mean to exacerbate your grief, but we need all the information we can get."

Getting no response as Owen's gaze was locked on the table in front of him—throat closed tightly on any word or sound that might escape— the officer sighed and reached into his pocket, pulling out a business card for a nearby hotel. "Here. You can't go home until we clear your house, but this hotel is nearby. Tell them I sent you, and they'll get you a room at a discount."

Owen's throat loosened enough for words as he reached out and took the card with shaking hands. He thanked the officer, who then left him alone in the cold room.

Owen sighed and leaned back in his chair, fingers tangling in knots as he pushed a hand through his wild hair. The officer, for all his gruffness, hadn't been cruel. He was doing his job. Owen repeated that to himself as he tried to fight back the anger and grief and overwhelming despair. He was doing his job, he was just trying to help.

Owen had been grateful for the distraction of the questions, even if he hadn't wanted to answer them. They kept his mind from the reality of his situation. Without being fully conscious of it, he made his way out of the station and called a cab to take him to the hotel advertised on the card.

***

To avoid confronting the vicious reality of his thoughts once he reached the hotel, Owen pored over small file the police had given him. He didn't allow himself to react to information on the sheets in front of him. Not while he couldn't do anything about it.

Still, it didn't tell him anything he didn't already know, and a part of him wondered why he'd been given it in the first place. It was practically useless.

The house was a wreck; there were clear signs of a break-in. The children were gone, their dog, Toto, hadn't been in his kennel, and there weren't any leads. Blood was found in the kitchen, but the labs didn't have any results on it yet. The police wouldn't let him help with the search, said he was too shaken up to be any help, and that it might be a while before he could go home.

A distant part of himself knew he should be scared. Tiffany was dead, their kids were missing, and these papers were the closest he could get to finding them. He wasn't, though. He didn't have the energy to spare for fear, so he searched everything he'd been given for information that wasn't there.

It didn't take long. Once he finished reading through the documents for the third time, he sat in the dismal hotel room staring at the drab wallpaper. He made no effort to fight when the darkness beckoned, and he let himself escape into the soothing grasp of a dreamless sleep.

***

Owen woke with a start. A freezing breeze came in through a window he didn't remember leaving open. He stood, muscles protesting every movement, and shuffled over to close the window. His head pounded, and as he rested his forehead on the cool glass, he pondered the window, before his eyes shot open and he spun around.

He scanned the room, over the bed, past the desk and the small pile that was his coat, and . . . there. There was something strange in the corner of the room. There was—he rubbed his eyes before he looked again. No, he wasn't wrong. There were eyes floating in a wave of shadows on the armchair. Eyes that were trained on him.

CHAPTER TWO

In Which Owen Makes New Friends

"There are to be several different species of fae with varying levels of humanity. The less human branches include a lizard species called dragons, a lupine species called werewolves, and two avian species called gryphons and harpies. At this point, we aren't sure how sentient these subspecies are, but some seem to be entirely animal, while others demonstrate various human behaviors such as basic communication. Further study will be needed to determine whether the creatures are still intelligent."

—Excerpt from the research journals of Jonathan Smith of SAFE

Owen blinked once, then again. The third blink flooded his system with adrenaline. He stumbled back against the window, trying to reconcile his mind with what he was seeing. The shadows shifted, and the dim outline of a person appeared.

"Who are you? What are you doing here?" he finally managed to say, frozen to the spot.

The shadow spoke, a soft lilting tone that floated on the air toward him. "Have no fear, Owen Williams. My name is Abey Two-Winds. I'm a shade of the Winter Court of Tearmann. I'm here to help you."

Owen tensed and forced back the acrid fear flooding his limbs. Everyone said shades were indiscriminate killers and invisible assassins. *Why was this one here?*

"Here to help me?" he said, narrowing his eyes. "How're you supposed to do that? How did you even get in here?" He inched toward the side table where he had left his jacket. His phone was in the front pocket; if he could call someone, he might get out of this alive.

"Looking for this?" The shadow laughed as the square block of his aging phone landed on the floor beside him. "It's dead, but you're welcome to try anyway."

Owen leaned down to pick it up and cursed when he realized the shadow was telling the truth.

"Tut-tut, such language, dear. What if your children were here to hear you?"

Owen froze. The blood drained from his face and his jaw dropped. If this thing knew where his children were . . .

"What do you mean?" he whispered. Mr. Jameson told stories about the fae. Stories about fae kidnapping whole families, brainwashing children into soldiers, killing humans for sport. He managed to find his courage and forced himself to ignore his screaming muscles as he leaped at the shadow and slammed his hands down on the armrests of its seat. "Where. Are. They?"

The shadow didn't solidify as Owen came close to the floating blue eyes. Its skin shifted, shimmering with the background as the creature moved. It settled back into the seat as if his sudden nearness were a mere inconvenience.

The shadow sighed dramatically. "And we were having such a nice conversation too."

It pulled back and kicked him in the chest. The blow to his injured ribs stunned him, knocking him back several feet. It moved quickly, taking advantage of his pained distraction, pressing his back against the wall and covering his mouth. The blurred edges of the shadow snapped into focus and revealed a muscular Native American woman dressed in skin-tight black shorts and a tank top.

"Look, your children are safe, but we have to hurry," she said, eyes blazing. "There are forces at work here you couldn't possibly understand." Her arm pressed harder across his throat, edging dangerously close to cutting off his breathing.

The woman, Abey, continued undeterred by Owen's lack of response and by the holes he was trying to drill into her skull with his eyes. "There are things we have to discuss before I can bring you to your children, and I would prefer to not do this standing. If I let you go, will you sit down and talk to me like a reasonable person?"

That was the last thing Owen wanted to do. Abey knew where his children were, had probably been the one to kidnap them in the first place. Who knew what twisted reason the fae had for taking them?

In the back of his mind, the faint beginnings of a plan took form. When Abey moved back to release him, he put it into action, reversing their positions. He grabbed her arms, twisted them behind her back, and shoved her against the wall. "The only conversation we will be having is the one where you tell me where my children are," he growled in her ear.

"Well," Abey said, shifting her weight. "Apparently we have to do this the hard way." She shoved him hard enough to knock him over before he'd even realized she'd moved. She pulled him up and smashed his face against the wall, pinning his arms behind his back with one hand as she did so.

Owen gasped as his broken rib creaked. Blackness edged his vision before the pain died to manageable levels.

"Stop messing around, boy. We don't have time for this. Answer my questions so we can all move on with our lives, all right?" she snarled, and squeezed his arms tight enough that he had to bite back a cry.

Biting back a curse, he twisted his face to the side to answer her. "Why should I listen to you? You broke into my room and attacked me."

"By all means, feel free to shout. I'll be long gone by the time help gets here, and you'll lose your only chance to see your children again."

Owen froze. The fae had effectively disappeared for fifty years. If Abey left and took the kids with her he'd never be able to find them again. He struggled to answer, pain stealing his breath away. "What," he said through gritted teeth, "do you want to know?"

"I need to know your feelings on the fae." Her hands tightened on his arms enough to make the bone creak.

"You broke into my bloody room," Owen said through a pained gasp. "Is this really the best time to be asking that question?"

"Irrelevant. Your children may be fae as well. I need to know your feelings about them at this moment."

He stopped struggling, his mind unable to process what she was telling him. "What do you mean?"

She sighed, spun, and threw him toward the chair. He fell into it, clutching his injured side. "They told me you lot had gotten smarter in the last fifty years," she said, lips drawing up in a sneer as she paced in front of him. "Your wife was one of us, so your children are probably faeborn." She growled. "Now answer my question."

He bristled, both at the contempt leaking through her words and the implication behind them. "It doesn't matter to me if my children are fae or human as long as they're safe and happy."

The shade smiled and her teeth shone in the dim light. "And would you continue to support your children even if they turned into the creatures of your nightmares? If they became something no longer even faintly resembling human? What would you do then, Mr. Williams?" Her demeanor had changed. She stood in front of him like she was facing an enemy on the verge of attack, staring into his eyes with all traces of good humor gone.

"They're my children. I would love them no matter what they became, no matter what they did," he answered, fingers tightening on his armrests.

"And would you leave everything behind for them? Abandon everything you know?" she asked, drawing closer to him with each word.

"Of course, but why would we have to leave?" he asked.

Abey laughed, a harsh sound that was the antithesis of the sweet voice she had used at the beginning of this strange interview. "Your children can no longer live in your world. Your committees and governments cannot hope to protect them from those that hate us."

He forced himself to his feet and grabbed her arm. "What do you mean they can't stay here? Who's after them?" Concern forced away the good sense telling him to get out of here while he still could.

Abey scoffed. "The people we went to war with never disappeared, Mr. Williams. They've been gaining strength since the war ended, and they are after the children of the fae. We had to take your children to keep them safe."

"You—you took my children? Where are they? What happened?" There was a fire burning in his breast, growing as he considered everything he knew. Blood, there had been blood in the kitchen. What did she know? Who was hurt? He pushed the overwhelming feeling down. He needed answers, and he wouldn't get them if he lost his temper and attacked the only one who could provide them.

Abey shook him off and moved away. "Don't worry, they're safe. But if we'd been a few minutes slower getting them out of the house, things might not have gone so well. As it was, one of our harpies got shot trying to get your dog out when SAFE—"

"Safe? Kidnapping my children won't keep them safe." His voice rose with every word, culminating in a barely contained shout.

"Not safe as in secure, idiot. S-A-F-E, the Society Against Fae Emigration. They've only been actively campaigning against us for the last fifty years. You've heard of them, right?"

"What do—no, they wouldn't do that. My neighbor is the president of the local chapter, and he's daft, but he wouldn't hurt anyone. Besides, how would they even know? It's not like the hospital—" His jaws clacked shut. The hospital would have reported what happened to Tiffany, and those reports weren't exactly secure.

She snorted. "Well, that explains how they got to your house so fast. Look, Williams, you are living in a dream. SAFE has been openly hunting us for years. We can't stop them because your government lets them fester, but we keep an eye on their activities. We've been staking out the town for months, and we knew we had to act quickly when we heard about your wife on the police radio." Her border flickered, bits and pieces of her vanishing and reappearing as she spoke.

"Anyways," she said when the worst of the flickering had stopped, "SAFE is the one who destroyed your home. Your children are in a warehouse a few miles from here, guarded by the rest of my team. They can't get them there."

He felt like the world had dropped out from under his feet as he stumbled back from Abey and fell into the chair. "Wait, you mean you kidnapped my children to stop them from being kidnapped? Do you realize how mental that sounds?"

"Yes, I know it sounds crazy, but I'm telling the truth." She shrugged and Owen, still trying to process her words, didn't respond.

"Look," she said, seemingly tired of waiting for his mind to catch up with the situation. "You've passed my tests. Either you come with me or you stay here, but you have to choose now. SAFE could be anywhere, and I don't fancy trying to run a rescue operation with such a small team." She didn't wait for him to answer before she went to the window and opened it again. "Follow me if you want to see your children again." She jumped through the window, her skin rippling as she faded from sight until her clothes were the only thing still visible.

He hesitated, on the verge of slamming the window shut and calling the police. Maybe Abey had been telling the truth and SAFE had tried to take them, but he shouldn't take her on her word. It'd only take a minute to charge his phone enough to call the police.

But all the same … he couldn't wait. By the time the police found where they were hiding, the fae would be long gone with his kids. He looked in the direction Abey had disappeared and wished Tiffany were here. She'd know what to do.

She wouldn't wait around for someone else to make a decision.

Cursing, he grabbed his jacket and his phone and followed Abey out the window.

***

"You do realize this is illegal, right?" he said as Abey hotwired a beat-up Chevy in the parking lot of a mostly abandoned apartment complex a few blocks away from the hotel.

"Owen, the parking tickets on this thing go back more than three weeks. No one is going to miss it. We'll be lucky if it starts, to be honest," Abey said, her face screwed up in concentration. "Now be quiet, I want to finish this before someone sees us." It took a few more minutes, but the car sputtered to life when she crossed the last two wires.

"Wonderful. It started. Now it just needs to stay together long enough to get wherever you're taking us," he said as he moved toward the passenger side door. A hand on his arm stopped him.

He turned to look at Abey, who smiled apologetically.

"Sorry, Owen, but I'm not allowed to show you where we're hiding."

She shoved a sweet-smelling cloth over his mouth and nose before he could react. His vision clouded and he stumbled against the car, struggling to hold himself up. He fell into Abey's arms as he lost consciousness.

***

Abey shook him awake in the dark car. "Sorry, but you haven't passed all the tests yet."

"Tests? What bloody tests? Didn't you say I passed the tests?" He felt like someone was pounding on his head with a hammer. He glanced around but couldn't figure out where they were. The dilapidated warehouses surrounding them could have been anywhere in the industrial district. Half the buildings there had been abandoned since the Fae War and the city hadn't gotten around to demolishing them yet.

"The tests. You passed my tests, but not the official battery. Every human who wants to help us needs to pass them if they want access to the safehouses. That includes parents, I'm afraid." She rubbed the back of her neck and shrugged.

"You couldn't have mentioned this before you knocked me out?" Owen glared at her as he brought his shaky and awkward limbs back under control. It seemed being chemically knocked out on top of a concussion and several blows to his ribs was a little much for his body to take without complaint.

"It's by order of the queen. She doesn't want a repeat of the Fae War, and that's easier to avoid if no one knows where we are or what our methods are," Abey said.

She scanned the area around them, for what Owen had no idea. It wasn't like the police bothered patrolling this part of town after nightfall. This place was even more abandoned than the apartment building where they'd found the car.

She grabbed his arm and pulled him toward a warehouse that was indistinguishable from the others in the darkness.

He stumbled behind her as she dragged him to a door hidden by tall weeds. He rubbed his aching and bruised arm while she forced the door open. He half expected it to squeal from disuse, but it seemed like the hinges were the only thing in this dump that were looked after. It opened without a sound.

As Owen's eyes adjusted to the darkness, the first thing he saw was the dragon curled around the only light source. The lamp was barely enough to illuminate the sheer size of the beast, and flickering shadows hinted at more beyond their borders. The dragon shifted and a massive foot with claws the size of Owen's forearm dragged along the ground, leaving deep gouges in the cement. Owen's eyes were drawn away from the foreboding sight by the five familiar shapes wearing pajamas sitting by its head.

One of the figures turned when they heard the echoing bang of the door clanging shut, and Arthur's voice carried across the room. "Abey, what's going on? Is that—Dad?"

"Arthur?" Owen croaked, falling to his knees in numb disbelief. A part of him hadn't really believed Abey could take him to them, but now that he was here … He forced himself to his feet, intent on grabbing them and never letting go, when a winged shadow roughly the size of Owen jumped from the ceiling and landed in his path. It screamed, a sound like a million nails running down chalkboards.

The creature had large brown wings that ended in taloned hands, while dark feathers covered its body except for its spindly avian legs. Pinched black eyes glared from a too-human face and screamed hatred from their cold depths.

Abey stepped in front of Owen, blocking the creature from his view. "Tony, that's enough. He's on our side."

The thing—Tony—stopped screaming. He stepped back but still refused to let the children pass. "Abey. You are back." His voice was hoarse and rough like he'd been shouting for a month straight. It sounded like he was forcing speech through muscles that weren't meant to form human speech. "This is their father?"

Abey nodded.

"You are sure we can trust him?" Tony said, blocking Owen again as he tried to pass. "The children told me he was helping that SAFE bastard the other day. You know how humans are. How can we be sure he is not on their side?"

"He passed my tests," Abey said as she stalked forward and shoved Tony out of the way. "If he fails Aaron's, we'll follow the plan. Let him see his kids."

Tony narrowed his eyes, the dim light reflecting off their obsidian depths, but he moved aside and allowed the children to run past.

"It's not my fault if the human betrays us." He flapped his wings harshly and flew to a rafter some thirty feet in the air, his glinting eyes following Owen in the darkness as he limped forward to grab his children.

"Dad!" The cacophony of his children's voices, overlapping as each tried to speak at the same time, sounded like heavenly music to Owen's ears. He never wanted to let them go.

The twins and Ashley grabbed him, hugging wherever they could reach, while Arthur came up behind them. He was carrying a crying Dorothy, who reached for Owen as soon as they got close enough.

Owen counted it as a blessing that none of them had thought to ask about Tiffany yet. Even the thought of breaking the news to them made him want to rip his heart from his body. He'd have to tell them, and soon, but for now he allowed himself to bask in the joy of having his children.

Unsurprisingly, it was Jen who finally managed to be heard over her siblings. "Dad, it was so cool. We were about to go to bed, but then we heard something break and Toto barking downstairs. Arthur went to see what it was and told us to stay in our rooms, but I followed him, and Ashley followed me, and there were these really weird shadow people and—"

David broke in, for once speaking over Jen. "Yeah, and those weird bird things. One of them broke the TV!"

Jen glared at David and kept talking like he hadn't interrupted. "The shadow lady told us we had to go with them because the bad people were coming, but Arthur told them no and was going to call the police, but then one of the bird people said we didn't have time and—" Arthur covered her mouth so someone else could get a word in edgewise.

"Why don't we let him sit down before we tell him the story, Jen? He looks a little beat up." Arthur looked meaningfully at the bruises on Owen's face. Ashley gasped and pulled the others away, a fear the twins didn't have turning her face white.

Owen took Dorothy, balancing her on his hip while shifting her away from his abused ribs.

Arthur set his hand on Owen's shoulder, trying to guide him toward the light. "Come on, guys. Let's sit down. We're all tired," he said. He wore a smile that didn't reach his eyes as he gestured toward the dragon with his other hand.

Owen hesitated. Everything he had ever heard about the fae told him to make a run for it while he still could. No one got away after the fae got their hands on them and whatever plan they had, he wanted no part of it. Even if Abey had taken him to the kids.

"Dad, it's ok," Arthur whispered in Owen's ear. The twins were already halfway back and it was only Arthur's hand that kept Owen from trying to grab them. "They're good people."

Owen bent his head toward him. "Are you sure?"

Arthur nodded and stuffed his hands in his pockets. "I wasn't at first, when they broke into the house. But Dad, they protected us. Those SAFE guys—they were trying to kill us. One almost got Dorothy, but Abey managed to get her out of the house." Conviction burned in his eyes, its fury matched only by the strength of his voice.

Owen took a deep breath and squared his shoulders. "All right, let's not keep them waiting. The sooner we find out what they want, the sooner we can get out of here."

"Dad, one more thing," Arthur said, glancing around to see if any of his siblings were paying attention. "What happened to Mom? Is she—?"

Owen cut him off. "Later. I can't—not right now. I'll tell you all later, I promise. But now we need to focus on what's happening here." He couldn't tell them, not until he was sure they were safe. And anyway, the others hadn't thought to ask yet. He could put it off for a while longer. Arthur would understand.

***

"Nice of you to join us, Mr. Williams," called out a tanned short man sitting by the dragon's head. Like Abey, he wore nothing but shorts and a tank top, but somehow he was showing more skin. "Jason Lucien, shade extraordinaire, at your service." His eyes twinkled as he bowed and swept his arms around him.

"I figure I'd introduce y'all to everybody." He pointed to each person as he said their names. "You met Abey, and Peter Jackman is the scary-looking one there, bless his heart. Both of them, fine shades. The dragon around us is Nathan Johnson, a good man once you get past the scales, teeth, and fiery breath."

"Bite me, Jason," the dragon said, opening one eye to glare at Jason as the Williams approached. His voice sounded higher than it should have, sort of like he'd been inhaling helium, but was just as rough as Tony's.

"Oh, you know you love me, you beautiful flying lump." Jason spun in a circle and pointed into the rafters when he stopped. "Moving on, the harpy who greeted you on your way in is Tony Carson, and really, he's shy—"

A rock flew out of the shadows at Jason, who dodged it without skipping a beat. "Also joining us is the other harpy, Isaac Rueben, who's hunting right now but should be back before sunrise. Last but not least, sleeping against Nathan's side is our siren, Aaron Rodriguez, who prefers A-a-ron—" The other fae snorted. "Shut up. You know he likes it."

A dark-haired young man in black shorts and a matching t-shirt— Peter, one of the shades—snorted again. "Or he's given up on convincing you to call him his actual name and is putting up with you until he can request a transfer to another team."

Jason waved, dismissing the younger shade's argument. "Nonsense. Everyone loves me; I'm hilarious."

Abey grinned, her blue eyes glinting in the dim light. "Why don't you wake him, then, since you're such good friends?"

"Hey now," Jason said as the blood drained from his face. "I may be everyone's favorite person, but even I know better than to wake Aaron when he's sleeping. I prefer not being poisoned, thank you very much."

Owen's curiosity got the better of him as he sat at the edge of the circle of light and shifted Dorothy to his hip. "Poisoned?"

Jason spun toward him, discomfort forgotten. "Sirens have poisonous claws, and they're very cool—"

"Shut up, Jason. They don't need to know that," Aaron, a man with thick spikes in place of hair and olive-colored scales, said in a sleep-roughened voice as he stood and stretched in one motion. He nodded toward Owen as a yawn split his jaw in two. "Is this him?"

Without waiting for an answer, Aaron walked over and stuck his hand out. "Aaron Rodriguez." His voice fell like music on Owen's ears and drew him in like a whirlpool.

Owen shifted his grip on Dorothy and shook Aaron's hand. "Owen Williams. You're the one who's going to give me those tests, right?"

Aaron stared at him without answering, his eyes weighing and judging. It was unclear what he saw that made him nod, but he did. "Well, let's get this over with." He walked out of the circle of light into the darkness beyond.

Owen's head swiveled toward Abey, hoping she could explain what he was supposed to do.

"He's the one to talk to if you want to come with us, Owen," she said, shrugging in an unhelpful manner. "I'd hurry. He might get impatient."

Owen passed Dorothy, who was reluctant to let him go, to Arthur. He took a deep breath as the children settled down next to Nathan, then followed Aaron into the darkness.

Once they were out of sight of the group and hidden by Nathan's bulk, Aaron turned to face him. "Mr. Williams, did Abey or Jason tell you anything about the tests?"

Owen shook his head and stuffed his hands in his pockets. "No, all Abey said was some queen won't let you talk about it." He looked around the area he'd been led to, trying to figure out what the testing would require. "Who is the queen? Abey didn't say."

Aaron nodded and began moving some of the boxes out of the way, clearing a space for the two of them. "The Fae Queen."

"The Fae Queen? What—who is she?"

"I can't tell you yet. You have to pass the tests."

"Tests?" Owen said, grabbing Aaron's arm as he passed. "What are these tests everyone is talking about?" He was tempted to start pacing himself, just so he could move. If he'd wanted to be terrified and uncertain about his family's future, he'd have stayed at the hotel.

Aaron held his hands up, trying to placate Owen. "Look, I know this is frustrating, but you have to understand. We're a secretive people for a reason, and if I could, I'd tell you everything. But I can't, so I need you to trust me." Aaron looked him straight in the eye. There was no humor in his voice, nothing to lighten the frightening level of gravity. "Will you trust me?"

Owen hesitated. Arthur said he trusted these people, and even David seemed comfortable around them. If his two most cautious children felt at ease here, shouldn't he? "Will it hurt? Can you at least tell me that?" he asked, shoulders drooping as he silently pleaded with the other man for honesty.

"It depends. Some people say it's like a dream; others, like a nightmare." The answer was, as always, lacking in any substance, but Aaron did have some air of earnestness about him.

"And you can't tell me anything else?" he asked, deflated.

"It's easier to fake the results if you know what to expect," Aaron said, setting a hand on Owen's shoulder.

Owen stared at Aaron, trying to measure him up, and made his decision. "All right. What do you need me to do?"

Aaron shrugged. "Hold still."

CHAPTER THREE

IN WHICH THERE ARE QUESTIONS ANSWERED AND ANSWERS QUESTIONED

"Some of the reborn have begun taking new names to reflect their new forms. Beira said this was a development we should officially approve of, and thus each of the founders has chosen a new name in addition to our given name. Thus, I am Lady Lorelei and Thomas is Lord Orpheus. Lord Chiron was the one to suggest the names. He said they were appropriate, considering what we recently found out. We knew our song could heal fae, but when we tried healing a human, they entered a hypnotic state and would do anything we told them to. This could be a major advantage in the war."

— Excerpt from the journals of Jennifer Thomson, Lady Lorelei

Aaron set his hand on Owen's forehead and started to sing. The sound wound through Owen's mind, confusing and scattering his consciousness as it settled in the center. His body sagged into Aaron's arms as the wonderful voice consumed him.

It was euphoric. The pain of his injuries faded away, and his eyes fell shut as the voice guided him to a protected place in his mind. Nothing could hurt him here: not grief, not loss, not worry. He was safe.

Now the voice was asking him questions. In a faraway part of his mind, he wondered if he had been drugged again, but this didn't feel like anything he had experienced before, even in his rather wild youth. Soon enough, even these vague thoughts drifted away as the voice consumed him. Who was he? What did he want? He answered the questions, wanting only to keep the voice happy. Whatever the voice wanted him to do.

Then the voice began asking harder questions: Did he blame the fae for what happened to his family? Did he hate his wife for not being what he thought she was? Did he hate his children? Would he hate his children if they became fae? No, no, he tried to protest, but his mind was so full. The voice pressed him to say yes, he would reject his children, they would become monsters, they might turn on him someday. Pain built behind his eyes with each refusal. The safe spot dissolved into torture and terror as every injury and hurt he had experienced in his life was resurrected to wound him anew. Broken bones, bruises, the heartache of leaving Wales for the last time, and the screaming grief of losing Tiffany all fought for his attention.

The voice pressed harder, and the pain in his head rose to a crescendo. Anguish filled every iota of his being, and had his muscles listened to him, he might have tried to jump away—but where would he go? The voice was everywhere. He may have screamed but he wasn't sure. He was missing something. Why would the voice want him to say these things?

The pain ebbed away and a soothing sensation replaced the biting, aching agony of before, as the voice changed its line of questioning. If the fae took them to their country, would he keep his silence about the locations of safehouses and villages? Could he be trusted with the secrets of the hidden people? Yes, yes, he would never betray them when they had protected his family. The voice, satisfied with his answers, withdrew from his mind.

Slowly, Owen came back to himself. They were still standing in the warehouse. Exhaustion wracked his frame as Aaron guided him to the ground.

"It's okay. The weariness you feel will pass shortly." Aaron sat down next to Owen, who rested his head against his legs and took deep breaths. "You did well. Most humans can't resist suggestion. You passed the tests."

Owen forced himself to sit up. "I passed?" he said, gasping for air between words. "How long was I . . ." he faltered, unsure how to phrase his question. "Whatever you called it?"

Aaron smiled and his shark-like teeth reflected the sparse moonlight. "Siren song is hypnotic. It's useful if you want to get answers out of someone without the trouble of interrogation." He stood, offered a hand to Owen, and pulled him to his feet. "It's been about twenty minutes, so we better get back to the others. That scream of yours probably scared the kids."

Nodding, Owen stumbled after him. It didn't feel like it had only been twenty minutes; the pain alone felt like it had lasted an inescapable eternity. He shivered and shook his head, desperate to force away the memory and everything it had dragged up from his mind.

The dim lamps felt like lemon juice in a papercut to Owen's tired eyes after the darkness of the warehouse. As the two of them stepped into the light, the children crowded around Owen, demanding to know what had happened in panicked and terrified voices. It took a few minutes for him to reassure them he was all right.

Satisfied, they led him over to where they had been sitting and settled themselves in a circle around him. If he hadn't been so exhausted, he would have laughed at the sight of Jen glaring at any of the fae who came close.

Aaron settled against Nathan's side. "All right," he said, pulling a silver flask from his jacket. "You have questions."

For a moment, the room was silent except for the occasional scrape of scale or claw against the cement.

"What did you do to my Dad?" Jen asked. The dark and threatening suspicion that filled her voice pulled Owen's heart to pieces. Why couldn't she have gotten a few more years of childhood before she realized how cruel the world could be?

Aaron took a swig from his flask before answering. "I hypnotized him." He stared at the flask like it contained the answers they wanted. "I had to. According to fae law, any human that wants to become an ally must prove themselves willing to protect our secrecy at all costs."

"Why do you need these tests anyway? Couldn't you have made him sign a contract or something?" Arthur asked, voice hardened by broken trust. "You hurt him."

Owen put a hand on Arthur's shoulder, trying to tell him it was all right without speaking. Their eyes locked for a few seconds before Arthur shook him off and sat down, glowering at the others.

Jason answered this time, crossing his arms over his chest and glancing away from the group. "Because of the war." The sentence brought darkness into the eyes of the gathered fae, who turned from the light. "During the war, we were betrayed by a group of humans who agreed to shelter fae young and their faeborn relatives. Towns that offered us shelter were bombed by U.S. forces. A lot of innocents, human and fae alike, were killed. We took steps to ensure it could never happen again."

It didn't seem right to break the silence that followed. There was an old pain in their faces, the sort of hurt time couldn't touch. As one minute dragged into the next, Owen found the courage to ask the question that had been gnawing at him ever since he'd heard about the tests: "What happens when someone fails?"

"In your case . . ." Aaron answered, rolling his flask in his hands. "You would have been taken to the capital because your children need you. If you had been a random human who wanted to help, I would've wiped your memory. It wouldn't be safe to let anyone not completely loyal to us know our secrets."

"What would happen if I broke that trust?" Part of Owen didn't want the answer, but a larger part of him wanted, needed, to know.

"Traitors get their memories wiped if they haven't caused too much harm," said Peter. "Otherwise, it depends on who catches them." His voice was cold, and a malice like none Owen had ever felt coated his words.

"What do you mean?"

"If their betrayal costs lives, rogues might hunt them down. If the Siren Corps can't get to them in time, traitors don't tend to survive." There was nothing kind about that smile, and it sent a shiver down Owen's spine.

"Peter, stand down," Abey said as she grabbed his shoulder.

Peter shook her hand off. "They asked. I was being honest."

"Now's not the time—"

Peter snorted and stood. Between one moment and the next, he vanished into the shadows of the warehouse.

"I'll go deal with him." Abey barely waited for Aaron's nod of approval before she vanished too.

"What was that all about?" Owen asked, staring at where the two shades had disappeared.

"His dad died on a supply run about ten years ago," Jason said, jaw tightening as he turned back to the light. "Our informant turned on us. Peter's older brother was the only survivor. By the time the Corps got there, the informant was in pieces around his apartment."

Owen's jaw dropped and he sucked in a breath. That had not been what he had expected to hear. That the fae could be killed, something everyone agreed was impossible, was surprising enough. That they could do something like rip someone apart was something out of the worst of the war stories he had ever heard. "In pieces?" he managed to whisper, stomach roiling at the thought. He dared a glance around the room and the kids weren't doing much better. "How could he do something like that?"

"We're not human, you have to understand that," Aaron said, eyes focused on something out of sight. "We can become so filled with one emotion that we can't feel anything else. To become so obsessed that nothing can distract us: not hunger, not grief, not injury, or reasoning. Only the satisfaction of our goal."

There was a beat of silence. "So, Peter's brother . . ." Owen couldn't bring himself to finish.

"Went feral and killed the informant, yeah," Aaron said, taking another sip from his flask. "When he came back to himself, he was never the same. He disappeared into the wilderness three years ago. We've been trying to track him ever since, but a shade that doesn't want to be found isn't going to be. His disappearance, and the death of their father, changed Peter. He takes a while to warm up to outsiders."

"No kidding," Owen whispered. "What's going to happen now?" He'd been avoiding thinking about the future, but he couldn't put it off anymore. Not after that conversation. If there was a chance that could happen to the fae gathered here, he needed to know about it.

"Well," Aaron said, shoving his flask back into his jacket as he stood. "It'll take most of the day to reach the haven, but the first safehouse is only four hours away, so the first group will leave tomorrow afternoon. The second group will fly out after sunset and meet you at the capital."

He walked to a small pile of bags stacked against one wall and pulled a battered notebook and a pencil nub from one of them. He gave both to Owen. "Our allies will try to get the rest of your possessions to you sometime in the future, so just list what you need for now. I'll be speaking with Jason, so give it to me whenever you finish."

Owen took the notebook and pencil in disbelief. That was it? Were they supposed to hide out here all day? Hope no one came for them? He got up to follow Aaron and demand more answers but stopped when David pulled at his sleeve.

"Dad? I need to ask you something." David chewed his lip and his eyes darted around anxiously. He opened and closed his mouth several times, once even getting as far as the first word before he was finally able to speak. "Where's Mom?"

Time slowed to a crawl. Everything he had tried to block out—his grief, his shock, and the aching, tearing loss that made him want to scream until there was no more air in his lungs—broke through his walls and flooded his chest with paralyzing agony. As he wrestled with his emotions, David's hopeful face fell. Owen tried to say something, anything to stop the heartbreak creeping over his children's faces.

"Daddy, where's Mommy? What happened to Mommy?" Dorothy asked, her tiny fingers tugging at his shirt. Ashley and Jen clung to each other for support as tears spilled down their cheeks. Arthur froze, face falling like the world had dropped out from under his feet. They knew. He hadn't said anything, and they knew.

He dropped to his knees and he pulled them into his arms, trying to find some semblance of calm for their sake, but his walls crumbled. "I'm sorry. I'm so sorry," he said, voice shaking and cracking. He pulled back to look into the eyes of his children, eyes that begged him to take back the words he hadn't even spoken yet. "Your mother . . . she was fae . . . she didn't . . ."

Like this sentence was the pebble that started the avalanche, his children began to grieve in earnest. Arthur's arms wrapped around Ashley, tears threatening to spill as he tried to ground himself. Ashley huddled into Arthur's arms and buried her face in his shoulder. She bit her fist to muffle the heart-rending sobs wracking her body. David's broken and gasping whimpers filled the air, his hair wild and eyes wide and vacant as he stared into the distance. Jen flung herself into Owen, desperate for some shred of comfort, of familiarity. And Dorothy, sweet Dorothy, she knew she had lost something, but she didn't know what. Where was Mommy? Where was Mommy? Over and over again she begged for her mother, yanking on Owen's shirt and demanding he take her to her.

As for himself, Owen forced back his own tears, shut the grief back behind his wall before it could crush him. He offered comfort so what was left of his family could mourn and heal while they still could. They couldn't go home anymore, the fae wouldn't let them, and there was no telling what tomorrow would bring. They were together for now and that was what mattered.

He wasn't sure how long they stayed there. Dorothy had cried herself to sleep in his arms, and the others were dead on their feet. The fae had withdrawn to a respectful distance from the mourning family, giving them space to grieve.

Jason noticed Owen's searching look and approached on silent feet. The quiet understanding on his face and the gentle set of his shoulders seemed out of place on a man who seemed to spend more time laughing and joking then being serious. His lips turned down as he directed them to the mats piled in one corner.

Owen nodded, too tired to question how prepared the fae were. He stood, shuffled Dorothy in his arms and pushed Ashley toward the mats, while Arthur took the twins' hands. They followed him, docile as sheep.

Arthur refused to go to bed after they had settled the other four, despite his obvious exhaustion. He said he wanted to help Owen make the list.

They crept back into the light and got to work. Jason said Nathan could only carry a few hundred pounds more, so they couldn't ask for much. First came clothes, both for winter and everyday wear, and then a small assortment of things that would make the transition easier. Dorothy's stuffed lion, Ashley's violin, Jen's drawing supplies, David's whittling kit, and Arthur's guitar. His and Tiffany's wedding pictures. He was about to give the list to Aaron when he remembered something.

"Who's going to take care of Toto?" The dog, a poorly named newfoundland/black lab mix, had been a Christmas present to the kids from Tiffany and him last year. He was fiercely protective of the kids, and it broke Owen's heart to think they had to leave him behind on top of everything else.

Aaron, gleaning something of Owen's thoughts from his face, smiled. "Your dog? He's riding with you. Isaac took him to get some exercise when he went hunting. They're due back any minute."

As if the words summoned him, a dark figure swooped through a hole in the ceiling, and in its arms was a massive wriggling shape. A frustrated voice floated down to them. "No, stay still, you mutt. Oh, queen's throne, I should have left you there."

It landed just outside the circle. "What should I do with the dog?" it asked Aaron in a deep voice.

The creature stepped into the light, carrying a squirming Toto, who seemed determined to lick every part of the harpy's face he could reach and only stopped when Owen called out his name. Toto froze as his mind processed the presence of one of his people before he renewed his efforts to get down. The harpy gave up his efforts to control the dog and dropped him.

Unfazed by the short fall, Toto leapt toward Owen, barking madly. Laughter bubbled from Owen's lips as he crouched to hug Toto. The rest of their lives were in shambles, but at least they still had this one thing.

Smiling, Owen turned to thank Aaron and the newcomer, but they were already deep in conversation. He swallowed back his thanks and waited for an opening. It'd be rude to interrupt, he reasoned, and besides, he could use this opportunity to learn something new about the fae.

Tony was big compared to this bloke. His bird and human features seemed discordant; they didn't fit together at all. His wings stuck out at odd angles and didn't sit right—Owen would've been surprised if Tony could pull them in enough to lie down—and his hands looked like the afterthought of some mad genius. It was almost like someone had mixed a falcon with a man to make him, with no concern for how he looked or functioned. To Owen, it seemed a minor miracle he was able to get off the ground.

This one, though, was a better blend of bird and human. He actually had arms, ones that were completely separate from his large, black wings. His chest pushed out more, like a proper bird's, and was mirrored by the large muscles on his back. A longbow was thrown over one shoulder and a quiver and a knife hung from his belt. He was the first to notice Owen's scrutiny and turned to face him. He threw out his wings and bowed.

"Hello, my friend. Nice of you to join us, although I must say I did not enjoy the company of your dog very much. The name's Isaac Rueben. I'm sure you met my comrade Tony, so I must assure you that not all harpies are quite as mean as he is." Isaac's eyes shone with barely contained mirth now that he wasn't dealing with Toto.

He turned to Aaron again. "Sorry about being late." He cast a narrowed glare at Toto. "But the dog kept chasing squirrels. I couldn't get him to stay still long enough for me to catch something."

After a few more explanations for why he was late and quips about his exact opinion of dogs in general, Isaac yawned, arms and wings stretching out behind him. "I'm going to bed. I assume Tony is nesting in the rafters again?" he asked, barely waiting for Aaron's nod. "Right, then. I'll join him there." Without another word, he flew into the darkness of the rafters.

Owen blinked as the dust settled. Toto had wandered over to Arthur, seeking attention, while Owen was distracted by the new harpy. He turned to Aaron. "Do you—what was that about?"

Aaron shrugged. "Remember what I said about fae having dominant emotions? Harpies are like that all the time. They're happy or sad or excited or angry with no room for anything else." He pulled out his flask and took a swig. "It makes living with them hell, but once you learn to manage the mood swings it goes easier."

He glanced down at the paper still in Owen's hands. "I'd make sure you have what you need for the dog on that list; it might be awhile before you can get any of it again."

Aaron waited for Owen to add those last few items to the list before he took it. He ran a critical eye over Owen and Arthur. "It's about four in the morning, and we have a long day ahead of us. You two should go to bed." He pushed them toward the sleeping area. "I'll wake you around eleven, now sleep."

Tired enough to admit Aaron had a point, they went without too much resistance. The twins had claimed one mat and were curled up into a ball in their thin sleeping bag. Ashley was cradling Dorothy on another; leaving two mats open for them. Arthur dropped off between the space of two breaths, but Owen lay awake for a while longer.

He stared up at the ceiling and resisted the urge to toss and turn. Grief he'd only been able to touch on earlier tried to break down his walls, but he couldn't give in to it yet. He had to look out for the kids, the only part of Tiffany he had left. Once they were safe and he knew they would stay human, he could grieve. It was just a matter of waiting that long.

Other worries plagued him too. Was he doing the right thing? He should have taken them and run while they still had a chance. Better yet, he should have called the police back at the hotel. As he replayed the day's events, exhaustion pulled him into an uneasy sleep.

***

Aaron shook him awake. "It's almost noon, Owen. Time to get up, we need to pack."

Owen forced himself out of his warm sleeping bag and stretched as Aaron moved on to Arthur. The light of the late morning sun lit the warehouse, showing its worn-down state in its entirety. Graffiti covered the walls and rusted equipment lay in various states of disrepair throughout the room. Holes dotted the ceiling, the largest of which was the size of a bus. Owen shivered. That explained why is had been so cold last night. Off to one side, the fae were gathered around Nathan.

It was shocking to see how much smaller Nathan was in the light of day. Last night, Owen would have sworn he was the size of a house, but he was only about fifteen feet tall and roughly thirty feet from snout to tail tip. Foot-long spikes ran the length of his spine, and his burnished bronze scales reflected the sunlight as he stretched his wings.

"Ah, wonderful to look at, isn't he?" Aaron said, coming up behind him. "Believe it or not, he's actually one of the more nondescript ones. There are some who can't leave the haven because they stick out so much." He clasped Owen's shoulder and pointed toward the kids. "Magnificent as he is, I'd get them up before the harpies eat all the food."

The kids were reluctant to wake, but between a groggy Ashley and himself, they managed to get them up with promises of food. Within minutes the entire Williams clan was stumbling on its way to the main group.

Abey intercepted them halfway there with two combs. Handing one to Owen, she grunted something about helping however she could and assisted him in taming Ashley's and Dorothy's wild bedheads. Owen, the boys, and Jen, each having short hair, ran a hand through the worst of the tangles and called it good. Now presentable, Abey allowed them to continue to the others.

Breakfast consisted of oatmeal and some dried fruit Jason had produced with a flourish from one of the many bags lying in a pile near the circle. Arthur and Owen gratefully accepted coffee from Jason, who swore he had had to fight off both harpies for it. Said harpies were perched on Nathan's back, bickering in a hooting language to each other, each with their own mug.

Owen's normally boisterous children sat in a subdued huddle away from the main group. Jen, the loudest of her siblings by far, barely spoke. David and Ashley were slumped on either side of her, picking at their food. Dorothy was the only one who seemed anywhere close to normal. She was playing with Jason, her grief forgotten for the time being. They were currently involved in a wild game of chase with Toto that had already laid waste to two stacks of boxes.

Once breakfast was finished, Owen and Arthur helped put away the mats and sleeping bags, leaving them hidden in the basement of the warehouse. Ashley made the twins help her wash the dishes and put away the food. Aaron told them not to bother with the food, as someone would be by to move it later, but Ashley, desperate for a shred of normalcy, ignored him.

"Are we allowed to ask about the safehouses? Or is that another thing we can only talk about someplace else?" Owen asked Aaron during a short lull in activity.

Aaron shrugged as he finished shoving the last of the sleeping bags into their bag. "Technically, no, but off the record, I can tell you we have them all over the country, maintained by our human allies. I'd tell you more, but even I don't know where any safehouses are, except the ones on our route and a few of the permanent ones."

"Why?" Arthur asked. His face was a blank slate, devoid of any signs of life, and a perfect match to his emotionless voice.

Aaron shrugged. "It's safer that way. As soon as a safehouse is compromised, we abandon it and set up a new one somewhere else. As a field commander, I know more than most, but only the Council and the heads of the Siren Corps know every safehouse."

"That makes sense," Arthur said, tilting his head to the side. "But what do you do if you don't have a safehouse to go to? Doesn't abandoning them make it harder to hide?"

"Well, yeah," Aaron said with a snort. "Which is why even our toddlers know how to survive in the wild. Hell, even Nathan over there could disappear for a few days if he found a big enough mud pit." He walked over to one of the tarp-covered piles lining the side of the warehouse.

He put a stop to the questions by pulling a large bundle of rope and leather out from under the tarp. "Oi, Isaac, Tony, get over here and help me with the saddle," he yelled at the harpies, who dropped their bags by the large pile next to Nathan's left foreleg.

He turned back to Owen and Arthur. "You might want to step back. This is a bit of a production."

The Williams stood off to the side as the fae unfolded a massive net with large leather patches tied into it. The harpies grabbed one end and flew it over Nathan, who now stood in the center of the warehouse. The shades stood on his back and positioned the net over his spikes, making sure everything fell where it needed to. The saddlebag patches hung along the edges of Nathan's spines, over his wings and out of the way. The bags were quickly loaded, and it wasn't long before there was no sign they'd been in the warehouse at all.

Nathan laid back down carefully, trying to find a comfortable position for his wings that didn't flatten the saddlebags. It seemed strange to Owen. "Aren't we supposed to leave soon? Why is he lying down?" he asked Aaron.

"We still need to get your things; besides, it's still too light out for Nathan to leave without being seen. Abey, the harpies, Nathan, and I will leave about an hour after sunset," Aaron answered as he checked his watch. "Your ride will be here in about twenty minutes."

Ashley frowned and looked over at where Nathan was still trying to find a comfortable position. "Then why did you put that saddle on him now?" she asked. "Wouldn't it be more comfortable for him if he put it on later?"

Jason sat by Ashley with a thud. "Yep, but it's better to pack now so we don't forget anything if we have to make a quick escape."

He leaned back and looked over at Nathan's laden form. Then he made a face at Ashley. "You know, you'd think the dwarves would have come up with a better design for this thing by now. Fifty years we've been up north, and still the best they can come up with is some leather bags and a thick net." He shook his head as he looked back at Nathan.

"We don't even get to ride him," he said, his lips pulling down into a frown. "The saddles that can take more than two people were deemed 'too dangerous' by the Powers That Be, and the gondolas are too bulky for covert use, so we're stuck with more traditional modes of transportation."

His show of exaggerated sorrow and irritation made Ashley laugh. Its unexpected bright peal rang in the stilted silence of the warehouse like a church bell.

Jason shook his finger at her and stuck out his lower lip, which only made her laugh harder. He turned to Jen, who was looking at them like they were insane. "She's laughing at me. Can you believe it?"

A smile crept over Jen's ashen face, and she too began to giggle. Jason, in turn, looked to David and Dorothy for sympathy to much the same effect, and laughter filled the warehouse.

Conversation flowed more naturally after that. Owen and Arthur chatted with Aaron about insignificant nothings while the girls and David bombarded Jason with questions about his home. It wasn't much, but it seemed to help keep their minds off their grief.

Jason seemed to understand what they were trying to do and did his best to keep up with their questions. He talked about the land around his home and his people's culture between anecdotes about various misadventures he had had over the years. Each answer seemed tailored to distract the one who asked it and to bring them out of their subdued shells. His gestures grew grander and his prose more unlikely as he built an entire world with each word.

He described cities carved out of living rock, villages where crops were planted on top of houses buried in the sod, the traditions of the wolf packs that roamed the wilds, and hunts that stretched into weeks in the cold of winter. He told of enchanting sirens and fearsome harpies, of the artistry of the dwarves and the brutality of the clashes of dragons and trolls, the mystery of the shades and the wisdom of the gryphons, and always dark hints about the war that drove the fae into their northern country. Undoubtedly, he would have continued forever had there not been a knock on the warehouse door.

CHAPTER FOUR

IN WHICH THERE IS AN EXPECTED JOURNEY

"We've located a place to settle in the northern Canadian Rockies and have begun construction. Most of the fae have already made their way there, but Lady Séaghdha and Lord Falk brought up the matter of new arrivals. We hear about more people changing each day, and due to our efforts to keep the location of our new home secret, we aren't sure how to get them from there to here. There are also a number of reborn who are concerned about family members still outside that didn't Change, so I'm sensing the possibility of a two birds, one stone solution."

—Excerpt from the journals of Beira Thomson, Queen Titania

The knock reverberated through the warehouse and scattered the fae. The harpies flew on silent wings and perched like gargoyles in the rafters. The shades stood guard on either side of the door, having moved faster than Owen thought possible to reach their posts.

Aaron pushed the Williams behind Nathan. He then pulled himself up on Nathan's back, using his spikes to steady himself, until he was in a position where he could see the whole warehouse.

Owen handed Toto's makeshift leash to Arthur and gestured for him to keep the dog silent while he peeked out from behind Nathan. He clenched his fists, wishing he had a weapon.

Abey approached the door on the tips of her toes as her skin faded in and out of view. She rapped her knuckles against the door in a short, brisk five-knock pattern. The person outside returned two short knocks and Abey opened the door a crack.

"When the king fell and the queen rose, who remained to bury their bones?" Her voice was light and uncaring, but the knife she held in her left hand was anything but.

"When the queen rode to war and the king lay in repose, no one remained to lay to rest their bones." The voice that answered was as dry as a desert in drought, although Owen could have sworn he recognized it.

Abey breathed a sigh of relief as she sheathed her knife. She pulled open the door, revealing the man behind it.

Owen's breath caught. He knew that man, recognized his graying hair and pot belly. "You—" Owen stormed out from behind Nathan and stalked toward the man, blood roaring in his ears. "You were the one who interviewed me yesterday."

The officer took a step back, face paling. Abey pulled him into the warehouse and toward Owen.

When the two parties met, the officer held up his hands and paired them with a timid smile as he glanced between Abey and Owen. "Sorry about yesterday, Mr. Williams, but we had to be sure. You needed to—"

"Take the tests. I know. They told me," Owen said, still seething, the blood burning in his veins, a scorching, vehement flame that threatened to consume him. He forced his hands into fists and resisted the urge to grab the officer by the throat.

This man had known where his children were, even as he practically accused him, their father, of trying to hurt them. He'd been the one to direct him to the hotel where Abey had found him. He had access to the hospital reports, and probably told the fae where they lived, let them take his children. Everything he had gone through since he had woken up in the hospital, all the stress, the terror, and the worry, could be pinned on the man in front of him.

The officer, face as white as chalk, took two steps back as Owen took two forward. "Hey now, I wanted to tell you, but—" He ducked behind Abey as Owen lunged at him.

Abey grabbed Owen's shoulders to stop him from making another attempt. "Owen, stop," she said, pushing him back. "This isn't helping things; you need to calm down."

Owen, who was still trying to set the officer on fire with his eyes, snarled. "But he's the one who—"

Abey grabbed his chin and forced him to look at her. "Yes," she said firmly, meeting Owen's murderous glare with a steady one of her own. "He was acting under our orders. Please don't kill your ride out of here."

They stared at each other for a time, a silent battle of wills.

Owen broke first, closing his eyes and turning his head. "Fine," he said through gritted teeth and shook Abey's hands off. He forced himself to breathe, trying to regain his composure. When he felt he could face the officer without trying to kill him, he turned back. "I apologize for how I acted." The words came like pulling teeth as he shot a nasty look at Abey. "After all, it wasn't your fault, Officer—?"

The officer nodded, brown eyes flickering between Abey and Owen. "No, no, it's fine. I'd, ah, I'd do the same thing if I was in your position. My name's Carson O'Neill." He rubbed a hand over the back of his neck and smiled again, more genuinely this time. "And hey, if it makes you feel better, you can punch me. Just nowhere anyone can see a mark, ok? Don't wanna have to explain that back at the station."

Owen considered decking him. No one would judge him, and he'd been given permission. After all, he'd kept the whereabouts of the children from Owen immediately after his wife was killed. No matter what Abey said, it had been his choice to do so. Really, he could do it—should do it.

But … the kids were here, watching him. Hitting O'Neill would make him feel better, but it wouldn't help anything. Besides, he should make an effort to practice the lessons he was always preaching to them. "No need. All is forgiven." He forced a smile and pushed down his perfectly rational anger.

Officer O'Neill's smile grew as he crossed his arms and nodded. He turned away from Owen, shoulders relaxing as he walked away. "Hey, Rodriguez, everything set to go? If you ever finish loading the van, we can get out of here before I die of old age."

"Hold your horses, O'Neill," Aaron said as he hefted a bag over his shoulder. "We're almost done. Don't you worry, you'll get to your fishing tournament in time." Aaron laughed as he threw his load down and then started walking toward Owen.

"We do need to get moving, though," Aaron said in a lower voice when he got close enough. "Officer O'Neill's van is parked outside, and he can't stay for long. Owen, you and your children need to get in the back."

"Wait. Aren't you coming with us?" Arthur asked, barging out from behind Nathan. His hands clenched into fists as he looked between the door and Aaron. "What's happening here?"

Aaron shrugged. "The harpies, Nathan, Abey, and I aren't going with you. We'll ride with Nathan and meet you back at Tearmann."

"Well, why aren't the rest of you coming?" Jen said, her smile disappearing as she narrowed her eyes. Whatever goodwill she had had toward the fae, and Aaron, in particular, had soured after Owen had been hypnotized, and Jason's stories weren't enough to restore it.

Aaron arched an eyebrow, tilting his head as he stared at the young girl. He crouched down to look her in the eye. "Jen, you have to understand that the harpies and Nathan can't fit in the van. It's my job to make sure they get home safely." His lips pulled up into a small smile. "I can't do that if I'm stuck in a van, miles away."

"It's like with Dad, right?" David said. The group looked at him strangely, and he rolled his eyes. "Like the other night, when Dad had to take care of Mom. He made us go with Arthur so he could help her. You're letting Jason and Peter protect us while you and Abey look after the others." His solemn blue eyes, his mother's eyes, shone in the soft light.

Owen's heart panged with grief that took his breath away. David was so like his mother. And now, when he and his siblings were all Owen had left of his beautiful wife, her traits shone starkly against what they had gotten from him. David may have looked like him, with his Welsh face and dark hair, but he shared his mother's eyes. And her heart. If any of his children had a chance of growing up to be as kind or as loving as Tiffany had been, it was David.

In his heart, Owen hoped those were the only traits his son shared with his mother. He would love his children even if they were fae, but they'd already lost so much because of this. Tiffany, their mother and his wife, was dead. They could never go home. Was it so wrong of him to wish they'd never have to face the struggles it would bring them?

Owen shook his head like it would also remove the stain of a moment of weakness. Like it would take away thoughts that even now sat curled in the back of his mind, a cobra waiting to strike.

Aaron coughed into his sleeve, providing a needed distraction for Owen. The normally composed man jumped up, eyes casting around as he tried to buy time, his scales flushing an interesting color. "I, I suppose you could phrase it like that. I mean, I wouldn't call myself a father figure . . ."

"At any rate," he said, recovering when he saw Jason leap out of the van. "You need to leave. Jason and Peter are traveling with you, that's what I came over here to say. Officer O'Neill will answer any questions you have about plans. I have to go."

Officer O'Neill returned as the Williams watched a grown man flee from an eight-year-old's innocuous observation. "Are you ready to go, Williams?" he asked, shrinking when the family turned their eyes on him. "The van's packed," he mumbled, jerking a thumb over his shoulder, "and I want to make it to Bayfield before midnight, if possible."

Owen nodded and directed the kids toward the van. It occurred to him that he should try to find out something about their travel plans before they left, even if he would rather eat nails than talk to Officer O'Neill any more than was necessary. "Where's Bayfield?"

"Wisconsin, near the border. It's almost seven hundred miles from here as the crow flies, or dragon, in this case." He laughed. "It's an eleven-hour drive. The drop-off point is a camp on the shore of Lake Superior, where someone is going to meet you to take you the rest of the way. The timing worked out perfectly since I was supposed to visit my brother's family in that area this week anyway."

"And you don't mind doing this?" Owen raised an eyebrow at him. It was hard to believe that he—that anyone—would go out of their way like this for them, for *fae*.

Officer O'Neill's eyes darkened and he half-turned his head away. "No, not at all. One of my friends turned into a werewolf when I was little, and I always thought it was stupid that she had to leave after she turned." He almost growled the last part of the sentence and his fists balled at his sides. "It's not right, what we did to the Fae. This nation was built on the principles of equality and freedom, but when we have a chance to test our beliefs, we fail—"

Arthur chose that moment to interrupt, yelling from the back of the van. "Dad, there's no car seat. Where's Dorothy supposed to sit?"

Officer O'Neill deflated and shrunk away from Owen as if he remembered that Owen was furious with him. "Err, sorry about that. I did try to find one, but there's only so much I could do without raising suspicion."

Owen grunted and cast a critical eye over the seating available to them. Padded benches lined the van, with a small walkway between them. Perhaps Dorothy could sit on his lap or lie on the floor. Without windows she might get carsick, but they didn't have any options. "We'll make do. I assume we're supposed to stay out of sight?"

Officer O'Neill nodded. "That's the idea, at least until we get out of the county. Right now, all of you are too recognizable. You were on the news this morning, Owen. Your family's misfortunes make for good television, apparently." He frowned and shook his head. "No, far better no one sees any of you. I let it slip around the station that I was giving a friend a ride up to Wisconsin, so one of the shades could sit up front for security."

Jason appeared at the police officer's shoulder, literally out of nowhere. "Yep, Ol' Petey will be sitting with the dog and Officer O'Neill, since he has better control over his blending and quite a natural gift with animals." He smiled brightly as he jumped in, slid past Owen, and sat on the driver's side near the front.

Ashley and the twins claimed the bench on the passenger side of the van, and Arthur, holding Dorothy in his arms, sat next to Jason. Owen settled by Arthur, taking Dorothy as he did so. Aaron closed the door behind them as the van roared to life. Cradling Dorothy to his chest, Owen tried to keep his thoughts from the future as the van took them away from the world they had known.

***

The first two hours or so of the drive passed in relative silence. The events of yesterday caught up with everyone, and what sleep they had gotten the night before proved insufficient. Officer O'Neill slid the dividing screen open and told them there were some blankets and camping pillows beneath the bench on his side. Owen and Jason passed them out and most of the passengers took the opportunity to sleep.

Several hours passed this way, but one by one, they woke up. Conversation filled the air as the passengers tried to keep themselves entertained. Arthur switched places with Owen and drew his siblings into a quiet game of twenty questions above Dorothy, who was still sleeping on a folded blanket on the floor.

Owen questioned Jason about Tearmann and the fae while the children were distracted. If they were going to live there, he needed all the information he could get. They had no idea what they were facing, and he wanted to be prepared.

"For the most part, people can live wherever they want, although most choose places that suit their physical attributes best or have a large population of their species, like the centaurs that live in the Summer Court or the angels in the Nead," Jason said. He seemed to enjoy talking about his adopted homeland, no matter what question was asked.

"What do you mean the Summer Court? And what's the Nead?" Owen asked. There were two havens, everyone knew that, but he'd never heard of a fae court before.

"Oh, those are what we call the havens," Jason answered, grinning broadly. "Inspired by legends of the fae, see? There were several courts of fairies, each named for a season. Tearmann, the capital, is in Canada, so we call it the Winter Court, while Daingneach, the Summer Court, is in Scotland which has slightly nicer weather." He crossed his arms behind his head and looked at the roof. "Bit silly, but the names stuck so what can we do?"

Humming, Owen leaned forward and set his elbows on his knees. "You said the centaurs were mostly in the Summer Court; how did they get there? Who decides if they can go?" He was vaguely aware of Daingneach—hard to miss it with the amount of controversy it generated each year—but the fae had mostly stayed within their borders while he'd been growing up. It hadn't been 'til long after he'd left Wales that they'd started mixing with the general population.

"Well, it used to be everyone went to Tearmann, but because of the number of fae from the UK, both governments decided it was easier to let them stay. Daingneach actually takes folk from all over Europe." Jason squinted at him like something had just occurred to him. "You know, you lot may end up there. They don't let many of us over if we're already in North America, but you kept up your dual citizenship, right? They should take you and your family back under the Expatriate Act of 2052."

Owen's jaw dropped. "We could go to Scotland instead of Tearmann?" he asked in a hoarse whisper. As far as he knew, the U.S. and Canada tried to keep the fae from leaving the haven. It didn't make sense to have them traveling back and forth. He said as much to Jason, who laughed.

"Well, on this end, we're not allowed to, but the UK is more open-minded, especially toward people who are from Europe. We have some of the larger and more durable dragons fly over once a year or so. They take supplies and passengers back and forth."

Arthur's stomach grumbled, cutting off Owen's next question. Laughing, Jason yanked the screen open to ask Officer O'Neill if there was any food.

"Sure, there's a cooler up here. I packed sandwich fixings and water bottles. We'll pass it back to you guys, just make me a sandwich, all right?"

Peter shoved the small blue cooler through the window and requested a ham and cheese sandwich for his work. Dutifully, Jason made him and Officer O'Neill sandwiches before asking the others what they wanted. Owen woke Dorothy to make her eat, unwilling to have her miss the meal, however small it was.

Dorothy made sure everyone knew her displeasure with being woken and was barely satisfied with the sandwich offered to placate her. She chewed it harshly and was in the process of working herself into a real strop when she remembered Jason could entertain her. She then commandeered his lap and begged for stories about the haven.

When Jen noticed Dorothy asking questions, she seemed to forget she was angry at all fae and started throwing questions at Jason faster than he could answer them. She dragged the others into the conversation too, effectively preventing Owen from finding out more about Daingneach.

Owen leaned against the wall of the van and rubbed at his eyes. Jason's words kept running through his head. There was a chance he could go home. Or at least near his home. The kids would adapt; they'd visited sometimes, even if it hadn't been recently, and it wasn't too different from America. They'd also have a chance to grow up around humans. Daingneach had open borders now and most of the UK accepted fae as part of life. If he had the chance, would he take it? Should he take it?

If he did it would get them away from these people. He'd never heard of the Daingneach fae kidnapping anyone, but then, he had never heard of the Tearmann fae kidnapping anyone either. They were so isolated no one knew how much they had changed in the last fifty years. But the fact they were willing to do so, even to keep them safe, was a major factor against them as far as he was concerned.

He'd gotten a third of the way through a silent argument with himself before he realized what he was doing and he let out a silent bark of laughter. Look at him, debating which group of potential kidnappers and monsters was the lesser of two evils. He put his head in his hands and bit down a scream. What the hell was he doing? Less than two days ago, he had been arguing with Tiffany about being late to Ashley's recital. Now, she was dead, and he and their kids were being dragged north to join a nation of monsters. No, not monsters, people thrust into an awful situation, but not human either. His stomach dropped to the floor as he wondered for the first time what the hospital had done with Tiffany's body. They burned fae, didn't they?

Arthur chose that moment to mutter in his ear. "So there's a chance we could go to the UK instead of the North American haven?"

Owen started and then kicked himself. Twenty questions wasn't an attention-consuming game. Of course Arthur, sitting next to him, had overheard the conversation. He replied in a low voice, "According to Jason, yes."

"That makes sense," Arthur said, nodding. "The UK passed the opposite of the relocation act about thirty years ago, didn't they? Instead of forcing the fae into the havens and keeping them there, they let them travel throughout the UK and choose where to live."

"Oh? How do you know so much about it?" Owen asked. He didn't think the schools in the States taught very much about the fae. He knew more than most as he'd been thirteen when Daingneach was established, but even the little he knew was a thousand-fold more than most of their neighbors.

Arthur shrugged, not quite meeting his eyes. "In my world history class last year." He scuffed his foot along the floor. "We had a debate about forced migration, you know, like slavery and the Trail of Tears. My side said that the Relocation Act did the same thing as the Indian Removal Policy."

"Oh? And how'd it go?"

"Well, the other team argued that at the time the precursor to the Relocation Act was passed most people agreed the fae were little more than animals, that at most we had to worry about disrupting local ecosystems." Arthur's eyes flicked toward Jason. "My team said that there was plenty of evidence, even then, that they were still sentient, and we pretty much illegally imprisoned them. It was a tie because the other side argued there was too much collateral damage to humans when fae were in the area."

"Well, that doesn't say much about what people think about the fae, does it?" Owen tried to joke, but it fell flat. They didn't need the reminder about why they were running.

"Dad? What do you think about the fae?" Arthur asked. He fiddled with the hem of his hoody without looking up. By now his shoes had rubbed long black streaks on the floor and showed no sign of stopping.

"What do I think?" Owen asked, eyebrows raising. He had never thought about it before now. The fae were something that, before Tiffany . . . well they hadn't made an impact on him.

It was true that popular opinion on the fae when he had been young had been negative, even when they had been mostly confined to the United States. The entire world had felt the consequences of the Fae War, of the defeat of the Stars and Stripes. He didn't think the U.S. military had ever recovered from the massacres at Breckenridge, Fort Carson, or Fargo, even now. But the fae had never been the aggressors. Every battle in the war had been provoked by humans. The fae would've preferred to live in peace, but out of fear of the unknown, they had never been allowed to.

"I never felt anything but pity for them, if we're being honest."

"Why?" Arthur asked.

"Well . . ." Owen said, trying to choose his words carefully. "They were locked in their havens regardless of how dangerous they were or if they fought in the war. No one on this continent will trade with them, so they only have themselves to rely on for survival." He paused to think, fully aware he and his family were now members of this group and assumed all the risks that entailed. "Yes, I pitied them. Even now, anti-fae sentiments are high, and they have no rights outside of their havens. Unless something major happens, like another war, nothing is going to change."

Arthur stared at the opposite wall and chewed his lip. "You know, I don't think I ever had that option, of choosing how to feel about them. They're like this giant elephant in the room," he said in a quiet voice. "I mean, no one knows anything about them besides what the government says, and it's taboo to talk about them." He bounced both legs now. "You guys, though, they at least mentioned them to you. You talked about them. The only reason we learned anything about them was because there was no way to outright deny they still existed. It's, you know, it's like I don't even know who these people are, and I might be one of them. Mom was, and we didn't know until it was too late. What if that happens to one of us, what if—" He broke off and didn't start again. Outside of their bubble, Jason was answering increasingly absurd questions about dragons.

Owen stared at his son, then set a hand on Arthur's shoulder. "I wish I could tell you everything was going to be all right, that I understand what you're going through," he said, keeping his voice low and even. "But I can't. My parents . . . well, you know that I never knew them. I can't tell you how to grieve when you lose one, or how to deal with the possibility the same thing could happen to you. The only thing I can do . . ." He paused, sighed, and closed his eyes for a moment. When he opened them again they felt dry and tired. "None of us knows what to expect in the coming months, but I will tell you this: No matter what happens I will do my best to be there for you and your siblings. No matter what."

Arthur stopped shaking and looked at him, his red-rimmed eyes wet. "Even if we all turn into dragons and have to go live in the nests on top of the mountains?"

Owen looked seriously at Arthur. "Yes, but I may need one of you to constantly breathe fire to keep me warm." His intense dislike of the cold was well-known, to the point he'd jokingly threatened to divorce Tiffany if her job required her to move farther north than South Dakota.

It was silly, but it worked. It got Arthur laughing, a deep belly laugh that turned his tears from sorrow to joy. "Thanks, Dad," he said as he wiped a tear from his cheek. "That helped."

***

After another thirty minutes or so of easy conversation, Peter announced they would be stopping at a safehouse to refresh while he and Officer O'Neill refueled.

A few minutes of scrambling to find shoes, jackets, and other possessions that had wound up in places they didn't belong, and everyone was ready. Jen, not used to being confined for such a long time, was bouncing in her seat, and more than once Ashley and David had to stop her from getting up to wait by the door.

The van pulled to a stop and they were let out in front of a small split-level home surrounded by a thick line of trees. Owen stretched carefully, trying to work out all the kinks in his back, while he examined his surroundings. The house was worn down, but well-tended, with fresh paint and exquisite woodwork on the porch and around the windows. If the gravel road was anything to go by, they were pretty isolated out here.

A harried-looking elderly woman with snow-white hair rushed out and her eyes followed the van as it pulled away. Once it was out of sight, she gestured for them to follow her. They hurried into the house after her.

The woman, who introduced herself as Clara Peters, relaxed as soon as everyone was inside. There were a few minutes of panic as everyone became aware of how badly they had to use the bathroom. The Williams introduced themselves and practically begged to use her bathroom in the same breath.

Owen made himself useful by helping Clara spoon chili into disposable containers in the kitchen while he waited for his turn in the bathroom, and Jason released Toto into the woman's fenced-in backyard. The dog rushed out, relieved himself on a tree, then took off after squirrels, chasing them up trees and barking like they were the devil.

Clara was a kind woman who filled the air with chatter and questions. She wanted to know if they were all right, if anyone was sick or hurt and needed medicine. How was their journey, did they need blankets or clothes, and would they like some flashlights? She had just picked some up. As nice as she was, it was a relief to get away from the constant barrage when it was finally Owen's turn to use the bathroom.

Sooner than Owen expected, but still not quick enough in his opinion, the sound of tires on gravel reached them. Jason crept toward the window on his hands and knees and peeked through the curtains. He breathed a sigh of relief. "Get up. They're here. It's time. No, wait, why is Peter coming in?"

Peter blew in like a hurricane, Officer O'Neill on his heels. Peter held a newspaper in one hand and he pulled Jason into the corner to look at it. He stabbed a finger at the newspaper while he hissed something Owen couldn't understand.

"Well, people," Jason said as he scanned the headline. "We have a slight problem."

CHAPTER FIVE

IN WHICH A JOURNEY
IS UNDERTAKEN IN PARTS

"The procedure for Possible Discovery During Relocation is simple: The commanding officer is to immediately begin contact down the line and change the pick-up point and safehouses. Two hours after the initial warning, all passwords and encryptions will be changed, as per normal procedure. Remember, at all costs, protect the civilians."

—Corps Training Regulations, IXVVI

"Your neighbor got a picture of us when we grabbed your kids," Jason said, rubbing his temple as he threw the paper aside. "He's claiming he called SAFE to protect them, but we got there first despite their best efforts." His lips turned down in a sharp frown, and the darkness that seeped from the cracks of his calm shell made him look like a different person.

"Well, they would've done that anyway, wouldn't they?" Arthur asked, eyes darting between Owen and the shades. He looked calm, but Owen heard the wavering note of anxiety in his voice and saw how his shoulders had tightened.

"Well, yeah," Jason said. "They blame us for every disappearance they think they can get away with. A lot of people think we kidnap humans to experiment on them, in no small part due to what they know about our creation."

"But this is different," Peter said. He was pacing the length of the living room and radiated nervous energy. "They have proof, and to make things even better, they also got a photo of you walking off with Abey. Oh, this is not good." He ran shaky hands through his long black hair, pulling it loose of its braid, and slumped into an armchair with all the grace of a beached whale. His body flickered in and out of sight as his breaths came and went in great shuddering gasps.

Jason knelt at Peter's side and whispered something in his ear. The disorientating flickering stopped as the heaving gasps slowed. Standing, Jason pressed his lips together and turned toward the kitchen.

Owen darted forward and caught Jason's arm. "What do we do?" He glanced at where the kids were huddled together. Right now the only thing that kept him from taking them and running was that the fae said they could keep them safe. *If they couldn't—*

Jason's eyes darted to Peter and then over to Officer O'Neill. "I'm not sure yet," he said under his breath. He pulled Owen closer and leaned in until there was barely any room between them. "Owen, they're saying you were in league with us. There's an Amber Alert out for your children, and you're wanted in connection with their disappearance and the death of your wife."

***

According to Peter, they'd barely managed to beat the news story. The hotel's security cameras had caught Owen leaving with Abey, whose vanishing body was undeniably fae. By the time they'd left the city, there was a warrant out for his arrest.

Peter, head still in his hands, summed it up succinctly: "Before we had to be careful; now this is the worst possible scenario. There was a bulletin on the evening news, for crying out loud. If someone catches even a glimpse of you, we're going to be in huge trouble. We haven't had to deal with that in almost twenty years—"

"Peter, enough. We stick to the plan. You know the rules," Jason said, voice echoing with authority. He raised his head and looked at Owen, searching and weighing. He nodded, apparently having made up his mind. He poked his head into the dining room where Clara had taken the kids and asked her to join them.

Jason wore a wicked smile when he returned to the group, one that said he'd seen all the horrors the world had to offer, and nothing scared him anymore.

Heart-stopping dread spread its icy fingers into Owen's chest as it dawned on him exactly what sort of people he was trusting with his children's lives. Jason Lucien acted like a joker, but he was a veteran of a war so brutal that people spoke about it in whispers fifty years later. A war that left one of the most powerful nations in the world devastated.

"Sounds like you have a plan, Jason. Care to fill us in?" Officer O'Neill asked. His arms were crossed and the fingers on his left hand incessantly tapped out a rhythm.

If Owen weren't so caught up in the fact that he'd be accused of murdering his wife, he'd have spared a thought about how bad this looked for Officer O'Neill. If they were caught, the best he could hope for was losing his job. At worst, there was a serious possibility he could be imprisoned. Fae sympathizers were not treated kindly by the court system.

Jason clapped his hands, still smiling in that terrifying way. "So, from a practical standpoint, this changes nothing. Admittedly, the cops'll be watching the Canadian border closer than a hen watches a fox, so we may have to change our meeting point, but the plan remains the same: don't be seen. If we get stopped, Carson and Peter will try to distract them, but it's best to assume the worst. Owen, Carson and I will show y'all the hiding places in the van before we leave. You need to make sure you can use them."

He turned to Clara, and his smile dropped away. "I know you hate using the radio, and I'm sorry for making you do it, but it's our only shot at changing the rendezvous point. Use code two and update them on the situation. Tell command to contact Percill with the new drop-off point."

Finally, he turned to Peter, who looked like he was one wrong move from hurling.

"I'm authorizing you to do whatever it takes to ensure the success of the mission," Jason said and took a deep breath. "I'll take the blame for anything you do as long as the children stay safe. Do you understand, Corporal?"

"Understood, Sergeant," Peter said. His skin stopped flickering, and even though his face was ashen, he looked calmer now that there was a plan.

The group broke up, each person going about their assigned tasks. Owen grabbed Toto from the backyard and ushered everyone into the van. The sun was setting, and the elongated shadows made the formerly cheerful-looking house look threatening in the deepening darkness. He was relieved they were leaving it behind.

Officer O'Neill made short work of showing Owen how the false bottoms in the storage compartments worked and made them practice getting in and out until he was satisfied. Still, once he was finished, he didn't leave like Owen expected him to. He rocked back and forth on his heels, looking between the Williams and the house, where the shades were still talking with Clara.

Then, he cursed and ran around to the front of the vehicle, yelling for Owen to wait before getting in. He returned with a small metal box and shoved it into Owen's arms. "It's my Dad's old pistol," he said, gasping for breath. "I had it up front in case—well, something tells me you'll need it more than me."

"Wait. What do you mean?" Owen said. He almost dropped the box as he darted forward to catch the other man by the arm.

"Look," Officer O'Neill said in a low voice, eyes darting to the shades again. "I've been doing these runs for the last ten years, and I've never had a problem before. But this? Something doesn't feel right."

"What do you mean?" Owen pulled back and followed the police officer's gaze. "Is something wrong?"

Officer O'Neill shook his head. "No, but it's—take it, all right? I'd feel better knowing you had something to defend yourself with, because . . ." He took a deep breath. "Jason and Peter will die before they let anything happen to your kids, it's their job. But you? You're human. They don't care as much about you."

"Good," Owen said without thinking. "I'd rather they protect my kids than me anyway." He'd come this far to protect them, and he'd do anything to keep them safe.

Officer O'Neill scowled, his frown cutting deep lines on his face. "I doubt the kids would agree."

Owen started to protest, but Officer O'Neill cut him off before he got more than a word out. "I know you can use this, I used to compete against you and your father-in-law. Keep it handy and pray you don't need it." Then, he turned on his heel and walked away without waiting for an answer.

Owen stood alone as the fading sunlight glinted off the box in his arms.

***

The van bounced along ill-kept roads as its passengers settled down for the next leg of their journey. Owen was curled over the small, unassuming box in his lap. A glance inside revealed a Glock and two magazines nestled in snug foam compartments. Bile surged up his throat as he stared at them. He didn't want to use these, didn't want to think about why he would have to.

He slammed the lid shut, hands trembling, and shoved the box to the side like doing so would take the danger with it. He'd been a decent shot before his father-in-law had died, but that was target shooting. He hadn't touched a pistol in years. He'd never even gone hunting. How was he supposed to—?

Worry tied his stomach in knots he didn't think would ever come undone. His thoughts ran in circles, repeating over and over again without end. If he couldn't trust the fae to keep his family safe, they were doomed. By now, everyone back home would know about Tiffany, and he'd burned any bridges he may have had by running. Most would've already labeled him a fae sympathizer—he'd be lucky if he wasn't arrested. No, there was a warrant out for his arrest; he'd definitely be arrested and then he'd lose the kids.

Owen wrenched his mind free of its spiral and forced himself to look at what the others were doing. Arthur, Ashley, and David were reading the books Clara had given them. Jen and Dorothy—hampered by a lack of interest in books and an inability to read respectively—didn't have anything to do. Jason was entertaining them with stories about some of his misadventures.

While they ate their now cool chili, Jason bemoaned an ongoing feud he had with one of the cooks back home. A feud which, in his mind, was why there was never any dessert when he was eating. Dorothy, in particular, thought that going without dessert was a harsh penalty for anyone.

Jason ate up the next two hours with his stories. People and places they'd never seen came alive to fight monsters and build castles. He even managed to get David to break out of his shell with eloquent descriptions of the main library. Books of all kinds were delivered annually by dragons from Daingneach, he explained, as if sharing a great secret, and they were closely guarded by the librarians to protect them from damage.

It had to come to an end, though. Jason needed to discuss precautions for their next stop with Peter and Officer O'Neill, and the Williams weren't privy to the conversation. Owen wasn't certain he wanted to be, as Jason cackled at a muffled suggestion from the front seat in a way that made his blood chill.

Unfortunately, Jason's sudden preoccupation meant that the easy and plentiful entertainment was no longer available. Fortunately, Owen didn't have to do much to resolve this. Arthur was able to distract Dorothy with a quiet, but heartfelt, reading from some fantasy novel, while Ashley went back to her own book. David chose to have a whispered conversation with Jen instead of reading.

Owen tried to read but wasn't able to focus. Some combination of exhaustion, grief, and the inattentiveness of being sedentary wouldn't let him focus for longer than a word or two.

After ten minutes, he gave up. Something was going to happen soon, he could feel it. It wasn't that his well-developed sense of catastrophe was making itself known with bells and flashing lights, even though it was, but rather his firm belief that trouble traveled in large groups, with a little bit of joy mixed in to throw you off.

Everything that's happened in the last few days is proof of how fragile life is, a voice that sounded like Tiffany whispered in the back of his mind. A measure of heart-wrenching grief threatened to overwhelm him at the thought, but he pushed it back down. He didn't have time for that. His children were holding things together, but they needed him to be strong. It was only a matter of time before that changed.

David and Jen plopped down on either side of him, jolting him out of introspection. Brown and blue eyes dug into his for several seconds before Jen broke the silence. "Dad? We're never going home, are we?"

Those whispered words smashed holes in the wall holding Owen together. No matter how hard he or his children wished, nothing was ever going to be the same. There would always be a Tiffany-shaped hole in their lives, and not even the faint hope of one day going home would cover it up.

"No, Jen, I don't think so." Owen's heart screamed in his ears and he was shocked the others couldn't hear it.

"Why? Is it because of . . . because of Mom?" David asked, like he was afraid even mentioning his mother's fate would summon all the dark things in the world to them.

"Your mom—" Owen choked, debating whether to tell them about Mr. Jameson and SAFE or to preserve a delicate lie where the law, not people they'd known their whole lives, sent them away from their home. Their eyes demanded the truth, but his heart wanted to keep them innocent for just a while longer. He stood on the edge of a precipice where either choice sent him down a path from which he couldn't return. In the dark corners of his mind, he wondered if the twins already knew what he was debating keeping from them.

Innocence wouldn't keep them safe.

"Your mom's death wasn't why we had to leave, or why we can't go back." He pulled them up onto his lap, their eight-year-old frames almost too large to do this, and looked them in the eyes. He needed them to understand now, before it was too late and they made the mistake of trusting the wrong person. "You have to understand there are people in the world that don't like people like Jason or Abey or ..." He swallowed as his heart reached into his throat like it intended to choke him. "Or your mother."

David bit his lip. "Why?" he finally asked out loud. "They don't mean to hurt anyone. Arthur said that they even live all alone to protect everyone."

"Sometimes people with the best intentions can still end up hurting others, David," Owen said softly. "That's what happened with the fae. They tried to tell people they wanted peace, but people believed them less each time they hurt someone. People wanted the fae to stop the Changes and didn't believe them when they said they couldn't. After a while, a group decided that if the fae weren't going to do anything, they would."

"And then we went to war, right?" Jen asked, her voice uncharacteristically quiet. Her solemn stare was something Owen would've expected to see on David. "That's what Mr. Jameson always talked about."

Owen's breath hitched. "Is that what you're worried about? People like Mr. Jameson?"

He was a fool to think he could've protected them from this. Mr. Jameson hadn't exactly tried to hide his less-than-stellar opinion of the fae from the children—or anyone else, for that matter. They got his mail often enough to know how many anti-fae groups he was a proud member of.

Owen forced himself to take a deep breath before he continued. "Mr. Jameson fought in the Fae War, and like most people alive at the time, he doesn't have a good opinion of the fae. Some of those people don't like fae even now. They hunt people like your mother because of it."

Jen wrinkled her eyebrows and tilted her head. "Why don't they leave the fae alone? Arthur said that they haven't left their home in years."

Owen opened his mouth and then closed it again. He wished it were that simple. The war itself, while passed off by most people as a matter of establishing rights and protections for the fae, was much more complicated than that. Even he didn't understand why there had been so much hate, and he had been raised in the aftermath.

He bent his head down and looked the twins in the eye. "It wasn't enough for some people." Jen looked like she was about to ask another question, and he cut her off. "A lot of people died in the war and some of the survivors are still resentful. People like Mr. Jameson think that the government shouldn't have called a stop when they did, they should've pressed on."

David tilted his head, his blue eyes searching for answers in Owen's brown ones. "What do you think, Dad?"

"The war was unnecessary," Owen said in a hollow voice. "A lot of people got hurt who didn't need to." He paused. No matter what he said, this wasn't going to be easy to explain. People were still getting hurt because of it. Nothing had changed. "As it stands, if the war had continued, I don't think it would have ended well for anyone."

"Why?" Jen and David asked at the same time, their eyes shining in the faint light.

It was quiet. Jason had finished his conversation with Peter and had closed the divider. Arthur and Ashley had put down their books and were watching the three of them silently. Even Dorothy didn't make a sound as she sat in her brother's arms.

The twins still stared at him, waiting for an answer.

"No one was winning," he finally said. "The U.S. and the fae were at a stalemate. There was no other way for it to go." Each pair of eyes on him burned.

Owen rubbed his neck and wished Jason would cut in. He knew Jason had been alive during the war from the stories he told, but he didn't seem interested in helping Owen out.

"After one of the last battles, some of the survivors wanted to make the fae pay, but any victory would have been pyrrhic." There was something hanging on the tip of his tongue, something that would explain everything.

Dropping her serious look, Jen crinkled her nose and pulled back. "What's pyrrhic mean?"

Owen answered her in a distracted voice. "It's a situation where the costs of winning are so high it may as well have been a loss." He shook his head, giving whatever he had been thinking about up for loss. "The last battle cost both sides in terms of life lost, but the fae won by the skin of their teeth and had the standing to demand peace talks."

"That's when they demanded their own country, someplace they would be safe," Arthur said like he was afraid that speaking would break the delicate spell that lay over them.

David was about to ask another question when Peter announced they were at their next stop. They got out of the van in front of a dilapidated barn and an ancient farmhouse. An untrimmed hedge, the only living plant Owen had seen on the farm, hid the building from the road.

A skeletal old man waved them into the house and introduced himself as Percill. He met questions with sullen grunts and suspicious glares while he ladled stew into chipped porcelain bowls. Once finished, he sat in a chair facing the door, a shotgun across his knees and two grizzled dogs at his feet, while Owen let Toto into the backyard on a long leash.

There was none of the ease they had felt at Clara's. The house was a wreck, with paint peeling from the walls and woodwork warped beyond belief. The furniture smelled of mold, was covered in dust, and made worrisome creaking noises when sat upon. Wind howled through cracks and broken windows and brought a chill barely restrained by the fire smoldering in the hearth. The less said about the state of the bathroom, the better.

It took a half hour for Officer O'Neill and Peter to get gas, but it felt like much longer. By the time they heard the crunch of tires on gravel, he was ready to walk to the haven himself if it would get them out of here. Something about the house—about its inhabitant—unsettled him. Even Toto was in a hurry to get out, rushing back into the van and laying his head on Peter's leg with a whine.

It had been dark for hours now, and the shadows swallowed any light that strayed beyond its borders. The moon hid behind a row of clouds and refused to share her face with the world below. Owen glanced back to the house and saw Percill's eyes glimmering in the black. That man, there was something off about him. He made Owen feel like someone was waiting just out of the corner of his eye to attack.

Owen shut the doors, only managing to shake off the odd tension the house and its strange inhabitant had left after the van pulled onto the interstate.

It didn't take long for Jen and David to decide that now was the time to continue their conversation from earlier. They had a brief and muttered conversation before sitting next to him again. They looked determined, and he waited for them to begin speaking.

"When we get there, to that place, are we going to be safe, like Arthur said?" Jen asked with a fire in her dark eyes.

Owen wondered if it made him a bad father that he hadn't noticed the innocence leaving her gaze. He wondered if she would continue on that path, if she would lose the parts of her that made her trusting and friendly, that let her have any faith in the world. He hoped not.

Dread stole his breath, threatening to drown him, and he wanted to hug his children and never let them go. They'd lost their mother and their home and were being forced into a strange land none of them knew. He wanted to protect them from all the harm the world would throw at them, but that wasn't an option anymore. They were on this path, and he was afraid of where it would lead them and who they would be at the end of it.

"I'd like to think so," he said, forcing the words past the lump in his throat. "Something tells me you can trust them." They could, but he couldn't.

"But if we can't?" Jen asked, her small fingers wrapping in Owen's shirt. "What do we do then, Dad?"

He stiffened, and the box with the gun pressed into his hip. "If it turns out that we can't trust them," he said carefully, "we'll find a way out of there."

A protective urge rose up inside of him, one that went beyond anything he had ever felt before. "I won't leave you there," he swore. "I'll die before I let anything happen to you, I promise." Something settled into place inside of him with that vow, a physical thing that would keep him bound to his children no matter what happened.

The twins' unreadable faces came to a silent agreement. David spoke first. His voice was quiet and hinted at knowledge of things no child should have. "It's ok, Dad. We know that."

"Yeah," Jen said, crossing her arms, "and we can protect you too."

Chuckling at Jen's enthusiasm, Owen said, "Oh, really? And what exactly would you be protecting me from? Cats? Bugs? Particularly persistent teachers?"

Jen scowled and hit his arm. "No, Dad. I mean that we can keep you safe. Just like you keep us safe."

When he saw her grumpy look, he considered feeling sorry for teasing her, but then he saw the grin tugging its way up her cheeks. He glanced at David, and that was all it took for them to break into laughter. Jen resisted for all of five seconds before joining in.

***

Owen was beginning to drop off to sleep when a loud curse made him jolt up. Peter shoved the divider back and shouted, "Lights behind us, get everyone into position and shut off the light, we don't have much time."

Jason cursed under his breath and jumped to his feet. "Everyone up, Owen, pull your kids off the bench and open it up. Younger kids first, like I told you, come on."

Owen leaped up and shoved the twins to the floor in his rush to get the false door open. Arthur yanked them to their feet as it swung open. The van had a false floor that hid a crawl space eight inches high. Enough for the little ones to hide—he and Arthur would have to crawl under the driver's seat.

"What's happen—?" David asked, voice still thick with sleep as the van slowed.

"Police, we don't know why they stopped us, but better safe than sorry. Take your sisters and crawl down as far as you can go. Ashley—now," said Owen shortly. He needed to gather up as much of their loose items as he could. There couldn't be any sign that someone was riding back here. It wasn't safe.

Jason yanked the bag from his hand. "Go, I can finish this. I'm not going down there anyway."

Arthur shushed a crying Dorothy, who was making grabbing hands toward Owen. "Dad, we need to go—"

"Yes, I know," he said. He dove for the box with the gun—why had he left it on the floor?

Arthur climbed into the crawlspace after handing a still sobbing Dorothy to Ashley and disappeared under the floorboards.

"Owen, go." Jason pushed Owen toward the still open bench on the left side of the vehicle as he pulled his shirt off and started fading away.

Owen stumbled forward and almost dropped the box as he clambered down and shut the bench above him. The crawlspace plunged into semi-darkness, lit only by light bleeding through cracks in the flooring. He could hear the muffled sound of Dorothy crying, of Arthur crawling into position and telling Ashley to hand her to him. The odor of the dust, raised by each of their movements, and the odor of unwashed bodies crammed in a small space made his nose twitch. He held back a sneeze as he fumbled with the box in his arms.

If ever there was a time, it was now. He wasn't sure what the shades would do if something went wrong but heaven help him, he was going to be ready. He needed to be. Pulling the Glock out, he slid a loaded magazine into place and set the box between his feet with trembling hands. His knees pressed against the underside of the bench and metal rivets dug into his back. He was supposed to be under the driver's seat, out of the way so the compartment's false bottom could spring into place, but he couldn't move. He had to protect them, he wasn't going to leave the kids between him and danger.

The light disappeared; Jason must have turned off the lamp. The van finally stopped, Owen could hear Officer O'Neill's muffled voice and Toto's whining.

HAVEN

Owen forced himself to take deep breaths. He'd hurt someone he didn't intend to if he couldn't calm down. *In and out, in and out.*

Muffled, nervous laughter came from the front seat. The floorboards creaked; Jason must have been getting into position. Owen rested his finger on the trigger. A shot would be deafening in such a small space, but he was willing to risk it.

The driver's door opened, and the vehicle shifted as someone got out. Why were they getting out? Arthur shushed Dorothy and her sobs quieted. Someone grabbed his leg, Ashley—she had gotten in before him. No, focus. He could hear the key scratching around the lock.

The back door of the van opened, and the light of a flashlight fell through the cracks. He debated trying to peer through the gap in the bench, because blast it, he didn't know what was happening. The voices were much clearer now.

"—can't be too careful," a female voice said. "Especially with fae, professional courtesy or not, you understand. We can't let those monsters get their hands on the kids."

"No, of course not," Officer O'Neill replied, calmer than Owen would have expected. "I completely understand—"

"Is this going to take long, Uncle Carson? I'm cold," Peter said, voice shaking.

"I just need to have a look around. You wouldn't believe the sorts of things those freaks have done to get people up there." The van shifted as someone stepped inside. "My boss said that he once found a whole truckload of them hiding in the back of a semi, crammed so close they couldn't breathe."

"Yeah, I can only imagine. We don't have too much of an issue with that back home." Officer O'Neill laughed, a tight and high-pitched sound.

The steps drew closer. Someone was moving things around. The bench rattled. "Do these things open?" the female voice asked.

"Uh, no. The seat's loose. It's been wonky for years, I keep meaning to fix it."

"Hm."

Her footsteps echoed as she walked away and the van shifted as she got out.

"Well, I can't find anything wrong. Get that taillight fixed, all right? We're cops, we have to set an example for the kiddies." There was a punching noise and Officer O'Neill grunted in pain.

"Sure thing," Officer O'Neill said. "Now, we have to get back on the road, so—"

"Holy shit," the woman screamed. "What's that?"

Owen heard a loud curse and footsteps shook the van. There was a loud crash followed by the sound of flesh hitting flesh. He wasn't sure how long he struggled with the bench, trying to remember how to open it from the inside. The gun got in his way and he almost dropped it when the bench finally opened and flooded the compartment with light.

"Everyone get out, Jason screwed up," Peter said, pulling Owen out with one hand.

Owen stuck the gun in his waistband with shaking hands and stumbled to the door. Jason and Officer O'Neill were crouched over a body. His breath caught in his chest. She was just doing her job—

"Owen," Jason said, looking very much like he wished he wasn't naked in below freezing weather. "Get down here, we need a hand hauling her back to her car. Peter, toss me my clothes."

"What happened?"

Jason snarled. "I flickered is what happened, and she caught sight of my outline." He picked up her wrist to take her pulse. "When she saw me, all bets were off. It's hard to explain a vanishing man in the best of circumstances, let alone when they're actively looking for one. I hit her between the eyes and Pete got her with a shot of ketamine while she was stunned. She'll only be out for the next twenty minutes or so by my estimation, so we need to hurry. Get her in her car and dismantle the radio."

Jason delivered the orders in a clipped voice, already walking to where Peter was holding his clothes. He dressed while Owen and Officer O'Neill carried the policewoman back to her squad car.

It was the work of seconds for Officer O'Neill to mess with the radio and hide the keys. "It won't stop her for long," he said, clicking the lock for good measure. "But it'll be enough. Tell Peter and Jason to take the van the rest of the way, I'll stay with her and provide a cover story."

"But—"

"No, go. I know what I'm doing. Jason will agree. Tell him to leave the van on the side of the road and I'll try to misdirect them as carefully as I can. Go."

Owen hesitated, but only for a moment. "Jason, Peter," he yelled as he ran up to them. "Officer O'Neill said to take the van and go."

Peter jumped out of the back of the van. "He did what? Queen's blood, hold on, I'll talk to him."

Jason pulled him back. "Nope, the man made his choice, and it's the best one for the situation. At least this way we have a chance of maintaining the contact. If he runs with us, he may as well kiss his life here goodbye. Get in, Peter, I'll drive. Owen . . ." He ran a hand over his face. "Just make sure the kids are ready. We're still a half hour from the drop-off point and we don't have any time to waste."

Nodding, Owen jumped into the van. The door shut behind him and seconds later they started moving. The divider slid open as he was trying to convince Dorothy she needed to put on her coat.

"Owen, from what we got from Percill," Jason said without looking back, "we're supposed to meet the transport at the lakefront. The meeting point is about a ten-minute hike from the drop-off."

"What? Can't we get any closer?" Owen asked as he finally managed to zip Dorothy's coat.

"Not without drawing attention to ourselves. It's easier to hide when you can't be seen from the road."

"Perfect," Owen said with a groan, "and how long will it take to get where we're going?"

"Another six or seven hours." The van swung to the right, knocking everyone to the floor. "It depends on the flight path. We can't use the normal route now that they're on alert."

Owen pushed himself up. "What do you mean?" he asked, silently making sure everyone was okay.

"Politically speaking, between you being seen and what just happened, it's like we tried to put out a wildfire with gasoline. We'll be lucky if they've only doubled patrols at the borders. If we're not, well, we may have to get creative."

Owen wanted to ask more, but Jason said the light in the back was distracting him, and slammed the divider shut. The Williams finished packing without speaking, too shaken to do anything else.

***

The walk seemed to take much longer than ten minutes, Owen thought as they followed Peter deeper into the forest. It might have been the cold air that made it feel like time itself was frozen or the way the thin beam of light from his flashlight cast ghostly shadows on the ground as they walked.

However long the walk was, it was still a surprise when Peter stopped the group at the frozen lakeshore. Jason was waiting for them, having gone to dispose of the van after dropping them off. How he managed to beat them there, Owen had no idea, but he was glad to see him anyway.

"What's going on? Is this the right place?" Owen asked through chattering teeth. A sharp wind blew off the lake and cut straight through his jacket. They couldn't stay out here much longer or the kids would freeze.

"Oh, we're in the right spot, sure as sunshine," Jason said, turning his flashlight straight up. He flashed it on and off in a pattern Owen couldn't follow before he spoke again. "It's just our ride is waiting for us to give the signal. Ol' Pete and I were trying to figure out what the signal was now that the plan's changed." He paused as he finished the pattern and then smiled at Owen. "No worries, though, we got it. He should be here any second now."

Owen strained his ears, but he couldn't hear anything. There was a strange sound, like sails flapping in the wind, but nothing he knew sounded like that. "Must be a quiet plane, then; I can't hear an engine, and I think we would have heard something by now."

Jason looked at him blankly. "Plane? What plane?" After a moment, he made a small noise of understanding. "We're not flying on any plane, Owen, nor any machine known to man or fae."

Wind from nowhere shook snow from the trees. A black shape moved through the night and blocked out the stars. Jason's white teeth gleamed in the darkness. "Owen, we're flying on old Thaddeus there."

The ground shook, knocking Owen down and frightening Toto into jumping behind the shades. Jason laughed joyously as a massive black dragon shook out its wings in the night.

CHAPTER SIX

IN WHICH THEY FACE
THE JAWS OF THE DRAGON

"The engineers finally took my advice and started designing a harness for the third-gen dragons. They're our biggest asset, literally, and it makes no sense that we don't use them. My grandson is one of their test subjects, and he says they haven't had much luck making it work so far. We can't use a classic saddle, as dragons couldn't fly wearing them. Now they're considering fastening a cage between the dragons' legs and around their stomachs to avoid interfering with the wings. It looks promising, but I'm concerned about how safe it's going to be."

—Excerpt from the journals of Danielle Burns, Lady Guivre

The dragon shifted its feet, trying to find a comfortable spot before dropping his head down to the three men. It pulled its lips back in a mockery of a smile. "Jason Lucien," it said, voice booming across the clearing. "You're late."

Jason beamed and laid a hand on the dragon's snout. "Thaddeus Green! It's good to see you; although, from a technical standpoint, you're the one who's late. We did get here before you."

Thaddeus rolled his eyes. "Well, it took you so long to get here I almost thought you weren't coming. Besides, I was hungry. Do you know how hard it is to hunt this close to inhabited areas? I was on my way back when I saw your signal." His large brown eyes narrowed. "What took you so long? You should have been here an hour ago."

Jason scowled. "We had a run-in with an unwelcome visitor. I had to show her the door."

Thaddeus snorted. "I bet you did. You didn't kill anyone, did you? The Corps won't be happy with you if you did—" He cut himself off with a huff and shook his head. "But we have to go. We can gossip when we land."

Jason stomped and glanced over his shoulder toward the children. They were all shivering, either from the cold or the terror. "I see what you mean. Which way is the door?"

Thaddeus raised a clawed foot; the dim light hinted at a shape strapped around his middle. "Forward as I fly, like always. Makes it easier for the passengers, you understand. You have the key?"

Jason nodded and pulled a large metal key on a chain from under his shirt and disappeared under Thaddeus's shadow.

There was a quiet scratching noise, followed by a loud clunk. A hinge squeaked as a hidden door opened. With a click, light flooded out from the compartment. Jason stood in the doorway, gesturing for them to follow him. "We haven't got all night. Get in here," he shouted and went further in.

Owen exchanged a look with Peter, who shrugged and made a pushing movement toward the door. Considering it sat under a dragon that made Nathan look small, the sight wasn't exactly welcoming. There was enough light to make out the shape—he thought it was a gondola. From this angle, he could see a single window set into the open door. Thick leather straps wrapped around Thaddeus's legs and disappeared upwards. The outside was painted a dark gray that almost disappeared into Thaddeus, so he couldn't see more than that.

Still, they had to go in, no matter how it looked. Owen rubbed his eyes. "Arthur, Ashley, get the others inside."

The crunch of their footsteps in the snow as they followed him was strangely reassuring, but he couldn't bring himself to look back as he dragged Toto behind him. If he was tired, the kids were bound to be exhausted, and he didn't have the strength to deal with it now.

Less than ten feet long and half as wide, the inside of the gondola wasn't much to look at. Wood crates and benches lined both side walls, straw poked through cracks in the wood and littered the floor, and wires and piping hung from the ceiling. An old intercom was embedded into the wall by the door, letting off the occasional crackle of static. The far wall had been converted into a tiny stove, which Jason was trying to light. Peter shoved past Owen, who realized he was still standing in the doorway.

Toto's leash dug into his hand and his whines grew louder as Owen pulled him in. It took all of Owen's strength to move him, but he eventually managed to fasten Toto's leash around the foot of a bench. Toto pulled against it, and the wood creaked against the strain.

Arthur came in while Owen was trying to calm Toto. "Jason, where should I put Dorothy?" he asked. His face was ashen and his arms shook under Dorothy, who had yet to remove her face from his jacket.

The twins ran in behind them, eager to see what the gondola had in store for them. Nothing was below their notice. They examined everything with the same excitement others showed toward historical wonders.

Ashley entered at a more sedate pace. She chewed her lip as she looked around before she narrowed in on Owen. Rushing to his side, she joined him in trying to calm Toto. She didn't look much better than Toto did.

Owen could sympathize. Between the rickety nature of the gondola, and the fact it was tied to a large reptile, it was hard to feel safe. He rubbed Ashley's shoulder as he stood and walked over to Jason. "Is this safe?"

Jason finished with the last of the complex system of ten or so locks and latches on the door before answering. "It's completely safe. We've been using dragons like this for the last fifteen years." He clapped Owen on the shoulder as he passed by. "Trust me, it may look shabby, but this thing is rock solid."

Owen grunted. That didn't make him feel better. It only took one crack somewhere for something shabby to become something ruined.

Ashley had managed to calm Toto, or at least stop him from trying to run away, but his panting had gotten heavier and louder. The dog was trying to curl up in her lap, but he almost dwarfed her and couldn't get far.

"I don't know what you want me to say," Jason said when he noticed Owen's face. "Outside of prayer, there's not much we can do if something happens. I haven't heard of a serious harness malfunction in years, if it makes you feel better." He sat between the twins and Arthur and rubbed his eyes. "Look, if you want to know how the harnesses work and what their safety ratings are, you should ask Peter. The kid knows as much about them as the dragons and dwarves that designed them."

"Really?" Owen glanced at Peter, who was fiddling with and muttering into the intercom. He hadn't expected the sullen young man to be so familiar with dragons. He seemed much more likely to stay with his own kind.

Although, what did Owen know about the fae? A day of travel with two representatives of a species didn't make him an expert. Even if he could count the number of times Peter had spoken to any of the Williams on one hand.

Jason shrugged as he took a small flask out of his jacket. "Yeah, kid loved being up in the Eyries. We were all surprised when he joined the Corps instead of becoming an engineer." He took a sip from his flask and might have said more, but the gondola lurched with enough force to knock anyone standing to the floor. Apparently, they were off.

***

Owen wasn't sure if he liked this form of transportation, even without taking into consideration his safety concerns. For one, he couldn't see outside, as Peter had fastened a curtain over the window to hide the lamplight. It was either a blessing or a curse—he wasn't sure which. The constant rocking alternated between sickening and frightening for at least ten minutes before they smoothed out.

The jolt caused by takeoff and the flapping noise of the wings, so much louder in here than it had been on the shore, terrified Dorothy. She started screaming and crying, which, in turn, made an already-panicked Toto go ballistic. His barking and howling scared her even more, a vicious cycle that took a half hour to break.

The constant jerky rocking and thunderous flapping made sleep difficult, even after Dorothy and Toto had calmed down. The older children managed to doze through it, but Dorothy, still cradled in

Owen's arms, wasn't as lucky. She kept falling asleep only to jolt up whenever Thaddeus flapped his wings.

Owen wrapped her as tightly as he could in two blankets Jason had given him and pressed her head to his chest. He may not be able to stop the rocking, but at least he could make it a little more comfortable for her. He leaned his head against the wall as the gondola rocked again. It was going to be a long night.

***

Owen bolted awake when the gondola shook, dislodging a still-sleeping Dorothy from his chest onto Ashley.

Jason stood next to him, hand outstretched to shake him awake. "Oh good, you're up. We're here."

Owen stared at Jason while his sleep-fogged mind struggled to comprehend what he was seeing. Jason was—they were—oh, they were here.

He jumped up and almost stepped on Ashley in his rush. They were here. They were safe.

His stubble scratched his palm as he rubbed his chin and wished he could shave. He didn't know what to expect from here on out, but he wanted to make a good impression, and he wasn't young enough to pull off two days of growth anymore. He allowed himself to fantasize for a moment about a hot shower before he dismissed the thought. If dirt and grime were the price he had to pay to keep his kids safe, he would never bathe again.

Besides, the kids were all still in the night clothes they'd been wearing when they left home. At this point, none of them looked respectable and he didn't think anyone would blame them for that. Or at least he hoped so.

Owen joined Jen in trying to rouse Arthur. The boy was almost impossible to wake most mornings, and it was a testament to how poorly he had slept that in less than ten minutes he was on his feet. That done, he went to speak to Jason, who had just started the complicated process of unlocking the door.

"So, where exactly are we?" His stomach growled. "And will there be food?"

Jason cursed as he struggled with the lock before answering Owen. "We've landed in the Eyries above the main city. There'll be someone here to show you around and get you settled, but Peter and I have to check in. They'll want to know why we had to call in at Clara's."

Owen's stomach sunk. "You're not coming with us? Why?"

Jason shook his head. "No, wish I could, though. We're a scouting team in the Corps," he said, cheering under his breath as a particularly stubborn lock fell open. "We were supposed to be keeping an eye on the local SAFE chapter, not picking up faeborn. We have to report to command now to explain why we weren't able to complete our mission."

Owen made a noise of understanding, but he wasn't sure how he felt about it. On one hand, it was understandable. They hadn't expected Owen and his family any more than Owen had expected this. But on the other . . . in the chaos and unpredictability of the last two days, Jason and Peter had been a source of comfort. Or, at least, Jason had been. He was pretty sure Peter scared Dorothy. And possibly the twins.

Standing, Jason laid a hand on Owen's arm. "Hey, it'll be all right. Shouldn't be too long 'til we're checked in, and anyway, we're grounded 'til the others get back. We'll find you later."

The door opened, and a pale, sickly light filled the carrier. Jason stepped outside and gestured for Owen to follow him.

Owen hesitated, one step away from the door when Arthur came up to his side, Toto's leash in hand. "You ready to go?" Something in his voice made Owen turn and look, really look, at him.

Arthur swayed on his feet and the bags under his eyes covered half his face at this point. He failed to bite back a jaw-cracking yawn.

"As I'll ever be," Owen muttered. He pulled himself straight, forced his shoulders back and tried to look awake. They needed him to be strong. "Ready, everyone?"

Dorothy's face brightened with the joy a new place brought her. He tried to smile back, but the muscles had forgotten how. Whatever face he made, it was enough for her. She grabbed his hand, darted forward, and pulled him out the door with her, giving him his first glimpse of their new home.

They were in a massive cave. Dim, flickering lamplight shone through countless doorways in the distance. Through the gaping entrance behind them, he could glimpse starlight, but beyond that, the outside may as well have not existed. There were no cars or planes, or even the distant hum of electronics. A breath or a footstep would echo off the walls for an eternity.

Though dark and foreboding, the room nonetheless exuded magnificence. The floor was worn smooth from years and years of countless footsteps, and half-seen murals covered the walls. Gryphons danced with elves up one wall; a dragon presided over a feast along another. Darkness turned images meant to be cheerful into foreboding and fearful things. A smile looked like a sneer, an offering hand like a fist.

"Oh, wow," Jen whispered. The room swallowed up the noise, a cathedral where sound was a blasphemy against the grand silence that filled it.

The spell that came over the Williams broke when Thaddeus started moving. His unsteady steps boomed and his tail scraped the ground, a *hssk, hssk* that rose to the ceiling and fell back down on them.

Turning to face the noise, Owen noticed a group walking toward them. Two hulking harpies carrying a box of tools chatted with shades, and bearded figures argued with giants that towered over them. Thaddeus lumbered in their direction, hindered by the gondola strapped to his chest.

"Thad!" shouted one of the short, bearded figures. "How was the flight? Not too much trouble?"

Thaddeus laughed, a sound like sandpaper. "Andrew, good to see you again. You here to help me get this thing off?"

The two parties met not far from where Owen and his family were gathered. Figures swarmed over Thaddeus and undid the harness that bound the dragon to his burden.

The man shook his head, black hair flying in all directions. "Nah, I'm here as an errand boy. Felicia says you need to hurry home."

The Williams stood to the side, completely ignored by the crowd standing not ten feet from them. Owen was beginning to wonder if he should do something when a red-headed figure finally noticed them. "Andrew, weren't you supposed to be taking the newcomers down to the third floor?" she shouted, jerking a thumb toward them.

The figure snapped his fingers. "Oh, right. I knew I was forgetting something." He turned back to Thaddeus. "I'll see you later. Hopefully, you'll have good news for me."

Spinning on his heel, he cupped his hands over his mouth. "Oi, Eoire, get over here. We got welcoming to do."

A tall, pale woman with brown hair pulled herself from the crowd and jogged over to the Williams.

The two reached them at roughly the same time. "Right, my name is Andrew Stephens," the short man said. "I can see you're wondering what I am. Well, I'm a dwarf. The woman beside me is Eoire Belfield, she's an elf. We will be taking you to registration and helping you settle into our fair city. Any questions?"

He wasn't more than four-and-a-half feet tall, while she almost doubled his height. The black mass of hair on his head had a life of its own, bouncing and curling in every direction, restrained only by a thick headband. His hair was matched by a thick beard that fell to his waist. Her hair flowed like a smooth river, chestnut strands dotted with small, intricate braids that disappeared into what fell loose. He was stout where she was slender, firm where she was graceful. In whole, they were a pair of opposites.

Jen's hand shot up, her exhaustion and worry disappearing when given the opportunity to sate her curiosity. "Mr. Stephens, Mr. Stephens!"

Andrew smiled under his impressive beard. "Yes, Miss Williams?"

"How do you know my name?" she asked, eyes wide as saucers.

Eoire smiled kindly. "We knew you were coming, sweetheart. What did you want to know?"

If possible, Jen's eyes grew wider still. She had always loved elves, the product of a steady diet of old cartoons and fairy stories when she was little. Being face-to-face with one must have been a dream come true. "Can I see your ears?"

Eoire blinked. Then she let out a musical laugh, bright and joyful.

It struck Owen like a physical thing, like wonder and innocence and peace wrapped in one sound. He stood tall, his strength renewed. Around him, exhaustion seemed to fall from the kids. Arthur smiled, Dorothy laughed, and Ashley lost her haggard expression.

Eoire drew back the hair that hung loose around her shoulders and free of her braids. She turned her head to better expose the graceful point of her ear to the group.

Jen's eyes shone. Her voice was as reverent as an eight-year-old's could be as she reached out with a shaking hand. "Can I—can I touch them?"

Smiling, Eoire bent so Jen could reach her ears.

Jen ran her fingers up Eoire's ear. Trembling fingers traced around the point and dropped back. "Can I be an elf?" Her whisper hung in the air, echoing with the memory of childhood dreams.

"We'll see," she said, her soft smile falling away. "We don't exactly have a choice in the matter."

Jen's smile faded. Disappointment crept into its place. "Oh, I understand." Her gaze dropped as she scuffed her shoe against the floor. "There's still a chance, right?"

"Aye, Miss Williams," Andrew confirmed in his deep bass that rung like a church bell next to Eoire's delicate chime. "Any of you could be an elf."

Jen nodded slowly, although she still looked dissatisfied with that answer.

Looking around the room, Andrew nodded to no one in particular. Thaddeus was dragging the gondola out of the room with his teeth, while the other fae sorted pieces of the harness. "Right, if that's all, we can begin the tour—"

"Are you made of hair?" Dorothy asked from Owen's side.

Andrew, in the process of turning around, stopped and looked back at Dorothy, his mouth opening and closing several times. "I beg your pardon, miss?"

Dorothy let go of Owen's hand and waved her own in the air. "You have so much hair. Daddy doesn't even have that much hair."

Andrew stared at her, then threw back his head and roared with laughter, the kind that made one want to join in. The few fae still in the room stopped to see what was happening.

Dorothy stomped her foot and crossed her arms. "It's not nice to laugh at people, Hairy Face."

Andrew pulled himself together until only a chuckle or two slipped out from his smiling face. "I'm sorry, my dear, but no. I am not made of hair, only rather hairy. See?" He knelt in front of Dorothy and pulled up a sleeve. His arm, while still incredibly hairy, was obviously flesh and blood.

The shine in her eyes was comparable to Jen's as Dorothy reached out and ran her fingers through the coarse hair. "It's so thick," she whispered. "Daddy, Daddy, look, I touched it."

"Yes, Dorothy, I see."

Dorothy turned back to Andrew, brows knotted together. "You're a lot hairier than Daddy."

Andrew almost started laughing again as he stood up. "I wouldn't doubt that, dearie; I'm a dwarf and he's a human."

"Are you all hairy?" Dorothy asked in the manner all children do when asking something adults would consider offensive.

"Oh, indeed. Some are even hairier, if you believe it," he whispered, like he was conveying some important secret that was on a need-to-know basis.

"Even your mommies?" she asked, bringing her hands up to cover her mouth.

Andrew's eyes twinkled as he nodded at her. "Of course, you can't be a proper dwarf if you're not hairy."

Eoire tapped him on the shoulder.

"Right," he said, shaking his head brusquely. "We have to get going. We're late as it is. Follow me."

Eoire laughed, smiling fondly as Andrew headed to the left side of the cave. "Come on. Once he gets going, he's hard to stop."

They came to an old-fashioned elevator. "All right, this is the Eyries," Andrew said as soon as they were all close enough to hear. "It's where most of the flying folk live, as well as the support staff that maintains the equipment. It's not technically in the city proper—that's further down the mountain—but it's still under the control of the queen and the Founders Council."

Owen stopped in his tracks. Toto hated elevators. How were they supposed to get him on as stressed as he was now? He'd throw a fit. "Hey, how's Toto going to—?" A glance backward revealed that the dog was no longer among their number.

Arthur shrugged. "Jason took him to the greenhouses while you were talking."

Ashley eyed the elevator as Andrew wrestled it open. "Are you sure this thing is safe? It looks like it's about to fall apart."

It wasn't an unfair statement. Rusted wire mesh covered the steel and wood framework of the elevator; at some point, it had been painted a cherry red, but time and use had dulled the color. Two lanterns hung from the ceiling, illuminating the rundown machinery. If Owen was being honest, it reminded him of an old mining elevator he'd seen when he was younger. He'd had ridden in worse, but not by much.

Andrew nodded as he hurried them into the elevator. "Definitely, this was built by first-generation dwarves. They're the great engineers of our people. It may look ugly, but that's because it's old. It'll do the job."

"The first generation? What does that mean?" Owen asked. He shivered and shoved his hands in his pockets. It was colder here than he expected.

"The first generation are the original fae," Andrew said. "Most of the older ones fought in the war, although some Changed after—"

"Someone who was originally human is considered first generation, Mr. Williams," Eoire interrupted. "If your children Change, they would be first generation."

"Does that have any impact on what they become?" he asked as he stepped into the elevator. That certainly got the kids' attention.

"A little, but only in the sense that their bodies can't handle the physical aspects of the Change as much as the later generations," Andrew said as he pulled the gate shut. "Thaddeus, for example, is third generation, and he and his wife are expecting their eggs to hatch any day now. They look nothing like their grandparents, or even much like their parents, and who knows? Maybe their children will look nothing like them."

"Why?" Arthur and Ashley asked at the same time.

"It's a little hard to explain," Andrew said, stroking his beard. "But I'll try. Half a moment, I need to get this going."

He latched the gate, pushed a button, and then flipped a lever. The carriage began the slow, clanging journey down with a great groan and a shuddering jump. "You might want to sit down," he said as he slid down the wall. "It's a bit of a trip and this thing only goes so fast."

"Where was I ...?" he muttered when the group was settled on the floor. "Oh yes, hyper-evolution. We think it's controlled by whatever triggered the initial Change because each generation has the same mutations. The first-gen dwarves were essentially hairy humans. A bit shorter and a bit denser, that's for sure, but not to the extent I am.

He hummed and pulled an intricate looking pile of rings from his pocket. The distant clang of machinery didn't seem to bother him. Perhaps, after so many years, he didn't even hear it anymore.

"I'm a second-generation dwarf you see," he continued after a moment. "Once removed from humans."

"And how were you different from your parents?" Ashley asked as she leaned forward.

She'd always been interested in genetics and family traits, Owen knew that. Compared to the rest of her family she was rather plain. Deep down, he thought she felt out of place, as her stringy blonde hair, thin lips, and wide-set eyes didn't fit with her siblings' more conventionally attractive features.

"Well, my parents had a bit more hair than usual, and my mother had a fine beard, but beyond their height they still looked human. I, on the other hand, came out small and stayed that way. I'm short for a second-gen; most of them are about five feet tall." He stroked his beard with one hand in an almost proud way. "I was also covered in hair more or less from birth and started growing a true beard when I was five. Let me tell you, it isn't easy to convince a five-year-old to shave. Eventually, my parents gave up, and I haven't been clean-shaven since.

"Anyway," he continued, his eyes dropping back to the ring puzzle in his hands. "Third-generation dwarves are even smaller; most don't get any taller than me. Their hair and beards are even wilder than mine and grow much faster."

"Do you know why?" Arthur asked. If he leaned any closer to Andrew and Eoire, he was going to fall over.

Eoire shrugged. "Like Andrew said, we think it has something to do with the Change. Each generation is different than the one before it. Dragons get bigger and fiercer, sirens get more hypnotic, and dwarves get hairier and shorter. We really don't know more."

"We actually thought centaurs were horse-like satyrs," Andrew said without looking up from his puzzle. "They're proper ones now, though. They have four legs and everything."

"Will it stop?" Owen asked. He got the feeling that even the fae didn't quite understand why things happened like they did, but he wanted to know all he could all the same.

Eoire opened and closed her mouth several times. Andrew bit his lip and exchanged a glance with her.

"We think it stops after the third generation, actually," Eoire finally said. "But we're not sure. We don't have many fourth-gens to compare. In the next decade or so that should change though."

"She's right," Andrew said, finally looking up. "If the hyper-evolution stops with the fourth, we'll probably stop counting them, but it's too early to tell one way or another."

It was quiet after that, except for the relentless bang of machinery. The Williams were trying to absorb the information they had been given while the fae waited for them to resume their questioning.

Ashley broke the silence. "Where are you taking us?" Her voice didn't shake, but Owen could tell she was wound tight enough to burst.

Eoire's face softened. "Down to registration," she answered in a calm and gentle voice. "We need to get you guys a place to live." She looked at Owen and smiled. "And besides, your father needs to find a job."

Ashley's shoulders relaxed, but it wasn't enough to rid her of her anxiety completely. Owen could still see it in her trembling hands as she fussed with Dorothy's hair. He put an arm around her and she leaned into him.

"What kind of jobs do you have?" Jen asked, leaping between Eoire and her older sister. Hero-worship like none Owen had seen filled her eyes with a radiant light.

"All kinds," she said, her eyes darting back to Ashley for a moment. "What your father ends up doing depends on his skills, but we have jobs in most fields. Now he's a single parent, too, so that puts some limits on what jobs he can take because he needs to take care of you. Most local employers are willing to work around a school schedule."

Owen's eyes widened. "Really?" he asked. "They're still not too good about that in the States." That was one way to put it. His shop covered its own expenses but wouldn't be enough to support a family. He'd have been lucky to find a job on a construction crew with his time constraints, even though he brought almost twenty years of experience as a carpenter to the table.

Andrew shrugged. "Well, we've only recently been able to establish an economy that could support small businesses in the sense you're used to. Those jobs need to be filled." The elevator ground to a stop with a screech that could have shattered glass.

"Queen's throne," he said, pocketing the rings. "I didn't notice we were almost there. Come on, time to get off."

Andrew blew out the lanterns, and he and Eoire ushered the Williams out of the elevator. They exited onto a porch overlooking the largest cavern Owen had seen in his life. Most of it looked natural, but it was clear care had been taken to expand it by opening tunnels and new caverns to the main hall. A draft blew up in his face as he inched toward the edge that carried with it the smell of fresh bread, wax, and smoke.

He stared at the buildings hundreds of feet below them, at the lights spilling out of windows and doors, at people as small as ants scurrying back and forth, at Andrew, and then back down again. Unable to tear his eyes away a second time, he heard rather than saw the grin in Andrew's voice as he spoke.

"Here it is, friends, the jewel of the havens of the fae, the hidden city of Tearmann."

CHAPTER SEVEN

IN WHICH THEY FIND THEIR PLACE

"We're taking advantage of a local mountain cave system not too far from the river fork where we've set up camp. The main cavern is massive, bigger than any I've ever seen, so we're planning to hole up for winter in there. The dwarves want to build the city inside the mountain and disguise entrances as natural caves where we can. All the same, the flying folk have decided to make their home on top of the mountain in caves that are only accessible through an all-but-impossible climb or a short flight. They want a more defensible location for the weak or young if we get attacked from the ground, and, I must say, I think it's a good idea."

—Excerpt from the journals of Elijah Stephens, foreman of Work Group 5

Owen felt very small as he stared at the glittering city. Far below him, dozens of rainbow-colored buildings were shoved up against each other like peas in a pod. Pillars and buttresses supported porches like theirs and occasionally doubled as bridges that connected tunnels in the cavern wall to the upper stories—except in places where the tunnels opened into the open air.

All sorts of people went about their business far below him, with no idea he was there. They moved in and out of buildings and tunnels that stretched into the unknown, never looking up or questioning. He wondered what they were doing and why they were out this morning. Were they students or teachers on their way to school? Shopkeepers running late to work? From this height, it was impossible to tell.

"Where's all the light coming from?" Ashley asked.

"Some of it comes from the solar tunnels—large skylights—and reflects off mirrors, but the rest is from torches, candles, and lamps." As he spoke, Andrew sounded very much like a proud father.

"Why don't you have lightbulbs instead?" Dorothy asked, grabbing Owen's hand. "Did your daddy say you couldn't touch them? Daddy says I can't touch ours."

"And smart your parents are, dear one. You're too little to play with lightbulbs," Andrew replied. The corner of his eyes crinkled as he smiled and pulled back from the edge. "But to answer your question, we don't have lights because we can't get them nor could we use them if we had them."

Andrew and Eoire dragged them away from the edge and toward a narrow staircase, barely two-feet wide, cut into the cavern wall. A rough, wooden fence lined with netting was all that stood between them and the long fall to the cavern floor. Owen gripped Dorothy's hand.

"Do you have any electricity here?" Arthur asked from behind Owen.

"We use generators in places where an open flame wouldn't be safe, but we don't have too many," Andrew answered. "The hospital gets electricity for obvious reasons, and some of the greenhouses are wired, but we also use the generators in the library. It holds all the books and knowledge we've managed to save in the last fifty years. It'd be a disaster if we lost a single book to a mislaid candle."

"The clans were going to wire the kitchens," Eoire said from the back of the group. "But we thought it might not be a good idea to make our food-production facilities dependent on it until we had a more reliable energy source."

"What are the generators powered with? I mean, gasoline's out. The fumes would build up to toxic levels in minutes," Ashley said. She, too, was somewhere behind Owen, but in his mind's eye he could see the way her forehead wrinkled and her fingers tapped her leg as she tried to work out the problem. She and Tiffany made the same face when thinking.

"No, not if we can help it," Andrew said, chuckling. "Too much gas messes with the ventilation system. There are a few hydro-generators outside the city we use for power." He sighed. "It's a pity we don't have more of them. Imagine what we could do . . ." he slowed to a stop, both in speech and motion.

Owen cleared his throat, trying to regain Andrew's attention and get him moving. "So, everywhere else uses lamps, then?"

"Hm? Oh, yes," Andrew answered, starting down again. "Some of the newer and fancier apartments are wired for electricity, but not many."

"Why don't you—" Arthur let out a yell as he missed a step and caught himself on Owen's shoulder.

Owen's heart leaped to his throat as he threw the hand not holding onto Dorothy out for balance. He turned to check on Arthur and everyone else behind him before his brain could catch up to what he was doing.

"Watch your step," Andrew threw back. "A fall here could be deadly."

"Ow," Arthur grunted, massaging his ankle. "I'm fine. Why don't you use it for lighting?"

"It's easier to manage," Andrew said as he picked his way down a particularly steep section of stairs. "Most rooms would be dark for lack of bulbs after the hospital and library got their share if we tried. The dwarven lamps work just fine for our purposes."

"What do you mean dwarven lamps? Are there elven lamps or dragon lamps?" Jen asked, pushing past Owen and Dorothy to catch Andrew by his arm. She was lucky Owen hadn't started moving yet, or she'd have knocked him and Dorothy over. There wasn't anyone to catch Owen if he fell.

Andrew slowed, wiped a hand over his face, and laughed. "Ah, of course. My apologies. He shook his arm free and pulled Jen up next to him. "The Change turned most of the innovative types into dwarves— we're engineers, inventors, and mechanics for the most part—so most fae innovations come from the clans."

Eoire scoffed and the sound carried forward like a flood.

"Uh, that's not to say that only dwarves design and build things," Andrew said quickly. "Eoire is the head mechanic for the courier branch, and there are plenty of other species in our ranks. The dwarves are just the most numerous."

Jen's forehead wrinkled in a perfect imitation of her older sister. "Well, why? I mean, whatever did this couldn't have made all the inventors dwarves. It doesn't make sense."

Owen debated telling her to be politer, but he was curious too. People were more willing to answer a rude question from a child than from an adult. Besides, he needed any information he could get about the Change if his family was going to stay here for any length of time.

"It's hard to explain," Andrew said as he rubbed the back of his neck. He continued down the stairs, Jen at his side, and his voice echoed back to the others. "The clans have done a lot of research on the Change: who it affects, why, and how it chooses. If we had better equipment or more resources, we'd know more, but we're rather cut off up here. As far as we can tell, whatever directs the Change sorts certain characteristics into certain species."

There were several seconds of silence when they came to a gate and Andrew unlocked it.

"At any rate," he said once he'd pulled it open. "Most children fall into the same personality types as their parents, so they tend to enjoy the same sorts of things and get the same sorts of jobs. That's why most dwarves are engineers or mechanics, like me."

The gate led into a room with six benches in even rows of two. Owen let out a happy sigh at the sight. He wasn't sure how far they had come, but his legs ached. He sank onto a bench, the respite almost euphoric, while Andrew and Eoire dealt with the locked door on the other side of the room.

"What happens if kids don't fit the categories, if they're not like their parents?" Ashley asked, her voice cutting off all other conversation. It shook, carrying the weight of years of schoolyard bullying, but beneath was steel conviction.

As he pulled a pebble from Dorothy's shoe, Owen wondered exactly how Ashley would react if Andrew gave an answer not to her liking. Ashley may look timid, but she was stronger than she looked and as set in her beliefs as a pastor on Sunday. After all, the only black spots on her school record were from fighting bullies. Somehow, he was never able to punish her when they got reports about it.

Andrew and Eoire paused and they turned to face Ashley. They exchanged a look, unreadable and solemn, before Andrew sighed.

He stepped up to Ashley and craned his neck to look her in the eye. She was at least a foot taller than him, but the height difference did nothing to cheapen his grave look. He exhaled, forcing the air from his lungs with all the weight of decades of marginalization and oppression.

"Ashley, children who don't share their parents' talents, skills, or interests are free to choose another field with the blessings of all involved."

Eoire knelt beside Andrew and set a hand on Ashley's other shoulder. "We're free to do whatever we want; no one has to do what their parents do. I mean, look at me." She gestured to her worn, stained overalls and leather apron. "I'm only second-generation and I'm a mechanic."

She chuckled. "My parents were soldiers, and the rest of my race would rather be up a tree than in the belly of a machine. My people may not understand my choices, but they respect them."

"You don't bother them, then," Ashley said, her shoulders visibly relaxing. "People that are different from you?"

"Child, if we spent our time fighting each other over our differences, we wouldn't have time to get anything done, and we'd be massive hypocrites to boot. Believe me, you have nothing of that sort to fear here," Andrew said, a small smile crossing his face, there and gone in an instant.

Ashley smiled back and the air lightened as she did. How long had she been stewing over this, Owen wondered, that she looked so different now?

The fae returned to the door. Andrew turned a combination lock and a slot appeared in the metal. Eoire gave a passcode to a gruff voice on the other side. The door opened on silent hinges, and they finally entered the city proper.

***

Andrew and Eoire led them deeper into the mountain, through several waiting rooms covered in murals and down a long hallway into a reception area.

Fifteen desks were scattered around the room, staffed by the strangest collection of creatures Owen had ever seen. He couldn't decide where to look first.

Scale, fur, and feather-covered beings danced around each other in a chaotic cycle, never missing a step. A harpy with brown wings took a letter from a green siren and leaped out a window, a shade in a flowery kimono passed a stack of folders to a walking tree, and a werewolf with red fur was telling jokes to two elves in a corner.

Andrew led them to the desk nearest them. The creature sitting behind it looked like no mythical being Owen had ever heard of. Brown hair grew like vines past its shoulders, and its darkened skin looked as hard and unyielding as bark. Each slow and methodical movement it made brought a creaking noise like wind shaking branches.

Owen's examination of the creature was cut off when it looked up from its paperwork and its dark green eyes peered over the rims of half-moon glasses as they approached.

"Stephens, Belfield," it creaked. "I assume these are the new arrivals?"

Eoire smiled at the creature. "Yep, sorry we're late. Sergeant Lucien said there were problems on the way over."

"Yes, I know," it said, lips turning down in a fractional frown. "One of the mechanics sent a flute message, as you should have." It turned to look the group over, silently judging them in a way that made Owen tense.

"Right, then." It sighed, a hollow, oaky sound. "My name is Derek Young. You may call me Mr. Young. To answer the questions I know you have, I'm a first-generation troll. This is the registration office. Here you will sign up for an apartment and school and get started on finding work. Any concerns before we begin?"

No one said anything.

Mr. Young shook his head. "Mm-hmm, yes—" He coughed. "Please sit down. This may take a while. Belfield, Stephens, I presume you two are their interim guides?"

Eoire nodded and presented a small envelope to Mr. Young. "Here's the interim notification; everything should be there," she said and turned to Owen. "I have some paperwork of my own to fill out, but Andrew will stay with you to answer any questions you have. I'll be back in about an hour."

She walked off without waiting for Owen to respond, leaving the Williams to begin the grueling process of signing up for housing, schools, food, and species qualifications. Owen didn't understand why they had to fill out the last one—they were all human—but Andrew said it would determine which apartment they got. Apparently, some species had a hard time living in humanoid-centric locations.

"You will all be required to take a series of seminars about the history of the fae and the different species before the children can take the placement exams and start school," Mr. Young said as he pulled a folder labeled cultural training from one of several identical piles on his desk.

"Are there any differences between American and fae schooling?" Arthur asked, leaning forward to look at the contents of the folder. "I mean, I'm a junior. Can't I just join the junior class here?"

"A fair few," Mr. Young said. His eyes lit up, and he turned the folder so Arthur could see it without having to strain. "As you can see here, we don't have access to the teaching materials most schools use. As such, our teachers focus less on the traditional liberal arts education plan and focus more on survival and practical skills. For example, there's a required class on wilderness survival and another on medicinal plants."

Owen blinked. He couldn't have heard that right. Sure, survival skills had their place, but they wouldn't help in the real world. "There's still math, science, and whatnot, right?" he asked, a scowl tugging at the corner of his lips.

"Of course," Mr. Young said. His eyes turned to Owen, hardening like tree sap in winter. "Our resources may be limited, but we take great pride in the quality of our education system. The queen herself assists with the history classes."

"I was told we could go to the UK because I was Welsh," Owen said before he could stop himself. "I need to know my children won't fall behind in their studies." He squeezed Dorothy to his chest. He couldn't let them stay here forever. They'd need all the help they could to adapt if one or more of them Changed, and that would be easier in Scotland. Back where they knew what to expect from people.

"Mr. Williams," Mr. Young said, his fingers tightening on the folder in his hand. "There's no guarantee you and yours will even be allowed to go to Daingneach, what with *your* situation, after all." His face didn't change, but his voice grew, a sound like wind rushing through branches. "Our status with the UK is tenuous; they're our primary legitimate trading partner, and we can't jeopardize that relationship. Without the medicinal and educational aid they offer, thousands would have to go without essentials—"

"Derek, enough," Andrew said, slamming his hands on the table. "People are staring."

Dorothy struggled against Owen's grip. "Daddy," she whined. "You're hurting me."

Owen loosened his grip. He hadn't realized he was holding her that tight. "Sorry, Dot," he whispered, rubbing her arm soothingly. "I didn't mean to hurt you."

"If the two of you are ready to act like adults," Andrew said as he slumped back into his chair, "why don't we move on to finding them an apartment? Remember, Derek, they have a dog."

Mr. Young narrowed his eyes but nodded. He pulled an unlabeled folder from his stack and dropped it in front of Owen. "This is a list of the apartments available for faeborn families. There's one in particular that will suit your needs. Three bedrooms, a full bathroom, a kitchen, and a living room. It's close to the southern gate and the greenhouses, which your dog will appreciate. Your interim guides will show you how the lamps and the laundry system work. Being so knowledgeable, I'm sure it won't be too hard for you to figure out."

"How much is rent? And how much do the utilities cost?" Owen asked, trying to ignore the way his heart sunk to the floor. None of his skills would be marketable in a place like this. He couldn't hunt and didn't know the first thing about farming. What happened to homeless people in a place like Tearmann?

"As a newcomer with faeborn minors, you'll be given an apartment," Mr. Young said. "Utilities come out of everyone's pay, provided they don't choose to live in one of the outlying villages or establish their own residences outside the mountain."

"And how many do that?" He hadn't known that was an option. How big was this place?

"Fewer than 60,000 people live in the capital itself. Most live outside or in one of the other citadels."

Owen asked a few more questions about potential living situations before he admitted the first apartment Mr. Young suggested was the best option available. Most of the larger apartments were inhabited already and the ones that weren't were too far from the greenhouses for Toto's comfort.

Mr. Young made an expression like he would have been lowering his eyebrows if he had any and shuffled through his folders. "The first thing you should know is that everyone who can work, must. We have no room for people who waste resources."

Owen could see Ashley fidgeting from the corner of his eye. Her eyes darted to Andrew, who seemed to be trying to set fire to Mr. Young with his eyes.

"Things aren't as rough as all that, Derek," Andrew said. "There's been no need for mandatory workforces in the last twenty years. And the council has been encouraging the educators to allow more freedom in choosing careers since the upper housing district was completed."

Mr. Young rubbed his eyes. "Despite what you engineers think, things aren't as perfect as they seem. We have no room for slackers, not when a single worker may mean the difference between starvation and survival for many of us, even now."

He proceeded to list everything Owen needed to do before he could get a job, preempting any attempt the others made to speak. Owen had to complete the same seminars and tests as his children, as well as one more for the human parents of faeborn children. Mr. Young insisted it was necessary, but the way Andrew snorted made Owen think otherwise.

"I know you think you'll be out of here soon," Mr. Young said to Owen once he had finished the winding lecture. "But in case that falls through, do you have any useful skills or are you all talk?"

Owen swallowed back a foul word. He should've held his tongue earlier. He had a sinking feeling Mr. Young could make his life very difficult if he chose to. "Well, I ran a carpentry shop behind my house back home—"

Silence blanketed the office as all eyes turned toward them. "You got yourself a carpenter over there, Derek?" a red-scaled creature yelled, razor-sharp teeth flashing in the lamplight. "We haven't had a new one in almost five years."

Owen blinked. That looked like a dragon, but she was … well, almost humanoid. And smaller than he expected.

The dragon jumped over her desk toward them. She would have towered over him had they been standing, and she moved like gravity didn't weigh her down. Shimmering red scales amplified the effect, making her look larger than life.

Andrew peered around Arthur and grinned. "Morning, Danica. How's the family?"

She shot a jagged, toothy smile at Andrew, returned his greeting, and looked back to Mr. Young. "Well, Derek?"

Mr. Young rubbed his forehead again. "Yes, Mrs. Moore, it appears Mr. Williams here is a carpenter."

The dragon—Danica—clapped her hands and turned to Owen. "Oh, wonderful, we don't have nearly enough of them, sir, and there aren't many people who are interested in the trade and capable of learning it."

She smiled again, revealing a plethora of sharp teeth, and stuck out a scaly, clawed hand. "Danica Moore, at your service."

Owen managed something resembling a smile. He reached up and gingerly shook the proffered hand. "Owen—Owen Williams, pleasure to meet you. Sorry, I'd stand, but with Dorothy, here—"

Danica made a harsh coughing noise that took him a moment to recognize as laughter. "It's completely all right. I had little ones of my own once upon a time; I know how it goes." She glared at Mr. Young. "You make sure the builders hear about this one. Richard says they haven't had a decent apprentice in years."

He grunted. "I know, Danica, but he still has to be evaluated. I'd hate to send him straight in only to discover he's an amateur."

"Whatever, Derek." She pulled a small card from the decorated apron she was wearing in lieu of proper clothing and passed it to Owen. "This is my husband. He runs a small construction company in one of the upper wings. I know you said you want to leave, but contact him and he'll get you set up. Derek was right about one thing, you'll probably be here a while." Once he took the card, she turned and walked back to her desk, her long, slim tail and wings swaying behind her with every step she took.

92

Owen turned back to Mr. Young. "I take it you don't have many carpenters here?"

Mr. Young shook his head. "No. There's more call for luxuries now that the major building has died down, you know, rugs, paintings, specialized furniture, and all that. There are also the normal maintenance concerns we have to consider that trained carpenters can assist with. Wood is one of the few resources we have in abundance, as you can probably guess. If you pass the evaluations, you will be working as a carpenter, I guarantee you that."

Each Williams was assigned an identification number in the next hour, beginning the records that would be completed the next day at the physical examination. Then they registered for the apartment and signed up for the seminars and evaluations. Owen wasn't sure if he had ever signed so many papers in his life, even when he had been filling out the dual citizenship paperwork. Finally, when his hand was about to fall off, Mr. Young declared they were free to leave.

***

Eoire rejoined the group as Andrew led them into another series of long hallways. Owen wondered if these hallways led to a cavern like the one they had seen before. It had looked like a proper city with buildings and paths and stores and people. All he'd seen since they'd left that cavern was an endless series of tunnels just like this one.

"No," Andrew said when Owen asked about it. "What we saw earlier is the market and town square. You can get to anywhere in the mountain from there and buy most anything you could want, but it's the only market we have. None of the other caverns in the area are safe enough to do that. Some are flooded or unstable; any building activity there could cause collapse or worse." He snorted. "We're lucky we found that one or we would have frozen to death years ago."

"Oh," Owen said, the unpleasant thought of the tunnel collapsing tying his stomach in knots. "Well, where are we now?"

"We're in the registration office, on the third floor in the western wing," Andrew said. His voice was lighter now that they were talking about the city again. "The city has six floors with four wings to each floor. The top floor is the Eyries, where the larger flying folk live."

"The cavern you saw is the center of the entire complex, and the Eyries are built in the mountain peaks," Eoire said when Andrew paused for breath. "In addition to the market, we also have the more practical tunnels that make up the wings of the cavern."

"Wait—" Jen said in a horrified voice. "There are more tunnels?"

Jen didn't like tight spaces—or being underground, for that matter. Owen thought it was because she'd gotten trapped in a wardrobe with a broken lock for most of the day when she was five. He'd had to take the whole door off to get her out.

"Yes, child, most of the city is underground, and there are a lot of tunnels," Eoire said and laughed when Jen's despairing groan echoed down the tunnel.

"Where are we going?" Arthur asked.

"We're taking you to get something to eat and then to your apartment," Andrew explained. "You lot have a busy day in front of you, and you need time recover from your journey. We're almost there."

They came to a massive stairway that Andrew said connected each of the floors, from the Eyries down to the greenhouses. Lamps hung on each landing and their light disappeared into the distance in either direction.

"What is this place?" Owen asked as he followed Andrew and Eoire down the stairs. His voice echoed and the sound disappeared into the distant mesh of movement coming from above and below.

"Didn't you hear him?" Eoire replied, slowing until the Williams reached them. "This is one of the Grand Staircases, from here you can reach every floor in the city."

"Even to the Eyries? That's got to be at almost half a mile from here." He swallowed and craned his neck back. He couldn't see where the stairs ended.

"Yep." She smirked. "Almost no one uses those stairs now that we have the elevators, but we keep them in good condition in case of emergencies."

"Can't the dragons fly people there?" David asked, pushing his messy black hair out of his eyes as he stared at the wall carvings. His left hand found Jen's right and he pulled her closer to him as they passed through a section where the lamps had gone out.

"Well, they could." Andrew chuckled, leaning close to David. "But what if there weren't any dragons on the lower floors? Only four species have wings, my boy, and it was years before the elevators were built."

They kept descending, each flight identical except for the carving on the landings. Supposedly, they were only going down one level, to the lower residential district, but after the first five flights, Owen had his doubts.

Andrew and Eoire filled the time by explaining how the city was set up and how to read the maps at each landing. A strong note of unmistakable pride filtered into their voices as they spoke, mixed with a small amount of competition as the two began racing to answer questions before the other.

So caught up in the lecture was Owen that he barely noticed they'd left the stairway and reached the dining hall. The smell of fresh bread and spices lingered around the doorway and pulled him in. His stomach growled as Andrew guided them through the line and thoughts of how the city was built were abandoned in favor of filling his belly.

***

Eoire and Andrew led them out of the dining hall once they'd finished eating and down another series of long, identical hallways. The kids stumbled into each other as they walked. Owen hoped they would have time to rest before whatever else they were supposed to do today. Eoire had mentioned a tour, and if the city was as big as they made it sound, his legs ached at the very thought of it.

Before long, they left the noisy hall behind them. The murals covering the walls, depicting everything from battles to landscapes, were faded and dull. Age and countless hands had robbed them of their color. People of all species lined the hallway. Adults, their hands full of groceries, stared at Owen as they passed, and a group of children played soccer down the far half of the hallway.

The group ended up walking right through the game. Most of the children scattered, but one, a harpy with blond colored wings separate from his arms, was braver than the others. He approached them, his wings fluttering behind him, and asked them if they were the ones moving into 1S30E.

Owen blinked. That sounded like an apartment number. He looked at Andrew for confirmation before answering that, yes, they were. The boy grinned and invited them to play soccer with him later.

"We haven't had anyone new here in ages, I can't wait to tell Lizzy I saw you first!" squealed the boy, his wings fluttering from excitement.

He and Jen were going to become great friends, Owen could tell. They were both chatterboxes who'd befriend anything that moved.

David promised that they would come out and play later if the game was still going on, and the group moved forward.

They passed a few more doors and took a turn down another hallway of apartments, decorated similarly to the one before it. Luckily, their door wasn't far from the turn. Owen was fairly certain Jen was actually dozing as she leaned on David's shoulder.

"Here, this one is yours." Andrew pulled a set of keys out from one of his pockets and unlocked the door. He gestured for them to wait a moment while he fiddled with the light. Owen heard several clicks, like two rocks banging against each other, before the apartment lights flickered on.

Andrew spent a few moments explaining how the light switch worked; Owen only paid enough attention to grasp that it might have to be struck several times before it worked. They were given a quick tour of the apartment and shown where they could find clean sheets. The furniture was old, and most of it didn't match, but the rug beneath their feet looked new.

Andrew and Eoire gave each other a look Owen was too tired to decipher. They then announced that they would finish the tour in a few hours. Apparently, the rest of the team was expected to arrive by then, and they would bring down the Williams' things at that time. In the meantime, they recommended that the Williams take a nap, a suggestion Owen approved of wholeheartedly.

CHAPTER EIGHT

IN WHICH THERE IS A PARTY

"… we aren't sure how this new government of ours is supposed to run. I've suggested establishing a democracy, but almost everyone I've spoken to is against it. No one knows what to do now that we actually got what we wanted. A lot of people are scared and looking for anyone who looks like they know what they're doing. I guess they think that since we led them during the war, we can build and run a nation, but I'm not so sure. We barely held it together back then. What do we do now?"

—Excerpt from the journals of Beira Thomson, Queen Titania

A bell woke Owen with a blaring ring that penetrated the murky depths of his mind no matter how much he tried to ignore it. There was a warm weight in his arms, too small to be Tiffany. Dorothy must have crawled into their bed. He threw a hand to shut off that blasted alarm clock before it woke her or Tiffany and hit air instead of his bedstand. With a groan, he pulled his head from the pillow and rubbed the sleep from his eyes.

A single glance was enough for reality to reassert itself. He wasn't at home, and he would never share a bed with his wife again. The bell rang again. Swallowing back his grief, he untangled himself from the blankets, careful not to disturb Dorothy, and crept into the hall.

"One minute, I'm coming," he said as he stumbled down the hall and toward the door, shaking his head to dispense the last of the fog of sleep. Out of the corner of his eye, he saw Arthur's bleary-eyed face poke out of the room he was sharing with David. Owen gestured for him to go back to bed.

He fiddled with the lock and pulled open the door, revealing the smiling faces of Andrew and Eoire. Without thinking, he slammed the door shut in their faces. He slumped against the door and rubbed his eyes. It was far too early for guests of any sort and they should know that. It was then he realized they were here to finish the tour and he needed to let them in.

He pulled the door open again, to see both of them wearing poorly concealed identical smirks. He paused, wondering exactly how to explain what happened.

"… Sorry about that."

They assured him that it was no trouble. Although they were clearly holding back laughter, Owen did notice that they made no effort to hide their grins.

"Right, I suppose you're here to finish the tour, then? Come in."

He shouldn't have sent Arthur back to bed; that boy was almost a zombie if he didn't wake on his own. It'd be impossible to get him up now.

Running a hand through his hair, he walked back down the hall. He knocked on the girls' door, and when he received no response, went in. He gently shook the shoulder of the lump in one of the beds. "Hey, time to get up, kiddos."

A red-eyed Ashley poked her head out from the nest of blankets. It took a few more shakes, but he got her moving. While she dragged herself from the bed he went to wake Jen, who complained but started getting ready.

Satisfied the girls were taken care of, he went to deal with the boys. To his surprise Arthur walked out of the boys' room, only slightly resembling the undead. He was followed by David, who—by comparison—was as fresh as a daisy. Both were dressed, if you could call their pajamas dressed, and making their way to the bathroom to tame their hair.

Pleased that Arthur hadn't gone back to bed and had gotten himself and his brother ready, Owen went to wake Dorothy. She'd burrowed herself under the blankets. It would've been cute if he weren't so tired. He had to pull her out and physically carry her out of the room.

"Arthur, are you and the girls ready?" he asked, wishing again he had the time and equipment to shave.

Arthur staggered out of the bathroom, rubbing a hand over his stubble. "Bathroom's free if you want. I'll get Dorothy ready," he grunted.

Owen handed the slumbering four-year-old to her brother. Now unencumbered, he felt his own chin, and three days' worth of stubble scratched his palm. He hoped someone had grabbed him a razor; otherwise, he was going to have to find out whether the dwarf outside would be offended if he asked to borrow one. He ran a hand down his pant leg, he could do with a change too. He'd been wearing these since the recital.

He hurried through his morning routine and splashed water on his face instead of taking a proper shower, then rushed out of the bathroom. It turned out he needn't have hurried, as Eoire and Andrew were in the middle of a wild story involving a gryphon, a centaur, and a herd of domesticated caribou from the sound of things.

"… and then Caiside gets the great idea of trying to herd the caribou toward Fedelmid, who has no idea what he was doing, but suddenly she has thirty caribou charging at her. She freezes, and Caiside, who is being absolutely no help, keeps sending them to her. So, she rears up on her hind legs and screams at the caribou, which, of course, terrifies them and sends them back at Caiside, who turns tail and runs back to the base with about half the herd following him in, and let me tell you, the mess those caribou made was like nothing I've ever seen. It took two hours to catch them all and get them back outside. Twenty-five years, and he's still in the stables for that one."

"Why didn't he run somewhere else?" Jen asked. She was staring at Andrew like he was insane. "Didn't he know they would follow him inside?"

"Well, no one ever said Caiside was the sharpest—" Andrew stopped when he saw Owen standing in the hallway. "So, Williams, now that you've gotten some beauty sleep, are you ready to finish the tour? I got people who want to meet you, and you're having dinner with Rodriguez's team, so we need to get the kitchen kitted out."

"What do you mean we're having dinner with them?" Owen asked, stepping into the room. "Jason and Peter mentioned they would stop in when we got settled, but all of them?"

"It's a fae tradition dating back to the founding of Tearmann," Eoire explained. "Newcomers have dinner with the team that brought them in, a welcoming party, if you will."

There was that feeling again, the same one he'd felt when they'd first met. Like there was a mind pushing against his own, except this time he felt subdued instead of happy.

He shook his head, trying to chase the uncomfortable feeling away. He wanted to ask Eoire about it, but the words wouldn't come. He couldn't speak. He forced his eyes away; the others were having the same problems.

Andrew stared at Eoire with narrowed eyes and put a hand on her shoulder. He whispered something to her. She paled and the feeling faded. Owen could breathe again.

"At any rate," she said, leaping to her feet. "We need to get going. Lots to see, you know."

Owen's stomach twisted. He forced the feeling down and moved toward the door. He must have imagined it; Eoire wouldn't do anything to them. They followed her into the hallway and he locked the door behind the twins, who were bickering about something Andrew had said. He swallowed. He needed coffee.

Andrew's eyes flicked back and forth between Eoire and Owen. "Eoire, take the kids to the marketplace. I've got a few things I need to talk to Williams about. We'll be right behind you."

She nodded and led the kids down the hall, back toward the Grand Staircase. Andrew waited until the group was ten or fifteen feet in front of them before he followed.

"So is this where you tell me about the raging inter-species gang war or anti-human prejudices?" He was joking, but his stomach tied itself into knots. Andrew had been open before now, answering any questions the kids had, but whatever this was he wanted to keep it quiet.

Andrew chuckled weakly. "Oh, no worries there, my friend, there've been no gang wars here in years."

"Oh, really? Well, that's quite a relief."

"No, no, no," Andrew said, his smile becoming more genuine. "The gang wars are on the third floor—politics, you see."

Owen squinted at Andrew, trying to decide if he was pulling his leg again. "You know, Andrew, sometimes I can't tell if you're being serious or not."

"Understandable," he said, shrugging. "But you may want to learn soon. Deadpan is in vogue in the capital, and most of us are rather good at it."

"Deadpan, huh? Anything else I should be on the lookout for?"

"Puns, mostly. They're a plague and curse upon the population."

Andrew's partial scowl was a thing of wonder. Owen hadn't been aware someone could put that much loathing in a single expression. Something like that could be rewarded in only one way.

"Are they that bad? I think you just have to take things pun day at a time, otherwise, people will pun all over you."

It was Andrew's turn to squint at him. Owen himself was struggling to maintain the façade of seriousness, a battle he lost when Andrew punched him in the side.

"How dare you make me listen to that monstrosity."

Owen would be having fun with this for a while, especially if the kids could be persuaded to join him in the wordplay. Nothing drew the Williams together quite like puns. There'd been a moratorium at the dinner table for a while after they'd driven Tiffany insane trying to outdo each other.

They walked on, the silence comfortable. Bits of whatever conversation the kids were having with Eoire drifted back. He thought he heard her mention that Caiside fellow again, so they must have been asking for more stories.

Andrew cleared his throat as they rounded a corner. Owen wondered if he was finally going to hear whatever had made Andrew take him aside in the first place. The jokes had been fun, but they weren't the reason Andrew had wanted to speak with him.

"Owen—" he stopped. Whatever he wanted to say, the words weren't coming.

For a moment, he wondered if he had hit home with the anti-human prejudice joke. His stomach tightened; were they going to make him leave? Had all of this been some scheme to get the kids up here quietly?

"Is there something wrong?" He was proud of how steady his voice was.

Andrew caught on to where Owen's thoughts had led him. "Williams, I assure you that we won't do anything to you or your family," he said. "By the queen's throne, you look like you think we're going to take them away."

"Well, what is it, then?" A strange combination of relief and desperation colored his voice as Andrew soothed a fear he wasn't certain would ever completely go away.

However much a population changed in fifty years, something like the Fae War didn't fade from memory, especially not here. Most of the humans who fought in the Fae War died in action and their stories with them. But here—here they were very much alive. Their stories had been told. And he was human. His children were human.

"The queen wants to meet you."

Out of all the things Owen had expected to come out of Andrew's mouth, meeting the queen fell somewhere below anti-human discrimination and above structural problems causing cave-ins. It had been a distant possibility but nothing he actually been concerned with.

He stopped mid-stride. After a moment, he realized that the spots in front of his eyes were from lack of oxygen and that he should breathe before Andrew called for help.

Somehow, he managed to garble together a sentence. "Me?" he asked in a high-pitched voice. "Why would the queen want to meet me?"

Andrew looked like he was on the verge of making him sit down and put his head between his knees. Instead of following through, he reached up and patted Owen's elbow. It entirely failed to reassure him.

"Well, it's not only the queen; the whole Founders Council wants to meet you," Andrew said. "But that'll come later."

"Andrew?" Owen managed to say after a moment of incredulous staring while he forced himself to breathe.

"Yes, Williams?"

"Never become a doctor. Your bedside manner is terrible."

Andrew paused and then nodded. "It's for the best that I'm an engineer. I'm told that they're not expected to know much about comforting people—or people in general, really."

Owen nodded. He was calmer now, but he made himself take another deep breath. "I want a better explanation," he said, looking in the direction the others had gone. "But we seem to have lost the group."

Andrew glanced in the same direction, not quite meeting his eyes when he looked back. "Well, it looks like we have. Come on, they can't have gotten too far ahead."

They hurried down the hallway, finally catching sight of the others after they climbed two flights of stairs.

"Oh wonderful," Andrew said. "I was worried they'd already gotten to the market. We really would have lost them then." He turned to Owen. "Now, as I was saying, the queen likely wants to meet you to talk about a proposition she has."

Owen looked at Andrew and then back at the kids. "And you couldn't you have told me this in front of my kids?"

"It's private, you see, and it's a service only you could provide."

Owen wasn't sure he was comfortable with the turn this conversation was taking. As far as he knew, the only other thing he could do that his kids couldn't involved woodwork. "And . . . what service would that be?"

"Well, surely that's obvious." Andrew snorted, raising his eyebrows when he caught sight of Owen's increasingly bewildered expression.

"Uh, no?"

There was a moment of mutual confusion before clarity filled Andrew's face. "Williams"—he hesitated—"you do know the queen's a vampire, right?"

A lightbulb went off somewhere. "So you mean she—?"

"Presumably, yes, as there aren't many humans in the city younger than seventy."

"But can't she—you know—with fae blood?"

Andrew shook his head. "She can't. I don't know the whole story, but I think someone died after she drank his blood."

"Someone—?"

He hadn't seen any other humans since they'd arrived. A cold, tight feeling plunged straight through him, and for a moment he forgot how to breath. They had to exist, they had to, otherwise the queen would be dead, but why hadn't he seen any?

"Do I even have a choice?" he asked raggedly. "I'm human, so I have to open a vein for her?"

"I'm not saying that. It's up to you and ..." Sighing, he massaged the bridge of his nose. "Just ... hear her out. Your appointment is at noon tomorrow. Either Eoire or I will come get you at eleven to escort you there."

Owen nodded and shoved his hands in his pockets to hide their shaking. He wanted to believe Andrew. He did, but he couldn't. There were too many dots begging to be connected, and he didn't like where any of them led.

He needed to get the kids out of here before they got wrapped up in all this.

They walked in silence to the market gate, where the crowd grew so thick Owen would've lost sight of the kids altogether if Eoire hadn't been so tall. Even from the hall, the deafening chorus of crowing hawkers and chattering pedestrians set his teeth on edge.

Andrew stopped him before he could work up the nerve to go in. "One more thing before we go in." His hand tightened around Owen's arm like a vice. For a second, Owen wasn't sure if he was going to say anything at all. "You can't ... we're trying to help you lad. I know you're hurting, but you need to keep that in mind. You and your family are going to be here a while." His eyes grew darker and his voice dropped low. "I know what you must think of us, but you can't fight all your battles on your own. It'll only end in pain."

The crowd flowed around them unnoticed. Andrew stared up at Owen for a long moment, something unreadable in his eyes, before he shook himself and turned to the market.

"Come along then, Williams. We've lots to see and not nearly enough time to do it."

***

That afternoon, they toured the marketplace, the schools, the farms and orchards, and any other place of interest their guides could think of. Along the way, Andrew and Eoire helped pick out basic necessities for the Williams's apartment and showed Owen how to arrange for delivery so he didn't have to lug everything around with them. If Owen had his way, they wouldn't be here long enough to need all this, but he didn't say that. For now, it was best to keep those plans close to his chest.

While Andrew was explaining to the children how to barter, Owen asked Eoire about payment. He didn't have any money, and the last thing he wanted to do was get into debt, but she brushed his concerns aside. Apparently, they had an allowance until Owen got his feet under him. As long as he didn't splurge on luxuries, they'd be taken care of.

After they finished their shopping, they went back to the dining hall for a late lunch. It was a tribute to how exhausted they had been earlier that it took until now for them to notice the murals and carvings covering the dining hall and most of the tunnels.

According to Eoire, the first of the murals had been painted not long after the founding and more were added to their number during the anniversary celebration. It was considered a great honor to be chosen to make that year's founding mural, and the artisans in the capital competed fiercely for it. The other murals and sculptures were the products of citizens who wished to beautify the capital.

After a brief detour down to the greenhouses, where an assortment of creatures had been helpfully entertaining Toto, they headed back to the apartment. Eoire and Andrew kept up a steady flow of facts and stories that kept the kids from lingering on how tired they were. Watching the twins fight over Toto's leash, Owen bit back a laugh. He hadn't felt this good in ages. If he closed his eyes he could imagine they were back home and at any moment Tiffany would call to complain about whatever work event had kept her from joining them.

Dorothy sprinted ahead, Eoire and Arthur at her heels. As they disappeared around the corner, their laughter echoing off the walls, Owen gasped. Spots danced in front of his eyes and he struggled to breathe around the tight knot in his throat.

Tiffany was gone. He stumbled against the wall and blinked back tears. God, had it only been three days? It couldn't have been. He wouldn't be laughing after three days, not when everything had gone to hell like this.

As he gasped for air, Owen's memories of the past few days passed his eyes like a dream. Had it been just yesterday that they'd landed here?

It felt like longer, a nightmare under rose colored glasses. They could never go home. *Tiffany was dead.*

He wished, more than anything in the world, that it was a horrible dream, that he would wake up and tell Tiffany that her cooking gave him nightmares. He would take a thousand nights of bad dreams if it meant she was still alive, still with him. But he couldn't wake up.

Somehow, his legs started working again and the tight feeling in his chest eased when he caught up to the group. By the time he passed the apartment door he'd locked the screaming bits of his heart away. He didn't have time for that now. The kids needed him.

Andrew and Eoire were demonstrating how to work the washing machine. It was a barrel with a strange collection of gears, cogs, and peddles that spun the clothes around and a press to get the extra water out. It required a manual to maintain, and they were expected to provide the upkeep themselves. From there, they went to the kitchen. The equipment there was much simpler: a wood-burning stove like his father-in-law had had in his hunting cabin, an ice box to keep meat cold, and a sink. A wooden box filled to the brim with firewood stood by the stove, ready to be used.

A knock at the door heralded an end to their lessons and the first of their deliveries. For the next half hour, the doorbell rang every five minutes like clockwork. There was a pile almost three feet high in the front hall when Owen pulled the door open one last time.

"Put the food in—Oh."

Aaron and Abey, weighed down by several bags and packages, stood outside with Tony, Isaac, Peter, and Jason. Aaron shifted his grip on one of the saddlebags slung over his shoulder. "Owen, nice to see you again," he said, smiling pleasantly. "Where do you want these?"

"Put the bags down in the living room, we can sort them out there." He paused, not sure if they knew the layout of the apartment. "Ah, the living room is this way, past the kitchen."

Variations of "got it" and "understood" assaulted him as the group tramped past. The bags were dumped in the living room, and the boxes, which held food nicked from the dining hall, were set down in the kitchen.

Jason followed the crowd in, dumped his bags, and made a beeline for a much more relaxed Toto. He'd had a blast playing in the greenhouses and was currently lounging in an armchair like he hadn't a care in the world.

"Oh, you got your dog back," Jason cooed, leaning down to scratch at Toto's ears. "Did you have a good time in the greenhouses boy?"

Toto's tail beat against the armrest as he smiled a doggy grin.

Owen, halfway into one of the bags already, hummed. "Seems so. I haven't seen him this relaxed in ages."

"Oh, there were a bunch of elves down there." Jason's smile was almost blinding. "Oh, that reminds me. The mechanics gave me something for you. Apparently, you left it in the gondola."

"Oh?" This bag was mostly toiletries. He made a mental note to have Arthur sort through it later. He had a system for it that Owen didn't dare disrupt.

After one last pat, Jason left Toto behind, plucked a bag from its semi-identical companions, and pulled out a familiar box. "Here, this is yours, isn't it?"

The gun. He'd forgotten it in the rush to get everyone out. "Yeah, uh, that's mine. I'll just—Let me put that in my room." The cold metal dug into his fingers. He would bury it in his closet. He wasn't sure what the laws here said about private weapon ownership, but until he did no one could know he had it. He wasn't about to give up his only means of protecting his kids if something went south.

Peter and Eoire commandeered the twins and Dorothy and took over the kitchen to cook while the rest sorted through the bags. Owen suspected that this was a clever way to keep the young kids out from underfoot while the rest of them were unpacking.

"We grabbed as much as we could, but after the news about you all broke, the police started watching the house," Aaron said, digging through one of the bigger bags. Both harpies had had to haul it in. From the mass of items, he pulled out a violin and a guitar case and handed them to their respective owners.

He ducked his head and rubbed his neck. "Sorry about shoving them in like that, but we didn't want to risk dropping them while in flight. The clothes bag seemed the safest option. Also—" He reached in again and pulled out a cloth bag. "I thought you might appreciate having some of your music with you."

Ashley's and Arthur's grins, previously in danger of splitting their faces in two, grew even wider. None of their siblings had shown any musical inclination in the past, and as Tiffany had been something of an audiophile, having their instruments back gave them a real link to their mother. After all, she'd been the one to help them learn most of their music. Owen could sing but wasn't to be trusted with an instrument more complex than a kazoo.

"All right," Owen said, interrupting their joyful conversation. "Let's get unpacking. Arthur, Ashley, put those in your rooms and someone keep an eye on Toto so he doesn't get in the way. We have a lot to do tonight."

They scattered into small groups. Arthur disappeared into the bathroom with anything with firm orders for everyone else to stay out, and Ashley took charge of the sorting.

"Owen, one moment," Aaron said, pulling him back before he could join Ashley. "I grabbed something else and I don't want it to be damaged. I'd feel better if you had it." For a third time, he reached into the bag and pulled out an item that made Owen's breath catch—a photo album, the product of Tiffany's brief scrapbooking phase. She hadn't been very good at it or very focused, so its pages held countless memories—baby photos, family holidays, school plays, and birthday parties— plastered in layers so thick you could barely see the pages beneath the pictures.

Words of thanks got caught in his throat. He reached out with shaking hands to take the album from Aaron. He traced the cover, embossed with their family name in gold paint on the brown leather.

"I—thank you. You have no idea what this means. I can't—" He couldn't thank Aaron enough. To have this bit of their family back, something that meant so much to Tiffany, it was something he could never repay.

"I'd want it if I were in your place," he said softly. He pushed Owen back toward his room. "Now put it away before something happens to it."

Owen nodded, throat still too tight to speak. He laid the album on his bed like it was glass. It was precious, the last they had of her. They would look at it later, as a family.

He returned to the living room, where the sorting had begun in earnest.

The whole mess was unpacked in less than two hours. It may not have been much, but it was more than Owen had been expecting. Their clothes were in their closets, their shelves littered with their books and knick-knacks, and a throw blanket Owen had gotten at Niagara Falls was draped over the back of the worn sofa. It felt like a home. Almost.

***

He hadn't had such an enjoyable evening in a while. Laughter slowly filled the apartment and lifted the gloom of its occupants. It was a nice distraction from everything else.

Over the stew that Jason and the twins made, the fae told stories about their childhoods and what it was like living in Tearmann. Abey and Jason talked about their lives before the war, being the only two present who were alive at that time.

Jen flat-out refused to believe the two of them when they admitted to being ninety-five and seventy-nine, respectively. This, of course, led to an all-around demand for the rest of the fae to reveal their ages, to various degrees of shock and incredulity.

Peter, after some good-natured ribbing, admitted he was only twenty-three. The cause of his embarrassment became clear when Aaron explained that third-gen shades were expected to live roughly two hundred years. In the eyes of the fae, Peter was little more than a teenager. Owen wondered aloud if Peter was even old enough to go on away missions.

Peter protested over the laughter that, yes, he was old enough, although Aaron said that it was only just, as third-gen shades were considered adults at twenty-two. This set off another round of laughter as Peter good-naturedly argued his point.

At some point, there was a call for music, and Arthur and Ashley were persuaded to pull out their instruments, not that it took much effort. For the next hour, they took requests from their siblings and the fae, who admitted to being out of touch with pop culture and mostly requested things that had been popular before Owen was born. They even played a few of Tiffany's favorite duets.

After one particularly rousing rendition of "Whiskey in the Jar," which was apparently a great favorite of the queen, Jason laughed. "You know," he called over to Owen. "You better keep an eye on these two, or otherwise the sirens will try to keep them to themselves."

Owen responded in kind. "Surely the sirens have enough singers and musicians to keep themselves entertained?"

Aaron shook his head. "Not really." He laughed. "Sure, singers we have plenty of, but instrumentalists are about as rare as vampires."

"Is it that hard for you to play instruments, then?" Ashley asked, pointing at Aaron's finned fingers as she sat down. Arthur was taking requests right now.

Aaron nodded but then shook his head. "Not quite. I mean, sure, there are some instruments we would have a hard time playing, what with the fins and all, but for the most part it's that we don't have any instruments to play."

Ashley nodded. "I suppose you didn't have time to grab many when you came up here."

"True enough. What ones we do have are in so much danger from the elements that we keep them protected and segregated in a dry and clean environment as much as possible. Only a few of us get the chance to play them. Those who do get to use them play at dances and the like, but not many are trained to use them properly."

Conversation died down shortly after this, as Ashley was called into service again to play a final duet with her brother. They finished with a flourish and a bow. The group applauded appreciatively.

Taking note of the late hour, they cleaned up from dinner and the party, and the crew left not long after. The apartment emptied, and the joy and laughter left with the fae.

The instruments were put away, showers taken, and stories read. After making a final check throughout the apartment, Owen turned out the light and fell into bed. He drifted off into the comforting arms of sleep, untroubled by dreams, nightmares, or intruding memories.

CHAPTER NINE

IN WHICH OWEN GETS
THE ROYAL TREATMENT

"So city planning is a pain. We've managed to throw something together, a city built in layers, but we don't have the luxury of waiting until it's done to move in. With this in mind, we're starting with the housing.. There are a lot of nice-sized caves at ground level, and we can expand them as we need to. Mostly, we want to get rooms hollowed out; we can sort out furniture and such later. Our current plan is a three-level complex (although Audhild is pushing for as many as six), the bottom floor being housing; the second, a hodgepodge of whatever we can fit there; and the third, a school or a library. Possibly both. We'll go from there and keep adding on, maybe even build Audhild's six-level monstrosity."

—Excerpt from the journals of Ryan Kordonowy, Lord Balder

For the second time in as many days, Owen was dragged from his sleep by a loud ringing coming from the main room. He threw back his blankets, dragged himself out of bed, and padded toward the front door.

A glance at the clock revealed that it was just past seven in the morning. Although he had no idea who was behind that door, he did know that he wanted to give them a piece of his mind. People were sleeping. For crying out loud, he'd been sleeping.

In this less-than-charitable mindset, he pulled the door open, revealing Eoire. She was far too happy for this time in the morning. He opened his mouth to speak, but stopped when he smelled the contents of the two mugs she was carrying.

"I'll forgive you for waking me up if one of those is for me."

Eoire raised an eyebrow. "And if it's not?" she teased.

Against his will, he smiled. "Well, then, I suppose I might have to kick you out until a more socially acceptable hour. Like, at eleven. When you were supposed to get here."

She laughed and handed one of the mugs to Owen, who gratefully accepted and led her into the apartment.

"Sorry if I woke you, but I figured you might appreciate the wake-up call either way. It takes a while to get used to telling the time under the mountain," she said, perching on the edge of the sofa where Toto was sleeping. He woke enough to shove his head on her lap, then went back to sleep.

"It's all right," Owen said, more awake with the promise of coffee. "It was past time for me to get up anyway." He shrugged, still fighting the urge to smile. Whenever Eoire looked at him, his heart started fluttering. Just like it used to when he and Tiffany were dating. He didn't like it. He was better than this . . . wasn't he?

She looked him up and down and giggled, scratching behind Toto's ears. "I can see that. Quite the late start this morning, isn't it?"

Owen realized at that moment that he was still in the T-shirt and shorts he'd worn to bed. "Er, sorry about that," he said, face flushing. "Give me a few minutes."

He downed the rest of his coffee in one gulp and hurried to his room. Settling for jeans and a white-collared shirt, he dressed and ran to the bathroom. Andrew had pointed him in the direction of a merchant selling shaving equipment and in the hubbub of unpacking he'd forgotten about it until now. It was a relief to be able to shave and get rid of the itchy growth on his chin.

Fifteen minutes after he'd left the living room, he strolled back in, feeling more like himself. During the short time he had been gone, Jen had fallen prey to her inner early bird and came in to sit with Eoire and Toto.

Jen's head jerked to him when he walked in. "Dad, Eoire says that there are self-defense classes here, and they even have Tae Kwon Do." Her grin was bigger than he had seen on her in days. "She says we can sign up for lessons. Can we, Dad? Can we?"

He smiled. "Well, I don't see why not, but . . ." He glanced at Eoire. "Is it safe?" From what he'd seen, most fae were stronger than humans, and his kids weren't fae. Not yet, anyway.

"Perfectly," Eoire said, nodding. "We pair the weaker fighters with those who understand their own strength. There's no need to worry about getting hurt."

He nodded. Logically, he had known that, as the fae had their own children to teach, but it had probably been years since they had worked with human children. "Well, I see no reason why not, in that case. Besides, it'd be good for you to stay in practice until we get to Scotland."

"Yes," Jen yelled, jumping up and down in her seat. "You'll sign David and me up, right? 'Cause Mrs. White said we were almost ready to advance to the next belt."

"Of course, although Eoire may have to help me," he said, "seeing as I don't actually know how or where to do it." He hadn't seen Jen like this since Tiffany died; he wouldn't have been able to say no even if he'd wanted to.

"Of course," Eoire said with a laugh. "I can take you down to the training rooms after your meeting."

Jen looked at her father with blank eyes. "What meeting, Dad?" she asked. "And why is Eoire here, anyway? No offense."

"Uh . . ." He wasn't sure what to say. Andrew had been adamant about not saying anything while they were there; he had even refused to answer questions Owen asked while they were shopping.

Eoire rolled her eyes and sighed in a put-upon manner. "Did Andrew say something about not telling them?" She threw herself back on the sofa, scaring Toto off. "You didn't have to keep it from them. He's being unnecessarily paranoid. Ugh, typical dwarf."

With another unnecessarily dramatic huff, she drew herself up and looked at Owen. "At any rate, we need to get going soon."

"But, Dad," Jen said, "where are you going? You never said."

He wasn't sure if Eoire had genuinely forgotten to answer the question, or if her whole spiel had been a clever way to make Jen forget she had asked something in the first place. Either way, it hadn't been helpful. He shuffled his feet and flailed around for words. "Um, well you see, Jen, there are some people who want to meet with me—"

Her eyes lit up. "Oh, to talk about grown-up things." She turned to Eoire. "Arthur said Dad would have to go talk to people this morning. He said Andrew told him Dad would be gone all day."

"Oh, did he now?" Eoire smiled, doing a reasonable impersonation of a cat who got the cream. Owen wondered if he should warn Andrew to keep an eye out for her today. That grin didn't suggest she had anything nice in store for him.

With a wary glance at Eoire's smile, Owen clapped his hands together. "Right, we should get going, I have a meeting. That is why you came, right? A full" —he glanced at the clock—"four hours before you were supposed to be here?"

"Oh, right," Eoire said, the tips of her ears turning red. "I thought I would take you around the third floor, introduce you to some people, that sort of thing."

"Right, and that had to be done today?" He looked at her, crossing his arms and smirking.

She shrugged and rubbed a hand along the back of her neck. "Um, yes, well I suppose this could have waited, but . . ." She trailed off into inconsequential muttering and then silence. A deep blush spread from her ears down her cheeks and neck.

Owen burst into laughter. Eoire joined in, followed by a confused Jen. The noise brought the rest of his children stumbling out of their rooms, yawning and determined to find out what was making so much noise at the ungodly hour of seven thirty in the morning.

Arthur stumbled over to Owen and asked what they were doing. He was much more aware than usual.

"Sorry, but you needed to get up anyway." He clapped Arthur, who squinted at him, on the shoulder. Owen gestured toward the clock, which did its duty of proclaiming the hour.

"Oh, right." Arthur grunted and looked Owen up and down, noting that he was already dressed. He made a vague gesture toward his own unshaven chin. "Your face, you shaved. Where did you get a razor?"

The last three days had seen the two of them commiserating on the trials of being unable to maintain their shared preference for being clean-shaven, so Arthur's betrayed expression was completely reasonable. Still, it made Owen laugh again. After he got himself back under control, he took pity on Arthur, directed him toward the shaving equipment, and handed Arthur his cup of coffee.

Arthur took the coffee without question and shuffled toward the bathroom, his siblings directing him around furniture and each other with an ease born of long practice. There was an informal family rule that you didn't let Arthur do anything in the morning without first making him take a shower or forcing a cup of coffee in him. He proved the necessity of this rule by running into the doorframe while trying to drink and walk at the same time. They were going to need to find a different way to wake him; coffee was more expensive here than at home, and he couldn't have a cup every morning.

Eoire, at least, found Arthur's slow journey toward consciousness entertaining. Owen couldn't blame her. They all had their own collection of Zombie Arthur stories they dragged out when he was being particularly obnoxious. Might as well let someone else collect a few.

"All right, kids, get dressed," he said, trying to get everyone back on track. "We should have time for some breakfast before I have to leave."

Eoire jumped up. "Oh, that reminds me," she said as she searched through her pockets. "Andrew told me to tell you that he'd like to take you on a more in-depth tour of the city after your physical examinations." She pulled out a tube, roughly six inches long and one inch wide, with a victorious sound. "If any of you are interested, we'll write him a note and send it down the tubes."

Seeing their expressions, which ranged from Ashley's interested look to Jen's blank confusion, Eoire elaborated. "The tubes are our messaging system." She held up the tube again. "This is a flute. You send them down pipes that run throughout the whole city, and you need to use certain ones to get to the right floors and wings. Once there, a messenger sorts them into baskets so they can be delivered. The whole process takes about fifteen minutes, but it's still faster than trying to run up ourselves, you'll have to agree."

If you asked Owen, the whole thing sounded needlessly complicated, but then, considering how big the city was and that they couldn't use electricity, it was probably the best way to communicate. At any rate, Eoire spent the next few minutes explaining the intricacies of the whole system to Ashley and the twins, regardless of his concerns. Dorothy, at least, was more interested in her eggs and toast than anything going on around her.

Arthur chose this moment to shuffle from the bathroom, clean-shaven and damp. He was now awake enough to make a beeline for the coffee pot Owen had prepared with him in mind, where a half cup still remained. He sat down as Eoire finished explaining the message system.

"Wait, what's happening? Why are we sending a message?" he asked, prompting another brief rundown on the messaging system and a renewal of Andrew's offer of a tour.

"Well, I wanna go," he said after he had drained his cup. "As long as you guys do too."

In short order, they decided they all wanted to go and Eoire wrote a message to Andrew. The twins and Ashley dressed quickly and went with her to send it, allegedly to see how the system worked in person. While they were gone, Owen helped Dorothy get dressed while Arthur washed the dishes.

By eight thirty, the Williams were all dressed and ready to leave; they just had to wait for Andrew to get their message and get down here. Eoire estimated that it would take less than half an hour for him to get the message and get down to the apartment, if he hurried.

In the meantime, they gathered in the living room and discussed what they wanted to see today. Requests varied from the library and the school to the greenhouses to the stables and back again. Dorothy wanted to see Eoire's house, but Owen shut her down.

"Andrew has quite the day ahead of him," Eoire said. "You guys are going to keep him running all over Tearmann."

Arthur frowned, cradling his empty coffee cup like holding it would reveal some residual caffeine. "Didn't you say that most of these are on the same floors?" he asked, finally setting his cup down. "Like, the training rooms and the greenhouses are both on the first floor, and the school and the library are on the . . . uh . . . fifth?"

"Glad to see you paid at least some attention to the tour yesterday," Eoire said with a laugh. "Yes, the school and library are on the same floor, although it's the fourth, not the fifth, and the training rooms for human-sized beings are on the second floor. Group exercises, like combat training or dance classes, take place on the first, which is where the greenhouses—" The doorbell rang, cutting her off.

"That can't be Andrew yet, can it? It's only been"—Owen looked over at the clock hanging on the wall—"fifteen minutes. You said it'd take him longer to get down here."

"Well, you won't"—the bell rang again—"know 'til you get it," Eoire said.

The bell had rung a third time before Owen reached the door. He was right, it wasn't Andrew.

Enormous golden eyes stared past a beak that ended with a wicked hook. The creature's arms shifted from feather to leathery skin and ended in taloned hands large enough to crush his head. Digitigrade feet covered in tawny fur drew the eye to the tufted tail twitching every few seconds beside them. Behind it, massive wings flared out, filling the hall. His knees went weak at the sight.

The gryphon, it had to be a gryphon, jumped when he pulled the door open and her wings flared out to catch her.

"Um, hello. My name is Elenor Rogers. I live down the hall," she said brightly.

"Owen Williams, a pleasure to meet you," he answered faintly, leaning against the door to hide how his legs were shaking. Cor, she was massive. "We've just finished breakfast, but we could scrounge something up if you'd like to come in."

"Oh, no, that's not necessary," she said, thrusting the pamphlet into Owen's chest. "I came over to invite you to a party! The Founding Day Celebration. The neighborhood does one every year, and ..." She babbled on and didn't seem to notice Owen's growing confusion.

"It starts at six in three days, right?" he said, cutting her off before he got even more lost. "I'll talk it over with the kids and let you know if we can make it."

"All right." Her smile, if it could be called that, could've powered a small city. "That'll work. I'll talk to you later."

"Who was that, Dad?" Ashley asked as he wandered back to the kitchen in a daze.

"Elenor Rogers, she lives down the hall." He slumped onto the sofa next to Jen, head spinning from the bizarre interaction. "She said there's going to be a party in the next few days, a local celebration."

Eoire jumped from her seat. "The Founding Day Celebration," she said with a squeal. "Oh, you have to go."

"What is it like your Independence Day or something?" Arthur asked from where he was playing with his guitar on the other side of the room.

"Something like that." She sank into her chair and turned to face him. "Founding Day is the anniversary of when we were legally recognized as our own nation."

Arthur nodded. "That makes sense—"

"Are there fireworks?" Jen interrupted. "There are fireworks on the Fourth of July back home, and we always went, even though Mom doesn't—" Her hand clapped over her mouth.

Silence fell, the kind people were afraid to break because it was holding back something much worse. Owen blinked back tears and tried to breathe normally as Jen shoved her face in his side. He chanced a look around. Arthur glared at the wall, away from her. Ashley clutched David to her chest and had buried her face in his hair. His eyes watered and he blinked the tears away. They needed him to be strong.

"I'm sorry, Dad, I forgot," Jen said, the sound muffled by his shirt.

Owen had known that a breakdown was coming, that the calm that had spread over his family wasn't meant to last. He'd tried to stop it, tried to stop Dorothy's wide-eyed stare, to stop David's tears and Arthur's anger.

Eoire didn't say anything at first. Her lips slowly turned down as she tapped a rhythm on her armrest. Then she sighed and leaned forward.

"Some years we have them," she whispered in a voice as soft as silk. "Most years, it's too cold out or too expensive, but when we can get them the whole town turns out to watch." She smiled and took Jen's hand in hers. "We couldn't get any this year, but I've seen the blueprints for next year's show and it's going to be amazing."

118

She drew the kids out of the impending darkness with an ease Owen envied. Every word made him feel calmer, like she was pulling the stress and grief from his bones, and he couldn't explain it. By the time Andrew finally arrived, she had all of them in stitches from about a particularly foolish dragon's adventures with a barrel of local moonshine, and the specter of Tiffany's death was banished for the moment.

***

After finalizing their plans for the day, the two groups went their separate ways. Eoire and Owen went up one floor to the political district, while Andrew and the kids decided to go down and work their way back up. Of course, they had to go to their physical examinations first, but a pack of werewolves had combat training today and David and Jen wanted to see it.

Eoire made good use of the short time they had before his meeting. Owen met political figures from each species, sat in on a short robbery trial, and toured the political district. He met generals and lawyers, guards and cabinet members, and a whole host of people there to petition the founders. His head was spinning with names, species, generations, and titles by the time he had to go to the queen's office.

Eoire led him away from the public offices and through a hall that looked like a combination of a conference room and a courtroom. It was a large space, twice as long as it was wide. Thirteen pairs of thrones lined the walls, six on either side and one at the far end of the room. In the dim light provided by twelve lamps, Owen could barely make out odd designs on each set of chairs, no two pairs alike from what he could see.

One set of thrones looked like they'd been burned and scarred repeatedly for years, and the wood had an unfinished quality about it that made his fingers itch for his tools. Another set looked more like perches than chairs, and there were deep scratches on the narrow seats. A third may as well have been grown where they sat rather than made, for all Owen could see any sign of a seam or chisel mark.

One pair, the ones at the far end of the room, stood out. They sat on a small raised dais, six inches above their fellows for no reason he could discern. No carvings or scratches marred their oaken surface, and there were no decorations to break the monotony. In fact, one could almost mistake them for something you might find in any home but for their grandiose backs.

He didn't have time to figure out what unsettled him about the two strange chairs. Eoire pulled him across the room, stopping in front of a pair of oak doors inlaid with copper reliefs. The left door had thirteen fae men—one of each species—and the right, a matching depiction of fae women. Through them, he could faintly hear raised voices.

For the first time in the short period he had known her, Eoire looked nervous, and it only made him feel a dozen times worse. The woman behind those doors was the most powerful person in the country—possibly the world if any of the war stories he'd heard were true—and she wanted to use him like a buffet. If Eoire was nervous, he was doomed.

The thought made his knees shake, and for one wild moment, he debated running. Just finding the kids and getting as far as they could. But as Eoire's fist made contact with the door, he knew it wouldn't be any use. They were trapped here. Even if they got outside the mountain, there wasn't anywhere to go.

A voice came from beyond the door and sealed his fate. Yanking Owen behind her, Eoire pushed the heavy door open and went in.

Owen found himself in a narrow room where each wall was covered from floor to ceiling in bookshelves and cabinets. From the first step, his nose was assaulted with the musty scent of hundreds of old books. At the far end, two women stood on opposite sides of an old oak desk.

One he recognized as a first-generation dragon. Her yellow scales matched her beaded leather tunic that tied below her upper wings, then again above her lower ones. Her tail lashed behind her, almost slamming into the desk with each move, and the thick strands of hair on head that almost looked like horns were raised up. Her yellow scales and lower wings glittered in the lamplight as a counterpoint to the dull beads. The other woman, tall and brown-haired, looked human.

But she wasn't. He ran his thumb over his wedding ring and wished it were silver. She was a vampire, one who wanted to drink his blood.

Eoire made an odd clawed fist and slammed it into her chest. "First Mechanic of the Couriers, Eoire Belfield, presenting Owen Williams as requested, Your Majesty."

The queen nodded and walked around the desk toward them. Drawing near, she addressed Eoire. "You're dismissed, First Mechanic Belfield. I'll return your charge to you when we're finished."

Eoire nodded and marched out, leaving Owen by himself.

The queen looked Owen up and down. He could have sworn that he saw her nostrils flare. After such a long period of time that Owen felt its only purpose was to make him feel uncomfortable, she finally spoke. "It's nice to finally meet you, Mr. Williams. My name is Beira Thomson, and I've heard a lot about you."

CHAPTER TEN

IN WHICH THEY TALK

"We buried Michael last week. Beira hasn't come out of her room since, not even to go to the funeral. She blames herself, I know she does. Whenever we try to see if she needs anything, she orders us to leave her alone. I tried to tell her Michael wouldn't blame her for what happened—he knew the risks when he volunteered—but she wouldn't have it. In all honesty, I think she's going to put a stop to the experiments like she wanted to before it all went downhill. Michael's death was hard enough, and he volunteered even when he knew the risks. I don't want to imagine how she'd react if she had to do it again. It might actually destroy her."

—Excerpt from the journals of Father Logan Johnson, Lord Wulver

Owen shook the queen's icy hand. A gaunt woman, she'd fallen victim to years of hardship that had stripped away anything fat or soft from her cheeks. She was perhaps an inch taller than him and wore dark clothes that, while simple, fit well. Her dark brown eyes had sunken into her snow-white cheeks and were framed by wisps of matching brown hair that hung loose of her long braid.

She dropped his hand and gestured to the dragon standing by the desk. "Mr. Williams, allow me to introduce Lady Guivre, my personal friend and one of the dragon founders."

The dragon snorted and smoke curled from her nostrils. "Don't listen to her. She pretends not to, but she likes all that unnecessary formality. Danielle Burns, at your service." She winked and her lips pulled back in a gruesome parody of a smile. "Call me Dani; everyone here does."

The queen sighed as she walked to her desk and sat, leaving a bewildered Owen with Lady Guivre. "It's your title, Dani, and as you're meeting him in a semi-professional manner, it seemed appropriate."

"Sure, I see how it is," said Lady Guivre, a snarl turning her words into weapons. "You can be Beira Thomson, but I have to be Lady Guivre. This is exactly what I'm talking about, *Your Majesty*, you're pulling away from us. We're your friends. You need to take a break—"

Somewhere in the exchange between the two, Owen regained his voice and latched onto the first word he understood. "Isn't the guivre a French dragon?"

Lady Guivre spun around, her grin impossibly wide. "Look at you! You know your stuff."

He wasn't ashamed to admit he squeaked when she grabbed his shoulders and spun him around, talons digging into his skin. When he made a complete circle, she wrapped her winged arms around him and rested her head on his shoulder. "Beira, he's so cute! Can we keep him?"

The queen rolled her eyes. "Only if you promise to walk him and clean up after him."

"Ew, no." Wrinkling her nose, she shoved him away. "I've changed my mind. You can have him."

"Why don't you leave, then?" the queen asked, raising an eyebrow. "After all, this is supposed to be his introductory meeting, sans one giant lizard."

"Hey, I'm warm-blooded," the aforementioned giant lizard answered. "But I'll leave if you want me to."

Lady Guivre walked to the door but stopped there, hand on the knob. She spun around and shook a finger at the queen. "Don't think you're going to get away with stopping our discussion like this. It isn't over, only postponed." Having said her piece, she stormed out, leaving him alone with the queen.

For a desperate moment, Owen wanted to call her back. He didn't know if she would help him if something went wrong, but he didn't want to be alone now. The door slammed shut with ominous finality, cutting him off from the outside world.

The queen waited for the sound to fade, then pointed to a simple, but sturdy, wooden chair in front of her desk. "Have a seat. We have a lot to discuss." She picked up a folder from the mess on her desk.

His eyes searched the room for something to defend himself with if it became necessary. Bookshelves straining under their loads and a glass cabinet that held a metal circlet on a dusty pillow lined the walls behind her, the only decoration in the barren room. There was nothing there that could help him, even if he could get past her.

He forced himself to move forward and fought the urge to run for the door with every step. The wooden chair creaked under him when he sat, protesting his weight. Too weak for him to use as a stake.

"I imagine that First Mechanic Stephens told you why I wanted to meet with you?" the queen asked once he had settled, putting the folder aside.

Owen coughed, a thick lump appearing in his throat. "He, uh, did mention something about it ..."

"And, in his usual fashion, I imagine he was as vague about it as possible?"

"Um, I suppose so?" He gulped and gripped the edge of his seat hard enough to turn his knuckles white. This was it, she was going to—

"Of course he did." She groaned and rubbed a hand over her eyes. "Probably scared you half to death, didn't he? Lord, we have to retrain that man." She leaned forward and folded her hands on the desk. "Listen, I don't know exactly what he told you, but this meeting was not to convince you to let me drink from you."

He jolted up halfway from his seat "It's—it's not?" Why else would she call him here to meet with her if not to make use of a fresh blood supply? It wasn't like he was anyone important, after all.

"No, it's not," she said. "This meeting is to discuss how you and your family are settling in and to answer any questions you have." Her voice had tightened and the folder in her hand bent under the tension.

Owen hoped he hadn't gotten the kindly dwarf in trouble. "So you're not going to try to—" He didn't know how to finish that sentence without offending the woman across from him.

"What, drink your blood?" she asked in a casual voice as she shoved the file on her desk into a drawer.

"Well, yeah," he said. "I don't see any other reason to meet me unless that was the end goal."

"Mr. Williams, I'll be completely honest with you," she said, smiling. "If one day you decide you want to be a donor, I'll be glad to accept, but I won't ask now or at any point in the next few weeks. Do you know why?"

He shook his head. Here he was, a human, sitting in front of someone who drank human blood to survive, and she didn't seem to think it was something to be concerned about. For someone who said she'd invited him here to answer any questions he had, she didn't seem keen on providing clarity.

She set her elbows on the desk and rested her chin on her folded hands. "For the same reason I don't make everyone obey my every whim. Because I believe that anyone in a position of power has the responsibility to put the concerns of their followers above their own needs, because I believe that people have the right to make their own choices, and because those I lead look to me to guide them."

That didn't do anything to clear things up. "So . . . you don't want to set a bad example?" he asked. He wrapped his fingers around the edge of his chair to stop them from shaking.

The queen laughed. "No ... Well, yes, but it's not the only reason I won't drink from you." She settled back in her chair. "Part of being a founder, and a vampire in particular, is the ability to control the other fae, even against their will. The difference between me and the other founders, of course, lies in the fact that they can only control those of their own species. I can order anyone to do anything, even kill themselves or their loved ones, should the mood take me."

His heart jumped into his throat and a chill crept into his bones as he stared at the unassuming-looking woman across from him. "You can order fae to do anything?" he asked. He tried to hold his voice steady, to sound braver than he felt, but he wasn't entirely successful. "Is that supposed to intimidate me?"

"No." She knit her eyebrows together and shook her head. "I would never do that. I meant that if I started abusing my power like that, others would follow. Imagine sirens and elves forcing others to serve them; dragons rampaging through the countryside, burning all in their path; shades taking what they pleased—" She stared beyond him, her eyes vacant. "It would be a free-for-all that would destroy us."

She shook herself and her eyes refocused on him. "I'm Catholic, Mr. Williams. As such, I believe that to use my power to make the fae obey me without great cause or to drink from someone without their consent violates their innate dignity as thinking beings. The ultimate form of disrespect, as it were. That alone would be bad enough without the side effects that come from drinking from someone directly."

There was something he couldn't explain, a niggling in the back of his mind that said she wasn't telling him everything. He was beginning to think he would never get a straight answer from her.

"All right," he finally said when it became clear she was waiting for him to speak. "What does your religion have to do with why I shouldn't worry about you drinking from me?"

She stood and poured two glasses of water from a pitcher on a table off to the side. She handed one to him and sat back down. He was about to repeat himself when she broke her silence.

"To answer your question, my beliefs prevent me from forcing someone to give me blood. It's my little workaround for the whole cannibalism thing."

"Cannibalism," he said as the blood drained from his face. "Who said anything about cannibalism?"

"Make no mistake about it," she answered without hesitation, swirling her water around in her glass. "I'm a cannibal. Sure, I can supplement my diet with animal blood and raw meat, I could even share a meal with you, but I need human blood to survive."

She set down her glass and leaned back. "I've spoken with priests and bishops, even had a letter exchange going with the pope for a while. What I do is necessary for my survival, but it is cannibalism, so we established guidelines to . . . lessen the weight of my guilt."

"What do—" he stuttered. "What do you mean, guidelines?" This didn't sound real. She was a vampire. She wasn't like the other fae, she preyed on people like him, on humans, and she expected him to believe some antiquated belief system would protect him? No, it couldn't be true.

"When the time comes," she answered, unable or unwilling to see the crisis of thought he was undergoing, "a volunteer, under no compulsion except their own free will, will go to the hospital. I then make a cut along their upper arm so no one else is complicit in the act. The blood collects in a bowl, which I drink before it has cooled. A siren sings the wound closed, and the volunteer leaves until the next time they're needed."

"You cut them?"

Beira chuckled and finally drank from the glass she still held. "We used to use a machine for donations, back when we first built this place, but we ran out of supplies and couldn't maintain it. It's gathering dust in a storage room for now." She stared into her glass as if pondering her own words and then sipped her drink again. "First Mechanic Stephens probably told you, but I can't drink from fae, directly or indirectly. It doesn't end well."

"How so?" he asked, curious despite the part of himself that wanted to run from this conversation.

"The short answer is that I release venom when I bite," she explained as she set down her glass. "A sedative that doubles as a slow, addictive poison. It kills humans within a few years if I drink continuously, a few weeks if I let them go through withdrawal instead. This is one of the reasons, besides my faith, we have donors bleed into bowls."

"Interesting, but it doesn't answer my question," he said. "What does that have to do with drinking fae blood?"

"I'm getting there," she said, chuckling hollowly. "I experimented with drinking fae blood, both directly and indirectly. The venom reacted poorly with their systems, driving them into aggressive, unstoppable rages." She stared at her glass. He wasn't sure she remembered he was there. "There were also the effects the blood had on me," she whispered. The words hung in the air like a death knell, all joy gone.

Despite the bit of himself that wanted to stop her there, that screamed it was none of his business, he asked her what she meant.

"It drove me mad. I hunted them down and destroyed them. I couldn't stop myself," she said, her eyes leaving the glass and fixing on his. "But," she continued, rolling her glass around in her free hand, "drinking in an indirect way wasn't any better. I killed them all and there was nothing anyone, even the other founders, could do to stop me. Fae blood will sustain me, but it's a death sentence to the one who gives it. Human blood is safest for all involved."

She looked away and drained her glass. "Almost by accident, we discovered I could live on a diet of mostly animal blood," she said when she had finished. "Of course, I still need fresh human blood at least once a month to survive. Having a younger donor, such as yourself, would be a boon I'll admit—most of mine are getting old—but I won't force you."

Silence fell. Questions danced in his mind, each shouting to be asked, but he didn't have the words. "Why?" It slipped out, he hadn't meant to speak. He wasn't even sure if he was talking about donating anymore. Why had this happened to him? Why did they have to come here? Why did it have to happen now, when they had so much back home?

"Mr. Williams," she said with a frown and reached across the desk to rest a hand on his. "I know this is hard for you, that you've lost so much in the last few days and you're trying to find answers wherever you can, but please, try to understand. I could no more force myself to hurt you or make you donate to me than you could hurt your children. It would be a direct contradiction of everything I was raised to believe and still believe to this day. Even as my donors age, even as the number willing to donate diminish with each passing year, I would never order them to continue. Doing so would be the antithesis of everything I believe." She pulled back. His hand felt bare without hers.

"Now," she continued, "did you have any other questions about the process?"

Owen shook his head. That was it? She expected him to believe her because she said she wouldn't? He couldn't . . . this couldn't be true. It was too clean, too easy.

"Why should I believe you?" His voice was hollow and harsh, riddled with exhaustion and shot through with confusion. "What proof do I have that you're even Catholic, or that you aren't trying to get me to lower my guard?" She was a vampire, he reminded himself. They fed on humans and he couldn't forget that no matter how earnest she seemed.

She stared at him as the last echoes of his speech faded, her mouth drawn tight and eyes narrowed. His heart sank. He'd angered her. His words had crossed an invisible line and now they were going to be kicked out.

"Mr. Williams," she finally said. "I can assure you that I hold the tenets of my faith near and dear to my heart. It is one of the few connections I have left to my family, to my home. I'm sure you can understand why that would be of value to me." The ice in her voice chilled the air. She glared, unblinking, at him. "I cannot force you to accept this as my answer, and I can neither provide proof of my devotion nor give you cause to believe me in the short time we have together today. Now, do you have any questions?"

He swallowed, recognizing the repeated question for the olive branch it was. His throat felt like sandpaper. He needed to watch his step.

"You said that sirens healed the cuts," he asked hoarsely, "but Jason told me they couldn't heal humans."

The queen nodded, accepting his truce. "That's correct, most can't. Second- and third-generation sirens have an easier time healing humans and faeborn than first-gens do, but it's not easy for most of them. The practice goes against their natural skillsets, you see. Captain Aaron Rodriguez, who led your team, is renowned among the Corps for his ease in healing and hypnotizing humans and fae."

She delved into the desk and pulled out a marked folder. "For example, I received a report that said you had several injuries—" She opened the folder and read from a handwritten page. "Including broken ribs and a concussion. They don't hurt anymore, do they? They haven't, not since you were given the tests?"

Owen opened his mouth to refute her, but snapped it shut. They hadn't, not since Aaron had hypnotized him, but he'd forgotten about them in the rush to get away, to keep his children safe. "No, they don't." He pressed a hand to the rib that should be broken.

"I thought so. Captain Rodriguez has always preferred to keep silent about his healing; he doesn't like to draw attention to his abilities."

"Why wouldn't he want to talk about what he can do?" Owen asked without looking up. The places where his other injuries should have been itched and he resisted the urge to rub them.

"We have our reasons for both our secrecy and our prejudices," the queen answered as she shoved the folder to the side. "The most compelling of which is our devotion to free will."

"But—"

She turned away as she went to refill her glass. His still stood untouched.

"According to Catholic teaching, to deprive others of their free will turns otherwise free-thinking and reasoning individuals into little more than slaves," she said as she turned back to the table. "Fae have no choice but to listen to the orders I or the other founders give. As such, we are prohibited from using that power under most circumstances." She sat down, and her glass hit the table with a loud thunk.

"Sirens who can hypnotize fae are in much the same boat as the founders," she continued, unheeding of water that had spilled from her glass. "To deny others the ability to make use of their free will is repulsive among the fae. Some leeway is given for questioning human allies and official oath taking, of course, but there are those who may seek to use it for their own ends."

Considering all he knew of the fae and their allies, Owen had to admit she had a point. A group of people like this, that had been kidnapped and experimented on, wouldn't take kindly to one of their own trying to control another.

"So that's it, then? The sirens aren't allowed to sing?" he asked, praying this would keep her mind from his gaffe. If he could keep her talking, perhaps he could make up for offending her.

She shook her head like the action would chase away bad memories. "It's not quite like that. Most sirens can only hypnotize humans or heal fae. They are generally accepted and their talents lauded for their use in protecting the country. It's rare to find someone who can do both and rarer still to find someone who can do both on each species. Captain Rodriguez is a member of a group that has fewer than a hundred members worldwide."

"So is there a committee that watches them or something, to make sure they don't abuse their abilities?" It didn't seem fair, to watch all sirens to guard against the actions of the few.

"No," she said, her eyes flashing. "No, we record their abilities as we do with all fae, but they are allowed to live as they will. Some flaunt their abilities and come to enjoy a strange state of pariahdom where people are wary of being alone with them or allowing them to sing in public gatherings. Others with special abilities, like Officer Belfield and other elves with their empathy, are also made aware of the consequences of abusing their talents."

He choked on his water. "Elves—Eoire's an empath?"

It couldn't be, he wanted to scream. Apart from her ears, she was normal, the most human person he'd met here. But, at the same time, everything he had felt around her made sense now. Why his grief only hit him when she wasn't around. Why happiness flooded him when she laughed or sadness when she frowned.

"All elves are. She is merely stronger than most," she said as a single eyebrow arched to the sky. "You may have noticed that you feel strange when she is around—"

"Like there's happiness that's not my own," he whispered, half to himself. He'd only known Eoire for a few days, but this felt like a betrayal. He had trusted her, left his children with her, and the whole time she had been manipulating them, using their emotions as her playground. What else had she done, what else could these people do that they weren't telling him?

When Owen finally lifted his head to look in the queen's eyes, he saw a sort of sadness looking back out, the kind that came from being let down by those you trusted. He wondered what had happened to put that sort of sadness there, one that he was sure was reflected in his own eyes.

"You've already experienced it, then." She started to reach across the desk again but pulled back.

He was glad of it, he didn't think he could bear her touch just then.

"You know," she said in a low voice, "some think Eoire was too young when she first took up her positions. She was thirty-five the first time she was elected first mechanic, and she's only been a guide for the last two years. To reach one of those ranks is honor enough, to have both is something usually reserved for those much older than her, with more experience."

She paused, and nostalgia replaced melancholy as she stared toward the door leading out of her office. "I remember her when she was young, always tramping about the Eyries and letting her gifts get away from her. She was a handful, even then."

It hit Owen as she spoke that this woman had been alive for a very long time, even if she looked younger than him. She had grown up in the world of humans, seen all the hate it could offer, gone to war, established a nation of refugees when she was half his age, and she had not let it to break her. That he would put his experiences against hers and claim his losses were greater, that wrongs done to him were worse, made him want to turn his head away.

She continued, oblivious to the twists and turns of his thoughts. "You know, I don't think she ever learned how to control her powers, not in the way she was supposed to. I'm not even certain she could, as powerful as she is, but then her position in the Courier branch isn't one that requires much control." When she met his eyes again the happy memories had fled. "I ask you not to hold it against her; she does the best she can."

Owen wasn't sure how to respond. On one hand, he didn't think he could trust Eoire after this. She should've told him. Now that he knew to expect it he could almost track the edges of Eoire's emotions, a bubble of calm that faded if he leaned forward. On the other … she had helped. Without her, his grief would've drowned him. He'd have lost control and the kids needed him.

"If it bothers you, I could have her reassigned to a different case until you and your family learn to shield against empathic intrusions." She made the offer as if he could be read as easily as one of the files she'd been looking at earlier.

Could she read his mind, he wondered, was that one of the hidden talents he would have to be on guard for? "No, no it's fine," he said, wishing he could calm his heartbeat. "She hasn't done anything that could get her in trouble." Except for all the times she had, he wanted to say but forced it down. He may not entirely trust Eoire right now, but better the devil you know than the one you don't, as the saying went.

"If you're sure," she said, waiting for his nod. "Then let's move on. How're you settling in?"

"We're fine," Owen said as he willed his shoulders to relax.

"The rooms are to your liking, and your guides explained how everything worked?"

"Uh, yes. Toto's going to be especially grateful for how close we are to someplace he can run around."

The queen's eyes glowed with mischief. It was rather unsettling to see. "Ah, Toto is it? I'd heard you had a dog. He's a—?" She left the words hanging in the air as a slow smirk spread her lips.

"A Newfoundland, black lab mix."

"Really? He must be big, then."

"Yes, my wife used to say he was half newfie, half lab, and half horse because he was big enough for three halves. Of course, as far as he's concerned, he's a lapdog." He wasn't sure where she was going with this.

"Why Toto, then? From what I remember, Toto was a rather small dog."

Ah, the name. Somehow, Owen was never ready for the name jokes. His cheeks turned a dark red as he explained. "We had a naming pool when we got him a year ago. Our youngest, Dorothy, was on a Wizard of Oz craze …"

The queen held up her hand, and a large grin revealed the points of her fangs. "No need to continue. I assume he's black, then, like Toto?"

He nodded glumly. "You have no idea how many jokes we get about it. It doesn't help that we lived in Kansas."

"Oh no," she said, hiding her laugh behind a hand. "That must have been awful."

It had almost been worse, he almost said. Arthur had wanted to call him Mr. Fluffykins. The thought made him smile and before he knew it he was laughing too, a sharp, almost hysterical sound that hurt more than anything else. He shouldn't be laughing, but he couldn't stop himself.

The air between them felt clearer when they finally stopped laughing. He still didn't fully trust her, but there was a sense of comradery with her that hadn't been there before. Like stories about dogs with silly names and sympathy for an elf who couldn't control herself had weakened the wall between them. He wasn't sure he liked it, especially considering what he had learned about fae abilities during this conversation.

"At any rate, was there anything else you wanted to know?" he asked.

The queen nodded, the mirth from earlier replaced with a frown. "Unfortunately, yes. I should have mentioned it earlier, but . . ." She stood, walked around the desk, and stopped at his side. "Mr. Williams, allow me to offer my sincere condolences on the death of your wife."

Owen's heart renewed its acquaintance with his stomach. Of course. Tiffany was the reason they knew about the Williams; the queen would want to know about her. Still . . . grief like none he'd ever felt tore at his heart. The kind that made breathing or thinking or living impossible, and not even the distant buzz of Eoire's emotions could calm it.

"Thank you, it—it means a lot." He clasped his hands in his lap, as much to do something with them as to stop the shaking. His wedding ring caught the light and the sight sent pain stabbing into his chest that felt like twisting knives as a thousand happy memories came rushing back. Each tore into him, a reminder of what he would never have again, how he would never see her smile, or hear her laugh, or hold her in his arms. A single tear dripped down his cheek, joined by others as his walls fell down. He bowed his head. He couldn't let her see.

She knelt in front of him and took his hands in hers in a way he supposed was meant to be comforting. "I've some experience with the loss of a loved one, I know how it weighs on you."

For one stark moment, Owen felt like giving in to his grief, like unleashing the full force of the gaping pit where his heart used to be on her. How could she know how he felt? How every moment the feeling struggled to overwhelm him and he felt torn every way? How tired he was: tired of being strong for his children, tired of having to decide who he could trust, tired of pretending he had everything together? He wanted to tell her everything for one wild moment. Then the moment passed and the feeling receded, pushed back down into the depths of his mind. His tears dried and his breathing slowed.

Where had all that been hiding, he wondered distantly. Had Eoire blocked all his grief away, hiding it behind that wall of false cheer until the distant edges of her control couldn't hold it back it anymore?

Beira continued speaking in a low voice, still quiet, still calming, like he was a spooked animal. "There will be therapists, counselors, people you and your children can talk to if you want. It's free, of course; they're part of a local charity organization for new arrivals."

There was a sort of sadness in her eyes. The lasting kind that never went away, no matter how long it had been. In some dark and angry part of himself, he was glad of the kinship their respective losses brought him, glad someone else had suffered like he was suffering now.

Owen managed to beat down the lump in his throat enough to speak. He needed to thank her for this, for the concern shown his family even when it was clear he didn't trust her. Back home, he couldn't have afforded for them to get that help, especially since Tiffany had been the real breadwinner of the family. His shop did little more than cover its own expenses. "I—thank you, Your Majesty."

Her lips curled into a mock frown. "Oh, don't call me that. I have a hard enough time convincing my students they don't need to bow every time I ask them a question; I won't take the title nonsense from you."

Almost unwillingly, he laughed, brittle and sharp, and his throat ached. "What do I call you, then?"

"Please, call me Beira, all my friends do," she said in a low voice as she got up and sat back behind her desk. "I expect you and I will become close friends in the future, Mr. Williams."

"Owen." It was a surprise to hear his name come from his own mouth. "If I'm going to call you by your name, it's only fair you call me by mine."

Beira smiled and leaned back in her chair. "Well, Owen, it appears we are at an accord. Did you have any other questions or anything you wanted to talk about?"

It was an offer for more than the standard meet-and-greet discussions, he knew. It was an offer for a shoulder and a willing ear. Something he couldn't explain told him that he could ask anything now and she would answer to the best of her abilities. Anything. Even how to leave.

"Beira—" The words caught on his tongue, stuck behind the name. They had reached a truce and he was tired. Did he really want to risk it by revealing he didn't want to stay here? That he wanted to raise his children among other humans? "Someone told me there was a chance we could go home."

Her smile fell. "Owen," she said slowly. "You do understand you're wanted for murder and kidnapping in the states, right? Even if you weren't—"

"No, not to America," he was quick to assure her. "To Daingneach, to Scotland."

"That's not much better." Beira rubbed a hand over her face. "The UK still has an extradition agreement with the U.S. Even if we could get the murder charge removed, there's still the kidnapping one to deal with and the integrated nature of Daingneach means I have less control there."

"But I didn't kidnap anyone," he said quietly, "They're my kids."

"Unfortunately, that's not enough," she said, pushing back her chair. "Faeborn children have always existed in a somewhat nebulous legal state." She walked to the bookshelf behind her desk, pulled a thick book from between two mostly identical books and returned, dropping the dusty tome on the desk.

"What do you mean?"

She found the page she was looking for and pushed the book toward him. "Here, read this, starting under Minor Citizenship. It should clear some things up."

He picked up the book and bent his head. "It is a well-known fact that every fae is a citizen of the havens, regardless of where they were born," he read aloud. "What is less known is how to treat the minor children of newly changed fae, who are often assumed to be faeborn while still appearing human. As detailed in the Tearmann Accords, section eight, paragraph eleven, these minors do not receive citizenship once a parent Changes and they are legally required to remain with the nearest human guardian—"

He stopped reading and looked up. "I don't see the problem. According to this I'm still their legal guardian. Once we explain things they'll have to drop those charges."

"Keep going," she said, waving a hand. "It's further down."

He wasn't sure where this was going but bent back toward the page nonetheless. "If their nearest human guardian chooses to travel to the haven with the fae parent, the minor children must remain with a guardian chosen by the state—" His voice cracked. No. This couldn't be right.

Beira nodded. "It gets worse," she said as she plucked the book from his hands. "In the event the fae parent or human guardian chooses to take the minor to a haven without permission of the federal government of whichever country they reside in, the leaders of the havens are hereby required to return the minor to their country of origin or be charged with aiding and abetting the kidnapping of minors, thus rendering all treaties, pacts, and international agreements void."

The words hit him like a hammer blow. "We have to go back?" he whispered. Aaron and Abey, they had told him that SAFE would try to hurt them. Once news got out about Tiffany no one would help them, he knew that. He had no way to keep them safe on his own. He'd have never come if he'd known the truth.

"You told us we'd be safe," he said hoarsely. "It's why I brought them here, I mean, why bother bringing us here if you were just going to send us back?" He sunk into his chair and buried his head in his hands.

"Because we have no intention of sending you back."

His head jerked up. "What do you mean? If they find us here, you could—"

"Lose the agreements that gave us the right to establish the havens in the first place, I know." She picked up the book again and flipped through some of the pages. "As far as the world is concerned, Owen Williams and his children never passed our borders."

He gaped at her. "So, you're telling me—"

"Legally, you and your children aren't here at all," she said with a Cheshire cat grin. "Say what you like about our tactics, but we would never leave faeborn children without protection."

"No kidding." He rubbed a shaking hand over his eyes and sighed. After all they had gone through he had still almost lost them. "How does this affect us getting to Scotland?"

"Well, you're going to have to wait until at least three of your children Change," she said, snapping the book shut. "At that point the Founders Council can make a majority claim and transfer your citizenship to the havens on the grounds that the rest are likely fae as well; then we can arrange for diplomatic immunity for you and get the charges dropped."

"And what are the chances of that happening?"

"More than 50/50 at this point," she said. "Since your wife Changed, the odds are higher than it is for the average faeborn. If at least two of your children also Change, it's likely all of them will."

He slumped back in his chair. He had known there was a chance that what had happened to his wife could happen to his kids, but to have it laid out in front of him like that was still heartbreaking. A 50 percent chance one of his kids wouldn't be human—and three had to Change before they could leave.

"There's no other way? Can't we change our names or something?" He'd meant it when he said he wouldn't abandon them if they Changed, but that didn't mean he wanted to hurry them toward it.

"I'm sorry, but—"

The door opened and they both turned to look. A young werewolf poked his head in. "Sorry to interrupt," he said. "But the banking ministers are here, and First Mechanic Belfield needs to take Mr. Williams to his physical."

"Wonderful," Beira said, assuming the powerful air she'd had when he'd entered, leaving no trace of the woman he'd been speaking to. "Tell them I'll see them in a moment."

She stood to put the book away and pulled a binder from the shelf. "Owen," she called over her shoulder, "it looks like that's all the time I have today, but we need to finish this discussion. I'll send someone by with times we can meet."

"That's it?" he asked, frozen in his seat. But he needed to make her understand why they had to leave, why—the werewolf coughed.

"This way, sir," the werewolf said, opening the door wider. "Her Majesty has work to do."

Owen nodded and forced himself to stand. She couldn't see him anymore, he had to leave. "I'll be going then."

As he moved toward the door, the queen caught his sleeve. "I meant what I said. It was wonderful to meet you." When she smiled the woman behind the royal mask peeked past. "I don't often get the chance to make friends. I promise I'll look into getting your family to Daingneach for you."

He forced himself to smile. This wasn't what he wanted, but it was something and it was enough to hope on. He let himself be led out of the office to Eoire.

"What did you talk about in there?" Eoire asked. Confusion and concern warred on her face and in the air around her. Now that he knew to expect it, it was almost insultingly easy to track where her feelings ended and his began.

"This and that." He had forgotten he was supposed to spend the rest of the day with Eoire. "She wanted to know how we were settling in, how the kids were taking it, about my family, things like that."

Before he might have tried to talk to her about it, but he wasn't sure how much of their friendship had come from him. The words weren't convincing, but Eoire did drop the subject, and they left the political center for the medical one.

CHAPTER ELEVEN

IN WHICH THINGS GET SHAKEN UP

"Jen raised the topic of new arrivals at our meeting the other day. Now that we've got housing sorted out, there's more time to talk about fae out in the world. Civilized places drop them off on the borders of our lands, sometimes even with some of their possessions, if they're lucky. The less civilized ones kill them and anyone associated with them. Keme suggested sending teams of shades out to keep an eye on potential faeborn, but most us aren't certain that's the best idea. We decided to leave the matter of hashing out how they get here and focus instead on the more immediate problem of what to do with them when they get here."

—Excerpt from the journals of Franklin Thomson, Lord Falk

Things settled into a strange but comforting pattern after that meeting. Either Andrew or Eoire would come get them around nine in the morning and spent a few hours walking with them around the city. Sometimes Jason or Abey would join them and tell stories about things the guides had missed. The afternoons were devoted to placement tests and learning about the cultures and physiologies of the fae. Evenings were spent as a family or meeting with their therapist.

Owen found himself with Beira in the little time he had to himself. At first, the meetings were planned—talks about how they were settling in and whatnot—but gradually eased into something more casual. Regardless, Beira seemed pleased to meet him wherever they were, whether that was in the markets, the dining hall, or even in the training rooms on one particularly memorable occasion when Jen misjudged a kick and sent David tumbling into Beira. The twins were very impressed that Owen knew the queen.

During one of their little run-ins, she even gave him advice for talking with Eoire about her powers. Thanks to her, Owen was able to get Eoire to promise she would make more of an effort to control herself around the Williams without horribly offending her.

True to her word, Beira never tried to pressure him into giving blood. She did introduce him to the other humans in the city, though, and they openly spoke about their experiences donating. The current blood donors belonged to a group they called the Foodbank, which scheduled the donations for Beira. They invited Owen to come back at some point, whether he decided to donate or not.

The peace lasted for a full three days. During that time, Owen qualified to work as a carpenter, the kids got placed in school, and Arthur decided to work as Owen's apprentice after class. They were supposed to go to the Founding Day celebration that evening. Then, of course, it all went to hell.

***

It happened in the middle of his first day at Richard Moore's construction agency. Jen had begun the Change. She'd collapsed during class and had been moved to a secure room on the first floor where she couldn't hurt anyone or herself.

Mr. Moore, a grizzled silver dragon with one eye, took one look at Owen's ashen expression and guessed what the paper in his hand said. Almost wordlessly, he gave Owen the next few days off, took his arm, and led him out of the workshop. If their pace gradually increased from a fast walk to a jog, neither of them commented on it, but by the time they hit the Grand Staircase they were running at a dead sprint.

They skidded to a stop in a long hallway with three iron doors on either side. The queen was already waiting for them, tension coiled in her shoulders like a spring waiting to snap. She looked up as they came to a stop and nodded grimly.

"Thank you for bringing him, sir. I'll take it from here."

Mr. Moore nodded. "Look after him, Your Majesty. He looks ready to do something stupid."

Owen would've protested but seeing as how the only thing keeping him here was Mr. Moore's firm grip on his arm, he really had no room to argue.

This had killed Tiffany. He hadn't been able to help her. She'd been fine one minute and the next . . . And now Jen was facing the same thing. Like hell would he let her face it alone.

Beira nodded. "I understand. I'll keep an eye on him, but I'm sure Owen would appreciate it if you stayed."

Mr. Moore glanced at Owen, who was only halfway paying attention to them. "I would," he said as his sharp teeth dug into his lower lip. "But I can't. We've got a lot to do today." He relinquished his iron grip on Owen's arm to Beira and slowly walked away, glancing over his shoulder as he went.

As Beira pulled Owen to a bench, a muffled scream reached them. With strength he hadn't known he'd possessed, Owen wrenched his arm free of Beira's grip and sprinted toward the sound.

"Jen, Jen, it's me," he yelled, pounding on the unmoving door. "Open this door, she needs me."

He spun, fists shaking at his side. He must look wild but he couldn't bring himself to care. Jen needed him.

Beira took it all in stride, his panic, worry, and fear not bothering her in the least. "I can't do that, Owen. If I open this door, she would hurt you—she wouldn't be able to help it. I guarantee that would bother her more than your absence."

"She's my daughter," Owen snarled. "I don't care. I have to be there." Another scream split the air, one that seemed so much louder from here and he shook with adrenaline.

Seamlessly, Beira shifted from the queen to the friend he had gotten to know over the last few days. Her hands came to rest on his, which were still gripping her shoulders. "Owen, I understand. Believe me, I understand, but I can't let you in that room."

His grip on her shoulders tightened to something he was sure had to be painful, but he couldn't make himself care. "Why? Why can't I be in there? She'd never hurt me." The words came like he was ripping each one from the place in his heart where Tiffany used to be.

"I told you," she said in a calm and even tone. "It wouldn't be safe for you, and it would be worse for her. There are trained professionals with her; they'll provide any aid she needs. You can help her best by staying out here where you'll be safe."

Owen fell to his knees as another scream made it through the door, stabbing his heart as surely as if Jen held the knife herself. "I-I-I—" There wasn't anywhere for him to go, and he didn't have an outlet for the energy pulling him to pieces inside. He wanted to tell her that he had to be with Jen, that she was scared, that he didn't want to—

Beira bent down in front of him and put a hand on his shoulder. "I know, but you can't help her by getting yourself hurt. Now come on; we're in for a long night."

With all his anger drained, Owen was as docile as a lamb as Beira pulled him to his feet and made him sit on a bench.

"You're staying?" he asked, somehow managing to feel surprised through the jumble of other emotions that were rolling through him like a tidal wave. "But you have to go to the celebration."

Beira smiled, exhaustion painting her face behind it. She had told him yesterday that she'd been preparing for the festival for weeks. For her to not go—was this that important to her?

"I try to go to every Change. As queen, it's my duty to protect and care for my people; as such, I need to know and understand them. It's why I teach in the high school and why I go to Changes, even when that means skipping other duties. The people understand, and one of the others is taking my place."

They were still close enough to the door to hear Jen's sobs. The sound wrenched Owen's heart in two, but he couldn't bring himself to move away. She wasn't screaming anymore, but like with Tiffany, in its own way, the near silence was worse. He almost wished they were further away, sitting on one of the identical benches outside the other five doors in this hallway.

"She'll be all right, Owen; some of the most experienced doctors and healers in Tearmann are with her. They've all been through countless Changes," Beira tried to reassure him. It didn't work.

"My wife died doing this," he said. "You think I can relax knowing what she's going through on the other side of that door?"

Jen cried out for Tiffany, and Owen's heart almost cracked in two.

"We should have had more time—" His voice broke, and he couldn't finish the sentence. He put his head in his hands. There hadn't been any signs, no headaches, or anything Tiffany had had. Nothing. This wasn't supposed to happen, not until they were grown.

Beira laid a hand on his shoulder, offering silent comfort while he wept. There was so much wrong in the world right now. His wife was dead, his family displaced, and now he couldn't even help his daughter when she needed him most. What use was he? Why had he even come?

Eventually, his broken sobs ceased, and they sat in silence. Owen was drained. He had no more tears left to cry, and there was nothing else he could do but shiver in a hall that hadn't felt cold before now. Minutes passed with little to mark them but the sobs that faded away. Arthur came down at one point, anxiously asking for an update on Jen's situation. Owen offered bland reassurances and sent him back to his siblings with a promise to send a note when he knew more.

Eventually, even Jen's sobs died away, and Owen was left to stare at the wall, resolutely not thinking about what that meant.

Perhaps it was inevitable that Owen and Beira would break out of their self-imposed silences. Unlike their earlier conversations, which flowed easily between them, now they couldn't seem to speak longer than a minute or two.

"Do you have any idea how much longer it's going to take?" he finally asked, staring unseeingly at the wall opposite them.

"Not really, no," Beira answered. "She's already gone past the time limits for elves, dwarves, and shades. Coming up are werewolves, trolls, and sirens."

"There's a tier system for species?"

"Of sorts. Sometimes there are outliers, but most of the time we can pin what species they'll be through how long it takes them to Change. And what they look like while Changing; that helps too."

"Oh. That makes sense."

"The next tier starts in about two hours if you're curious."

Silence.

"Are you feeling better?" Beira asked. "I can send for tea if you want."

"Tea would be nice."

Beira signaled a shade who'd been standing unnoticed off to the side. They didn't speak until he reappeared with a pot, two mugs, and a small bag of sandwiches. They ate while attempting conversation for the third time.

"Are you all right? You looked tense earlier," he asked over his tea. It was weak but hot. A perfect distraction.

She shrugged. "I'm fine. There was some bad news earlier, an accident with a human hunter out on our borders. Usually, the Canadians keep a respectful distance from us, but this guy didn't realize how close he was to the border. He was aiming at a deer and accidently hit a troll instead."

"Oh?" The familiar churning in his stomach returned tenfold and he set his tea down.

"This hasn't happened in almost thirty years, so you can get rid of that look." Beira's voice got distant, like she was back in whatever meeting had taken place after she received word of the shooting.

"Are you going to prosecute him?"

"What? Oh, yes." She had jumped when he spoke, and it had taken a second for her to answer. "The hunter killed someone, however much she looked like a tree. Her family explained the situation to him, and he agreed to come in. Says he feels horrible, and the elves confirmed it. We've sent word to the Canadian government and invited them to send officials to oversee the proceedings."

"I see. How do you think they'll react?"

"Who? The Canadians?" she asked, sipping her tea. "They have a mellower attitude toward us than the U.S., but there's still some residual distrust. They'll send someone to make sure we're not sentencing this guy to death and try to get us to release him into their hands."

Owen winced as Jen pleaded for help beyond the door. The sound shouldn't carry this far. "And how will you punish him, prison?" he asked to distract himself. "Do you even have a prison?" That sounded like something Andrew would have pointed out.

Beira laughed, a quiet, bitter sound instead of the open, joyful one he was used to hearing. "Oh, we have a prison system. Works as forced labor, though. Prisoners work on community projects like building new housing or farms. Half the wages they would have gotten gets put aside for their use when they get released, but the other half pays for their detainment. This guy will get six months or so, and we'll end up sending him back to Canada to serve his sentence."

"That's all?" Relations might be tense, but murder was murder.

Beira shrugged again and pulled a sandwich from the bag. "It was an accident. Even some of the fae mistake third-gen trolls for plants sometimes. Their natural camouflage is second to none, and from a distance, it's likely that he didn't see her," she explained as she poured another cup of tea. "Besides, it's important we keep good relations with Canada, as they do surround us on all sides. It wouldn't do to go overboard with sentencing this guy; he feels guilty enough, and doing so would only anger our neighbors."

"So that's it?" Owen asked. "He killed someone."

"Not at all," Beira said. "Even back in the States, something like this tends to be punished lightly. If anything, he's facing a longer sentence than normal, since he was within our borders without permission."

That display of calmness and logic pulled the wind out of his sails. "What was her name?" he asked, desperate for something to cling to. If this woman's killer was going to walk free, then the least he could do was remember her.

"The troll? Amelia Bickler. Her meme runs several outposts along our borders. They said she was traveling between two of them when she was shot."

"Oh." There was a pause before something occurred to him. "Wait, her *meme*?"

That brought a chuckle out of Beira, who seemed inordinately gleeful at his confusion. "Yes, we couldn't resist."

As Owen still looked confused, she continued. "Riling people up online was called trolling, and trolls usually used memes. Once Lady Eri and her son, Lord Bress, decided they'd like their species to be called trolls, Orpheus said that a group of trolls should be called a meme. That particular meeting rapidly devolved into fighting over what you called each species when they're in a group. We never did get rid of meme, though."

"What are some of the names you decided on?" he asked. At this point, he would take any distraction.

Beira leaned back against the wall and stretched her long legs out into the hallway. "Well, some are obvious. A group of werewolves is a pack, centaurs are a herd, it's a flock of harpies and a choir of angels. Others were us having fun in the meeting or common opinion overthrowing what their founders wanted. For example, dragons are a flight, sirens are a school, shades are a collective—"

"A collective? Who came up with that?" he asked with a hollow laugh, copying her pose.

"Taylor, if you can believe it. That is, Lady Enenra," Beira said, correcting herself smoothly. Owen only had a slightly better idea who Lady Enenra was, but it was the thought that counted. "Cameron, Lord Keme, wanted to be a shadow of shades, but no one else did, thank God."

"What do you call a group of vampires, then?"

She shot him a betrayed look, although he wasn't sure why. "It's stupid. I voted against it."

He smiled back in a way that was slightly maniacal. Perhaps his exhaustion made him more petty than usual, but either way, anything that embarrassed her this much had to be worth it. "Oh, then I have to hear it."

She tried to demur, but he needled her until she agreed to tell him. "Keep in mind, I voted against any names for a group of vampires, since I'm the only one, but I was overruled."

"You're stalling. It won't work."

"Very well, if you insist. It's—it's—" She ducked her head and refused to meet his eyes. "A group of vampires is called a court," she muttered all in one breath.

"Well, it's not that bad," Owen said slowly. He couldn't see why she was so embarrassed.

Beira looked like she would have been blushing had she had the ability, but her nature left her without it, according to a cheerful explanation she had given to Owen the previous morning. "If I'd had my way, a group of vampires would be a coven, if we had a name at all," she said, not looking up from the floor. "But at the time, the sirens wanted it, and the dwarves are clans, which was my second choice. Lord Orpheus decided that, since I was going to be queen anyway, it made sense to call any other vampires my court. The rest—" The door to Jen's room swung open.

Owen jumped to his feet, heart in his throat, as a siren with jet-black scales opened the door to Jen's room and limped into the hallway. "She's done," he said as he wiped his hands on his apron. "And she wants to see her father."

***

Owen forced himself to wait for all the attendants to leave before he went in. A large cot with thick leather straps, some almost torn in two, stood in the middle of the room, the only furnishing except for some small wooden cabinets along the far wall. He zeroed in on the cot, or rather, the blanket-covered lump lying on top of it. Jen.

He reached out, hesitating as his hand hovered over her blanket-covered shoulder. It wasn't every day that your child completely changed species, after all, and he—and he wasn't actually even sure what she was now. He'd forgotten to ask, too caught up in how fast everything was moving.

He took a deep breath and finished the motion. "Hey, Jen, you doing all right?"

No response. He tried again and sat next to her on the edge of the cot. "Come on, Jaybird, talk to me." The nickname got her shaking.

"I'm sorry," Jen said, the sound muffled by the blanket.

"Sorry? Sorry for what?"

"I ruined the party."

"Party? What—?" Oh. The Founding Day celebration. They were supposed to go to the neighborhood party, but Owen had to send the others with Arthur and Elenor.

"Jen. Look at me, Jaybird," he said, rubbing her shoulder. "It's not your fault."

The shaking didn't stop, and hitching breaths began to accompany it.

"Come on, little Jaybird, you didn't ruin anything. In fact, Jason said that it's considered an honor to Change during the festival."

"We were all gonna go together, then I got sick and we couldn't go. I ruined it." Her hitching breaths became sobs and twisted his heart in ways he hoped he would never feel again.

"Hey, hey, hey," he whispered, rubbing a hand along her back. He waited for the sobs to die down as he searched his mind for an appropriate topic. "You know, Arthur said that the neighborhood is planning to throw you a party when you feel better. He told me this was the first time someone had Changed during the festival in sixteen years, and everyone was excited."

That got Jen's attention. She shifted under the blanket, and a lump that might have been her head came to rest on his knee. "A party? Why? I ruined everything." She sniffed. Her voice was still croaky and hoarse in the way of someone who'd been screaming.

"They feel bad you missed the party," he said, trying to sound more excited than he felt. "The neighborhood kids want you to feel welcome, too, so they convinced their parents to throw it." He huffed, his smile becoming genuine. "He said they called it a birthday party."

"A birthday party?" She giggled a bright, albeit teary, sound. "That's silly, my birthday isn't 'til June."

She still sounded scared, but that was understandable. This was hard enough for Owen, and he wasn't the one changing species.

"I know," he said in a high-pitched voice. "I tried to tell Arthur that, but he insisted they said that was what they called it." He sighed mournfully. "I'm sorry, Jaybird, you're just going to have to deal with two birthdays from now on."

"Does this mean I get presents twice?" Jen asked, shifting under the blanket.

He could picture the way her eyes were narrowed now, and the suspicious look she must be giving him that matched her tone.

He pretended to consider it, screwing his eyes up and rubbing his chin, fully playing the part even if Jen wasn't looking at him. "You know, I don't know. I mean I suppose—"

"And I don't even have to share with David." She laughed, the sound muffled by the blanket, but as clear as a bell to him. It was working.

"You know," she whispered, her laugh disappearing, "I've never not shared something with him. It'll be weird."

"I know how you feel," Owen said as he patted her shoulder. "I mean, having to put up with all this extra fuss, but if you're set against it, I suppose I can ask Elenor to cancel it . . ."

A hand darted out of the blanket to smack his leg, too quick for him to see. "Dad, no!"

"No, no, no, if you're this set against it, there's nothing else to do. We'll have to cancel. Such a pity. The neighbors were looking forward to it too."

"Dad, I want the party," she whined. "I want to meet everyone."

For a moment, Owen thought Jen was going to take the blanket off, but the motion stopped almost as soon as it had begun.

"Do they really want to meet me?" Jen asked, her voice small and hesitant. She curled into a ball and pulled the edges of the blanket under her.

"Of course they do," Owen said, dropping the high-pitched voice. He couldn't joke about this. "You're a wonderful person, why wouldn't they?"

The shifting stopped and Jen uncurled a little. "It's just—I'm not— I haven't seen anyone like me."

Owen's eyebrows shot up. Their neighborhood was one of the most diverse he'd ever seen. He'd counted three languages between the five species who lived in their hall alone, and Jen was worried because she didn't look like them?

"Jaybird," he said, rubbing his thumb in slow circles on her shoulder. "Whatever you are, whatever you look like, I guarantee these guys have seen it before. And anyway, it doesn't matter. You'll always have me."

"Even if we have to leave?" she asked in a small voice.

"Especially then, because it would mean that you were strong enough to leave a situation that wasn't good for you and people that didn't appreciate you."

Jen dug her face into his thigh.

"Please, listen to me, Jen," Owen said, resisting the urge to pull her up. "There is no force on Heaven or on Earth that would make me hate you or give up on you or drive you away. You're my daughter, my little girl, and I love you in ways I can't even describe."

She didn't move as the last echoes of his proclamation drowned in the silence. Then the blanket shifted. "I think I'd like to come out now," she whispered. "When I get out, don't say anything right away, okay?"

Jen pushed Owen away, but he didn't resist and slid off the cot to stand. The blanket pulled one way and then the other. Then it slid off, falling to the ground, and he got his first look at what she had become.

Shaggy fur the same honey-blonde as her hair covered her body, longer on top of her head, but thin on her face and hands. From the way her legs bent, Owen thought she would walk on the balls of her feet for the rest of her life; he could almost hear the clack of her claws against stone. Twitching ears rose into furry points on the side of her head. Her nose—her whole jaw, really—protruded like a snout and fangs poked out over the edge of her lower lip. There was little left in her that had been there before that night.

He searched for his child in the face of the creature in front of him, and even with all the changes that had been wrought, he looked and knew her. This was his daughter, and beneath the fur and fangs and claws, she was still there, no matter what she looked like now.

A small part of him ached for who she could have been, would have been, without the Change. She could never go back home now, would never live a normal life. He grieved because they would never know if she would look like her mother or what she would have grown up to do. So many opportunities were gone, her options were so limited now, and his heart broke at the thought—but she needed him. He couldn't linger on what could have been.

Owen smiled, the blinding, joyful one Tiffany had called his dazzle-me smile. This was still his daughter, still Jen, and she needed him. "Well, I can't say I've had too much experience with werewolves before," he said. "But I'm up for the challenge if you are."

Her eyes lit up and she smiled a toothy, jagged grin. She flew across the small space between them, tottering on new legs, and threw her arms around her father's waist.

She was his daughter and she needed him, he repeated to himself as he picked her up and swung her in a circle. She was his daughter, and he would turn this mountain into rubble before he let her down.

CHAPTER TWELVE

IN WHICH THERE IS A
HAIRY SITUATION

.

"How exactly are we supposed to manage Changes? They're violent more times than not, and as it stands, we've had three sirens almost die because well-meaning bystanders tried to help and almost fifty of those bystanders got injured in the process. We need a safe place where they won't be bothered by other people and put my healers at risk. One of the dwarves said there were several storerooms that are empty right now. Those are strong, isolated, and most importantly, lock. Let me put my healers in there; it'll keep other people safe. The safety is worth the lost space, don't you agree?"

—Excerpt from the letters of Jennifer Thomson, Lady Lorelei

They separated when the door opened, and an elf, who introduced himself as Travis Stark, entered. He said he was here to take some measurements and deliver clothing to replace the tattered garments still clinging to Jen's frame. Owen was treated to a lengthy lecture about her needs as a werewolf as he helped with the measurements.

She could wear most shirts, but pants would be touch and go. She didn't need shoes and her fur would thicken during winter. Owen needed to make sure her claws were trimmed to a healthy length, get something for her to chew on when her teeth fell out, and arrange for pack bonding sessions. Jen turned around to dress while the two men talked, revealing another thing Owen would have to watch out for.

"You have a tail," Owen said dumbly, pointing at the offending appendage.

"I do?" She dropped her new shorts as her hands flew to her rear.

The way she twisted and turned reminded Owen of Toto chasing his tail; he put a stop to it before it could make him laugh. "Pull it in front of you," he told her, ignoring the way the elf sniggered behind them.

Jen took his advice, craning her torso to see it better. She examined it carefully and ran her free hand through the hair. "Dad," she said, turning to him with horror in her eyes. "How do I wear pants now?"

His jaw snapped shut as he turned to Travis, who picked up the shorts Jen had dropped.

"No need to worry," Travis said, turning the shorts so he could see. "There's a hole."

True to his word, there was a small hole for the tail a few inches below the waistband. It took a moment, but Jen managed to figure it out without too much help. While she was distracted Owen questioned the elf on how to alter her clothing to fit.

The rest of the lecture didn't take long. Armed with a thick folder and stern instructions to get help if he had any more questions, Owen and Jen were shoved out of the room so the elf could clean it.

Beira jumped up when they came out and walked toward them. She wore the stiff expression that Owen called her Queen Face, as this was something of a formal ceremony. The Welcoming, she had called it during one of their stilted conversations earlier.

Beira nodded at Owen and bent her neck enough to greet Jen. She then looked him in the eye. "Owen Williams, your daughter is too young by our laws to care for herself. Do you swear to care for her, to provide for her needs, and teach her our laws as the leader of her pack until such a time as she can learn on her own?" Her voice echoed down the corridor, hanging in the air like mist.

"I swear," Owen said in a stiff voice. He'd been told a little about this ceremony, enough to know how he was expected to answer. "She will never know want or be without love, and she shall be taught the law while under my care."

Beira smiled. She turned her head back to Jen and continued. "Then, Jennifer Williams, I welcome you to Tearmann as a member of your father's pack in the name of the Fae Queen's Court and the Founders Council. In these names and my own, I swear to lead you and your people well, to provide for you as if you were my own kin. Do you accept my vow?"

Jen looked at Owen uncertainly. With a jolt, he remembered she hadn't been told this was going to happen. There'd been no time.

"Go ahead," he whispered to her.

She looked back at the queen. "I do. I accept I mean," she said as her claws dug into Owen's trouser leg.

"Then I leave you to your kin," Beira said and stepped back. "Owen, I need to speak to you soon about Jen's needs now that she has Changed. Stop by my office after you get off work tomorrow."

Owen blinked. The shift from queen to friend was jarring enough to startle him. "Um, all right," he said, shifting his feet. "Does five thirty work?"

Beira nodded, congratulated Jen, wished them goodnight, and walked off, leaving them to find their way back to the apartment on their own.

***

Owen knew it had only been three days, and he couldn't say what was normal in a place like this, but still, he had never seen the halls this empty. It was almost two in the morning, but he'd have thought there would be guardsmen on patrol at the very least. The halls lost what little sense of warm invitation they had during the day in the wee hours of the morning. The scattered lamps became safe havens between the long stretches of utter darkness. Noises he would have sworn were just in front of them disappeared when they turned the corner and shadows flicked out of sight when they drew near.

Jen walked so close to him he stumbled over her paws several times, and she maintained a death grip on his left hand that threatened to break bone. His heavy work boots clomped loudly to the counterpoint of her claws clattering on the stone. Owen was glad to finally reach their apartment, where he could shake off the unease of the empty hallway.

David slammed into Jen as soon as Owen opened the door, hugging her with all his strength. His face pressed against her shoulder. "Are you all right? Arthur said—"

"I'm fine, really. Just a little tired," Jen said with a soft growl. She guided David into the boys' room, still whispering in his ear.

Owen, in the meantime, had walked over to Arthur, who was contemplating his mug while holding Toto back from ambushing Jen. "Well, it seems like you've got the situation well in hand," he said as he passed boy and dog on his way to the coffee pot.

He picked up the pot, empty but for the residue from the last batch. If the warmth it let off was any indication, that hadn't been too long ago. "Dare I ask how many pots you drank?"

Arthur ducked his head away from what his children had dubbed the "seriously?" eyebrow. "Only two. Ashley helped before she took Dorothy to bed," he said as he let Toto go. The dog wasted no time running to scratch at the door the twins had vanished behind.

At that moment, Owen finally realized everything that Ashley and Arthur had to deal with today. "Ah, and how did Dorothy take it?" he asked, rubbing the back of his neck. "The news, I mean?"

Arthur sighed. "She didn't understand what I was talking about when I said Jen couldn't come, and I didn't want to bring up Mom—" He choked up and rubbed a hand over his cheeks. "I didn't want her to think that Jen would die like Mom, although I'm not sure she understands what that means." Arthur's voice cracked and bitterness filled the spaces it left behind. "She was asking where Mom was yesterday. Ash and I tried to tell her that Mom wasn't coming back, and she thought it was because she did something wrong. She kept crying and telling us she would be good if Mom came back. And today? Today it took us twenty minutes to convince her that you weren't gone too."

Each word hit Owen like a physical blow, chosen to strike where it would hurt him most. The party today was supposed to be their first real family outing since they'd gotten to Tearmann, and he'd left Arthur and Ashley to take care of the others so he could go to Jen.

He didn't know what to say, how to start. He only knew he had to do something before it got worse. "Arthur, look, I'm sorry. I should have been there—"

"No, no, it's fine," Arthur said harshly. "I'm just . . ." He sighed, put his head in his hands, and took deep breaths. After a few seconds, Owen realized he was crying.

"I miss her. I miss her so much and I don't know what to do about it. It's like—it's like you don't care, like you don't miss her, and that's not true, I know it's not true, but I still—" he sobbed between hitching breaths. "How do you do it? I'm barely holding it together, and I only have to worry about myself, but you—you have to worry about all of us, and you—" There was a moment's pause as his tears overwhelmed his ability to speak, one filled by Toto's whines as he tried to comfort Arthur in his own slobbery way.

Owen stared at his sobbing child, speechless. Arthur—and Ashley, and David, and all of them—had been so brave. He'd forgotten, somehow, that they'd lost as much as he had, more even, and they had managed to keep going, to take care of each other while he'd been distracted by other things.

"I miss her too," he said, keeping his voice low. "I miss her more than words can describe. Every day, I wake up and I think it must be a dream, that the last few days were nothing more than a nightmare, only to turn around to see her side of the bed still made." His throat tightened against the words; he forced them through with the desperation of a drowning man.

"Sometimes, I'll be working or talking with someone, and I'll turn around to ask her a question, and I remember she's not there and will never be there again and it hurts." It did. Even now, the thought of never seeing her again tore at him and made him want to scream until his throat bled.

"How did you make it stop?" Arthur asked, wiping tears away.

"I didn't," Owen whispered, unable to speak louder. "I couldn't. I let it build inside me until I thought I was going to burst. And then—" he hesitated.

"Then what?"

Owen pulled out a chair and sat across from Arthur. "I ran into the queen in the market the day after our first meeting. She was staring at one of the statues in the square."

"The memorial statues?" Arthur asked, eyes still damp.

Owen nodded. "She told me that this one belonged to a werewolf named Michael, her old fiancé. His death sent her into a destructive spiral where she made 'a host of bad decisions', in her own words. She only snapped out of it when those decisions killed a few people."

Owen paused, possibly for dramatic effect, possibly trying to get his thoughts together—even he couldn't tell. "She told me those deaths made her realize that she couldn't do that anymore. She couldn't hold her pain inside and try to deal with it herself. So she stopped. She went out, helped people, and let go of a little of her pain each day."

"How?"

"She said she started journaling again, something she'd stopped doing after the war, and she talked to people. She volunteered to be the person I could talk to, offered to buy me a journal too, come to think of it." The memory made Owen laugh, but the sound was sharp and brittle.

"And that was enough?" Arthur asked, arching an eyebrow.

"She understands," Owen said in a low voice, running his thumb over his wedding ring.

Neither Owen nor Arthur broke the silence that followed. Owen was consumed with his own thoughts, and judging from the way he was staring at the wall, Arthur was as well.

"Arthur," Owen finally said. "I know the last week has been rough, and I haven't been here as much as I should, but you should know you can talk to me. I want to be here for you and your siblings in any way I can, even if it means skipping work or putting off going back altogether."

Arthur took a deep breath and raised his head. "I think I'd like that," he said in a small voice. "If we could talk more, I mean. We never ..."

"We never talked much at home," Owen whispered. "There was always—"

"Something else." Back home there was always work or school or practice or one of his siblings to stop them from talking, and now this.

Owen used to make the time to talk to each of his kids every day, ask them how school was, what their friends were doing, that sort of thing. Lately, though, he hadn't had the time. He was always too busy, and his relationship with them had suffered for it.

"It's late," Arthur said, making a show of checking his watch. "I have school in the morning."

Owen raised a hand to stop him before he had even managed to rise from his seat. "Beira—the queen, that is—said to tell you and the others you don't have to go to school tomorrow. She said it's to give you time to adapt."

"Really?" Arthur asked, sinking back into his seat. "But shouldn't we go anyway? To normalize the situation and make it easier on Jen?"

"Your sister grew fur, paws, claws, and a tail in the course of a few hours," Owen said bluntly. "I don't think there's any way to normalize it."

Arthur tilted his head and then nodded. "Fair enough. Are you going to work tomorrow, then, or did Mr. Moore give you the day off as well?"

"The next two days and longer if we need it."

There was something different about Arthur now, something Owen couldn't explain. He tried to pin it down, that elusive change in his son that was both obvious and subtle. It was in the way he carried himself, in the way his eyes looked at his father, in the confidence and maturity that shone in his actions far beyond others his age.

He was a man now, Owen realized with a jolt, his mouth falling open in a small 'o'. The events of the last week and the responsibilities laid upon Arthur's shoulders—ones Owen had put there—had hardened him, made him grow in a way few people could lay claim to. In a way that would break most adults.

"Look at you," he whispered, every word laced with the melancholy every parent faced the first time their child looked at them as an adult. "You've changed. You're grown now."

Arthur opened his mouth.

"No, let me finish," Owen said before he could speak. He took a deep breath, trying to force down the lump in his throat. "I'm ... so proud of you. I know I haven't always been as clear as I could be, but I need you to know that."

The words poured from him now, wild and untamed, and perhaps it was the late hour or everything that had gone wrong today, but this needed to be said. "I don't know what's going to happen in the days to come, and I know you're walking down a path I can never follow, but I swear I won't leave you to face all this on your own again."

He never should've left him in the first place, but living in the past was the best way to destroy the future. If he wanted to fix this, he had to start here.

Arthur answered in a voice like steel. "I know, Dad but ... you need us too. We're a family. We're not going to let you take everything on yourself, not even to protect us."

There it was. It was finished. Arthur had taken his words and internalized the meaning behind them, shoring up his spirit and leaving behind the last bit of childhood that clung to him. He stood alone, the softness of the world they had left behind gone and the harshness required to live in their new one taking its place.

He sighed and, glancing at the clock, said, "Well, now that that's out of the way, what do you say you and I make our way to bed? Dorothy's going to be up bright and early and it'll take both of us to deal with her."

Arthur made a face. "Ugh, she's going to be impossible. Yeah, that's not what I meant, I'm leaving her to you. Night, Dad." Without another word, he turned tail and raced toward his room.

"Not so grown up then." Owen laughed, shaking his head. "I've no idea where he gets that from. It certainly wasn't me."

CHAPTER THIRTEEN

IN WHICH OWEN
CAN'T CATCH A BREAK

"In the last week alone, there've been three accidents caused by the reborn trying to use their new abilities. To make things worse, the more territorial species keep getting into fights. Individually, these problems would be a handful. Together, we're almost overwhelmed. Titania told Séaghdha to arrange a training regimen for Changed while Ailell and Aelfric are looking into establishing colonies similar to Paxton. This would allow the more aggressive folks to branch out, establish their territories, as it were."

—Excerpt from the journals of Gabriel Clark, Lord Gabriel

As expected, Dorothy was up and about a few hours later. Arthur and Ashley refused to get out of bed, leaving Owen to deal with her by himself. So much for not letting him take everything on himself.

And so, running on four hours of sleep, Owen had to convince Dorothy that the furry girl sitting next to David and muttering over the block of wood that was his current project was her sister. She took the news better than he might have in her place. Apparently, she knew it was Jen because the hair was the same. Would that all their problems were so easy to solve.

Toto took to it even better than Dorothy. He ran to Jen as soon as she left the boys' room, and after carefully sniffing essential areas, immediately tried to lick her face.

Owen had to pull Jen off Toto, to their mutual displeasure, after they started wrestling on the living room floor. It was only then that he was able to push Dorothy and the twins out the door. They needed to get to the cafeteria by nine if they wanted to beat the crowds, and they were nudging perilously close to the limit. He shouldn't have bothered, though, as what should have been a short twenty-minute trip turned into an odyssey all its own.

Jen gloried in the attention her new looks got her as they ate. It seemed like the whole neighborhood—and half the bloody mountain—came to see her during their short meal, to offer their congratulations and inquire about how she was settling in. Owen was debating how to best forcibly separate Jen from her admirers so they could get home when salvation came in the form of a stocky mechanic.

"Williams! I need to speak with you, get over here."

Owen breathed a sigh of relief and walked to where a small pack of werewolves and their canine companions were showing Jen how to "use her nose properly." How that involved rubbing a piece of cheese in a line around the room was beyond him, but it made sense to them. "Jen, it's time to go. You can play with your friends later."

"But Dad," she said, pulling off her improvised blindfold. "Can't I stay here?"

"No, Jen, we have to go." She probably could have stayed, but the memory of her screams were too close for Owen to be comfortable letting her out of his sight in public. "Andrew needs to talk to me, and Arthur and Ashley need breakfast, remember?" He held up two wrapped bagels as a reminder.

"Oh, all right," Jen said, turning back to the pack of dogs and werewolves. "My dad says I have to go. I'll see you later, though."

The werewolves agreed, howled their goodbyes, and scattered. One, a gray-haired first-gen, made plans with Owen to meet later for another session before he disappeared into the crowd.

All-in-all, it took ten minutes to extract everyone from the crowd and follow Andrew out into the hallway. "I'm sorry it took so long," Owen said once they'd made their escape.

"It's fine," Andrew said with a wave of his hand. "You looked like you were getting overwhelmed and I was happy to provide an escape."

He glared back into the crowded dining hall. "This always happens when someone's reborn. People get excited and the poor soul who grew fur becomes a local celebrity. Don't worry, it'll die down in a week or so."

"Will they still want to play with me?" Jen asked, her ears twitching.

"Oh, the city werewolves will without a doubt," Andrew answered, beckoning them forward. "They're a welcoming bunch and they like knowing all the werewolves in the city. Of course, some of the packs further out in the country are more insular, but they shouldn't bother you too much."

Happy to have someone with inside knowledge on how the pack system worked, Jen monopolized Andrew's attention for the entire walk back to the apartment.

***

It took a week for things to settle down again. Jen had to spend two days learning how to be a werewolf before she could return to school. All that meant was a group of wolves took turns teaching her how to manage her newly enhanced senses, groom herself, and keep track of her claws. None too soon, in Owen's opinion, as she'd already shredded two cushions and left a collection of small scratches on pretty much everything in the apartment. Still, it was strange how fast things went back to normal, even if Jen now shed more than Toto.

"I know I shouldn't complain about it," Owen said to Beira. "But it doesn't feel right. It's like—agh." He thudded back in his seat and massaged his forehead.

Beira had invited Owen to her apartment for tea after their meeting and he'd accepted, more out of curiosity than anything else. As bare as her office was, he hadn't expected the chaotic mess of Beira's living quarters. A housekeeper, she wasn't. By her own admission, doing the dishes was about as much as she could manage.

A single mural, a massive rendering of the founders not long after Tearmann was completed, covered the entire ceiling. That was the only place it could go, as the walls themselves had been hollowed into shelves. Which, speaking of, half the books in Tearmann had to be in here, stacked on the floor, holding up a wonky table, and spilling off the shelves. Owen had never felt more like he was at risk of being crushed by an unstable pile of books.

Across the small table in her living room, Beira nodded as she poured the tea. "I know what you mean. I felt the same way after we settled here."

Owen raised an eyebrow as he reached out to take his tea. "Oh?"

She huffed, forcing the air out with a tired sigh. "Before we came here, and even for years after, I was always busy, always working. I felt adrift when we settled." She chuckled bitterly and wrapped her hands around her mug. "We'd been in a constant state of turmoil for, oh, twenty years or so before that, and I didn't know what to do with the sudden calm. I had time, time to reflect, time to—" She stopped and stared at the bottom of her mug. "I was lost like you are now," she continued, her voice dropping to a harsh whisper. Cracks spread in the clay under her fingertips. She stared, not in fear, but at something unknowable beyond the surface of her tea.

"Beira? Are you all right?" Owen asked. Past her shoulder, one of her ever-present aides, today a young second-gen shade who normally waited just out of sight, took a cautious step forward, his hand outstretched.

Owen's question broke Beira's concentration, and her hands loosened enough for the mug to drop from nerveless fingers onto the table inches below. A deep and ragged breath tore through her. Owen exchanged another glance with the aide, wondering if they should have called whatever passed for emergency services here.

Deep breaths turned into dark laughter. Beira ran a hand over her face. "I'm sorry," she said between chuckles. "I didn't mean to do that."

She picked up the cracked mug, which was now leaking tea, and drained it in one gulp, heedless of how it still steamed. "Anyway, I meant to tell you that I understood what you were going through. My therapist said it's pretty typical for people who go through high-stress situations."

"What, like PTSD?"

"Post-Traumatic Stress Disorder was, and remains to be, a common problem among first-gen, especially for war veterans."

"Right. That makes sense." He nodded and then sipped from his mug. He wasn't surprised to hear she had PTSD or even that it was common. From what he'd heard, his family's journey here was tame compared to what some had gone through, even with the added danger of his being seen and the encounter with the police,.

A harpy a hallway over told him her mother had been rescued from a SAFE research facility. One of the dwarves he worked with told stories about fleeing his hometown on foot with little more than the clothes on his back. A centaur he met in the cafeteria one afternoon said all of her aunts and uncles had been killed by a roadside bomber in Pakistan while being shipped to Tearmann in a livestock truck. Few of the settlers had happy stories associated with their journeys here, and even when Tiffany's death was taken into account, the Williams's was easier than most.

"What did you do to stop it?" He wasn't sure why the conversation made him want to duck his head, but his eyes traced the Celtic knot engraving in his wedding ring so he wouldn't have to look at Beira.

"I talked to people," she said, grabbing a scone from their dwindling pile. "Therapy is a thriving practice among first-gens, as I'm sure you've noticed, but more than that I stopped shutting myself away. I got a job that wasn't leading people."

"That's right; you're the history teacher," Owen said. "Arthur and Ashley said they like your classes."

"No, I didn't start teaching right away." She chuckled and stood to throw her broken mug in the trash.

His eyes snapped up. "Really? What did you do then?"

"I was a historian before all of this," she said as she returned with a new mug and poured a fresh cup of tea. She considered her scone for a moment before she dunked it and continued speaking. "My parents were Arthurian scholars, so I guess I was raised in it. I had received a position on a dig in Scotland when it all went south. After we were settled, I went back to it."

It didn't seem right to break the silence after her pronouncement, although Owen wanted to ask her what she meant.

"You know," Beira said as she leaned back and crossed her arms over her chest. "They say history is written by the victors, but that's not true. History is written by those who are left. We won the war but withdrew afterward. With no one to say otherwise, we became the bad guys. After we settled, I decided to fix that."

"Is that why you became a teacher, to remind your students what the fae went through?" Owen asked, leaning forward. That would be what he would've done. People were too quick to forget.

"No," she said. "I became a teacher because I'm selfish. I needed something to remind me why I fought in the first place. I became a teacher because I needed them to remember the other side has a story too." She stopped to take a sip of her tea, then said, "And also because I found I really do enjoy teaching."

She set her mug down and smiled. "But I digress. I realized I was dividing events into before and after, which created a disconnect between events. By bringing them together, I was able to process them."

"So that's it, then? More of what I've already been doing?" Here he'd been thinking Beira was about to drop some great secret she'd found for dealing with her grief, but all she had to offer was the same things his therapist had been saying.

"More or less." She shrugged and took another bite of her scone. "Listen, Owen, there's not anything more we can do. We don't have access to the medicines and cures of the outside world, so we have to make do with what we have. New blood brings in new knowledge, but rarely does it correlate to what we want or need."

"I know. I'm sorry," he said, giving in and looking away. "It's just—" He stopped, unable to put his feelings into words.

Beira's eyes softened. "You want this to be over, to go back to how things were before."

"Yes, but—no." Owen was truly fed up with feeling helpless all the time. It was like he was a child again, throwing a tantrum because he lacked the words to explain what was bothering him.

"Look," he finally said. "I don't regret coming here, really I don't. The havens are the safest place for the kids, and I'll always be thankful for that protection even when we leave, but I wish—" He took a deep, cleansing breath. "I wish Tiffany was here." He didn't say that if she was here he probably wouldn't be pushing so hard to go to Scotland. Any place where he had his wife and his kids was home to him.

Beira reached out and laid a hand on his. "I would've liked to have met her," she said in a low voice. "She sounds like an amazing person."

"She was," he answered, smiling ruefully. "Although the two of you would have hated each other. She was strong-willed, to say the least." It hurt to talk about her, but it was a relief at the same time. Having someone who understood—like Beira, who'd lost more than her fair share of loved ones—was cathartic. She knew what it felt like, could understand the things he didn't say and make him admit the things he didn't want to.

"Surely you don't think I would dislike her simply because she might oppose me. I assure you, I'm an adult," she said in a haughty voice as she looked at him down her nose.

He laughed. This was the part of their banter he enjoyed: The back and forth as they gauged each other's moods and adjusted accordingly, never too serious, never too stupid.

Beira knew how dwelling on the past made him melancholic and teased him to bring him out of his foul mood. He tried to fulfill the same function for her but didn't have the advantage of either knowing her for a long time, as most of her friends did, or having seventy years of life experience to draw back on as she did.

"Oh really"—Owen met her haughty look with his own raised eyebrow—"then I suppose arranging for several buckets of water to be placed in strategic locations throughout Dani's quarters has nothing to do with your prank war?"

"I assure you there is nothing untoward happening. Lady Guivre sent me a message and I answered in kind. It's a matter of politics." She acted convincingly affronted at the suggestion of any wrongdoing on her part, but he had been present for both the incident that led to the buckets and the aftermath. The image of Beira sprinting away from a soaking-wet dragon to avoid a hug was one that would stay with Owen forever.

"Sure you did," he said, rolling his eyes.

He glanced at the clock on the far wall. "At any rate," he said as he set down his mug, "I promised Ashley I would be back by five to help with the party decorations."

The time it took for Beira to drop her faux disdain and offense would have been impressive had he not seen it every day since they had met. "Jen's Changing party is today, right? Is she excited?"

"She's been bouncing off the walls all week," he said with a scowl. "The heads of a local pack are coming over to formally offer their assistance with her training and to recognize the Williams line among the packs." He knew he sounded irritated. He was happy that Jen was settling in so well, and even happier that she was smiling again, but from what he had seen, there was less pomp and circumstance at a presidential inauguration. He hated parties.

"Now, Owen," Beira said as she waved a finger at him. "You know that we need to keep track of who's related to whom. We haven't had a new line for any of the species in years, and this is an important opportunity to introduce her to local authorities of her species."

This was the third time they'd had this conversation, and Owen couldn't say he was any more pleased about what this opportunity represented than he had been the first time.

The packs were sending representatives for one reason and one reason only. To poach Jen away from him. One day, Jen would join one of the city packs, whether through marriage or friendship, or leave the city to start her own. The bonds of the pack were imitated in their family group, but one day that wouldn't be enough and he would lose his daughter.

In a way, he had already lost her. She wasn't human anymore. She was part of something he would never be able to understand, would never be able to appreciate in the way she did, and try as he might, he couldn't stop thinking about how things were different now. He still loved her with all his heart, but he mourned the person she could have been had none of this ever happened.

He rolled his eyes to shake off his sudden bout of melancholy. "I know that, but it doesn't mean I have to approve of them bringing their sons along. She's eight."

Beira laughed and called him a curmudgeon as he gathered the notebooks and blueprints that were the real reason for this meeting and stuffed them into his bag. "That reminds me," he said as he tried to catch a sketch that was making an escape attempt across the table. "Jen wants to know if you're coming to the party."

"After she made me that lovely invitation? I wouldn't miss it for the world," Beira said over her shoulder as she brought their mugs to the kitchen sink. The books piled everywhere around her apartment absorbed enough of the sound Owen had to strain to hear her. "I'll try to drop by a little after seven." She walked back to his side, wiping her hand on a rag as she went. "Do you mind if I bring Balder and Audhild with me? Balder said he wants to meet the 'crazy carpenter' who designed the tents."

Owen stopped to consider it. Lord Balder and Lady Audhild, the dwarven founders, oversaw all of the public engineering and construction projects for the havens. He didn't want to bring work home with him, had promised it in fact, but this could lead to a job for him in Daingneach. Jen would understand. "Well . . . Jen doesn't think work has a place at parties, so as long as they keep the business talk to a minimum," he said, trying to calm the rapid beating of his heart. "I see no reason why they shouldn't take advantage of the open invitation."

Beira beamed and clapped him on his shoulder. "Wonderful, I'll let them know after the cabinet meeting tonight. He was impressed with the steps you took to make them accessible for various species, though, so you won't escape without at least a little shop talk, I'm afraid. Now, I believe I'm keeping you. Tell the children I said hello and I'll be by tonight."

Owen said goodbye and maneuvered around the stacks of books, papers, and knick-knacks scattered throughout her living room. With a final wave, he opened the door, and began the long descent to the second floor and the frankly frightening party plans Ashley, Eoire, and Elenor had put together.

***

After much careful deliberation, the three minds behind this endeavor had decided to hold the party in the cafeteria instead of their apartment. When he asked why it had to be so large, Eoire insisted the first Changing party was always a big deal and that subsequent anniversaries were smaller, more intimate affairs. He had tried to argue for a smaller party anyway, as they didn't know any people here and he didn't want to overwhelm Jen, but he'd been loudly overruled.

In accordance with this decision, the cafeteria was decorated to the extremes. The mural and carvings on the walls had been cleaned, the tables were set with fancy tablecloths and settings, the kitchens had gone all out on food, someone had provided far more alcohol than an eight-year-old's party warranted, and there was even a small band in the corner providing music. It felt more like a festival than a party, and he half expected someone to pull out a kissing booth or try to pin a tail on someone.

Jen, of course, loved the attention. Her fur had been brushed until it gleamed, and she was wearing a dress a few of the neighborhood grandmothers had made for her. She dragged Arthur around by his arm, introduced him to the few people he hadn't met before, and pulled him out to the dance floor. David, upon seeing her enthusiasm, had taken the coward's way out and hid under a nearby table whenever Arthur looked like he was about to make an escape attempt. Owen thought he might have to go free him soon.

"You know, if you keep standing in the corner glowering at everyone, someone might think you weren't enjoying yourself." Andrew's voice at Owen's elbow from out of nowhere almost made him jump.

"Andrew, I didn't see you come in. And I'm not glowering, that's my face." Owen scowled when he realized his drink had spilled onto his sleeve. Perfect. This was why he hated parties.

Andrew made a show of squinting at Owen. "Lad, are you trying to claim you're one of those poor unfortunate souls cursed with a face that looks angry all the time? Because, while I've only known you for a short time, I can say with confidence that it's a lie." He sipped his drink and smiled over the rim of his mug. "Now, what's got you up in arms at your daughter's party?"

Owen's glower softened into exasperation as he leaned back against the wall, out of sight of the rest of the room. "It's nothing," he said. "I just don't like crowds. Don't get me wrong, I'm happy for Jen. but it's hard to keep track of everyone like this. Besides, I don't like having my family's private affairs splattered everywhere for everyone to see."

Andrew snorted. "Your daughter turned into a werewolf, you're a carpenter when we have a shortage, and your family are the first newcomers we've had in years in a place where everyone knows everyone. It's a little late to keep things quiet. Face it, Williams, you lot are doomed to a life of being minor celebrities."

"That doesn't mean I have to like it," he muttered, trying to blend in with the wall as three of the neighborhood fathers and two grandmothers made their way in his direction.

They stood in silence as the group passed by their alcove.

Speaking of local fame," Andrew said once they were gone, "rumor around the third floor is a certain carpenter submitted a design that's got the rangers in an uproar."

"They're making such a big deal out of it," Owen said, his scowl coming back with a ferocity that could've curdled milk. "It's not like it's a new or revolutionary design, after all." He had submitted a design for an aerial tent for the scouts to use after Mr. Moore had suggested it. He would never have believed his stupid sketches would get so much attention.

Andrew chortled. "It is to us. We've been out of touch with the rest of the world for fifty years now. I've seen those designs, and we've got nothing like them."

"It's a portable, hanging fort," Owen said and took a sip of his drink. "One of my foster homes had one when I was growing up. It's not like it's breaking new ground. You lot have plenty of forts." He bit down a groan when he realized his glass was now empty and he had to make the choice between going thirsty or braving the crowd.

"Our forts are built into trees, and most of them are hardly what you'd call comfortable or stealthy." A new voice coming from Owen's other side did make him jump. "Yours will keep our patrols warmer and safer than current designs, and with a few adaptations, they can be used in other environments as well." He was glad his glass was already empty.

The speaker was a stout first-gen dwarf approximately a foot shorter than Owen with sun-starved skin and the squashed appearance of his species. Unlike most of his kin, his blond beard was almost nonexistent, limited to a small goatee and a five o'clock shadow. The dark-skinned woman accompanying him, also a first-gen, was remarkably petite for a dwarf, normally a stout and full-figured people. Her curly black hair was cropped close to her ears, in contrast to her companion's elbow-length mane, and she had an elaborately braided mustache.

"Ryan's right, Williams, although he doesn't understand as much as he thinks he does," the woman said, smiling pleasantly.

"Er, right. And you are?" Owen managed to say when he finally decided he had no idea who these people were. The curse of being well-known was that you never knew who you were talking to even if they always knew who you were.

"Oh right, introductions," the blond dwarf said, slapping his forehead. "My name is Ryan Kordonowy, officially known as Lord Balder, dwarven architect. My friends call me Ryan." He bowed and gestured for his female companion to go, although Owen now had a pretty good guess who she was.

"My name is Alva Amundsen," she said, bowing as well. "They call me Lady Audhild, dwarven engineer. Please, call me Audhild, I prefer it to my given name." Now that Owen had more of an opportunity to hear her speak, he detected a faint African accent, although he couldn't place it precisely.

"A pleasure to meet you. I'm Owen Williams. Sorry, but if you don't mind me asking, where are you from, Audhild?"

The petite dwarf laughed. "No trouble at all, I get that question from most new arrivals. The name doesn't help things, of course. I was born in Namibia. My father was part of a humanitarian project, met my mother, married her, and had me. I got mixed up in this nonsense when I came to America to study abroad. And to answer your next question, no, my parents died before any of this happened, so they're not here. Ryan's are, though."

Ryan nodded. "Mom's a dwarf like me, but Dad's human."

"Uh," Owen managed, looking around for Beira. She was supposed to be here so he wouldn't have to deal with this on his own. "You two were supposed to come with Beira—the queen, right? Where is she?"

Audhild laughed again. "Her Majesty got caught up in the crowd trying to speak to Jen. She sent us your way and told us to ask you about the forts. Speaking of, how are we supposed to lift them into the trees or cliffs or wherever we hang them?"

This Owen could do. This was work, not small talk, and even though he had promised to keep it to a minimum, Jen would understand if he participated in a little bit of shop talk as long as he didn't start it. "I've seen elves lift two-hundred-pound blocks of stone with little to no trouble," he said, setting down his glass. "These forts weigh barely twice that. A simple pulley system would allow them to be lifted, moved, and hung with ease."

"Perhaps so," Ryan said, raising an eyebrow. "But what if we can't find trees strong enough to take that weight in addition to one of our gryphons, hm?"

"Come on, surely you can see how the forts can be lightened or fastened onto the treetops, increasing the amount of weight they can safely bear, in addition …"

Owen lost himself in the talk between himself and the three dwarves, and the conversations moved from discussing his forts onto how exactly the mass lighting systems worked, and from there to the benefits of different methods of trash disposal used in the city. Owen only understood about two-thirds of it, but it was fascinating nonetheless. Despite his earlier grim mood, he began to enjoy himself and even emerged from the corner to debate the various benefits of burning garbage versus re-using it.

The conversation would have likely continued until the end of the party had Ryan not hit his companion on the arm. "Audhild, look. We're in for a treat." He gestured toward the stage, where the band was inviting guests to come and sing. A small horde of teenagers egging Beira onto the stage had drawn his attention.

"What's she doing?" Owen hissed in Andrew's ear. As far as he knew, Beira avoided the spotlight as much as possible. She even kept her birthday a secret to avoid the people making a fuss about it.

Andrew rolled his eyes at the spectacle as the queen was finally convinced to take the stage. "They want her to open the singing for them. It's something of a tradition at Changing parties for the highest-ranking person present to humiliate themselves by singing a local folk song. You can't get higher than the queen."

Andrew waved a hand at Ryan and Audhild next to them, who cackled as Beira spoke to the band. "Those two are only happy they weren't asked to do it. Now hush, we need to at least pretend we're paying attention." Owen wanted to ask more, but Andrew shushed him again and waved toward the stage where the queen had started to sing:

> "There once was a king among bandits old
> Who had a cat named NineFold
> Oh, King of Rogues, the young tom said
> I know a place, of yellow and red
> Listen well and bend your head
> The only tenants of this place tend the dead . . ."

172

Owen furrowed his brow. He knew this song, but he hadn't heard it in years. Where...?

> *"And with a cat-like grin*
> *And a rapid spin*
> *Old NineFold told a tale*
> *About a place past river and dale*
> *Where gold and emeralds ran in streams*
> *Riches beyond your wildest dreams . . ."*

It couldn't be . . . that movie hadn't come out 'til he was ten, and the fae didn't have the technology to see it anyways.

He turned to Ryan and Audhild, who were both watching him instead of Beira. "I wouldn't've thought you lot knew this song. It only came out thirty years ago."

"Oh, the person who wrote the book the movie's based on is one of us. She manages her writing through one of our allies down south," Audhild answered as her grin became alarmingly large. Was it normal for someone to show that many teeth?

Owen almost dropped his drink. "Really? But wouldn't we have heard about that? I mean, I know the author wrote under a pseudonym, but every known fae is recorded in the registries."

"Oh," Ryan said with a laugh. "It's completely possible. The writer was so fame-shy her agent never saw her face, and the money she made was deposited in a bank account under a different name. It was simple for our agent to take it over."

Owen narrowed his eyes at the two grinning founders. "You're messing with me, aren't you?"

"No, we're not and that's the best part," Audhild said earnestly. He did get the impression she was silently laughing at his confusion, though, so he refused to engage either of them in conversation again until Beira was finished.

> *". . . The brothers wept as one lay bleeding*
> *Binding the wound and beginning down,*
> *The brothers, king and cat, watched the dawn*
> *Rise over mountains and world of Yorn."*

Beira finished to a smattering of applause and made her way to their table. The scowl she wore as she took the open seat across from Owen was enough to curdle milk.

"A fat lot of help you two were," she said to Ryan and Audhild. "You left me to fend them off by myself."

"Well, your ladyship, it seems like it worked well. After all, we amused ourselves at your expense," Audhild said as Beira's scowl deepened. Ryan didn't even bother trying to defend himself. He just laughed.

"At any rate," Beira said as she turned to Owen. "It's time for your favorite part of the evening. Let's go meet the pack dignitaries."

He groaned and thumped his head against the table. He had almost managed to forget that he had to do that. Blast, why couldn't Jen have been a shade? They had far fewer rituals.

CHAPTER FOURTEEN

IN WHICH THINGS CHANGE
BUT ALSO STAY THE SAME

"There's been more fighting this week between the Changed and the battleborn, as they've begun calling themselves. One of the battleborn sirens told a dwarf to jump in a lake. He's fine, except for some frostbite, but he's demanding retribution. I agree that the siren should be punished, but that won't solve the lingering issues. The elves aren't helping matters, either. Any fight with an elf in the area is always at least three times worse. Something needs to be done. None of the younger newborn, fae or battleborn, know how to control their abilities, and they're causing havoc. Someone's going to get seriously hurt."

—Excerpt from the journals of Beira Thomson, Queen Titania

Owen wondered if he would ever witness one of his children beginning the Change when the news came less than a week later. Arthur and David had collapsed within minutes of each other, this time in the apartment while he was across the city helping at a worksite. By the time Mr. Moore finished saying Owen could leave, Owen was halfway across the worksite in a headlong dash through the crowd.

The boys would survive, he knew that now. Jen was waiting at home for him, living proof that Changing wasn't a death sentence, but he couldn't shake fear. Even if the kids had help Tiffany hadn't, he wasn't going to let them go through it without him.

There was a stitch in his side by the time he reached the Changing rooms. As was to be expected by this point, Beira was waiting in the hall outside.

"I'm curious," Owen asked, gasping for breath. He should be asking about the boys, but he was out of breath and for some reason this was the only thing he could focus on. "How is it you always beat me here? Do they—ha, do they tell you first or something because I'm—I'm almost positive you had a meeting today?"

Beira jumped. Odd, he would've thought she'd have heard him coming.

"Oh, no," she said in a flat voice, turning back to her papers. "The meeting was canceled. One of our patrols didn't report back. Enenra, Keme, and Aelfric took a team to check it out."

"Oh." He eased onto the bench next to her. "Is it serious?

"It's probably nothing," she said, paging through her notes. "But one of the gryphons found something near where they disappeared and it's got Aelfric up in arms. It's likely he's just being paranoid, but the fuss the Americans raised about your family had us concerned enough to check it out."

She paused and turned to him. "That reminds me. If all goes well this evening, I should be able to submit the paperwork for the majority claim this week."

Owen choked on air and had to struggle to remember how to breath properly. "The majority—you mean?"

"Yep," Beira said, her lackluster gaze going back to her papers. "Since three have Changed, we have enough of a claim on your family to get citizenship, the first step to getting you to Scotland."

"You mean it? I can't—I don't even—" Owen had almost forgotten about the majority claim, the first step to clearing his name, to going home and getting his kids somewhere they would be safe and still be able to live something like their old lives. He ran his hand through his hair, turned to thank her properly, and—stopped. "Are you all right? You look tired."

That was an understatement if he had ever uttered one. The bags under her eyes, already as big as dinner plates, looked like bruises on her paperwhite skin. Her hands shook as she flipped through her papers and her eyes kept fluttering shut. Had she even slept since the last time he'd seen her?

"Oh, I am," she said without looking up. "This week has been busier than usual." A yell punctured her sentence, the first since he had arrived.

Owen flinched. That was Arthur's voice; he was certain of it.

"Oh, I'm sorry," Beira said as the last of Arthur's scream faded away. She shoved her papers into their folder and set it aside. "I'm here for you, and I'm working instead of helping."

"No, it's fine," Owen said, although he flinched when another scream shattered the peace. "It keeps my mind off things."

Despite that hollow assurance, or perhaps because of it, the conversation between them didn't pick up again. The silence was punctuated only by Arthur's deep yells and the occasional quieter ones coming from David across the hall.

"Who's watching over the other three?" Beira asked after a few minutes. "Will they be all right with you staying here for however long this takes?"

The sudden question startled Owen so much he almost fell off his chair. From the way she had lapsed into contemplative silence, he had thought they would spend the evening without exchanging another word.

Still, he hadn't been lying. This was easier when he didn't have to go through it alone.

"Oh, one of our neighbors, Elenor, offered to watch them. Ashley said she and Jen might come by later to see how things are going." Owen had stopped by their apartment to check in before coming down, but Ashley had the situation well in hand and sent him to wait with the boys. "When Arthur realized what was happening, he sent Ashley to Elenor's with Dorothy so she wouldn't freak out. Jen went to find people to help the boys down here."

Beira nodded. "I see. Overall, they're not struggling to adapt to life here, though?"

"As far as I can tell." He shrugged. "Jen is having an easier time than I dared hope, and they're all enjoying being back at school, strange as that may sound." He kicked his legs out and folded his arms across his chest as David screamed for him. His fingers dug into his arms so hard they almost drew blood.

"I imagine it gives them something to focus on," Beira said as she massaged her temples. "The last two weeks have been rough."

"They have, but there's something here for each of them that takes their minds off of it."

It was true, they had each branched out, desperate to cling to something of their own when things were so unstable. David was taking classes on local medicinal herbs and how to use them. Jen and Arthur both preferred the more physically taxing classes, like bow hunting and scouting. Ashley studied under the local music teachers, seeking solace in the movement of her bow, and Dorothy, well, she and her stuffed lion spent most days with him at work or in their apartment being watched over by the growing number of neighbors at her beck and call. She liked being surrounded by people.

They settled in so well that he was hesitant about making them leave again. Their lives had already been upended once and living with the fae wasn't nearly as bad as he'd worried it was going to be. They could be happy here, if they wanted to be.

Owen and Beira fell into silence again. Why couldn't they manage to keep a decent conversation going at these things? Admittedly, the background ambience of screams and sobbing didn't do much to encourage conversation, but—no, that was a good excuse.

"You said there was some trouble out on the borders," he said, raising his voice to speak over the screams. "Is that something the rest of us need to be concerned about?" His fingers dug into his arm again as another scream pierced the air. He resisted the urge to check his watch; it was too early.

"No, but Aelfric wanted to check it out anyway," Beira said in tired voice. Her left hand inched toward her folder. "He's in charge of the rangers, and he takes care of his people. Losing an entire patrol hit him hard."

"You've lost a lot of people recently. First that troll, now this."

"I know," Beira said, groaning. "That's not all, either; things have been going wrong at both havens for the last few years. Enenra and Balder came over from the Summer Court as ambassadors, since the U.S. is putting pressure on the UK to close Daingneach's borders. A result of your rather dramatic departure, I'm afraid. It's likely nothing will come of it, but as closed off from the world as we are, we need to pay attention to what news we can get. There were supposed to be meetings all week, but now this has fallen into our laps. I'm not sure what will happen now." The words came like she was tired of trying to hold them back. She brought both hands up to rub her temples.

Owen took a moment to mull over the information he had been given. Not for the first time, he wished that the fae had more in the way of computers and other electronics. Being so out of the loop put him on edge.

"Did we cause much trouble for you?" he asked, resting his elbows on his knees. "Leaving like we did?"

Sighing, Beira rested her head against the wall. "No more than usual. This was always going to happen; they were always going to crack down on us. If not for your family, then for some imagined offense given however many years ago. The last fifty years has given each side time to lick its wounds but also time to dwell on the past. The time has come for something to give."

Her words had all the éclat of some ancient proverb, but dramatics aside, they didn't clear things up at all. A habit of Beira's, so it seemed. When she lost herself in thought rather than finish whatever she was saying, Owen nudged her to get her attention.

Beira stared at him, all trace of humor or goodwill gone from her face. "This is a dying city, Owen, and we a dying people. We cannot survive if the world continues to cut us off. Each year we lose more people to diseases and injuries we can't cure with song or what little knowledge we ourselves possess. Trade from Daingneach helps, but they cannot offer too much without hurting themselves."

If Owen had held some hope that Beira would relax as she vented, he was sorely disappointed. If anything, she got worse the longer she spoke, like some long and deeply held rage had finally found an outlet and was trying to break the dam. The darkness in her words pressed down on him, a physical weight crushing him like a vice. It promised vengeance for past wrongs and justice for the oppressed, a force that couldn't be stopped.

"You must understand, Owen," Beira said, unheeding of the effects brought by her words. "Change is coming. Those who drove you here won't give up that easy. We fought them to a standstill once, but I fear the next battle will require more than we can give." Impossibly, her voice

179

grew and grew, pressing down until he felt he couldn't breathe, and she kept going. "The winds of war blow, the battleborn cry for vengeance, and daily the whispers of freedom from our human oppressors grow. Soon we will outgrow what safety Tearmann offers us, and I fear what will happen to our people when we face the coming storm."

Almost as suddenly as it had begun, the maelstrom stopped, and Beira collapsed against him. Each breath came as a great heaving gasp, but still, she spoke.

"War comes, my brother, and I fear I am not strong enough to lead them this time."

Beira's harsh breathing filled the air, and Owen didn't dare to break the silence for fear she would speak again. Whatever that was, it had drained her. His heartbeat was so rapid and so strong he could have sworn it was bruising his chest. He had no idea what had just happened, but most fae wouldn't take finding him and the queen like this kindly. He was looking for the aide that normally followed her when a large first-gen angel turned the corner.

The angel, a stereotypically tall, blond, and winged Adonis, broke into a sprint when he saw them and fell to his knees once he reached them. If Owen hadn't been so worried about Beira and the boys, he would have marveled at the angel's speed. Almost as soon as his knees hit the floor, he grabbed the near-unconscious Beira's wrist and checked her pulse.

The angel glanced at Owen, bright wings fluttering behind him, and demanded he explain what had happened. As Owen had no clear idea himself, the explanation was lacking.

"She was talking with me, and all of a sudden, she got, I don't know, dark. Her voice got weird; she said some strange things and collapsed."

The angel cursed. "When you say 'dark,' did it feel like you couldn't breathe?"

Owen nodded, glancing between Beira, the angel and the boys' rooms. He couldn't remember the last time he'd heard a scream. "Well, yes. What happened?"

"She did something stupid," the angel said, wearing an expression almost as dark as Beira's voice had been. He stood, Beira in his arms, and moved toward the stairs.

Owen knew the chances of anyone in the capital hurting Beira were less than slim to none but wasn't willing to let this stranger take his friend away. He surged to his feet and grabbed the angel's arm before he could get too far. "Wait, who are you? Why should I let you take her? There are healers here."

The angel shook Owen's hand off and glared at him, a look that would have set him on fire had the angel loosed some of the power Eoire had said could flatten buildings. "You will release me," he said, the strength of his words practically compelling Owen to obey. "I am Lord Gabriel of the Founders Council. The healers here cannot help her, and I have to get her to those who can."

With those words, Lord Gabriel ripped his arm free and sprinted toward the stairs, leaving Owen alone with only the sound of the boys' renewed sobs to keep him company.

***

The remaining hours before either one of the boys emerged ticked by slowly. Jen and Ashley joined Owen four hours after he had first gotten the message and three after Beira had collapsed. Jen insisted they would have arrived earlier, but Dorothy hadn't wanted to go to bed and they'd had to stay with her 'til she did. Elenor was with her now.

He tried to send them back, but they came prepared with arguments, blankets, and pillows. Within minutes, the girls overwhelmed his half-hearted rebukes and set themselves up for the long haul.

They didn't speak much, but the silence was comforting in its own way. Even Jen seemed happy to curl against Owen and sketch instead of incessantly chatting, although Owen was certain that had more to do with her nagging worry for David than anything else. She confirmed this by unconsciously digging her claws into Owen's leg whenever David's hoarse voice reached them. Not being able to help David had always bothered her, and tonight was no exception.

"Jen, you don't have to be here," Owen said, running a hand through her hair. "David would understand."

Jen rolled her eyes. "You don't understand, Dad. I have to be there for him. He couldn't be there for me because he had to take care of Dorothy, but that's ok. He'll be scared when he gets done if I'm not there." She huffed, curling even more into his side as another muffled scream reached them. "Besides, Dad—" Her voice cracked. "I promised I would take him running with me when he got done."

And there it was. Jen and David were convinced that, as twins, they would both be werewolves. Owen, Andrew, Eoire, and Eleanor had each tried to bring them to terms with the idea that it might not happen with minimal luck.

"Jen, you know that he might not be like you."

She leaped off Owen's lap, heedless of her scattering pencils or of disturbing Ashley on his other side. "He will be," she said, snarling. Fire flashed in her eyes as her tail slashed through the air. "Jason told me species run in families, and we're twins so we're already alike."

Owen sighed. He wasn't in the mood to have this argument again, but he had been the one to bring the topic up, so he was the one who had to deal with the consequences. Even if they involved an angry, lupine eight-year-old. "I know what he said, but that's not always the case—"

Whatever he would have said was cut off when a feathered head poked out of David's room. Owen hadn't even noticed the screaming had stopped. The gryphon beckoned Owen toward him with one claw.

"Leave the girls. He wants to talk to you first." He wouldn't meet Owen's eyes, instead pulling back and leaving Owen to comfort the girls before he went in.

Owen couldn't remember a time when David had chosen to share something with him instead of Jen. "They probably want me to sign something and make sure I know how to handle him," he said, forcing a smile. "Nothing to worry about, right?"

"That's right," Ashley said when Jen tried to protest. "Eoire said they have to limit how many people are around right after the Change so they don't overwhelm him. We'll sit here and come in when he's ready." Her equally forced smile may have fooled Jen, but Owen could tell her thoughts ran along the same vein as his.

David hadn't been in there long enough to be a werewolf.

***

Owen was struck by déjà vu as he walked in. The gryphon and two sirens had taken the opportunity to slip out as his eyes adjusted to the dim light, leaving the elf who'd been there after Jen's Change to clean the room. What was his name? Trenton? Tom?

David sat on the cot in the middle of the room, the blanket slung over his head like a hood. It seemed David had taken after Jen in this. Quiet sniffles carried across the empty space to Owen.

Owen caught a glimpse of a pale, human hand holding the blanket shut as he sat down, and he knew why David was crying.

"David, she won't blame you," he said, reaching out to settle a hand on David's bony shoulder.

One of the few things that had kept the peace in the family since they had arrived was the knowledge that they would be together, that nothing would separate them. They were united as the only human family in the capital, and even after Jen had Changed, they had thought they would have time to come to terms with the idea of separation.

Owen didn't think the possibility of being different species had even been a serious concern for the twins. To have that dream—that ideal—shattered so thoroughly, to have to face the stark possibility of their own needs forcing them to live apart, was heartbreaking. After all, there were still three Williams left. If it could happen to Jen and David, it could happen to any of them.

Well, this conversation wasn't going to be pleasant no matter what. Now Owen had to work his way through the aftermath without tearing his family apart.

It began when the blanket fell from David's head and Owen got his first look at his son's new form. He didn't actually look all that different. His hair hadn't spread and his skin remained free of scales. There were no new limbs or gills peeking out from his neck.

He was slightly longer of limb than he'd been before, sort of stretched, like someone had pulled his limbs through a taffy puller. His eyes shone in the dim light, two minimoons reflecting the lamp light back into the world. But most telling, most heartbreaking, were the two pointed ears sticking out of his messy black hair. His son may not have been a werewolf, but all the same he'd become the only thing he could that Jen wouldn't be able to forgive him for.

"David—David, it's not your fault—" Owen rushed to say, but the tears rolled down David's cheeks faster than before.

"But Dad, she wanted to be an elf," David said through great heaving sobs. "And I—and I promised her that I would be a werewolf and that I wouldn't be an elf because it would make her sad that I was and she wasn't and—" He threw himself into Owen's chest and sobbed into his worn shirt.

This was worse than Owen had thought. He had known that Jen and David had been conspiring for days and that Jen had taken to trying to teach David how to be a werewolf, but to try to direct the Change? To reject what it made you as it made you? Owen may not know much about the whole process, but everything he had heard or discussed with those more knowledgeable than him had said that was a monumentally bad idea.

They should've known better. He should've talked to them more, put a stop to this long before now.

Those that tried to control the Change inevitably suffered more than others. This was a genetic process that ripped people apart and rebuilt them from their DNA up. It couldn't be stopped, couldn't be bargained with. Those that tried were never like normal fae. They looked and acted differently, and their bodies were almost always grotesque and deformed.

And David had tried to do it.

Owen raised his eyes to the elf in the corner. David was still sobbing and unable to answer him, but the elf could tell him what had happened.

"As far as we can tell, he was actually more successful than others who've tried it," the elf answered. "That may have something to do with how young he is, but I digress."

Owen's heart sank further still as the elf took a battered clipboard from the table behind him. This wasn't going to be good.

"From what we can tell, there are a few differences between him and other first-gen elves. For example, the bottoms of his feet are padded, and he has rudimentary claws on both his hands and his feet. His teeth are still human, but that might change as he ages and loses them," the elf read, his voice tinged with something that was either condemning or admiring.

The question of how he felt was answered with the elf's next sentence. "It's actually impressive, you know. The practice of trying to guide the Change was never formally outlawed, even if those on top disapproved of it. We could never get enough research on the topic to fully understand it, although many people tried. But, you should know"—he paused, his teeth worrying at his lip—"what your son did, guiding it like he did, should have been impossible. It never ends that well. The ones that try end up looking more like the battleborn than anything else."

Owen shuddered and pulled David closer to his chest. The battleborn weren't fae, not technically. They were relics of the Battle of Breckenridge, the last battle of the Fae War. No two looked the same and few resembled their parent species. Many had died in agony, unable to adapt, and others had taken their own lives rather than live in their new forms. He didn't want to imagine one of his children as one.

"But he looks normal," the elf continued as he ran a hand through his messy red hair, heedless of Owen's worry. "There's no trace of the sores or tumors that characterize the battleborn. The sirens in here earlier said that they'd never seen one like this. He's perfectly healthy. If anything—" He stopped short and paced around the room, too excited to go on.

"If anything, what?" Owen asked, shifting David onto his lap. His son wasn't what he should be, and he wanted to know everything there was about it. David's health could be in danger, and all this man could focus on was how interesting this whole thing was. Of course, his excitement literally charging the air was not helping matters.

The elf stopped and looked at David, a gleam in his eyes and the air shimmering with his enthusiasm. "His abilities, the elven empathy, they're far more developed than they should be. You can't tell because I put a block up, but he made Ezekiel, the gryphon, sob after he finished Changing. Normally, elves can't affect other people for weeks, but he did it in moments. Whatever he did enhanced his abilities beyond anything I've ever seen."

The silence that followed was so complete Owen almost thought he'd gone deaf. Even David stopped crying as the words sunk in. The air around the elf was still filled with the electricity of his excitement, which combined with Owen's sinking dread in ways that made him want to vomit.

David was powerful, more powerful than any of these healers had ever seen. Whatever he had done had worked, if not in the way he intended. Werewolves were stronger than the humanoid species, and now David was stronger than most elves.

"Am I stronger than Eoire?" David asked in a small, scared voice.

Owen swallowed. Eoire was the strongest empath among the elves, as far as he knew, and she had taken the time to sit down with the Williams after his first meeting with Beira and explain the careful politics behind elven and siren abilities. If David was as strong as this elf was claiming, there would be trouble ahead.

"Not yet," the elf answered, shaking his head. "Perhaps in the future, if your abilities keep growing."

"What does this mean then?" Owen croaked, struggling to picture the power the elf was implying David might have. Eoire impacted anyone within fifty feet of her whether she wanted to or not. If David was anywhere near that powerful now . . . Cor, there was no way he'd be able to live in Scotland. It'd be insane to let him out of Tearmann until he was grown.

The elf—Travis, that was his name—shrugged. "For now? Nothing much. He gets lessons on controlling his abilities from the Athrawon, those who teach us how to control our emotions, and he goes back to his life. Some of the others will want to examine him—"

Owen's head snapped up and his eyes shot flames. If he'd been an angel, Travis would've been dead, turned to a pile of ash on the floor.

The air around them became calm, completely devoid of the excitement of before as Travis raised his hands to placate Owen. "Nothing invasive. They want to make sure that he's healthy. Anything else is completely up to you—and, well, him, but mostly you."

Owen breathed a sigh of relief and he leaned down to kiss the top of David's head. If there was one thing he should have learned to count on in this city, it was the emphasis on free will and the intense dislike of being treated like a lab rat. No one would force them to do anything. They were safe.

"How will these changes impact his development?" he asked after a moment.

Travis shrugged again. "We'd need to look more closely at them, but that can be handled later. We already know he's healthy, and now he needs comfort more than he needs to be examined. I just need to take some measurements, and then you can take him home. Try to get him to the hospital in the next few days, where one of the sirens can examine him and tell you more."

Owen wasn't able to get anything more out of Travis. Instead, the two of them helped David dress and finished a rudimentary examination of David's differences.

It was only as they were about to walk out the door that David stopped. His head was bowed, and he looked like he may start crying again.

Owen knelt in front of his son and waited for him to speak.

"Dad, what do I do? I tried, but I messed up. And now—" His voice cracked and a single tear dripped down his cheek. "Now we're not alike anymore."

At some point in the last two weeks, Owen had thought his heart couldn't break anymore. Blast, he should have stopped this nonsense before it got this far. "Hey," he whispered. "Is that what this is about, that you don't look alike?"

David shook his head, tears streaming down faster than he could wipe them away. "No." He took a shuddering breath. "No, it's not that. It's—Elves aren't like werewolves. My teacher said that they don't think the same, they're different inside. Jenny and I—we're twins. We're supposed to be alike, everyone says so, but now we're not." His bottom lip trembled and he only lasted a second before he gave hoarse cry and threw his arms around Owen's neck.

Owen tried to comfort him and rubbed soothing circles into David's shoulders as he cried. His voice cracked and broke and the sobs sounds like nails running down a chalkboard, but somehow he still had tears to cry. Eventually, even those died down to the occasional hitching breath, but David kept his head pushed into his father's shoulder.

"David," Owen whispered when he was comfortable enough to risk speech. "This won't stop you and Jen from being twins. You were still twins, even though you didn't look alike when you were human, right? She has blonde hair and you have black, and she was bigger than you.

But you were still twins, still family. It doesn't matter what you look like or what you are as long as you know that."

"But we're different—"

"Listen," Owen said. He needed to finish what he was saying before it was too late to convince David it was all right. "People are different, everyone. They don't stop being them because something changed. You and Jen were always you and Jen, and you will continue to be you and Jen, even though you look different than before. That's not a bad thing. Life would be boring if everybody were the same, wouldn't it?"

David pulled back from his father and wiped his tears using the cuff of his sweater. "But Dad, I don't want everybody to be the same. I want to be like Jen."

"But David, you wouldn't be you if you were like Jen," he said, grabbing his son's chin and turning it up. "Don't you think she would prefer it if you were you instead of someone else? She might be sad you can't go on runs like you planned, or compare fur, or tails or, whatever else you wanted to do. She may even be angry for a while, but one day she will be so thankful that you're an elf, that you're you. And no matter what, she will love you as you are, I promise."

David looked at him with wide, tear-stained eyes. "Do you really think she'll still like me?"

Owen chuckled and leaned forward to kiss David's forehead. "Of course. She's your sister. That's what they do best."

A bright laugh burst out of David and he covered his mouth to hide a smile. Owen felt a sharp burst of joy and a part of him wondered if Travis's block was still in place, but he didn't really care. David was happy now.

"Well then, David." Owen stood and messed David's hair. "Let's not keep them waiting."

***

True to his predictions, Jen—despite the tears threatening to fall—managed to look, well, not happy, but not upset that David wasn't a werewolf like she was, although some of her concerns were alleviated by David showing her his additions. His claws were a big hit, at least, as well as his padded bare feet. Owen debated whether it was his imagination or not that David's hair seemed thicker, but he didn't care to check.

Citing the late hour, he suggested the girls and David go to bed, but was overruled. They refused to move while Arthur was still in trouble. Faced with such a united front, Owen had to concede.

By his watch, it had been approximately seven hours since this whole debacle had started. According to Beira, the next tier was passed at the twelve-hour mark, and after that—well, after that, he would send them home no matter what happened.

They passed the time with games both old and new. Tag had been ruled out, as none of them wanted to get lost in the tunnels or be too far away to help if needed, as well as most singing or running games. Ashley offered a compromise and suggested the twins play a hearing game where she would walk away 'til one of them could no longer make out her breathing.

It was staggering how well they could hear now, Owen mused as Jen gave up in a fit of mock outrage when Ashley was fifty feet away. He would have to remember that if he tried to keep anything from them.

Arthur's voice gave out two hours later, which gave them some peace, even if it was worrying. Jason had said the silence meant that the Change was drawing to a close, but Owen took it with a pinch of salt. According to Beira, the screams, like everything else concerning the Change, depended on the person. They could debate symptoms and timetables all they liked, but nothing was set in stone. Whatever the silence meant, he was glad of it. Things were calmer when they weren't trying to ignore agonizing screams.

Eventually, though, the games stopped, and Ashley, Jen, and David came back to Owen. The twins curled up around each other and fell asleep, and Ashley took up her book again at his left side. It was almost anticlimactic when the door to Arthur's room opened.

A battered elf Owen didn't recognize limped out around four in the morning and told Owen he needed to go in alone before stumbling off.

Owen stood, reassured the others that everything would be fine, and entered, wary of what he would find there. The other healers left as he walked in, leaving a siren behind to finish up.

Arthur made no attempt to hide his new condition, a refreshing change from the twins' secrecy. A blanket was folded at the end of the cot, and a shirtless Arthur sat in the middle, staring at the wall in front of him.

Arthur's skin was gray and sickly and his hair had fallen out in clumps. From Owen's angle, he couldn't make out any new limbs or odd glowing, but there was something on his neck that could have been gills. Arthur didn't look like any of the first-gens Owen knew.

"They said my skin will slough off in the next few days. Scales will replace it if that's what you're wondering." Arthur's voice was . . . alarming. He didn't sound hurt or scared or concerned. He sounded empty.

None of his characteristic cheer or wit were present. Even the obvious hoarseness couldn't account for how dead he sounded. There was nothing in his voice, no inflection, no emotion.

"So you're a siren, then?" Owen asked as he eased down on the cot next to Arthur.

Arthur nodded without moving his eyes from the wall. It was more than a little unnerving. Owen turned to the only other person in the room, a siren he'd seen in passing in their neighborhood. He might be able to explain what had happened.

"He's struggling," the siren said as he stuffed dirty sheets into a bag. "Sirens feel things differently. It has to do with our song. Humans are especially vulnerable, though, so he's trying to not affect you."

"What does that mean, exactly?" Owen asked, half-standing. "I thought siren abilities didn't kick in for a week or so." He glanced back at Arthur. Was he different, like David, he wanted to ask.

The siren nodded. "That's mostly true. It takes approximately six days for the full impact of our abilities to touch us, but fresh as he is he could do something. He'll spend the next two days recovering with you, but then he'll need to go with some of our singers to learn how to control his abilities. Your other boy, the elf, will need to go away as well. They have to learn to control themselves before we let them out in public."

Owen nodded numbly. He had known that this could happen. At one of their talks, Beira had spent twenty minutes going over the various training regimes first-gens had to go through before they were considered fit for society.

Werewolves, dwarves, and the like could go out right away, as their issues lay with their senses and their muscles, but elves, sirens, angels, and dragons had to leave while they came into their abilities. There was just too much risk to the public for them to stay in populated areas.

"I understand," he said hoarsely. "Is there anything else I need to know?" Fear and worry and anger mixed themselves into one giant mess, a ball that felt trapped in his throat.

The siren nodded again. "His teeth are going to fall out in the next few days, so you need to keep an eye on what he eats while his new ones grow in. There's not much else you can do for him, but try to make sure his scales are clean and that he doesn't pick at his skin. We don't want him hurting himself."

There were a few more instructions relating to things like diet and dental care, but soon enough the siren finished the last measurement. He gave Arthur a pair of shorts, as his skin was too sensitive to wear much until his scales grew in, and shoved them out the door.

CHAPTER FIFTEEN

IN WHICH OWEN LEARNS THINGS
HE WISHES HE NEVER KNEW

"We've managed to stabilize our population centers in the last few years. Most of us live in Tearmann, but the angels and the battleborn struck out on their own. I wish they had waited; Beira isn't well. She doesn't have the energy to deal with establishing two settlements in addition to her duties here. It's concerning that she's been getting sicker and sicker for the last decade. I don't want to consider it, but if she doesn't get better, we may have to take extreme actions."

—Excerpt from the journals of Gabriel Clark, Lord Gabriel

Jen was not happy when she heard her brothers had to leave, something she made known as often and loudly as possible and nothing Owen said made any difference. She had made her decision and would not be swayed. As far as she was concerned, anything that made David leave her sight wasn't worth learning.

She kept complaining even after Andrew and Eoire came to take Arthur and David to their respective training facilities, biting and snapping at anyone who came close. Owen was more than a little concerned that this would bring back her dark feelings toward the fae; luckily, that didn't seem to be the case. Instead, desperate to forget they wouldn't be there when she got back, she spent as much time as she could out of the apartment.

He brought it up during a chess game with Beira in her apartment, something they'd picked up when Beira had learned he played. Apparently, she hadn't had someone new to play against in a decade. "I'm worried about them, Jen especially, but Ashley and Dorothy as well. Having the boys gone hasn't been easy for them."

"They're young," Beira answered, the first time she had spoken since setting up the chess board. "They'll recover, but it will take time." Her voice was stilted and formal, with no attempt to put him at ease. She was fidgeting too, something she never did. Owen was about to ask about it, but she saved him the trouble.

"I wanted to apologize for my actions the other day. I wasn't . . ." She faltered and looked away. "I wasn't myself. It won't happen again."

"What exactly did happen?" he asked, daring to look up. He'd wondered but hadn't wanted to bring it up. "That angel—Lord Gabriel—he didn't tell me anything. And you look fine now."

She looked more tired than usual, he didn't say, but the frightening paleness was gone.

"Gabriel worries," she said, smiling weakly. "He was a biologist before this, and he knows more about our physical makeup than most, including our weaknesses." She moved a bishop, putting Owen into check. "He is the head of the healers and physicians in the capital, though, so perhaps I should listen to him more than I do."

"A biologist?"

"Yes. There was some debate about it when the matter was put in the hands of the Medical Corps, but most thought he was a better judge of how each of our nonhuman bits went together than anyone else. Our medical professionals were limited to human anatomy at the time, and most of our vets had specialized in small animals. He was able to marry the two professions in a way that meant he was best suited for the position."

"Oh," Owen said, dropping his gaze back to the board. His cheeks burned. He should've known Lord Gabriel had been elected. That was, after all, the way of things among the fae. You had to earn a position if you wanted it, and corruption or nepotism were severely punished. For rulers who had complete control of their followers, the founders were remarkably devoted to making sure their power wasn't abused.

"If it makes you feel better, he doesn't think he should have the position either. He plans to step down after the next election cycle."

"Oh? Why is that?" Most people didn't like giving up power once they had it, even if they hadn't wanted it in the first place. "Is he stepping down because they found someone better?"

"He wants to retire to a more research-based position now that we have more people trained in fae medicine." Beira said as she picked up a captured knight and rolled it in her palms.

"I see." They played a few more turns in silence. "What's the difference between physicians and healers?" he asked, moving his king behind a rook.

"Pardon?"

"Physicians and healers. You've mentioned them several times, but I'm not certain I know the difference between the two."

Beira looked up from the board, a single eyebrow arched in surprise. "Healers are those who can provide some natural ability, such as the sirens and elves," she said. "Physicians are trained in medicine, although many use the two terms interchangeably."

Owen was going to lose; it was only a matter of time and how much she wanted to humiliate him. He was debating whether to move his rook or risk his queen when he realized Beira had never answered his first question.

"What happened to you? You never said—although you don't have to answer if you don't want to."

Beira leaned back in her chair. "No, it's fine." She sighed and massaged her temples. "You deserve an explanation."

Owen waited for her to continue and lost his rook and two pawns in the meantime.

"What do you know about vampires?" she asked abruptly, fiddling with her copper bracelet.

"Besides the obvious?" Owen asked. He tented his fingers as he considered his next move. "Well, you're the only one. You have some kind of control over the other fae, although I'm not sure if it extends to the other founders or not, and the humans think you're dead." He shifted back in his seat and examined the board. Perhaps it was time for him to surrender. There was no way to salvage this situation.

"What about the vampires of myth?" Beira asked.

He snorted. "What, like Dracula and that nonsense?"

She nodded, a quick and jerky gesture.

"Oh, well"—Owen paused, digging through his memory for the last time he'd actually read or seen anything about vampires—"they need to drink blood, like you, although most can only drink human blood, and in large amounts. They can't go out in sunlight, be near garlic or holy objects, don't reflect in mirrors, and they tend to be charismatic."

"Odd," Beira said as she captured his last pawn, leaving Owen with his king and queen. "You left out the one thing that everyone comments on, the only other thing that I have in common with mythological vampires."

He shifted in his seat. "Oh? What'd I miss?"

"Owen," she said, finally looking him in the eye. "New vampires are made, not born. I'm the only vampire by choice, not nature."

"And? Are you getting lonely?" he asked, raising an eyebrow.

"How many founders are there, Owen? Not including myself, of course." Beira moved her knight, putting him into checkmate and taking him out of his misery.

"Um . . ." He counted in his head. "Twenty-two, two for each species."

"And doesn't it strike you as odd that there are two of every other species but not vampires?" She picked up the captured king and rolled it between her fingers.

"Well, I suppose it is, now that you mention it." His breath caught at the implication. "Wait, are you saying that there's another vampire out there?"

"I was not supposed to be the only one, no."

"So there isn't another vampire?"

Beira set the king back onto the table and leaned back into her chair. "No, there's not. And if I have my way, there won't be. If I'm being honest, there can't be. Not yet."

"Why is that?" From what Owen could tell, having another vampire certainly wouldn't harm anything. It might even help matters.

This was the first time in their acquaintance that Beira looked at him like he was an idiot. "Owen, vampires aren't like the other species," she said slowly. "We're the controllers, the alphas. We can order other fae to do anything. Not just the founders, like with the other species, any vampire could order any fae to do anything they wanted. There cannot be another vampire until we know they wouldn't abuse that power, something easier said than done. But even so, we need one desperately."

That wasn't a comforting thought. Owen had known that Beira was powerful in the same way he knew water was wet or Arthur needed coffee in the morning before he could be trusted with a razor. Sort of out of the way, something you didn't think about until someone reminded you of it. She could order anyone, his children even, to do what she wanted. Up to and including self-violence, if even half of the stories and her repeated warnings were true.

"Why?" he asked hoarsely. The thought of another out there with Beira's power filled his mind with gruesome images. He barely trusted her with it. "Why do you need another?"

"Several reasons." Beira stood and began to search through the numerous stacks of books, papers, and files in her living room. "First and foremost because there is no one who can overthrow me should it become necessary; I am under no delusions about my own fallibility. Controls need to be in place should something happen that necessitates my removal. Second, as it stands, the fae will die to a man if the vampires die out. We are intrinsically linked, and the fate of one is the fate of the other. Finally, and perhaps most importantly, the strain of being the only vampire is killing me. Unless we find another, I will die within the next fifty years and with me the fae."

She made a small victorious noise as she pulled a battered green notebook from a teetering stack of files. She dropped it on the table between them. "This a collection of notes recovered from Nathaniel Smith's labs. Do you know who that is?"

Owen blinked at her, jaw silently working up and down. She was dying, and if she did, the fae would die. Three of his children would die if she died. "No, no, I do not know who that is. And—and what do you mean find another? I thought that there were no others. What does this have to do with you collapsing the other day? Why are you telling me this?"

Beira knelt at his side, pushed his head between his knees, and ordered him to take deep breaths. "I'm getting there, but you have to calm down. Here, I'll get you some water."

His hands shook as he took the glass from her a minute later, drained it, and collapsed back into his chair.

This was not information he wanted to know. She could make other vampires? Fine. She needed to make another vampire, one who could potentially lead the fae in an involuntary civil war against her, or she was going to die and all the rest of the fae were going to die with her? Not fine. No, this was too much.

Beira must have thought he looked better because she started speaking again. "I'm connected, after a fashion, with each fae. There are more than a million of us worldwide, so you can imagine how overwhelming that can be. The strain of handling it by myself is part of the reason I collapsed." She paused and chewed over her next words. "The thing is, that connection is what keeps the fae alive. We tried removing it in the beginning, but every test subject died within minutes."

"So"—he made himself take a deep breath—"would having another vampire help fix it? Would it stop the deaths?"

"Honestly?" She shrugged. "We don't know for sure. Once again, this"—she grabbed the notebook on the table to his left and shook it in front of him—"is all we know. Nathaniel Smith is the man who created us, the founders at least. These are his notes, what little we were able to recover from the lab after he died. We burned the rest."

That got Owen's attention. "His notes? On how he made the fae?"

Nathaniel Smith was a name he knew, now that he thought about it, the rogue scientist who'd made the first fae. The man himself had been dead since before the war, but his lab had been raided before the end of it by researchers trying to find weaknesses. He didn't think anything of value had been found. If that little green notebook held what Beira seemed to think it did, there was a reason for that.

"Yes. There was a method behind his madness, at least as far as the founders were concerned. The mental load for each species was supposed to be split between the Founders, although having a male and a female was allegorical on his part. It fed nicely into his god complex. Male and female he created them, and all that." There was more bitterness in Beira's voice than Owen would have expected, but Nathaniel had ruined her life—and the lives of thousands of other people, come to think of it.

"So what happened to the male vampire, then?" Part of him knew the answer already, as several different puzzle pieces had clicked into place, but he had to ask anyway.

"Oh, Nathaniel was supposed to be the other vampire, the king to my queen, as it were," Beira said as she stood and went back to her chair. "It didn't work. He didn't have whatever it was that meant he could survive the Change. His death triggered the Change worldwide, although it was smaller than his notes indicated it would be. Some of our researchers theorized that there are supposed to be more of us since it's genetic, but because he died and left us without a male vampire it wasn't as widespread as it was supposed to."

"So what? Does that mean that a new vampire would—?" Owen couldn't even get the question out. It had been chaos the first time, even with the relatively few fae involved. The world hadn't gotten any more accepting either; a resurgence of Changes might even lead to another war.

"Theoretically, at least," she said, slumping back in her chair. "Hopefully, society will have advanced far enough by the time such a step becomes necessary that things won't happen the way they did last time. But I'm not too hopeful."

"Christ, how do you even go about finding these vampires?" Owen asked, wiping his forehead. "Do you bite some random human, or are only fae able to survive it?"

"No," she said. "Normal humans aren't compatible with vampirism. We tried, they have to be faeborn at the very least or they'll die, like Nathaniel. And fae who have already Changed aren't options either."

His jaw dropped. "But—I thought you couldn't tell who was going to be fae until they had already Changed, barring tracing family lines," he said, the words falling out of his mouth in a jumble. "No one can trace it."

"Eh." Beira tilted her head. "That's not strictly true. I can taste whether someone is faeborn through their blood and make a guess as to what they'll be, but we can't test everyone like that. Even most faeborn aren't compatible."

He leaned forward, tented his hands, and looked at her between his fingers. "So you're telling me you have no way to tell who can be a vampire, but if you don't find one, then you'll all die."

198

"More or less, yes."

Owen ran a hand over his face. "How do you even know that other vampires exist? What if Nathaniel intended for the two of you to be the only ones?"

"No, I know there are other vampires. Do you honestly think a man smart enough to create twelve unique sentient species wouldn't take into account the possibility of the leaders dying? He made sure there would be vampires, but he also made sure they were hard to find so they couldn't be used against him."

The silence between them was deafening and the tail end of her outburst hung in the air.

Truly, this was the most energetic Owen had ever seen Beira, and it was done to defend a man she rightfully hated. But it wasn't defense so much as desperation. Her eyes were blown wide and begged him to believe her, to validate her search, since the lives of every one of her people relied on her success.

The clock on the wall rang the hour, reminding him that he had to make his way back home soon. But he couldn't leave yet, not when he had so many questions left.

"Why are you telling me this?" he asked. He hadn't factored worrying about a species-wide extinction into his evening plans.

"Because you deserved an explanation, because I trust you, because you're my friend. Do I need a reason? I have a thousand more if you need to hear them."

"What was the other reason you collapsed?" he asked. "You said that the thing was part of it but not the rest." His mind drifted, filled to the brim with questions he had no answers for and questions he didn't want the answers for.

"Oh, that." Beira turned her head and picked at a loose thread on her chair. "I was thirsty."

"You were thir—oh." Owen pushed himself back before he could stop himself. Gripping his armrests, he swallowed and tried to remember how to speak calmly. He trusted her now, he reminded himself, and she'd promised she wouldn't drink from him. "Are you . . . feeling better now?" This was the first direct reference to her drinking that she'd made since their first meeting. And what an uncomfortable one it was, as she had had her teeth far too close to his neck for his peace of mind when she'd collapsed.

"Yes," Beira said, quick to reassure him. "Gabriel grabbed one of my donors and a few rabbits. Don't worry."

"Did the, uh, stress make it worse than normal?" Owen asked as he slowly sat down again. "The thirst?"

"A bit," she said, nodding. "The longer I go without a partner, the shorter the time between my feedings. The connection can overwhelm me when I'm not at my strongest. Anything I said during that time was influenced by the multitude of minds."

Beira was entirely too blasé with this topic for Owen's comfort. The collective will of an entire people sometimes overcame her and made her do creepy things like spout dire apocalyptic prophecies, and she acted like it was nothing. He would have been more concerned had he been in her shoes.

He let out a sharp laugh. Was this his life now? A month ago, he'd been worrying about whether he would be able to finish his latest commission on time. Three weeks ago he'd just wanted to find his kids after Tiffany died. Now he had to worry about the early death of not only his children but an entire culture and whether the woman across from him might give into her baser urges, and not in a fun way.

His entire life had been uprooted, and he couldn't help but feel he was coming closer and closer to losing his children each time one of them Changed. Jen spent more time in the company of other werewolves than she did at the apartment, and he didn't even want to think about what things would be like when the boys came back. It was hard to look at the mess that was his life now and not feel like everything he was trying to protect was slipping through his fingers.

"Is there anything else you want to get off your chest before I leave this evening?" Owen asked and swallowed to relieve his parched throat. "I mean, we've covered your dating troubles and the potential extinction of the fae."

Beira laughed, echoing his earlier hysteria, which made him feel bad. He was in no way impacted by this situation to the extent she was. How exactly did one deal with the fate of literally hundreds of thousands of people hanging over their head?

"No, I think you covered everything. Although there is one other matter." That made Owen look up. Nothing that had been discussed today was comforting. "Nothing earth breaking, I assure you; you can stop looking at me like I'm about to drop a nuke on you. The council wants to meet with you in three days' time."

"Oh, is that all?" he asked, sinking back into his chair and rubbing his eyes. Andrew had mentioned that the council would likely want to meet with him when they'd first arrived. He had been expecting this, but not now.

Another glance at the clock told him he needed to be going if he wanted to eat dinner with his children. He was glad to take the excuse to leave. He needed time to think, to process what he had been told.

"Owen," Beira said, stopping him at the door. "I hope this goes without saying, but I'd like you to keep the things we discussed here quiet. And the collapse as well. It wouldn't go well if people heard that the only thing keeping them alive was giving out."

"I understand," he said, taking a deep breath and releasing it. They should know, he wanted to say. She didn't have a right to keep something like this from them. "I won't tell anyone, I promise. Is there anything else?"

Beira's eyes filled with relief and she dropped her arm. "I'll drop by your apartment when the boys get back home. I need to perform the welcoming ceremonies, as I wasn't able to the other night."

He nodded, said goodbye, and left, eager to get away from the apartment, which felt increasingly small, and the woman with the weight of the world on her shoulders.

***

It was nearing nine in the evening when Jen finally came home. He could hear her outside the door, thanking the people she had spent the day with. Dorothy had gone to bed an hour ago, and he had sent Ashley to his room so she could do her homework without waking her sister. He needed to have a talk with Jen, and it was better it was done alone.

The door squeaked open, accompanied by the quiet clicking of claws. He waited until Jen had closed the door before speaking. "Jen. How was your day?" He would have laughed at the way she jumped on any other day, but he wasn't in the mood after what he had learned that afternoon.

"It was fine," she said without meeting his eyes as she hung her jacket and bag with her drawing supplies on the hooks by the door. "I went with some of the other werewolves at school to a nearby spring."

"Were there any adults?" It never used to be this hard to talk with Jen. Hell, they hadn't been able to keep her quiet. Just one more way they'd all changed since they'd come here.

Jen shrugged as she padded past him into the kitchen, where Owen had left a sandwich for her. At least she came back into the living room with it instead of escaping to the boys' room, where she had been sleeping since they'd Changed. "One of the pack elders was there, the Olson pack, I think."

"Are you going with them again tomorrow?" he asked once she had finished eating.

"Maybe," she said, eyes downcast. Why wouldn't she look at him? "One of the trolls invited me down to look at the livestock. I might go with him."

Owen sighed, both tired and concerned. Things had never been this hard before. "Jen, is everything all right? You haven't been yourself recently."

"I'm fine, Dad. Just tired." Her smile didn't reach her eyes.

"All right, if you're sure," he replied, forcing himself to drop his defenses even it did nothing to quell his worry. "I'm going to bed soon, but I'll be out here for a bit longer if you need anything."

"Yes, Dad," Jen said. She was almost to the boys' door when he called out again.

"You do know you can talk to me about anything, right?"

For a moment, it looked like she was going to take him up on his offer. Hope rose in his chest only to be squashed when she shook her head instead.

"I know," she said. "And I will, but I'm fine."

Owen nodded and tried not to look crestfallen. Perhaps he would have better luck in the morning. Worries consumed him, rolling and rocking in his stomach, and would have stopped him from sleeping even if he had wanted to. He stared at the door for a long time, lost in his thoughts as he considered all he had learned that evening and everything he wished he could forget.

CHAPTER SIXTEEN

IN WHICH OWEN MEETS
THE OTHER PEOPLE IN CHARGE

"It has been decided that we need a central government. As there are twenty-three people conveniently arrayed in positions of authority, there seems to be such an infrastructure already in place. Of course, most of us have been working as generals and leaders already, so it's not all that much different. Someone came up with the great idea to call us the Founders Council, as it's a council made up of, wait for it, the Founders. Tacky, I know, but it could be worse."

—Excerpt from the journals of Stephen Andrews-Conway, Lord Aelfric

The next two days came and went much the same as the days before. Jen was anywhere but the apartment, Ashley went to school and helped take care of Dorothy, and Owen went to work. Evenings were spent in their own corners of the apartment, without much interaction. Life slowed to a crawl, and one event bled into the next with little to distinguish them. The prospect of the council meeting the morning of the third day brought a relief from the monotony.

"Now, you remember the rules when you're at Mr. Abnell's?" Owen asked Dorothy as they walked out of the apartment, heading toward the small daycare where she would spend the day.

"Yes, Daddy."

He laughed and mussed her hair. "Oh? And what are they?"

They'd had this discussion every time she had stayed with Mr. Abnell. It wasn't that he didn't trust her; it was that she was her mother's child and prone to forgetting silly things like safety precautions when she saw something interesting. It was in everyone's best interest that he kept reminding her.

"Stay there, get a grown-up if someone gets hurt, share my toys, and listen to Mr. Abnell," she listed off as her eyes almost rolled out of her head.

"Good, but you've forgotten the most important one, I'm afraid." He schooled his face into a serious expression, suppressing the urge to smile when she screwed her face up in concentration.

"Oh yeah," she said as her eyes lit up. "I need to have fun!"

"Of course," Owen said, laughing as he swung her up onto his hip. "How could you forget that? It's the most important thing anyone does in their day. Now, what're you going to do today, Miss Dot?"

And so the conversation continued, with Dorothy chattering about her toys and how many games she was going to play. Owen almost wished the walk was longer when they reached the daycare, as Dorothy was in the middle of a spirited re-enactment of one of her friends playing a trick on another.

"—and then Jingyi cried and Toby tried to make Abel give it back and Mr. Abnell had to come over."

"Oh? And what did he do?"

"He put Toby and Abel in timeout while he helped Jingyi pick up." She spoke of their punishment with all the levity of someone describing the fate of some heinous criminal, a mass murderer perhaps. She would have gone on, but she realized where they were.

"Mr. Abnell, Mr. Abnell," she yelled when Owen pushed open the door to a brightly painted room full of wooden and stuffed toys. "Daddy says that I get to stay with you today. Is Jingyi here? And Henry? And Sophie? And—"

"My dear," the elderly werewolf said as he set his book aside. "I'm afraid you're the first one here, although the others won't be long. Why don't you go pick out the game we're going to play this morning as a special treat?"

Mr. Abnell shared a toothy grin with the bouncing four-year-old. His long canines and other wolfish incisors peeked past his lips, something that would have made Owen uneasy if he hadn't had at least seven different people tell him how protective werewolves were of children.

To hear the stories told about Mr. Abnell alone, you would think he had ripped soldiers apart with his bare hands to protect little fae children. Admittedly, that wasn't something Owen would put past him, as Mr. Abnell hadn't let himself go to waste as he had aged. Even approaching his twelfth decade, he could probably take on most of the younger werewolves and a good portion of anyone else who wanted to challenge him.

Dorothy hugged Owen tightly before she raced to the toy box with single-minded devotion.

"I'll be back for her when the meeting is done," he told Mr. Abnell as they watched her dig through the toys. "Andrew said that's usually about five, although I don't know if I have to stay the whole time."

It took a great deal of effort, as it always did, but Owen pulled himself away and walked to the political district on the other side of the third floor. If he hadn't spent the last few weeks learning to navigate the warren of rooms and hallways that made up the third floor, he would have gotten lost; he almost did anyway and only managed to find his destination five minutes before the meeting was supposed to start.

A bored-looking harpy sitting at a desk in front of the council chamber waved him in, far too used to him breezing past with Beira over the last few weeks. Owen paused outside the heavy doors, his hand poised to knock. Council meetings etiquette hadn't been covered by Beira or his etiquette seminars, and a sudden case of nerves struck him. He swallowed, forced himself to open the doors, and stepped into a veritable wall of sound.

All around him, first-gens of all species talked over each other. At one end of the room, near Beira's throne, Lady Guivre was speaking with a red dragon that had to be her husband, Lord Fafnir; across from them, Lord Balder and Lady Audhild were arguing with a young troll, Lord Bress, and next to them, two centaurs were animatedly discussing poetry.

There were more founders in this room than he had ever seen in one place. He felt lost in the cacophony. Or at least he did until Lord Bress noticed him frozen in the doorway.

"Oi, Aud, is this him?" Bress jumped over the railing between the founders' chairs and the open floor and bounded up to him.

"James Cooney, pleasure to meet you. You must be Owen Williams, then? I've heard so much about you."

And now Owen had to change his first impression of the man because now he reminded him of an overeager puppy more than anything else. He also hadn't stopped shaking Owen's hand.

"Ah, yes. It's a pleasure to meet you too, Lord Bress." That made Bress wrinkle his face in disgust like a cocky and brash twenty-year-old.

"Ugh, don't call me that. I get enough of it from everyone else."

A giant of an elf, likely Lord Aelfric, scoffed and drew Owen's eyes toward the corner where he'd been hidden. "You know that in all official functions our formal titles must be observed, Bress."

Bress dropped Owen's hand and spun around. "But Stephen, Beira and the notetaker aren't even here yet. We don't have to be all formal."

As if his words had been a summons, the door to Beira's office opened and the woman in question stepped out, followed by a plump, nervous-looking blonde elf carrying a thick folder. The last bit of their conversation carried into the room as Beira walked her companion to the door. "... Remember to get the condolences to me by tomorrow afternoon. I'll sign and deliver them myself. Send the first builder to me in the morning; we need to go over mine safety measures."

"Understood," the elf said. "I'll get the paperwork to you as soon as possible." The door closed behind her with a thud, and Beira slumped against it, rubbing her forehead.

After a moment, she looked up and glared at the other founders. "Seriously, guys? She was nervous as is, and you lot have to go and make things worse by going quiet when we come in? Now I'll have to apologize to her."

There was a fair amount of awkward shuffling and refusal to meet her eyes going on between the founders.

Lord Bress rubbed the back of his neck. "Sorry. You kind of came in during a lull in the conversation. We didn't mean to make her uncomfortable."

She rolled her eyes as she walked across the room. "Yes, there was a lull because Mr. Williams came in." She looked at Owen, concern turning her scowl into a smile. "Incidentally, how are you? These lugs haven't managed to scare you off, have they?"

"Oh, uh, no. It's fine," Owen said. "We were just saying hello."

Beira nodded and made her way to her throne, the simple one on the raised dais.

It must have been a cue, as everyone sat when she did. He noticed that a few thrones were still empty, the perches he'd seen on his first visit among them. Presumably, they were for the founders still in Daingneach.

Beira's voice snapped him from his thoughts. "Owen, please sit down." She gestured toward a simple chair in the middle of the room. He sat, keenly aware of every eye on him. Across the way and next to the empty throne by Beira, a small shade sat ready with a notebook to take notes on the meeting. The shade smiled at Owen when he noticed him looking.

"All take note," the shade announced, his pen poised above the page. "This meeting has been called to discuss the state of the world outside our borders. Those present please state your names for the record."

Lady Guivre, seated to Beira's right, spoke first. "Lady Guivre, of the Dragon flights."

The red-scaled dragon next to her spoke next. "Lord Fafnir, of the Dragon flights."

"Lord Wulver, of the Werewolf packs," a grizzled werewolf with one eye said from their right.

And so it went, from one to another. Aelfric of the elven tribes, Balder and Audhild of the dwarven clans, Orpheus of the siren schools, Amaltheia and Chiron of the centaur herds, Bress of the troll memes, Raphael and Gabriel of the angel choirs, and Enenra and Keme of the shade collectives. And of course, Queen Titania of the vampire court.

Lord Balder and Lady Enenra stood at the end of the official introductions and announced they were present on behalf of the fae of Europe and Daingneach. Once everyone finished, they sat and the meeting began in earnest.

"Mr. Williams, tell us as much as you can about the current political situation in the United States, at least as it relates to the fae," Lord Keme said, a barely concealed note of glee in his voice.

What followed was a rapid-fire series of questions Owen hardly had time to answer coming from each corner of the room, half of which he had no answers for. Each founder had their own agenda and questions they wanted answers to. The only one who abstained from the deluge was Beira, who, having had plenty of time to ply Owen with questions during their meetings, seemed content to wait out her colleagues' curiosity.

Over the course of the next three hours, Owen answered questions about the current presidential agenda; the various fae interest groups in the United States; the probable impact of his wife's Change and their subsequent journey to Tearmann; the economic and environmental recovery from the Fae War, and the Battle of Breckenridge specifically; and a whole host of topics he wasn't sure related to the actual issue at hand.

"Yes, as far as I know, most genetic experimentation ceased after the war, even the projects not related to the human gene code. No, scientific development didn't stop, although it did suffer from the economic impact and a backlash against anything involving human experimentation," he rasped out another answer to Lord Gabriel's varied and plentiful questions about scientific advancement. Blast, he'd been a carpenter. Why would he know anything about genetic variance?

Lord Keme opened his mouth, presumably to reiterate the same questions he'd been asking for the last three hours in hopes that Owen would remember something new about modern military tactics, only for Beira to raise a hand in the air.

"We've picked Mr. Williams's brain for long enough. Besides, Mr. Sikes is almost out of paper. I move for a fifteen-minute recess."

The motion was seconded, and the founders scattered, leaving only Owen and Beira in the council chamber. Almost against his will, Owen collapsed against the back of his chair then raised a hand to mop the sweat off his forehead.

A dark chuckle filled the room, forcing him to look up. Beira was sprawled over her throne, a complete dichotomy to the stark posture she had held seconds earlier.

"Was it just me," she asked, "or was that more exhausting than it needed to be?"

"I don't know. Keme could have repeated himself again, and Bress could have derailed the conversation a few more times. It could have been worse," Owen said in a dark voice, all respect and awe of the founders destroyed after three hours of answering increasingly inane questions.

Beira made a noise of agreement. "Despite what he sounds like, Keme is one of our best military minds. He's just a little thick sometimes."

He forced himself to sit up. "So can I go now?" he asked. "Or will there be more questions after this? And will lunch be provided?"

"Not yet," she said as she sat up as well. "Aelfric said one of his spies is supposed to arrive at any time now, and Keme thinks you could provide a useful firsthand interpretation of whatever they report. Of course," she said, shrugging, "I can't imagine you'd be able to provide anything unique in that department, but I won't stop him if he thinks it'll help. And yes, there will be food in an hour or two."

"Wonderful. So I'm stuck here for the foreseeable future, then?" He groaned and dropped his head in his hands. He had things he wanted to do today that didn't include being stared at by the most powerful people in the country. You'd think they'd never seen a human before.

Beira nodded over her steepled fingers. "It looks like that might be the case," she said. "I wonder if the kitchen will send up sandwiches or stew—" The doors to the council chamber burst open and bounced off the wall from the force.

Lords Keme and Aelfric stood in the doorway, each clutching a stack of papers. Aelfric stalked toward Beira with the grace of a prowling panther. His pitch-black hair flowed out behind him like a cape. "My scouts have reported back. We have evidence that a group in the United States has violated the accords." As the words left his lips, ice flooded Owen's veins.

The Tearmann Accords were the peace agreements signed at the end of the Fae War that stipulated, among other things, that research on fae was to cease, their borders were to be respected, and no fae was to be held against their will by any organization involved with a signing nation. Violating them was as good as a declaration of war, everyone knew that.

Beira grabbed the papers with a jerky hand and read them through, letting out a curse as she reached the end. "How long ago was this report written? The scouts who delivered the message, where are they?" Her eyes glinted with something that looked like fear but shone like determination as she grilled them.

The crashing noise had drawn the other founders in, and once they grasped the urgency of the situation, all joking ceased. Bress helped Owen haul his chair off to the side, as apparently his aid was required for planning for possible counterattacks, but they needed the middle of the room to plan.

Truthfully, even if Owen had anything to contribute to the conversation, he wouldn't have been able to. Speech flowed so rapidly from founder to founder that at times it was all he could do to keep up. Plans were swiftly made and just as swiftly discarded, only to be remade when someone came up with a new angle to approach them.

Send a flight of third-gen dragons to raid the installation or a team of angels and dragons to completely wipe it off the face of the earth. Infiltrate, expose, invade, overrun—it went for hours. Meals came and went, lamps were replaced at regular intervals, and still they argued and planned. Were he a poetic sort, Owen would've said that war raged in front of him, armies defeated and reborn as whole campaigns were planned out in meticulous detail.

It was late when the founders agreed on a strategy and the meeting ended. The founders, their generals and assistants, and the unfortunate notetaker abandoned the hall for the warmth and safety of their beds. Once again, Owen and Beira were the only two left.

Owen was about to leave himself when Beira called out to him from where she was organizing the last of her notes. "Stay behind a moment, if you don't mind. I'd like to have a word with you."

He wanted to go to bed and opened his mouth to tell her so, but the look in her eye made him nod instead. He grabbed a stack of her notes and followed her into her office.

Whatever she wanted to tell him, she didn't seem to be in a hurry. She stacked her notes and files on the corner of the desk and pulled a whiskey decanter from a cabinet.

"Can I convince you to indulge? I don't often drink, but today was . . . well, it was something." She barely waited for his nod before pouring a finger's worth of whiskey into each tumbler.

Owen waited for her to finish her drink and pour another one before he spoke. "So, not that I'm not happy to see you, but it's late and I want to go home, so if you could . . ." For a moment, he thought she wasn't going to answer, and he debated downing his drink and leaving.

Beira stared into her glass like it held the answers to all her problems, but she couldn't see them past the liquor. "I never wanted this," she whispered as she set her glass aside. "Not war, not this separation between humans and us, not any of it. Truth be told, I would have been happier if I were the elderly woman I actually am, not—this." She gestured around her office with a limp hand. Her words carried the weight of her years and her sins. "But nothing was ever accomplished by wishing things were different," she said, picking up her drink again and draining what was left. "War beckons now as it did fifty years ago. Nothing will stop it."

The amount of bitterness and resignation in her voice shocked Owen. He may not have caught the details of what had happened, but this was not the Beira he knew.

He surged forward, conviction buoying his words against the venom of hers. "Why do you have to do it? The accords say any move against you counts as an act of war, but you don't have to strike back. Talk with the government, the people, anyone. War won't make the lives of those here any easier. It'll only make things worse."

Beira laughed again, a sound like nails being dragged over a chalkboard. "War *is* inevitable. Perhaps if we hadn't isolated ourselves, let them turn us into the monsters they tell their children about, things might be different, but one way or another, war would have come in the next decade anyway."

"Why? Why does it have to be war?" Owen demanded as he slammed his fist on the table and almost spilled his whiskey. "Go out, show them there's nothing to fear. Daingneach helped the fae of Europe become accepted. Why can't Tearmann do the same?"

"Owen," Beira said as she poured herself another glass of whiskey. "Daingneach was established before anti-fae fervor rose so high. Then we could travel between the two havens. We had trade and people may not have liked us, but we weren't feared. People saw the fae of the Summer Court and learned to trust them."

Her lips curled up in a sneer. "In the U.S., they're afraid. We're the boogiemen, the monsters under the bed. Our isolation, which was intended to help them heal, taught them to fear us. They pass laws forbidding us to travel or even leave Tearmann. Every year more and more groups test our borders in search of the capitol, and to have a fae relation or to even betray pro-fae sentiments is to risk alienation or imprisonment." Her breathing was harsh and her words sharp. She gripped her glass hard enough Owen was concerned it might shatter. "They treat us like animals that need to be exterminated, and we have no say in the laws they make to restrict us."

He tried to speak, but she was louder.

"Did you know that we've tried to send ambassadors to Washington to establish an embassy for the last ten years? The Canadians accepted us well enough, but as far as the U.S. is concerned, it would be better if we didn't exist. So, yes, Owen, war is inevitable, for when those in power deny a group their rights, there is always backlash. And for what they've done—" Her voice cut off. She stood and paced across the room.

"What did they do?" He knew that something had happened to the patrol, something that had violated the accords, but nothing specific.

Beira stopped and faced him, her eyes lit with the fires of rage. "They took them. Two were killed, and we found their bodies dumped in a gorge ten miles from the border, but the other four were captured and taken to a research installation in Minnesota."

For a second time that evening, ice filled Owen's veins. He choked on his drink. If the patrol had been taken for research, then war was inevitable. Border violations, even combat could be forgiven, but never that. The first war had started over fae being used as guinea pigs, and almost half the accords were devoted to the consequences should it happen again.

War loomed on the horizon, not just between the fae and whoever had attacked, but between the fae and the world. If it could be proved that a group in the United States was behind this . . . His heart sank at the thought of what this evening meant for his family and for all the families of the fae.

"You're sure?" he whispered. "What am I saying? Of course you're sure." He set his glass on the edge of her desk and put his head in his hands. They had taken them for research, even knowing what would happen if they were caught. What else would they do if given the opportunity? Would they attack the capital itself or begin raiding the outlying settlements?

Some of the plans made during the meeting made sense now. Work on improvement projects, like his tents or city beautification, had been halted, effective immediately. The Corps would be deployed to each settlement, to provide protection and evacuation aid as needed, and all teams in the U.S. called back. All nonessentials would be withdrawn to the capital, Nead, and Paxton, the three great citadels of the Winter Court. The livestock herds would be separated and the farms hidden. The fae were preparing for war.

His breath came in short, quick bursts. With great effort, he lifted his head and looked Beira in the eye. "So that's it, then?" he asked. "You raid the installation and hope for the best? Hope they won't retaliate?"

"It's all we can hope for." With those words, some of the heat left her and she shrunk into her chair. She pulled her knees to her chest and wrapped her arms around them. "I don't want this any more than you do, but we don't have a choice."

He swallowed and took a deep breath. "Then what's the most likely response?"

"SAFE did this," Beira said in a quiet voice. She rested her head on her knees and looked at him, her eyes bereft of hope and optimism. "They've got allies just like we do, only theirs are out in the open. If they decide to retaliate against our retaliation, the U.S. will declare war on us, either as a separate party, because we harmed U.S. citizens in an 'unprovoked attack' on the research installation, or because of the kidnapping of your family, or to support SAFE's efforts to eliminate us. No matter what, there will be war on two fronts."

"I can't believe it's come to this," he whispered, deflating back into his chair. "There has to be another way."

Beira bristled, her voice lined with daggers, each word was chosen to hurt. "And what would you have had me do? Wait for them to slaughter us and our families in our beds? Lie down and let them bury us where we lie? They want to wipe us out, Owen, us and anyone associated with us. I don't want a war, but there are going to be casualties no matter what we do, and frankly, war has a lower body count for my people."

"But can you afford to have another war?" he yelled, her venom feeding his. "Look around you; you hide in your cities and in your citadels, and scrape by for a living year after year. Many places tolerate you, but most of those places are looking for an excuse to get rid of the fae. I won't allow my children to be put in the path of a war we cannot win." He wanted to scream, to shake her and make her see that this wasn't the right way forward. There was far more at stake here than four people's lives. The fae couldn't survive a prolonged war. She knew that.

"We have no choice, Owen." Her fingers dug into her desk and left deep imprints behind. "They have our people, and we swore that no one would ever be left in the hands of *researchers* again." She spat the word out like poison. "They are my people, and I will not leave them behind in that hellhole. And if that means war, then so be it. They will learn what it means to anger the fae."

Silence rang between them, the last echoes of their arguments fouling the air. Neither was willing to give ground to the other, so they sank into their chairs, silently agreeing to put the conflict aside.

"I know you didn't call me in here to argue philosophy or to drink whiskey. What do you need?" Owen finally made himself ask as the silence stretched on.

"Well, it hardly matters now," Beira said, pinching the bridge of her nose. "But in light of today's events, I wanted to ask you if you would consider becoming a donor."

Owen was going to refuse on principle, but he stopped to think. Most of his concerns had been removed the first time he had met her, and the rest had been eroded over the course of their acquaintance.

His children wouldn't be targeted if he chose to not donate. Beira had demonstrated clear control over her bloodlust with the exception of the incident during the boys' Change, and even then she had resisted drinking from him. No one in the capital treated the process like it was anything more than donating blood or giving someone medicine, but at the same time, no one tried to pressure him into allowing it.

He opened his mouth to accept and shut it again. There was more to consider about this than whether he was comfortable doing it. If he allowed it and gave her a fresh blood supply, was he tacitly giving approval to her actions? Did he want her to be strong enough to participate in the war she said was coming? Would she have more breakdowns like the one from before if he didn't, or had that been a fluke?

"I'm not opposed to it," he finally said. "But I need time to decide. Things are different now. Can you give me until tomorrow?"

Beira's eyes widened and she smiled. "Of course, take all the time you need," she said. "Send my secretary a message no matter what you decide. I don't know how much time I'll have for socializing in the next few days."

"Right, then." He finished his drink and stood. "I should get back. I'll let you know by tomorrow."

The clock chimed and Beira's head shot up. "Blast, I didn't realize we'd be here so long," she said, jumping from her seat and almost knocking the whiskey decanter over. "I'm sorry for keeping you. Go, get home."

He nodded goodbye and made his way out of the office and down to his apartment, where his family and his bed were waiting for him.

***

Owen entered the apartment as quietly as he could. Everyone should've been in bed at this hour, but he didn't want to wake Dorothy—or anyone else for that matter.

It turned out he needn't have bothered. The girls were curled up together on the couch. Jen jolted up when he tripped on a pair of shoes left in the entryway, dropping her sketchbook to the floor and waking Ashley and Dorothy in the process.

He was treated to a minor stampede when the girls realized who was in the doorway, each throwing their arms around as much of him as they could reach. Their voices overlapped in their hurry to make sure he was all right.

"Where were you? We were so worried—"

"I thought they took you too—"

"Mr. Abnell waited with me all day, but Leyley came and got me—"

His stomach twisted into knots. He had completely forgotten to send a message. He dropped down on one knee and ran a hand through Dorothy's hair. "Hey, hey, hey, I didn't mean to worry you," he said. "There was some bad news during the meeting that made it run late. I didn't have a chance to send a note. I'm sorry."

"What happened?" Jen demanded. "You were supposed to be done hours ago."

Their searching, questioning eyes made him wish he could tell them, but he didn't dare. It was bad enough that his dreams would be plagued with battlefields and bullets tonight, he wasn't going to inflict that on them. "One of the patrols reported back," he said carefully. "A group on the border ran into trouble, and they wanted my advice on how to deal with it."

"Do you have to go to another meeting tomorrow?" Ashley asked, fiddling with the hem of her sweater.

"No, I have tomorrow free."

What would happen to them if the fae went to war? he suddenly wondered. His hand froze in Dorothy's hair. Ashley was old enough to help the Corps in noncombat positions, and Jen would want to help the scouts. Arthur was old enough to act as a distraction or even to fight. They would undoubtedly want to use David's enhanced empathy in combat, even though he was still a child. An elf who could affect other Fae like that would be devastating on the battlefield. And Dorothy— Dorothy was so young, young enough that she would be sent to one of the hidden fortresses with the other children. These next few days could be the last he saw of his children.

"What do you say we go on a picnic tomorrow to make up for this?" he asked. "Jason said one of the greenhouses has been turned into a park for everyone's use, and we haven't done anything like that in a while."

Jen rubbed a hand over her eyes. "It won't be the same," she said viciously, shaking her head. "Arthur and David won't be there. And neither will—neither will Mom."

"Hey," Owen whispered, turning Jen's head to look her in the eye. "That doesn't mean we can't do anything we used to do because it won't be like it used to be. Besides, the boys are supposed to come home tomorrow evening; we can have a game night with them."

Dorothy clapped. "Oh! Can we have pancakes with blueberries? We haven't had pancakes in forever."

"We'll see, but I'm sure I could arrange for pancakes at some point in the next few days." He had time with them now, he reminded himself, and nothing was going to stop him from enjoying it. "Now come on. It's late and going to the park is no fun if you're too tired to enjoy it."

Ashley and Jen clearly weren't convinced, but they didn't comment on how forced his cheer sounded. Within minutes, the three girls were ready for bed, and Owen indulged Dorothy's request for one story and then another. He could admit to himself that he was dragging this out, reluctant to kiss his girls goodnight and go back to his empty room.

When he finally managed to drag himself from their room, he went back to the living room. Mindlessly, he picked up some of the accumulated clutter that went with living with children as he turned over the events of the day and Beira's request.

It wasn't much, what she was asking, he reasoned. If she was strong, then that meant there was less of a chance that the war would drag on and his children would get hurt.

Really, she wasn't asking for much.

The decision was easy. Finding a pen, some clean paper, and a spare message flute was harder, but he got the message off before he could change his mind. He had just come back into the apartment and was locking the door when Ashley came out of the girls' room.

"Dad? What were you doing?" She looked him up and down, like she was searching for injuries.

Owen shrugged. There was no reason to conceal this from her. "Beira asked me to do something for her. I sent her a message with my answer."

"Really?" Her eyes narrowed. "What did you say?"

Perhaps it was the alcohol or the late hour, but he laughed when he told her. "I said yes and asked her where and when. Goodnight."

"Dad, wait—" Ashley's cry stopped him in his tracks. He turned to look at her where she stood trembling in the doorway.

"What is it?"

She paused, refusing to meet his eyes. "Nothing. It's—can we talk?"

He nodded. He went back to the living room and sat on the couch. "Of course. What's up?"

Ashley sank down on the opposite end of the couch, as far as she could get from him. "You scared us," she said, tears glimmering in her eyes. "You said you'd be home before dinner. I had to get Dorothy by myself and even Mr. Abnell didn't know where you were."

His breath caught in his chest. "Ashley, I didn't mean—"

She jumped up, cutting off what he had started to say, and paced across the living room. "No, you don't get to talk yet," she snarled, fists shaking at her side. "You left us alone, again, like you did when Jen Changed. Like you've done since Mom died. We had no idea what happened or where you were. Do you have any idea what that was like?"

"Ashley"—he stood and grabbed her shoulders—"I'm sorry, I didn't know the meeting would take that long. It was supposed to be done hours ago, but something happened and the queen wanted my advice."

"What would they need you for?" she snapped, knocking his hands off of her. "I can't think of anything that they would need your advice on, Dad. You're an immigrant who barely got a high school education."

"Ashley, enough," he yelled. He took several deep breaths, trying to force himself into some semblance of serenity.

She stared at him, tears in her eyes and spilling down her cheeks. "Why?" she asked, a stifled yell that pulled his heartstrings. "Why didn't you tell us where you were? We were so scared something had happened to you, that—" Her words dissolved into sniffles and then sobs as she sunk into herself.

Owen dared to grab her again and pulled her against his chest as tight as he could. "Ash, it's okay. It'll be all right. I'm not angry. The queen needed me. I couldn't leave."

"We needed you too, Dad," Ashley whispered, almost too quiet to hear. "Why weren't you there for us?"

He wanted to answer, wanted to explain that there hadn't been time and that everything had happened so fast, but he couldn't. The words wouldn't come. Between what he had agreed to and what he had learned that night, there was too much going on inside of him to reduce to a simple explanation. His tongue bound, he was forced to listen as Ashley sobbed into his chest, heart aching as he offered what little comforts he could.

CHAPTER SEVENTEEN

IN WHICH THERE ARE NEWCOMERS

"They're experimenting on us. They promised it was over after they acknowledged our sentience, but lo and behold, any group that can get their hands on fae starts right in with trying to test our pain tolerance or some other such nonsense. Perhaps this wouldn't be so bad if they didn't treat us worse than the animals they house us with. If they didn't vivisect us and dump our bodies in mass graves with one hand and preach about how much they're helping us with the other. No more. Something has to give and it won't be us."

—Excerpt from the journals of Beira Thomson, Queen Titania

The boys returned the next evening, with two first-gens who introduced themselves as their teachers, and a long list of new appointments, lessons, and rules. The teachers offered to stay and go through their lesson plans with Owen, but he refused. It was enough his boys were back; he could meet with them later and work out the logistics.

Dinner that evening turned into a celebration. He made blueberry pancakes, baked a cake, and mixed punch from an odd assortment of fruit juice a woman at the shop had forced on him.

Arthur helped Owen fend off Jen and Dorothy's pleading requests to try the batter while Owen cooked. His training had done a lot to help him adjust to his new life and his new look. Gone was the melancholy and apathy that turned him into an unmoving wall after he'd Changed.

219

The last of his skin had fallen off while he'd been gone and burnished ivory scales replaced it. Even his hair had grown back different, each strand a half-inch thick and stiff as stone.

On the other hand, while most of Arthur's Changes had been visible, David looked almost exactly the same as when he had left, at least on the outside. Jen had grabbed him the moment he walked through the door and flat-out refused to let him out of her sight for the rest of the evening.

A week ago, he'd have done everything in his power to escape. Now, he smiled serenely and let her pull him around. His teachers said his control was amazing for his age, but they'd still blocked off most of his abilities for safety's sake. Even with the block, snatches of emotion occasionally broke through, wafting through the air like smoke.

Overall, Owen would say the party was a success. They played games and told stories, each impossible and loud and entirely their own. Halfway through, Arthur dared to challenge Jen's creative interpretation of the rules and started a loud debate that raged for a half hour and ended when David tag-teamed with his sisters to force him from the game.

At midnight, he had to put his foot down and send everyone to bed despite loud pleas for just a little longer. It was late, he insisted, and they all had to be up in the morning.

By the time he'd managed to wrangle them all into their beds, it was almost one and he ached with exhaustion. He could still hear giggles and laughter filtering through his door, but he couldn't bring himself to care. They were home. They were happy. They might be tired in the morning, but they'd be here. For now, that was more than enough.

***

The city was positively buzzing the next day with news of coming arrivals. The research installation had been raided the night before. A team of shades, sirens, and elves had broken in, erased any information they could find, set fire to the facility, and were now on their way back to the capital, rescued fae in tow. It turned out that, in addition to the four patrolmen, there had also been seven other fae, some apparently held captive for years.

The news set every patriotic heart in the capital ablaze, and there was open talk in support of war in the streets. Weapons that hadn't seen use in years were pulled out and repaired, veterans saw their stories brought out and examined like they had never been before, and stored food filled every available space. The training rooms had never had so many people in their self-defense classes before, while the dwarven clans were doing everything in their power to shore up weaknesses in the city's defenses. To live in the capital was to eat, sleep, and breathe the oncoming storm. Owen hated it.

Mr. Moore'd been contracted to assist one of the clans with expanding the livestock pens, which meant everyone had to help with the heavy lifting. Owen spent more time with his coworkers in the two days they spent working on that project than he had since he'd started working there, and he got good at ignoring their gossip. All they talked about was what they'd done so far to prepare for the war and how much more they wanted to do.

Well, that and the new arrivals, but those two went hand in hand, didn't they? They were the reason they were going to war, the reason the uneasy peace that had held for the last fifty years was being broken. They were why children and those unable to fight were being evacuated, why the patrols had doubled in number and frequency, and why everyone who was able was training to protect themselves.

Other preparations were being made too. Healers of the mind and body were preparing for the worst, apartments for the new arrivals were being furnished in the safest parts of the city, research into any relations they might have among the fae already present was ongoing, and everywhere people were talking about them. All this talk made him wonder if something similar had happened when the fae had heard about his family.

After all the excitement, it was almost anticlimactic when the escapees finally arrived. They'd landed after midnight, clinging to the dragon harnesses with the team that had saved them.

They were a bedraggled bunch, from what Owen heard the next morning—covered in scars and half-starved when they met Beira in the Eyries for the welcoming ceremony. A technician said he saw some of them burst into tears when she promised them her protection. No one knew anything else. They had been sequestered by the healers, and the general populace was ordered to give them space. No one expected them to be out and about for at least a few more days.

That was why it was such a surprise when the gryphon limped into the shop that day, barely able to stand straight. Her fur and feathers were worn and tattered, and she had been shaved to remove mats. She had three large scars running across her lion-like face, the largest of which went from her temple to past her chin.

She zeroed in on Owen, who'd been allowed to work on his commissions while the rest of the crew wrangled with some of the barricade gates by the market, and limped toward him, making her way past the myriad of equipment and half-finished projects scattered throughout the shop. When she reached him, she stood in silence, head tilted expectantly.

"Sorry, can I help you?" Owen asked after the silence had stretched on past what was polite.

She rolled her eyes in a half-familiar way and tapped a collar he hadn't noticed before. It was linked to what looked like—was she wearing a shock collar? She was, a metal shock collar like they would put on dogs, except this one was attached to a battery three times as big as any he'd ever seen a dog wear.

"Oh, I'm sorry," he said as he jumped to his feet. "I didn't notice. Are you all right? I don't have the tools to remove it—"

The gryphon rolled her eyes again and put a taloned hand over his mouth to silence his babbling. When she looked certain that he wasn't going to talk again, she removed her hand and started gesturing.

She pointed back and forth between him and her, made a circle, and pointed toward the door.

"I'm sorry. I don't—"

She shook her head, pointed at him, and then toward the nearest outer wall.

"Oh," Owen said, finally realizing what she was trying to say. "I'm from out there, like you? Yes. My family and I came up a few weeks ago after my wife died. We were the first new arrivals in a while. My guides said it was odd that they found our groups so close together."

She made a circle over his head and set her hand flat at various heights around him like she was measuring something that wasn't there. Ah, she was asking about the kids.

"Yes, I have five children," he said. "The oldest turns seventeen in a few weeks. The youngest turned four almost two months ago. Three of them have made the Change already. My oldest is a siren, and my twins, who are eight, are a werewolf and an elf."

She made more hand gestures, and he decided he'd had enough.

"You know what? Can you write? I have a pen and paper around here somewhere . . ." Owen dug through the clutter at his workstation. Technically, he wasn't supposed to use this paper for anything but drafting his projects, but Mr. Moore wouldn't mind him using it for this instead. Hopefully.

When he managed to unearth his paper from underneath the remnants of his lunch and a pen from his toolbox, he handed them to her with a bow. "For you, my lady."

She rolled her eyes again and snatched the pen and paper away. She had a hard time forcing her fingers into the proper position to write and managed a strange clawed position that pained him to look at and rendered the writing almost illegible. When she finished, she shoved the paper at his chest and he had to work to decipher the scribbles.

"Why did you bring them here? They were safer where they were."

Owen looked at her and shook his head. "No, they weren't. My neighbor, Mr. Jameson, hated fae. He called in a group that wanted to kidnap them."

He'd come to terms with a lot of things over the last few weeks. One of them was that people like Mr. Jameson existed everywhere. Even if they'd escaped from SAFE, they might've lost Jen to the Change like they'd lost Tiffany. He didn't even want to think about what might've happened to the boys.

The gryphon huffed silently and grabbed the paper. *"How do you know? I heard it the other way around. The fae were the ones who kidnapped them."* She wrote and shoved the paper back at him.

Owen let a single bark of laughter. "No, you heard wrong. The fae saved them. They gave me a choice, said that if I didn't think they would be safer with them, we could go. But I know what those sorts of groups do to fae after they Change. Why is it so hard to believe they wouldn't do the same to ones who haven't? Beira says that they want to know everything about the fae, and the chance to observe them mid-Change—No. I did the right thing by letting them bring us here."

He'd never have seen them again. Once the boys changed, they'd have taken all of them and left him to rot if they didn't kill him first.

"The queen? How're you on a first-name basis with her? I can't imagine she spends much time with those who aren't fae. They aren't her concern."

"We're friends, I'll have you know," he snapped. He took a deep breath and started again. "It's hard for her to form friendships when the fae have to obey every word she says. I'm not fae, so I don't have to worry about that. And as for humans not being her concern, she moved her people up here so the humans would feel safe."

The gryphon lifted her lips in a sneer as she scribbled on the paper. *"And yet they fear us. If she'd stayed instead of running before the dust settled, they wouldn't be so scared of us."*

He took the paper and squinted; the words had bled into each other. "No, that wouldn't have worked," he said, looking up. "Humans hated the fae after the war, everyone knows that. They didn't even build Daingneach for more than a decade. If they'd stayed, the humans never would've had time to heal."

"War. Is. Coming. If she believed that she could make them accept the fae, then why did she jeopardize it by rescuing us? Your children are in greater danger than they ever were before they left home." The page had almost ripped in two from the pressure she had exerted on it.

"Because she believes no fae should be treated like that and if we let them do it, they'll never treat fae as equals." He shoved the paper back at her. "Even if she wanted to, she couldn't have left you. The people wouldn't've allowed it. They all lost someone to the old research centers—I know if my family was in your place, I'd risk everything to save them. In fact, I'd wager every person here would say freeing you and the other captives was worth the risk."

The gryphon glared at him as he stood, chest heaving from the exertion of his defense. Slowly, she picked up the paper and started writing again. Once finished, she slammed it into his chest and stalked out of the shop.

With shaking hands, Owen read the paper she had thrust at him. On it, there was a single line:

"And I would wager that every single one of us would have preferred it if she'd let us rot instead of risking war and our extinction."

CHAPTER EIGHTEEN

IN WHICH WAR COMES

"Despite what Orpheus says, we will never be safe enough to forget about security precautions. There is always a chance someone will find Tearmann, and we can't leave it undefended when that time comes. The guards can only do so much, so we have to find a way for civilians to protect themselves. The evacuation tunnels are a good start, but we need something more concrete. I have a few ideas, like gates or weapons caches, that Beira might find interesting. I'll talk to her about them in the morning. She's always more agreeable before open court."

—Excerpt from the journals of Stephen Andrews-Conway, Lord Aelfric

Dinner was quiet that night. The Williams ate in the apartment instead of the communal dining halls for once, and Owen was enjoying not having to shout to be heard. Dorothy was in the middle of regaling the table with a detailed account of everything she'd done at daycare that day, with Arthur egging her on unashamedly.

Try as he might, Owen couldn't focus on her story. He kept running over his encounter with the gryphon in his head. She reminded him of someone and he couldn't figure out who. He could count the number of gryphons he was on a first name basis with on one hand.

"So, Dad," Jen said during a lull in Dorothy's storytelling. "Antony said that his dad saw one of the new arrivals come in to talk to you today. Is it true the researchers put them in shock collars?"

He stopped, his fork halfway to his mouth. "Where did you hear that?"

"Antony told me," she said, taking a bite of her spaghetti. "His dad works with you and his mom is one of the healers assigned to the new arrivals. He said the gryphon was the only one who's left their apartment since they got here."

"Jen, you shouldn't gossip," Owen said sharply, setting his fork down. "How would you feel if people talked about us that way?"

"But Dad," Arthur said, a mischievous gleam in his eye, "they do talk about us like that. Every day. Until now, we were the most interesting thing that's happened around here since the angels moved out."

"And you've come home complaining about it every day since we got here, Arthur," Owen said, pushing his food around his plate. He had been hounded about the gryphon enough after she left by his coworkers and what felt like half the mountain. "Think about how much worse it is for those poor people. They deserve their privacy and, with it, our respect."

"So that means you won't tell us anything about her?" David asked.

Owen looked up to answer and saw that they were all looking at him with varying degrees of expectancy. Except for Dorothy, who was playing with her meatballs.

"All right." He sighed, bringing his free hand up to rub his temple. The kids were like wolves with a scrap of meat when they wanted to know something, and they'd gotten a taste of blood. "Listen closely. I'm only saying this once. Yes, I saw the gryphon today. She had a few scars but looked healthy. I don't know if it was to stop her from talking, but she was wearing what looked like a shock collar. We had a short conversation through notes."

He waited a moment for any other questions. When none came, he stood and went to the kitchen. His appetite was gone, so he might as well get some work done. "Mr. Moore asked for my help planning out some drafts," he threw over his shoulder as he rinsed his plate off. "I'll be in my room if you need anything."

***

Exactly none of the gossip had died down by the next day, and Owen spent much of the morning fending off the curious and the inquisitive. From what he'd heard, he was the only person outside the healers who had seen the newcomers, let alone spoken with one.

It wasn't an honor he was happy to hold, as it meant people were traipsing in and out of the worksite all day while he was trying to work. Did Andrew and Eoire have to go through this, he wondered, biting back a curse as Mr. Moore chased a harpy away. If so, he needed to buy them something nice. It was unbearable.

What's worse, the gossip mongers constant badgering meant that barely anything got done. The whole crew would have to stay late if they couldn't get moving soon.

Finally, after sending the harpy away for the third time, Mr. Moore sent Owen home. With him gone, there was a chance the gossips mongers would leave them alone long enough to get the job done.

Owen started the long walk back home from the worksite and grumbled about nosy fae as he went. He was debating whether it would be worth stopping by one of the dining centers for dinner when a piercing wail filled the air.

The evacuation alarms, he realized with a start. They weren't supposed to have a drill today, were they? No, that was—Almost without thinking, he sprinted down the hall, and frantically tried to remember where the kids had planned to spend their afternoons. He was halfway back to the apartment when the ceiling collapsed.

The impact knocked him off his feet. For a moment, there was complete silence. Then the screaming started. Owen forced himself to his feet, squinting through the dust filling the air as figures dressed in combat gear poured through the hole in the outer wall.

For a moment, he couldn't believe what he was seeing. Then he watched a soldier fire six shots into a centaur with a foal strapped to her chest, and shove her out of the way and the world jumped into motion.

Without thinking, he threw himself at the nearest soldier and into his worst nightmare. He'd been in countless barroom brawls, spent years scrapping with the other boys in his foster home, and boxed with his father-in-law until his knuckles bled, but he'd never seen anything like this.

All around the same situation was playing out, men and women fighting for their lives against this unrelenting force. Near him, a werewolf fought against six men to protect two elven children; a centaur slammed his hooves into a helmet, shattering it and the skull beneath it, in an effort to reach a foal that was screaming for its mother; and a collective of shades blinked in and out of sight, dropping clothing as they went, to distract the soldiers filling the hallway long enough for others to get away.

It was a fight like none Owen had ever seen, one they had no chance of winning. Claws, wings, and hooves were all well and good, but they didn't provide much protection against bullets. The last of the barricade doors slammed shut behind him just as he pulled an unconscious troll past the threshold.

"What the hell happened?" he shouted as a gryphon took his place supporting the troll.

"We got attacked, idiot," a dwarf in a scout's uniform said, then spit. "Looks like those SAFE bastards want their pets back."

He couldn't have silenced anyone better had he dropped a grenade in their midst.

"SAFE, here?" an elf said as the shirt she'd been ripping into bandages dropped from nerveless fingers. Her terror stained the air with a bitter, overwhelming flavor. "I thought they couldn't find us, no one knows where we are."

"Well, they found us. Probably followed the captives here." The dwarf growled and grabbed hold of a limping shade to help him away from the barricade.

"So what are we supposed to do? There are people still out there, and the barricades won't hold forever," Owen yelled at the retreating dwarf's back.

"Then defend them," the dwarf said without turning around. "Give people time to escape into the tunnels. I need to find whoever's in charge. We're running blind without the scouts."

The words were enough to galvanize those left into movement. Teams were organized to take the wounded to safety, while others held the barricade.

Owen's first thought as everyone split around him was to find the kids. He still wasn't sure where they were, but he had a few good ideas. Dorothy would be at daycare and Mr. Abnell would make sure she got into the tunnels if Arthur hadn't already gotten her, and Ashley had said she had homework to do so she should be at the apartment. The twins would be harder, since Jen had mentioned having a myriad of plans that took them all over the mountain, but Owen was confident one of the neighbors could point him in their direction—

"Where're you going?" said a voice in his ear. Its owner, an elf dressed in a Corps uniform, grabbed onto Owen's shoulder.

"To find my kids. I can't do anything to help here," Owen said, shaking the hand off. If he was lucky, the staircase on this side hadn't been blocked off and he could get home in a few minutes. He needed to hurry, who knew how far the soldiers had gotten. A hand at his elbow stopped him and physically pulled him back to the elf's side.

"You can't be serious," the elf hissed, grabbing Owen by both shoulders. "We need all the help we can get."

"And I'm just one human," Owen hissed, yanking free again. "I'd do more good if I found my kids and got out of the way." The fae could take care of themselves. The vast majority of them had lived through one war already. His kids didn't have that luxury, and he needed to find them before one of the soldiers did.

"There's a group of soldiers guarding the barricade," the elf said, his words enough to stop Owen in his tracks. "If they get through, then they have a clear shot to the living quarters. From there, it's only a matter of time before they find an entrance to the evacuation tunnels."

The evacuation tunnels were supposed to be safe and impossible to find if you didn't know what you were looking for, but he had a point. If even one soldier got past this barricade, any civilian stick outside the tunnels was a sitting duck. The barricades wouldn't protect them long, the soldiers had already broken through the mountainside.

"Will this take long?" If they weren't stopped here, those soldiers would kill him long before he found the kids. He'd help here and then he'd leave.

"Not more than ten minutes, if luck is with us. Come on, we're gathering over here."

Owen grabbed a retreating harpy to take a message to the kids as he went toward the gathering crowd. He had no way of knowing if the harpy would actually find them, but he'd take that chance. If he was going to do something this stupid, he didn't want them waiting for him.

***

A wiry blond elf put his hands on the door. "I sense ten minds past here." His eyes slid shut. "They're waiting for us. We have to be careful."

"That's it?" asked a third-gen werewolf midway through shifting forms. "There must have been thirty before. Where'd the rest go?" She fell forward as her black fur thickened and her bones cracked into place. In her place stood a wolf as high as Owen's shoulder.

"Must've gone for reinforcements," said the dwarf to Owen's left. He fingered the knife at his belt and frowned. "We should attack before they get back."

Privately, Owen agreed. If the soldiers wanted to breach the barricade, they'd need more than ten men. Between everyone here, they had an axe, two knives, and a werewolf. They needed to attack before they were even more outgunned.

"No," the elf said. "Not for reinforcements. They're—queen's blood, I can't see it. The emotion is too complex."

"What can you see?" Owen asked before the dwarf could speak again. They were wasting time. The longer they waited the longer those soldiers had time to prepare.

"Anger. Anger and regret. Greed, they want something. They aren't being allowed to get it." The elf's eyes shot open. "Looting. They're missing out on looting."

The wolf, now joined by two of her brethren, growled. Her lips pulled up over her teeth as she pawed at the ground.

The dwarf spat. "I agree with Rhon."

The elf spun. "No, we can't. We need to make a plan. They want to kill us."

"They're already killing us, we can't wait anymore," another elf, this one as broad as an oak with hair and skin to match, said. He shoved Owen aside to get to the front of the group, almost knocking him to the floor. "We need to get out there now, Ishmael."

"I know, but if we go out there, they'll slaughter us. We need—"

"Listen to them. They're laughing, you think I can't hear their joy?" the dark-haired elf said as a snarl crossed his face. "I've never been so disgusted in my life. They want to kill us, and what's more, they're happy to do it—"

"Enough, we have to move," the dwarf said.

"It won't do anyone any good if we get ourselves killed," the blond elf said, wringing his hands. "We need a plan."

"And I have one," the dwarf said, wearing a smile that showed too many teeth. He turned on Owen and shoved a finger into his chest. "You, human. How do you feel about playing bait?"

***

It should have been simple. The elves would get the soldiers to look away from the door for long enough that Owen and two shades could sneak out. Owen would lure the soldiers away from the door so the fae fighters could get into position. The shades would wait for the elves to disorient the soldiers and disarm them while they were disabled. They would only fight if the elves couldn't maintain control. No one was supposed to get hurt.

Things started to go wrong the moment Owen slid under the barricade. The shades had already disappeared, and he was alone for all intents and purposes. The others hadn't even let him have a knife before they sent him out. For this plan to work they couldn't suspect Owen was a combatant. He hadn't gone more than three feet toward the soldiers before he was spotted.

"Wait, please," he shouted, raising his hands as high as he could. "I'm human, I need your help. They have my family, we need to hurry."

A soldier wearing a sergeant insignia raised a fist. "Hold your fire, men."

Owen held back a relieved sigh and jogged toward them. "Thank god, we've been trapped here for ages—" He froze as the soldiers raised their weapons again. Behind them, he saw the tell-tale glimmer of moving shades.

"Smith, Montgomery," the sergeant said, his voice layered with suspicion. "Search him. Make sure he's telling the truth. You, don't

232

move or we will fire." Two soldiers, indistinguishable from their fellows, slung their rifles over their shoulders and broke from the crowd at the sergeant's command.

Owen swallowed. "I'm not armed, I need your help." His heart sank as they came closer. They needed to look away from the door. The fighters couldn't move if the soldiers could see them.

"So you've said," the sergeant said as his men reached Owen and started roughly searching him. "But we need to be sure you aren't one of these freaks."

"I'm not, I swear—" Something slammed into the back of Owen's head and his vision went white. A blow to his stomach sent him reeling to the floor.

"That's what they all say, freak," the soldier who'd hit him said. Her lips twisted into an ugly smile as she wiped his blood from the butt of her rifle. "You think we can't tell the difference?"

The sergeant laughed. "Good job, Smith. I didn't think he'd actually fall for it, but you know what they say. These savages aren't very smart."

The soldiers laughed and their voices echoed off the broken walls. One kicked a fallen troll, who screamed and tried to crawl away.

"You're right, Sarge," he said through his sniggers. "They still make good hunting though." He raised his rifle at the troll, who was sobbing and begging for mercy. He fired once, twice, three times, the sound reverberating enough to deafen Owen.

The troll stopped moving after the first shot and stopped crying after the second. The third made the body jerk, but she was already dead, one more body among the dozens in the hallway. Blood, slow and thick as sap, stained the ground.

The sergeant swore. "Damn it, Reynolds, you know not to waste ammo. It's a frigging tree, it's not going to fight back."

"Ah, come on, Sarge," the soldier who fired said. "We cleared this section, we're not going to see any more of those beasts. Might as well have some fun while we can, right?"

For a moment, Owen saw a body kneeling by the downed troll. It flickered, there and gone in an instant, but it was clear.

"Please, I need your help, they have my family." It hadn't worked before and it wasn't going to work now, but it might be enough to keep their attention on him.

One soldier, his jacket coated in a substance Owen didn't want to think about, snorted. "Again with that bit, you think he'd give it a rest."

"But I'm not—"

"Lesson one, freak," the sergeant said, pulling a large knife from a sheath at his waist. "Everyone knows fae don't take prisoners. Lesson two, even if you were human, you'd have to be fae-lover to be alive and those aren't worth the time to save."

Every sense went into overdrive. The smell of blood, thick and cloying, mixed with sweat, tears, and gunpowder. Colors were too bright against the backdrop of cold stone. The soldiers' jeers and the scrape of their boots was as loud as the gunfire in the distance. His clothes felt like brands against his skin, his hands scraped against the ground, and everything felt too cold, too tight.

They were going to kill him just like they'd killed that troll. Like they were going to kill anyone they found, human or fae. And he'd been willing to let it happen if it meant he could find his kids.

Something inside Owen broke and loosed a wildfire in his chest. He pulled himself up straight and spat at the sergeant. Grinning viciously, he snarled. "Then you better pray you kill me in one shot."

He couldn't fight, there were too many guns aimed at him, and they'd shoot him dead before he could reach the barricade, but he wasn't going to die quietly. Let the others say he'd done his best to protect his home.

As the split slid down his face, the sergeant raised his knife and— something hot and wet splashed across Owen's face. The air shimmered and everything descended into chaos.

The fae attacked.

Owen moved without thinking. The sergeant was dead, his throat slit ear to ear. Grabbing the fallen knife, he threw himself into the fight.

It was like a movie. Time slowed to a crawl as the werewolves turned into walking bloodbaths, tearing through human flesh like it was paper, while the shades, visible only by the blood dotting their skin, ripped weapons away. The dwarf had gotten an axe from somewhere and was hacking at the legs of those the elves incapacitated.

234

It was over almost as soon as it had begun.

Shaking, Owen slumped to the ground when a shade cut the last throat. His heart pounded in his ears. There was blood on the knife. How many of those soldiers had he killed?

"When I said distract them, I didn't mean try to get yourself killed," the dwarf said, wiping the blood off his axe. "Still, it got the job done."

Owen let out a broken laugh. "Is that what happened?"

The dwarf's gaze fell down as he fingered his beard. "It's not your fault. When Rhon realized you were stuck, she suggested the elves get the soldiers focused on you. Anger and hate are easier to enhance from a distance."

Owen's head snapped up. "You did what?" The troll's jerking body played one repeat in his mind and he almost threw up. They could've gotten him killed.

"It got them close enough for the elves to distract them. You were never in any real danger."

Owen wanted to protest, but the words caught in his throat. He saw that death play over and over again, but her body became his. His body became Arthur's. Arthur's body became Ashley's, then David's, Jen's, and Dorothy's, one by one. Owen's knees shook, and he almost fell down again. That could've been him, that could've been one of his children.

Rhon, the werewolf with black fur from before, pulled at the dwarf's sleeve with her teeth. When she had his attention, she started growling.

The dwarf nodded. "Yes, I know."

She growled and pawed at the ground. Her head swung between Owen and the dwarf and then back to the barricade.

"I'll ask him, but I'm not sure what good it'll do." The dwarf shoved Rhon away with one hand, his fingers lingering for a fraction of a second in the fur before they dropped away. "Now, go help the others. See if you can find anyone still alive."

"What did she say?" Owen asked as the werewolf bounded away. "Why did she look at me?"

"Rhon says she can smell children on you." He didn't meet Owen's eyes as he cleaned nonexistent blood from his axe. "She thinks you should leave before you get hurt."

Owen's heart dropped and he scrambled to his feet. "I ..." He couldn't go back now.

Those soldiers laughed as they killed an innocent woman. They didn't care that she was a person, that she had a family and a home, and they'd made it clear they'd do it again if they could. He couldn't stand by after that, not if he wanted to look Dorothy or Arthur or any of them in the eye again.

"No, I'm staying."

Those soldiers were wrong. The fae weren't monsters, they were people struggling to survive, like any other. He couldn't stand by while families like his were torn apart.

Besides, his kids weren't alone. The fae protected their own and now it was his turn to repay that favor.

The dwarf hung his axe from his belt and smiled. "Then let's get moving. We have a lot of mountain to cover."

***

They found their rhythm after that battle. They went section by section, closing off the barricades and trapping both fae and soldiers inside. The elves distracted the soldiers, manipulating the weak into a catatonic state, which gave the fighters time to get into position. Owen played bait and lured soldiers to the others with pleas to rescue imprisoned humans or by pulling them away from injured targets. Any guilt he might have felt disappeared after the first time he came to a group torturing a siren and her child.

It was unfortunate, but whenever they ran into a group like that, the elves had a harder time controlling the soldiers. Most of those groups died.

Every so often, they ran into a group with a similar plan. Those with sirens didn't even bother fighting. After all, there was no need for violence if the soldiers were happy to lay down their arms when asked; they were there to carry the wounded and restrain the captives.

That wasn't to say it was all easy. The large entrances to the Eyries had been targeted, trapping the dragons and gryphons inside and depriving the fae of their air force. The soldiers didn't always go down easily to the emotional manipulation or the hypnotism for whatever reasons, and apparently, they would rather die than be captured. After the second one blew himself up, they learned to send the shades in for the grenade belts.

***

Owen's legs ached. He'd lost count of how many times they'd had to fight, how many soldiers they'd captured or killed. The group grew whenever they came across survivors and now numbered in the thirties.

The soldiers had not been kind to the city. They'd passed hundreds of dead and dying. Holes in the floors and walls made movement uncertain, and some soldiers had left traps behind them. As the group grew, he'd been called to action less to play bait and more to check if areas were stable. Never had he been as glad of his background in construction as he was today.

He was picking his way across a decimated tunnel by one of the Grand Staircases when the wall next to him exploded. The blast knocked him into the bullet-ridden wall, perilously close to the landing entrance, and a squadron of soldiers poured through the hole.

Owen forced himself to his feet as the first soldier rushed at him with a knife. He deflected the first strike, and the knife flew from the attacking man's weak grip. The other members of his squad rushed at the fae with the desperation of dying men. Behind them came a small pack of werewolves, their teeth and claws bloody.

The soldier attacking Owen threw himself at Owen's waist and knocked them into the landing, which looked like it had been the victim of a grenade or two. The sounds of combat halved. It was just them, alone in the guttering light of dying lamps.

The landing was riddled with rubble and holes, adding danger to each movement. They rolled on the floor, first toward the gaping hole in the stairway, then back toward the fight. Owen got on top and punched the soldier in the face, then was knocked back and received the same treatment, only to slam a rock into the soldier's temple.

Owen managed to get to his feet seconds before the soldier and kicked him in the face. The blow was technically underhanded, but at this point Owen didn't care about being fair. He grabbed onto Owen's legs just as the ground under their feet gave way.

They fell into the blackness, ten, twenty feet, it was impossible to tell. Owen slammed into the ground hard. Something in his leg snapped and he almost blacked out as he rolled to a stop. The soldier was not so lucky, and his screams continued for three long seconds until they ceased with a sickening thud.

CHAPTER NINETEEN

IN WHICH THEY FIND EACH OTHER

"Some of the humans who came up with their fae friends and family have offered to give Beira their blood. She's been trying to live off animal blood, like in those stupid vampire books, but it isn't working. She's starving, but she's more concerned with the health of the humans than with her own. We'll all die if she does, but she still refuses to drink. She says she doesn't think she'll be able to stop. I've managed to get her to agree to a series of experiments about her blood drinking, so it's progress at least. Maybe she'll agree to drink from the fae instead?"

—Excerpt from the journals of Michael Jones, advisor to the queen

Owen sat outside an emergency clinic, blinking blood out of his eye while he pressed a cloth to a cut on his forehead. He was lucky that he only had a few cuts and a broken leg. Six more inches to the left and he'd have missed what was left of the staircase and fallen to his death.

He wasn't sure how much time had passed, but he knew that much of the mountain had been retaken. They'd taken a lot of casualties though, and no one knew how many people had been taken captive. His erstwhile teammates had dumped him outside an emergency clinic before they jumped back into the fray, and he'd been trying to piece the gossip he heard into something useful. It was there Arthur found him.

"Dad, are you all right?" Arthur asked when he ran up to Owen. "I looked everywhere for you when Mr. Moore said you weren't with the rest of the crew—"

"Arthur—Arthur, I'm fine." Owen gasped when the hug squeezed fresh bruises. "They said—ah, they said I'd be fine. Besides, a few cuts won't kill me and my leg doesn't hurt much."

"Oh my god, did I hurt you?" Arthur leaped back and pulled Owen's hand out of the way so he could examine the still bleeding cut. "Why haven't they healed you yet?"

"I'm human, remember?" he said with a grunt. "Besides, there are loads hurt worse than I am. One of the doctors splinted me up. I'll be fine. Where are the others? I thought you were supposed to stay in the evac tunnels."

Arthur eyed him skeptically but lowered his hands and sat next to him, out of the way of the fast-moving crowd. "Ashley and the twins are at home, and Dorothy should still be with Mr. Abnell. I was on my way to pick her up when the alarms sounded and I got grabbed to help with the healing. A harpy told me you were with a search-and-rescue squad and pointed me in your direction. I've been looking for you for the last hour."

Owen closed his eyes and breathed a sigh of relief. Elenor would make sure the ones in the apartment got to the tunnels and away from the fighting, and Mr. Abnell would die before he let any of his charges get injured. This was the best way to make sure they were safe short of keeping them with him.

"Are you safe here?" Owen asked, his eyes flying open. "I know the fighting moved away, but still—" His stomach clenched. If Arthur was here, he was in danger. The search-and-rescue squads would recruit anyone, Owen was a prime example of that, and the mountain wasn't safe anymore. Floors were unstable, walls had been knocked down, and who knew how many soldiers had escaped. "You haven't tried to join the fighting, have you?"

"No." Arthur shook his head as he slumped into the wall next to Owen. "I've been with the healers the whole time. Whenever someone came at us, a battle siren would sing and they'd fall over. I want to learn how to do that."

That eased his worries some. Arthur wouldn't lie to him, even to make him feel better. "No using it to make me agree to things. I'm sure that there's a law against that somewhere."

240

"Father dearest, are you implying I would so grossly misuse my abilities?" Arthur asked, making a show of looking hurt. "And for such little gain—I am shocked. Shocked, wounded, and offended. Would you really accuse your own son of doing something like that?"

"If it were David? No. You? Without hesitation and with the full backing of anyone who's ever met you," Owen said as he pulled back the cloth to check if his cut had stopped bleeding.

Arthur frowned, finger held up to protest, and then dropped it. "Yeah, you know what, fair point."

Arthur could only stay with him for a few minutes before one of the healers called him away. Apparently, what he lacked in actual skill in healing, he made up for in a stunning ability to harmonize with the other sirens. It enhanced their abilities through a process Owen couldn't even begin to understand.

Owen watched the sirens do their work while he waited for Arthur to get free again. It was like something out of a fantasy novel. Injuries mended before his eyes, wounds closing into scars, and scars disappearing into unblemished skin.

Still, it wasn't all-powerful. Sirens could mend bone and skin, but they couldn't regrow something that had been lost and they couldn't repair anything that was damaged beyond use. A shade who had been blinded by shrapnel would never regain her sight, for example.

Arthur had been paired with a small brown siren and an elderly human doctor. The doctor would examine the injuries and tell the sirens where to focus while he patched injuries that weren't life-threatening enough to require healing.

While Arthur was helping to mend a nasty broken arm, a grim-looking shade covered in blood, dust, and debris ran through the door asking for the Williams.

"Over here," Owen called. "I'm Owen Williams. What did you need?"

The shade ran toward him and skidded to a stop. "The queen sent me," he said, panting as he wiped sweat off his brow. "I have news for you about your children."

The blood drained from Owen's face. They were supposed to be safe—no one had said the living quarters had been penetrated—those were supposed to be too deep into the mountain for explosives to reach. But Dorothy—had something happened to Dorothy?

"What happened? Tell me!" His broken leg protested as he forced himself to his feet, but he ignored it and grabbed the messenger's shoulders, tempted to shake him until he got answers.

"Let go of me and I will speak," the shade snapped, knocking Owen's arms away. "Listen, they broke through one of the barricades and got into the business district. The daycare was one of their first targets. They would have gotten everyone had your son not distracted them—"

"Arthur? But Arthur's here—how could he help?"

"Not Arthur, the other one, David. He's alive, but he was badly hurt. The queen is with him and sent me to get you and the other boy. You need to hurry."

Owen's breath slowed. His heartbeat pounded in his ears as each second stretched into infinity. David. David was hurt. How? He wasn't supposed to be—he was supposed to be safe in the tunnels below the mountain or in the apartment.

"Where is he?" he asked, hands clenching uselessly at his sides. David had gotten hurt and he wasn't there to stop it. He needed to be there now—the thought repeated over and over. The messenger pulled Arthur out of the group of healers, and Owen watched as the blood drained from Arthur's face in turn. The next moment he was at Owen's side, helping him keep up with the messenger.

Oblivion threatened with each step. The splint helped, but he shouldn't have been walking. They stumbled down a set of mostly intact steps and banged his leg into the wall. He almost screamed as darkness beckoned at the edges of his vision. He sucked in a breath and willed the pain away. He couldn't deal with it now. David needed him.

Fortunately, the daycare wasn't far after that. A cluster of healers, parents, and children gathered by the rubble that had once been shops and houses, standing around—oh no.

A small hand hung off a table, pale and weak, white sheets and bandages failing to stem the crimson tide. Three sirens sang, a desperate choir echoing in the destruction as they fought to undo the damage time had wrought. Arthur abandoned Owen and raced to join the singers, his voice raised to the heavens, a plea, a prayer to spare his brother's life.

Owen froze, ten feet from the group. He watched a drop of blood drip from lifeless fingers. Even from this distance, he could make out dozens of bullet holes, too many to count, that covered David's torso. Fragments of bone poked through a massive wound in his leg, ignored for the moment while they tended to the larger injuries. There was—there was no way David could survive this. This was too much for anyone to survive, too much for all the sirens and all the medicine in the world to fix.

He made himself take an aching step forward. Over and over his broken leg reminded him this was real, ripping away the fragile hope that he had never left his bed this morning.

The injuries were worse this close. Owen caught glimpses of shards of metal and something beating under David's ribs that shouldn't be seen. They hadn't covered anything, the better for the sirens to see what they were doing. Owen collapsed into the chair Beira had vacated when he arrived. She had a hand on the lead singer's shoulder, he noticed, and her eyes were screwed shut.

"What happened?" he asked without taking his eyes off David.

"They came in looking for Dorothy through one of the escape tunnels." Mr. Abnell's voice came from behind him, hoarse with grief and rage. "The soldiers came through just after. I tried to hide them, but the tunnel collapsed with only half of the students through. We were trapped—" He swallowed like he was fighting back tears. "David said he could distract them. I should never have said yes, should have made him hide with the rest, but it worked, they never saw us."

"If it worked, then why is he hurt?" Owen reached with a shaking hand to stroke blood-soaked hair. "What happened to him?"

Mr. Abnell made a pained noise, like every injury on David's body was mirrored on his own. "When they didn't see any of us, they decided to shoot anyway," he said. "In case we were hiding in the walls or something, they said. I tried to protect him, but I was too slow. He was right in front of them, and they tore him apart."

"And what happened to them?" he asked, turning dead eyes on the man he had relied on to protect his children.

"Have you ever seen what werewolves do to someone who hurts a member of their pack, Mr. Williams?" Mr. Abnell growled. "I assure you they didn't die easy. Your daughter and I made sure of that."

Some part of Owen wanted to yell at him for denying him his own shot at the bastards, but the more rational part wondered if that meant the children saw several grown men literally ripped to pieces. Not without reason were the werewolves the most feared of the fae foot soldiers.

"A search-and-rescue squad came through not long after," Mr. Abnell continued. "Their sirens stayed to help save him, and the rest found the children's parents."

So that was why the rest of the parents were already there. It made sense. They wanted to make sure it wasn't their child bleeding to death on a makeshift operating table.

"Has he woken up?" Owen asked, turning back to the table. He counted the beats between each rising and falling breath, unsure what he wanted the answer to be.

"No." A new voice, Jen's voice, came from his elbow. It was enough to make him look away from his dying child. Blood coated the fur around her jaw and her claws. Her voice was hard, and he mourned her childhood, another victim of this attack.

Without speaking, he pulled her into his lap, uncaring of the blood staining his clothes. She broke, the walls holding back her trauma crumbling down as she collapsed into his arms. Ashley came to his other side with Dorothy and joined in, wrapping her arms around them all like somehow this would keep her family whole and safe.

Owen wasn't sure how long they stayed like that. The crowd left, and more sirens joined the growing choir at David's bedside. The sound was beautiful and bounced off the walls in harmony with the screams and distant gunfire, but he knew they were only delaying the inevitable. Sirens could mend bones and cuts, but they couldn't work miracles. Even the most skilled couldn't sing a shattered bone into place in time to mend the holes it left behind.

The change was so small he might have missed it if he hadn't been looking. David's breath became shorter and more labored. "Daddy? Dad, is that you?" he whispered as his eyes cracked open. "Where's Mom? I want Mom."

"David, David I'm here," Owen said, grabbing David's cold hand. "You're safe; you did so good." His voice broke. This was it. His son was dying. These were his last words. Arthur dropped out of the choir and rushed to join them, kneeling with the rest of his siblings as David struggled for air.

"I did good? Then we won? They're all safe?" His voice gained a little lucidity, and he smiled. Then it fell. "I'm dying, aren't I? That's why you're all sad."

Owen opened his mouth to answer, but nothing came out. Tears streamed down his cheeks as he nodded, completely unable to hold them back as he admitted the bitter truth in his heart. He had known, been preparing himself since he had first seen what had become of his son, but he hadn't wanted to believe.

Some part of him thought Dorothy shouldn't be here for this, and Jen shouldn't have to watch her twin die, but the greater part didn't want any of his children where he couldn't see them. Besides, they had come this far and he was too selfish to send them away.

"Oh," David said. He coughed and blood dripped from the side of his mouth. "At least this way I get to see Mom again. Do you think she'll be proud of me?"

"Of course she will," Arthur said when it became clear Owen couldn't respond. "She was proud of all of us." He was crying too, and the tears made tracks in the dirt on his face.

"Ok." And just like that, David accepted his death. No fighting, no fuss, like that was all that was needed. "Hey, Dad? Look out for Jen, okay? She'll be sad when I'm gone."

Jen made a noise like she wanted to speak, but the only thing that came out was a choked-off gasp.

"Of—of course I will," Owen said, somehow finding his voice. "I'll never leave any of you alone again."

"And we'll take care of him, David, just like we said. No one will hurt him either." Jen grabbed David's other hand and clutched it like she could hold his spirit in his body. "You promised. You can't go."

David smiled again. His breaths were slower and shallower than they'd been a minute ago. "Good. You should take care of each other. I can't do it anymore."

Shakily, Owen leaned forward and kissed David's forehead. "I love you, David."

"Don't be sad, Dad," David said as his eyes fell shut. "I'll get to see Mom again." His smile grew faint and his voice dropped to a whisper. "I love you too, Dad. I love Jen and Arthur and Ashley and Dorothy. Can you tell them for me? Don't be sad. I'm going to see Mom now."

With those words, David Williams breathed his last breath. Owen put his head in his hands and screamed.

***

Beira threw Owen over her shoulders when his legs refused to bear his weight and carried him back to the apartment, so hollow and empty now with one less resident. Even Toto, who one of their neighbors had returned to them, sensed the change. He kept running around the apartment, searching each room and always returning to David's. *Where is he*, Toto asked in each whine, *where is my boy?*

Almost mechanically, Owen went through the actions Beira directed him to before she left to meet with the other founders. He showered. He ate. He comforted his children. News passed through one ear and out the other with little of it sticking.

If he listened, he could swear he still heard fighting in the distance, past that corner, and up those stairs. It would never leave him. Beira returned as the clock chimed two in the morning and sat next to him at the kitchen table. She made them tea and waited for the storm to break. Like many things, it started with a whisper instead of a shout.

"How did this happen?" Owen's voice was dead. Something was growing in him, something to fill the void, but it was too young to name yet, too unformed.

Beira's shoulders slumped. "As best as we can figure," she said, swirling her tea in her cup, "there was a tracker in the collars. The scans didn't pick it up, but it led them here. The whole thing was a trap and, fools that we were, we walked right into it."

"Were the captives on their side, then?"

There was no question about who they were. SAFE couldn't have made a firmer enemy of Owen had they tried. That unformed thing in him turned to rage that said there was nothing that would make him forgive what they'd done. He wouldn't be satisfied 'til every single piece of their organization was destroyed and its leaders were dead at his feet.

He was going to destroy them one day, destroy them like they had destroyed his family.

"Not as far as we can tell. The captives fought as hard as any of us when the soldiers broke through, harder in most cases. None of them wanted to go back." She paused and stared at the bottom of her cup. "We think that the tracker was activated when we took off the collars this morning," she said in a low voice. "But we won't be sure until the dwarves reverse engineer it."

"And what will you do now? They have hostages." With every word, that rage, that desperation grew, filling him, consuming every thought.

"That's why I'm here instead of with my generals," she said resolutely, setting her tea on the table. "Most of my donors were injured in the attack and any healers that could help them are busy elsewhere. I can get the dragons out, I can find our missing people, but I can't do it without human blood. Animal blood keeps me going, yes, but I'm much stronger when I'm eating like I should."

"How are we doing this?"

There was no question about whether he was going to let her drink. It made sense, what she was asking. He wasn't hurt that bad and now had a personal score with the force that had attacked them. At this point, he would provide the knife and bowl himself or offer his neck if it meant stopping those bastards from ever hurting anyone else again.

Beira grimaced. "It's not exactly safe to use my normal method at this point since I can't heal you, but we don't have a choice. Half a liter should be enough. Any more and I risk sending you into shock." She stood and took both their mugs to the sink. "We should do this in your bedroom. It'll be more comfortable for you and it's less likely one of your children will walk in on us."

Owen nodded without putting much thought into the matter. She would drink, he would stay, and she would go get the people who did this. Simple.

"Perfect." Beira pulled him to his feet. "I don't want to leave you alone, and I don't think you would want Arthur to have to help with this, so I took the liberty of arranging for someone to watch you. A gryphon, one of the newcomers. She told me the two of you had met before."

His head shot up. If the gryphon had survived, then perhaps something good had come from this night. He nodded numbly, and Beira went to the door to invite the gryphon in.

The gryphon looked even more bedraggled than she had when he first met her. Her fur and feathers were singed and a fresh scar laced its way down her left side, disappearing under her dirty leather apron. She followed them into his room and made a beeline for his desk, where she seemed content to glare at the two of them.

Beira eased him onto the bed, mindful of his injuries, and spent a minute or two finding a comfortable angle for him to hold his arm while he bled into the bowl. Once satisfied, she pulled a clean knife from a box in her bag and made the cut on his upper arm.

The blood started flowing immediately, and Owen watched it with a morbid fascination. It should've hurt, but it didn't. At least not more than he was already hurting.

Nothing felt right about the whole experience. On one side of him, a vampire was waiting for her dinner, and on the other, an angry gryphon was watching the whole thing and sulking. It was almost funny, he hadn't had a grown woman in his room since his wife had died, and now he had two and neither wanted to be there. He was glad when it was over.

Beira licked the entry wound to stop the bleeding, saying that since the venom was only released in the actual act of biting, she was free to make use of the coagulants in her saliva to close the wound before she wrapped it. It tickled.

Once the cut was tended, Beira guided Owen into a horizontal position and got off the bed. She carried the bowl like it was filled with the most precious resource in the world. To her, it probably was.

That should have been the end of it. He lay on the bed floating through the haze of semi-major blood loss. He was nodding off when the gryphon broke her silence.

"So are you two a couple now? Isn't that a little fast?" Her voice was hoarse, almost to the point he couldn't understand her, but the fire was clear.

He threw a half-hearted glare at her, too tired to get worked up in the tizzy that statement deserved. No one would ever replace his wife. "We're friends," he said. "None of the others were in a fit state to donate. And I wanted to play a part in bringing down those bastards."

"None of this would have happened if she'd left us there," she said like he hadn't spoken, her tail twitching beside her. "Now they have hundreds of fae in exchange for eleven."

"As we've already discussed, that was never an option. They were always going to come," Owen said, forcing himself into a seated position. If they were going to talk, he wanted it to be on equal footing. "This only made them move their plans up a bit."

"And how do you know that?" she asked. She jumped to her feet and knocked her chair to the floor as she paced. "If she'd left us there, none of this would have happened. They were happy with what they had, who they had. They came across the patrol by accident, they weren't trying to find anymore. If she had left us there, none of this would have happened and our son would still be alive—"

"By accident? How many more patrols would they come across by accident? SAFE wasn't even supposed to be on our border—" His rant died in its tracks. It couldn't be, he had to be imagining it. A combination of blood loss and grief was making him see things. She was dead and the best his broken mind could come up with to comfort him was putting his wife's voice in another woman's body. And yet . . .

Tiffany had been a gryphon, screamed the part of him that desperately wanted to believe this was real. The gryphon across from him was healthier than the other captives, and she'd sought him out, taken the time to find him when she should have been recovering. Her eyes were so familiar, that wonderful blue he'd fallen in love with twenty years ago.

"When were you going to tell us?" he asked in a broken voice. This wasn't real—it couldn't be—but right now he'd take his comfort where he could, even if it was a hallucination of his dead wife.

Tiffany shrugged, the action dragging her wings across the floor. "I don't know. They told me the fae kidnapped you and they brainwashed you into letting them take our babies. I needed to see for myself."

He fell back into a prone position. "So you came to see me. I'm guessing you didn't like what you found."

She shrugged again—no, wait. She was shaking. "The tracker went off when the collar was removed," she said. "I didn't know they would do this. They said they would come and take my babies home, make us human again. I didn't know what they planned. Mr. Jameson—"

Owen snorted. "I should have known he was involved in this. Let me guess. The familiar face comforts the poor kidnapped woman, giving her a false sense of security. Did I get it right?"

"I know," she screamed, her wings flaring out and knocking the lamp off Owen's desk. "I know I'm a fool and I shouldn't have trusted him. If I had any idea what they were going to do, I wouldn't have done it. I would have told them—"

Owen forced himself up onto his elbows and glared at the ghost of his wife. "You don't get it, do you? It doesn't matter now. Nothing matters. David is dead and you could have stopped it." She was dead, she couldn't have stopped it, this was his fault—

"I'm sorry," she repeated, sobbing.

All at once, everything went out of him and left him empty again. He fell back onto the bed and laughed, the broken and hysterical sound of a man who had lost something he thought would outlive him. Every injury, every ache and pain, screamed as he did, but it didn't matter. His son was dead, nothing could change that, but here he was arguing with someone who wasn't there.

"Do you know he was asking for you right before he died?" he asked through his laughter. "The first thing he said when he woke up: *Where's Mom, I want Mom.* And right before he died, he said he was happy because he got to see you again, did you know that?"

"I would have given anything to be there for him, to trade places with him," Tiffany said, rushing toward the bed. She stopped, barely inches away, silently begging for understanding he didn't want to give, as tears leaked from her eyes and soaked her fur.

Owen's laughter stopped; he brought a hand up to stroke her face but fell short. She wasn't there, he didn't know why he'd tried to wipe her tears away. "Take care of him, won't you?" he asked softly, closing his eyes. Even if it was a hallucination, it still hurt to look at her. "I couldn't do it, so it's up to you now. Keep him safe until I get there."

His world exploded into a kaleidoscope of pain as a slap resounded through the room. His eyes shot open and he stared at Tiffany—real and whole and here.

"Don't you dare say that, don't you talk like that," Tiffany growled, her hands balled up like she was going to hit him again. "We need you, you can't leave us."

"You're here," he breathed. Ecstasy warred with his grief and rage. She was here, she was back, she hadn't died, she—he surged up, ignoring the way his wounds screamed and blackness threatened, and wrapped his arms around her. "You're really here," he whispered, digging his fingers in her fur. It was rough and dirty, but *real.* "I thought I'd gone mad."

Tiffany stiffened, like his touch hurt. "You'll open your wounds again, and the kids still need you," she said, gently pushing him back onto the bed.

"They need me?" He let himself get pushed down without a fight. "What about you? David's dead, Tiff, they need both of us."

Tiffany shook her head and backed away, lips wobbling like she was about to burst into tears. "No," she said in a quivery voice. "I've done enough harm. If I'd just told someone what had happened, if I'd warned them, they might have been able to stop the attack. David might still be alive if I'd just—"

Owen pushed himself to his feet and put a hand over her mouth. "SAFE would've come anyway." Spots danced in front of his eyes. "We couldn't have done anything to stop it, and even if we could—" His throat closed, and he swallowed back the lump that formed. If he'd gone home instead of going out with the search-and-rescue team he could've stopped it. "We raised good kids, ones that want to help others and David saw his chance to do that. Even if he'd known what was going to happen, he would've done it anyway. It was just the kind of kid he was."

Slowly, Tiffany started shaking and wrapped her arms around Owen. They sank back onto the bed. He wasn't sure how long they sat there, comforting and being comforted, but eventually he had to speak.

"You need to tell them," he whispered in her ear. "The kids. They deserve to know."

Tiffany started, almost pulling out of his arms. "Owen," she said, her voice rough with tears. "I can't. They would hate me. I couldn't stand that."

Slowly, Owen dropped his arms and moved away so he could see Tiffany's face. He hadn't bothered to look closely at her before, at the differences wrought by Change and captivity. There wasn't much left of the woman he had fallen in love with.

Golden fur the same color as her hair shifted into amber feathers dotted with white on her shoulder blades. Her wings were taller than she was, peeking out past her shoulders like unwelcome guests, and trailed along the floor when she moved. Her tail, just visible from this angle, ended in long feathers instead of a tuft and twitched every few seconds. Her face—the only thing he knew there were her eyes, eyes he had once compared to the sea after a storm in a fit of drunken romanticism. They were set deep into the feline face of a first-gen gryphon.

He searched that face. There were the wrinkles at the corner of her eyes from laughing, the set of her mouth when she was upset, and bits and pieces of the woman he loved scattered in the face in front of him. It was different than it had been, but then, so was he. Nothing was ever going to be the same, but that didn't mean they couldn't try to build something new in the wreckage.

"My love," he whispered, kissing the back of her clawed hand. "We've spent too long apart. The things that happened today happened, and we can't change that. The only thing we can do is promise to be there for each other in the future. Stay with me tonight." The last part slipped out without his permission, but he couldn't bring himself to regret it.

Slowly, gently, Tiffany nodded, her tears dampening the fur on her cheeks. She crawled next to him and placed her head on his chest. It was too much, it wasn't enough, and it was perfect. Today had been hell, but something good had come out of it, and that was enough for him, it had to be or he'd break. He fell asleep listening to the sound of his wife's breathing.

CHAPTER TWENTY

IN WHICH OLD WOUNDS
ARE REOPENED

"The accords were signed today. Not every nation signed them, of course, but enough to make a difference. We're protected now. No one can hurt us anymore; the world won't stand for it. It's a wonderful feeling. To top it all off, Canada gave us some territory for a fae homeland, although we have to share it with the First Nation tribes in the area. Somehow, I don't think that'll be a problem. We know too well how it feels to lose our home. I don't know what's up there, but whatever it is it's the first step toward a new world. A new home."

—Excerpt from the journals of Beira Thomson, Queen Titania

At some point, vague estimations about losses began circulating. Some said there were as many as three thousand dead. Others, less than five hundred. Everyone agreed about the captives, though. Two hundred and forty-seven fae of various species had been taken during the battle, loaded onto cargo helicopters like cattle.

Beira had rescued most of the captives herself by ripping away the rubble covering the Eyrie entrances and leading half the able-bodied dragons in a counterattack that caught SAFE just before they crossed the U.S. border. But there were still groups coming in that had saved themselves. Final estimates put the remaining captives at twenty-eight, and already there were whispers about rescue attempts.

Still, the mood in the capital was grim. Every captive that returned was a reminder that others were still imprisoned; every crack, hole, and piece of rubble removed was a home or shop destroyed. There were so many funerals that they had to be held as mass services, entire neighborhoods coming together to mourn their loved ones.

Tiffany came clean to the kids the next morning. They hadn't believed her at first. It seemed like too much to be real. That they had gotten their mother back should have been impossible, but that it came on the heels of David's death . . . Nothing was worth that.

The kids took Tiffany's return with varying levels of grace. Dorothy seemed to think that because Mommy came back that David would be fine too. She spent as much time as she could in the apartment, stubbornly insisting she needed to be here when David came home. Not an hour went by where she didn't ask if he was going to be back soon. Owen was tired of trying to tell her otherwise.

Jen alternated between tearfully hugging her mother and screaming at her. She blamed Tiffany for David's death, like getting her mother back had cost her her brother. The death of a child or a sibling may be painful, but she had lost her twin, the other half of herself. That was a wound that couldn't be soothed.

Ashley became even quieter and faded into herself more with each passing day. She spent her days helping restore the burned library and avoiding the apartment when Tiffany was there. Consequently, bound to the apartment as he was, Owen hardly saw her. On the rare occasions he did, he hardly recognized her. Gone were her smiles and her cheer, a dead soul waiting for her body to catch up.

And Arthur—Arthur sang himself hoarse in the clinics. He left early each morning and didn't come back until he was forced away. He turned away each time he saw Tiffany and left when she tried to speak to him. His brother was gone, his mother was back, but as far as he was concerned, she may as well have stayed dead.

Owen wondered if, deep down inside, Arthur blamed them for David's death. The return of the captives and Tiffany had heralded the attack, and he had chosen to go out fighting instead of trying to find his kids. He couldn't blame Arthur. He blamed himself, after all.

***

254

There is no feeling in the world like losing a child, Owen thought as he dressed for the funeral. He'd lost friends, family, and even his wife for a while, but nothing compared to the aching void that had settled in his heart, to the crippling inadequacy that plagued him every hour of the day. If he'd been faster, stronger, better, if he hadn't tried to fight, David might still be alive.

David's funeral was one of four being held in the cafeteria, still decorated from the last party held before the attack. It felt like half the mountain showed up. People of all shapes and sizes were flowing out the doors. Even a small dragon had managed to cram herself in between the tables. He wasn't sure why people wouldn't leave him alone.

They must be looking for someone else, he insisted to several people before Arthur led him away. One of the other funerals. They couldn't— they didn't know many people. It had to be a mistake, they couldn't be here for David.

The funeral passed in a blur. The only thing he could focus on was the small wooden coffin that held David's body. Speeches and readings went unheard, condolences answered without thinking. He understood now why Ashley withdrew. It was so much easier to deal with the stark reality of David's loss if he didn't allow himself to feel. But he couldn't work on autopilot forever. Eventually he had to come back to the cold reality where he only had four living children and the other was lost to him forever, but for now, he was content to live in a haze. For now, he could pretend everything was fine and he wasn't falling apart.

***

"Jen let me in," Arthur roared from the hallway, a loud banging echoing around the apartment. "I need to get ready."

Owen limped from his room and caught hold of Arthur's wrist. "I'll handle this," he said, adjusting his crutches. "Find something to wear in my room and we'll be right out."

Arthur snarled, an expression that was unforgiving and ugly and entirely unsuited for his face. "She's not letting me in, Dad, and I need to get in there. I need to—I need to get something of his."

"And I said I'd handle it. Let me know what you need, and I'll make sure you get it. For now, give her space and go help your mother with Dorothy. This is hard for her."

"Like it isn't hard for the rest of us," Arthur said as he shook his arm free and stalked away.

Owen gently knocked on the door. "Jen? It's Dad. Will you let me in?"

"No. You're gonna make me go to that stupid memorial," she shouted, her voice muffled.

He sighed and leaned his head against the cool wood. "Look, if you don't want to go to the memorial, you don't have to, but please let me in. I'd like to speak to you." Nothing happened at first, but the quiet pattering of Jen moving across the room and the lock turning reached his ears soon enough.

He eased the door open and walked into the room, careful not to startle her. It turned out he needn't have worried. After unlocking the door, she'd run back across the room, leaped into what had been David's bed, and buried herself in his blankets.

Clothes were strewn everywhere, making every step a dangerous one for a man on crutches. When he reached David's bed, he sat on the edge and set his crutches beside him. Torn papers filled with half-hearted sketches littered the floor and the bedcovers.

"So are you going to tell me what this is all about, or do I have to guess?" he asked when Jen didn't give any indication she'd heard him enter.

A quiet, mournful growl came from beneath the mound of blankets. "I don't wanna go to the memorial. It's stupid."

"Oh? And why do you feel like that?" he asked mildly, too tired to be upset.

"Because it's stupid." The mound shifted toward him. "Putting their names on that stupid wall won't bring any of them back."

"You're right, it won't," he said, setting a hand on her head. "But it will help keep them alive in our memories."

There was so much more going on here than a simple matter of remembering the dead. This ceremony was a chance for all the fae to unite as they hadn't in years. Ambassadors from Nead, Paxton, and the larger villages had been arriving all day, and the smaller villages around the mountain had been emptied.

It would be an opportunity to remember the lost, yes, but also the future they died for. To show the fae their queen wasn't afraid of what the future might hold, that despite it all, the fae were strong. There were so many things he wanted to tell Jen, but he was too tired to find the words for them.

Regardless, Jen peaked out from under the heap of blankets and glared at him. "I don't care. I wanna stay here," she mumbled, as she rubbed tears from her eyes. "David won't be there and he should be and it's my fault. I should have protected him." She sniffed, tears turning into aching sobs.

He let out a deep breath and pulled Jen into his arms. "Oh, Jen," he whispered into her ear. "It's not your fault any more than it's mine, your mother's, or Mr. Abnell's. The only people to blame for David's death are the soldiers who killed him."

"You don't understand," she said as she lost the battle to hold back her tears. "I told him we should go get Dorothy, so it's my fault he's dead. I'm a murderer."

"And if you hadn't," he said, pulling her back to look her in the eye, "then Dorothy or Mr. Abnell or any of the other children would be dead instead. If you hadn't, he might have gone on his own or someone else would have gone in his place. We can play the 'what if' game all day, but it doesn't change what happened, and what happened doesn't make you a murderer."

"I killed those men," she whispered, so quiet he could barely hear her. "The ones who shot him. That does."

His heart stopped. Mr. Abnell said both he and Jen had attacked the soldiers. Curse the man, why had he done that, why hadn't he stopped her? Owen took a deep breath. Panicking wouldn't help Jen.

"You listen to me, Jennifer Edith Williams," he said. "You are not a murderer. Those men are the murderers. I wish, with all my heart, you hadn't had to do that, that there was any other option, but you did what you had to do. You protected David and the other children long enough for help to arrive."

"But it wasn't enough," she said, playing with the loose strings on his sweater. "David still died and those soldiers got away. I couldn't protect everyone, not like you."

"You don't have to protect everyone," he said. He couldn't believe she was so focused on being like him—No, that wasn't what this was about.

"You're eight years old and you shouldn't have to protect anyone. You did what you could and more than most people would ever ask of you. At your age, I wouldn't have been able to do what you did."

He didn't think she believed him, but she smiled sadly.

"If you say so," she whispered, "then I guess I'll go to the ceremony."

She slid out of his arms, off his lap, and padded to the door. It took a moment for his brain to catch up with what was happening.

"Wait a minute," he said as he pushed to his feet.

"What?" she asked, turning back to him, one hand on the doorknob.

His leg twinged as he leaned down to pluck a clean sweatshirt from a pile of David's clothes. "It's going to be cold," he said as he threw it at her. "Wear this."

Jen caught the sweatshirt with one hand and stared at it. A small, teary smile made its way across her cheeks. She let go of the doorknob and threw her arms around him. "Thank you, Daddy."

***

The whole city must have come, Owen thought as he stared around the square, Tiffany and the kids pushed so close to him he could've dropped his crutches and still stayed on his feet. Fae filled the room, thousands sitting on every available surface, hanging from the balconies, flowing out into the hallways, and peeking through holes in the walls. Even the centaurs, gryphons, and larger trolls were carrying people.

But for all the people here, the market had never been so quiet. No one was hawking goods, no children were playing, and even the sounds of movement were somehow stifled. There was little chatter that all but stopped the moment the queen glided onto the small stage in front of the memorial wall.

Beira wore a light blue dress edged with tawny fur. Birds danced around the hems in silver, and flowers covered her draping sleeves in royal blue. Her hair hung loose, peppered with white starflowers, and flowed like water when she moved. But most striking was her crown.

Owen had never seen her wear her crown, which normally sat in a locked glass cupboard in her office. The silver circlet had no adornment, no jewels or gems of any sort. It was made to stand on its own, much like the people it represented. It shone against her dark brown hair and glimmered in the lamplight like a beacon standing against the darkness.

She took her place center stage and stared out into the crowd, her hands folded in front of her and shoulders bowed with grief.

"I stand here before you today because of the terrible attack that took place four days ago," she said, the amplification system bringing her voice to every ear. "A reprisal for our rescue of our brothers and sisters from their hands, the hands of those who only mean us harm. They invaded our home, killed our families, and took our friends hostage. Tearmann will bear the scars from this attack for years to come.

"I come here today to say that we will not allow their suffering to have been in vain." She took a deep breath, and continued, a tiny tremor shaking her voice. "Even now, we are working to rescue the captives and find those responsible. Our allies have brought word of this attack before the world, and for the first time in half a century, they stand tall and proudly proclaim that they will no longer stand for our mistreatment." She paused as excited murmurs swept the crowd.

"Fifty years ago, the world claimed we were little more than animals, and not worth human dignity or respect. Those in power stood aside as we were systematically kidnapped, tortured, and murdered. Our kind were bought and sold as pets and curiosities to be displayed in zoos or to be used as labor. For years, we endured abuses at the hands of those who did not understand us while they tried to exploit us. We did not allow it then, and we will not allow it now." Her voice grew harder with each word, a testament to what her people had suffered.

The air vibrated with excitement in a more literal sense than Owen was used to. People had started moving and whispered to each other in the stillness, never loud enough to drown out her words.

"Some places have opened their arms," she said, silencing the whispers. "Allowing us to establish our sister city of Daingneach while we worked to learn from our past mistakes. Unfortunately, not everyone has taken such wisdom from the past. In the years since we withdrew from the world, the United States of America has tried to minimize us, to belittle and restrict us. They allow the abuses that began the war so many years ago to flourish without consequence." Angry shouts interrupted her speech, and she was forced to raise a hand to silence them before she could go on.

"Those who ordered this attack suffer under the delusion that we are animals, that what makes us different robs us of that which makes us thinking beings. They think that this has weakened us, that we are afraid and unable to defend ourselves. They have damaged our walls and destroyed our homes, but they have not broken our will. We will rebuild. What was made weak will be strong again, and they will learn why the fae are not to be trifled with." The words fell like a blow, a promise made to all who heard that this would never happen again.

Thunderous applause filled the room, a roaring sound that shook the air. People filled with the fire of patriotism forgot their fear and remembered why they were proud to be fae. She raised her hand again, bringing the applause to a sudden halt.

She didn't speak, but in the silence of the room, she began to sing. First, she sang alone and her voice hung in the air, but one by one, like a wave, the rest joined her in a fiery chorus. It was a battle hymn, an anthem, something each fae rallied around even as their city crumbled around them.

> *Remember where we came from*
> *Remember where we've been*
> *Remember who we've become*
> *And recall all we have seen*
> *We are the people forgotten,*
> *Returning to darkness and night*
> *Though we stand alone*
> *We remember, and so we fight*
> *Remember the hate we've been shown*
> *Remember the blood-stained blade*
> *Remember we were vanquished once*
> *Now never again shall we fade*
> *We are the people forgotten,*
> *Returning to darkness and night*
> *Though we stand alone*

We remember, and so we fight
Remember what is lost can be found
Remember that wounds can heal
Remember that we all are one
Together we are tempered steel

The last words faded into a triumphant roar that only ended when she held up her fist, demanding silence. The entire room waited with bated breath.

"I come before you as your queen," she said, her voice shaking from the strain of holding back her tears. "But remember that I am one of you and your losses echo as my own. Four days ago, we lost hundreds of proud fae. The village of Glenhold was destroyed completely when they fired upon it, and many more perished when the explosions caused collapses around the mountain. The names of those lost will be recorded on the memorial wall alongside those who died in the Fae War." She stopped. First one tear, then another, followed by an unending stream she didn't seem to notice that fell down her cheek and stained her bodice.

"But among those lost there are those who will be remembered as heroes. Like the heroes of the Fae War and those who have died doing amazing things for our people, the heroes of this battle will be honored with statues around the market square. I do not have the time to read off the names of all those we lost, as much as I would like to, but I will give the names and stories of the brave men and women who gave their lives so that others might live." She pulled a scroll from her sleeve, rolled it open, and read off it in a strong, clear voice.

"Patrick Shea, a gryphon who held off ten attackers so that his students had time to escape. Letha Meindl, a troll who collapsed the escape tunnel in her home, trapping herself in the process. Ashlynn Smart, a siren who used her song to guide the attackers away from her coworkers. Zechariah Mcfarlane, a dragon who raised the alarm when the business sector was breached. Felicity Sloan, a centaur who threw herself at oncoming forces so others could escape behind the barricade. And David Williams, an eight-year-old elf who gave his life to protect the children at his sister's daycare. Long may they be remembered."

The sentence was repeated by everyone in the room, a prayer and a promise, yet the eagerness and excitement from earlier swelled beneath the surface. As he took Tiffany's hand and squeezed, Owen felt in his bones that the outcome of this gathering would be felt around the world for years to come. From today on, nothing would be the same.

"Long may they be remembered in our actions and in our words, and may their sacrifice be honored," Beira said as six limestone pillars, each standing six feet above the crowd, were unveiled. "We have much to do to rebuild our homeland, just as these pillars need much done before they are complete. Let them stand in memorial for as long as fae walk these halls. Let this night be kept in remembrance for time immemorial." She walked off the stage to join her people in solemn observance as the first names were added to the list of those already carved on the wall.

CHAPTER TWENTY-ONE

IN WHICH
THE WORST IS YET TO COME

"We need a memorial of some kind, Beira, someplace people can visit to mourn those we couldn't bury. There's a wall in the main cavern that could work for this purpose. There's nothing major going on behind it. I checked, and it's large enough for all the names to fit. A lot of brave people like General Locke or Amy Fields lost their lives doing great things, the great heroes of the war. They're a part of our history, and they need to be remembered; their stories need to be passed down to our children. We need our own heroes, and they're ready for us, waiting. There's room in the cavern for a wall of names, like Aelfric suggested. Promise me you'll think about it?

—Excerpt from the letters of Father Logan Johnson, Lord Wulver

Two months passed and the mountain came back to life like a beast rising from hibernation. The walls were patched, shops reopened, and plans for future defenses were finalized. Every day more names were added to the wall and the pillars revealed their shape as the artisans lovingly cut away the excess stone. Being the smallest, David's was finished first, and today Owen was getting his first real look at it.

David smiled widely; his features—elven, human, and that little bit of him that was werewolf—all arranged as they had been in life and immortalized in stone. His ears poked through a messy mane of hair and his pointed canines peeked out from under his upper lip. The statue even held out a clawed hand like an offering of aid. The base had four bronze plaques, one on each side, detailing who he had been and what he'd done in the dominant languages of the fae.

Owen hated it.

Well, that wasn't true. David deserved to be remembered, and there were many things he liked about the statue. For example, the artisans had used a picture of David that the Williams provided to carve the face, so it was accurate at the very least. It almost felt like he was looking at his son instead of cold rock.

He just hated more things than he liked about it. He hated the stare that no artisan would be able to make anything other than blank. He hated that it showed an eight-year-old boy who would never turn nine. He hated that it was necessary.

Beira found him glowering at the statue in the middle of the square. He supposed he stood out since he was the only one standing still. All around them, people ushered to and fro, construction workers, hawkers, and shoppers going about their lives.

"Is it not to your tastes or is something else making you glare holes into the statue?" she asked, smiling softly at him.

"No, it's fine. I just wish it didn't have to be here," Owen said, keeping his eyes on the statue.

"I know what you mean." She nodded at where a group of workmen were removing a lingering pile of rubble. "As good as this whole business has been for the economy, I would have preferred if SAFE hadn't tried to solve our economic woes this way."

His head snapped toward her. "So it was SAFE, then?"

"Yep," she said, snapping the P. "The reports are in, and they confirm what we already knew. SAFE organized, paid for, and sent the attack on Tearmann with the intent to kill or capture as many fae as possible since we attacked them first. The U.S. is, of course, denying any of it ever happened, and they're not allowing us to search for our missing people on U.S. soil." She shrugged and bit her lip. "I mean, it's not like we were going to wait for their permission anyways, but still, it does tell us where their loyalty lies."

"I see. What's the plan, then? Find your people and hope they don't attack again? Or are you going to go to the UN?" he asked, turning back to the statue.

"A little of both, actually, but there's something else I need to talk to you about. Walk with me?"

Owen paused, trying to remember if he had anything he was supposed to be doing today. Mr. Moore point-blank refused to let him back to work for another month, the kids were either at school or at work, and Tiffany was on the other side of the mountain helping repair some of the tunnels.

"Well—," he said with a shrug, "it isn't like I have anything better to do with my time. Where to?"

"My office, if you don't mind," she said, already turning away and leaving him no choice but to follow her. "You've heard the reports, right? About the new fae?"

"Yeah," he said. "Something about more Changes?"

"Correct. Since the attack, we've been receiving reports of Changes happening on a scale we haven't seen in years. The teams we have out right now can't keep up with the demand, which leaves the newly Changed and their families vulnerable to SAFE and other interested organizations. The Corps generals and I are putting together more teams to help handle the overload." She glanced at him from the corner of her eye. "We were wondering if you or Arthur might be interested."

"Me?" he asked, eyes wide and brows raised. "Don't I still have warrants out for my arrest?"

"It's not like we're asking you to go dancing naked across Times Square or anything," she said as one eyebrow arched up. "You and your family are the most well-known of the recent arrivals. Seeing you might make this whole process easier for newcomers."

Owen opened and shut his mouth several times. On one hand, she had a point. Fleeing across the country, attacking a police officer, and getting accused of murder had put his face on a lot of televisions. A familiar face might make things easier for scared newcomers. At least, unless someone took his being accused of murdering his wife and kidnapping his children seriously. On the other hand, he didn't want to leave his family for that long. Those missions often went on for months and his leg had barely healed.

"I can't say for Arthur," he said, rubbing the back of his neck. "He's seventeen now, and he has to start making these choices for himself, although I won't say I'd be pleased with him if he did. He hasn't had any of the training required, and he only just came into his power. Aren't there are other people you could send?"

"Oh, there are," she said with a nod. "We're sending half of them. The rest are providing security to the capital and the major cities. The rest of the teams will be filled with young elves and sirens. They need to know the risks of misusing their abilities."

"So you test them on humans?"

"No," she said as she shoved an elbow into his side. "You know I didn't mean that. They're being sent as observers unless something goes wrong, in which case the lessons they learn will come in handy."

They walked in silence for a while longer.

"What about you, Owen?" she asked as they turned a corner. "You've said you don't want Arthur to go, but you've had some combat training, and you have the advantage of being human, unlike most of our agents."

Owen laughed tiredly. "Honestly, I'm not sure. If you think I can help, then I want to go, but I don't know if I can leave Tiff and the kids that long. I might also be of more use here. I'm a carpenter, after all, and we've got a long way to go before we're done with rebuilding."

"Understandable. It's something to keep in mind for the future, though," Beira said as they approached her battered office doors. "Do you mind coming in? There's something I have to show you."

Owen nodded and helped her force the damaged door open. Once they had managed to slide in, she walked to her desk and pulled a familiar green notebook from a drawer.

"Do you remember the conversation we had after I collapsed?"

"Of course. I had nightmares for three days," he answered, following her to the desk and sitting in his usual chair. Between finding out the fae were linked to her, that she was slowly dying, and that it was essentially impossible to find another vampire to help her, he hadn't been able to forget.

"And you remember what I said about the vampires?" She fidgeted with her bracelet.

"Yes," he said slowly, his eyes darting between her and the notebook. "There are supposed to be two, but you can't find—" His mouth dropped open. "You found one, didn't you?"

She nodded as she sank into her chair. "I had the opportunity to check his blood when we were attacked. I pulled out Nathaniel's notes afterwards to double check my theory—but yes. I believe I may have finally found another one."

"This is fantastic," he said, not even bothering to hide his broad grin. "Who is it? Was it one of the soldiers? It had to have been; there've been no other new humans here besides me, and you've tasted my blood."

"No, it wasn't one of the soldiers," she said, burying her face in her hands. "I didn't drink from any of them."

His smile fell away. "Well, then who is it?"

Her hands dropped from her face so she could stare at him with an unobstructed view. "Owen," she said like he was a particularly slow child. "I only drank from one person throughout that whole course of events, and that was you."

His brain shut off, refusing to comprehend what she was telling him. He wasn't—she couldn't be—several seconds ticked by where they simply looked at each other. Then he fainted.

***

An indeterminate time later, Owen woke to a pitcher of water being dumped on his face and Beira standing over him.

"Sorry," she said. "You fell out of your chair and I wasn't sure what to do."

He took her hand and allowed himself to be pulled to his feet and led to his abandoned chair. "What happened?" He groaned and rubbed the back of his head. "Did I hit my head on something?"

"Well, you did make a nice smack when you hit the ground," she said as she went back to her chair. "You passed out after I told you—"

He held up a hand to stop her there. His stomach tightened and bile rose in his throat. "Never mind. I remember."

"And?"

267

He took several deep breaths. And then several more before he could attempt speech. "You can't be serious," he exploded. "You must have gotten it wrong. There's no way I could be a vampire. I'm not even faeborn."

"I'm not wrong about this. I've tasted vampire blood before. I know what it's like," she said, crossing her arms and glaring at him.

"You—you know what it tastes like?" he said. "But you said you hadn't found any vampires. That's why this whole search you were doing was such a big deal, remember?"

"It's complicated, Owen. Most of my donors who have fae relations are actually vampires, but the traits for each species are set by the traits of its founders. I'm the only vampire, so the people who fall into my category are like me." Her hands came up to clutch at her arms and she shivered. Her voice dropped to a near whisper. "You may not have noticed, Owen, but I have issues. I couldn't just pick the first one I found or we would've been in even more trouble than before. You're only the second relatively stable one I've found in fifty years."

Owen had to admit that Beira probably knew what she was talking about. But still … "The other donors are good people, Beira; any one of them would have made a good leader. Why put the fae through so much when you could have picked one of them?"

"Every single one of them has issues, things that wouldn't make them very good vampires," she said as she turned and ripped a binder from the shelves. She opened it to a list of names and shoved it toward him.

"Fred is bipolar," she said, pointing to the appropriate name on the list. "Jake has anger problems. Miguel has attempted suicide three times in the last two decades. Talon, Steve, Tony, Daewon—every one of them has problems they have a hard time controlling, and you know why we can't let someone like that into power." She pushed the binder off the desk, leaving it to drop on the floor.

"But you—when you first came here, you were lost. Your wife was gone, and you and your children had been ripped from everything you ever knew, but you didn't let it control you. Other men would have been destroyed by what you went through, even before you lost David—"

"Don't you bring him into this," he growled, half-rising to his feet.

"My point is, you're a survivor." She fell back into her seat and covered her eyes. "Instead of giving up or wallowing in your misery, you look for ways to work around it."

"Why are you telling me this?" he asked, slumping back into his chair. "Are my options leave the capital or become a vampire? Pick one, 'cause you can't stay here if you say no?"

"No, no, of course not," she said, eyes as wide as saucers. He almost felt a little guilty for suggesting it. "I told you about my idea in case you wanted to get out of the mountain, but I won't force you either way."

He forced himself to calm down and took several deep breaths. "You said I was the second, what happened to the first?"

"He didn't want the position," she whispered, her eyes downcast. "Said he didn't trust himself with that much power. He moved to Paxton forty years ago to remove himself from the temptation."

"So I can say no, then? What will you do if I do?"

"Keep looking," she answered without hesitation. "One of the soldiers we captured could be a match or someone one of the teams brings back. I lucked out on you, but that doesn't mean there aren't more out there."

"So the choice is between me, a man who doesn't want the job, and some hypothetical stranger you find in the future. Wonderful." Owen groaned and rubbed his temples.

"How are you even sure I'm a 'relatively stable' person?" he demanded. "What if I have temper issues or I beat my wife or I'm a drug addict or some other thing that would disqualify me?"

"Well, if you have temper issues, you keep them under wraps, because not much stays hidden in this city. You don't beat your wife or kids or one of the werewolves would have ripped you apart by now. You're definitely not addicted to anything or you would have gone through withdrawal, and anything else I'm sure we could deal with," she said, checking each protest off with nonchalant ease as she leafed through the green notebook.

Owen stared at her. She was so calm about this. Couldn't she remember how she'd felt when she had been turned? The thought of living like she did, forced to drink the blood of others for however long she lived, possibly forever, made him want to vomit. He didn't want to outlive any more of his children.

"Owen," Beira said, closing the notebook and pushing it away when she noticed his struggle. "Like I said, I won't force you into this. The decision is up to you. If you say yes, I will give you the right to retract right up to the moment I begin turning you; if you say no, I will never mention it again."

She was so earnest, staring at him with eyes that begged him to believe her. He knew that she wouldn't force this on him, just like she hadn't forced him into giving her his blood. The problem was he wasn't sure what to do with this information.

He wasn't a good fit for ruling, not the way she was. She was kind, gentle, and understanding but hard as steel when she needed to be. She was smart, wise, and willing to make the hard decisions. This was a woman who led a revolution and tore her people a place in a world that hated them.

Owen was not that sort of person. He was a father, and the hardest decisions he had to make were whether he said no to Dorothy's pleas for a third candy bar or whether he trusted Arthur with his new car. He wasn't a general or a leader, and he had no business running a country.

But some part of him wanted to say yes. To join his family among the ranks of the fully-fledged fae, to protect them from those who hated them, to protect children like David so they never had to worry about their lives being taken far too soon. He wanted revenge for David's death too, and to make sure his family could never be hurt again. He wanted so much, and that was why he couldn't say yes.

"I'm sorry—I can't," he whispered. "I can't do it. If I had that kind of power—it would corrupt me, and one day you would have to put me down. I'm exactly the wrong sort of person you would want for this job. I want to help you, but I can't do it at your side."

Beira smiled sadly and accepted the answer without protest. Owen knew she understood, better than anyone, why he couldn't say yes even when the lives of his family, of their people, were at stake. "Very well. I do hope you will still consider being one of my donors, though; we lost too many in the attack."

"Of course," he said, deeply relieved she hadn't tried to change his mind. "It's no trouble. I may not be able to rule with you, but I'll help you however I can."

"I would expect no less of you, Owen Williams," she said smiling sadly. "Now, I've kept you long enough. I have work to do that I've been putting off for far too long. Tell your family I said hello, won't you?"

"Sure," he said as he forced himself to his feet. His legs shook beneath him. She was already buried in one of the countless folders perpetually stacked on her desk. He continued without thinking. "Oh, hey, Beira, come by for dinner one of these days. I make a mean meatloaf, and I'm sure the kids want to see you."

She looked up from her work and smiled. "I'll have to do that. Would Tuesday work? That should be enough time for you to tell your wife you're having dinner guests."

"I'll see you then." He walked out and closed the door, relaxing as it clicked shut. Leaning against the cool wood, his eyes slid shut and he took a deep breath.

He was faeborn, as odd and improbable as it sounded. More importantly, he was a vampire—or at least he could be one—and he had chosen not to. *He had chosen to stay human.*

He fell to his knees, grateful that the doors were thick enough Beira wouldn't be able to hear him. He had said no, he thought hysterically, failing to fight the laughter that bubbled up inside him.

It was just so funny. Back home, he was no one, the immigrant husband of a software programmer, but here he was one of the few people who could save them all. Heavens, it was like a bad young adult novel.

He didn't know how long he sat there. His legs had gone numb and his throat ached, but he couldn't move. At some point he'd started crying and the two contrary emotions waged a war that turned his stomach into knots. It was a long time before the last echoes of his laughter faded away and longer still before his tears dried.

He'd have to move soon. Beira couldn't be expected to stay in her office forever. She was the only person who might understand how he was feeling but that didn't mean he wanted her to see him like this.

The distant sound of voices was what finally drove Owen to his feet. He took a moment to gather himself, then checked his watch. *It's almost five thirty.* He needed to hurry if he wanted to get Dorothy and pick up groceries before dinner.

Dodging around rubble carts, Owen moved as fast as he could. A quiet chuckle bubbled out of his chest as he moved, and he didn't try to stop it. *Him, a vampire.* He couldn't believe it.

The world had come apart at its seams and now this had landed in his lap. It was too much to think about, horrifying and hilarious at the same time. People stared at him as he ran past, a grown man laughing to himself like a child, but he didn't care. They had no idea what he'd just learned and what he'd just done.

He was a vampire.

He was, and he'd refused to become one. This should scare him, but instead he was flooded with a strange sense of relief. He knew where he stood and, come hell or high water, he'd made his choice.

About the Author

Ceril N Domace is an accountant, the owner of a grumpy senior collie mix, and a half-decent fencer.

As a lover of fiction works great and small, Ceril has been reading age-inappropriate fiction since her father failed to pull *The Silmarillion* from her grubby little fingers at age five. As a grown-up accountant, her spreadsheet compiling gives her plenty of time to make plans for a fantastic world that isn't plagued by balance sheets . . . and also has dragons.

On the rare occasions she manages to free herself from an ever-growing and complex web of TTRPG, Ceril enjoys taking walks and griping that all her hobbies are work in disguise.